"Why do you think someone wants to harm you?" he asked.

"I witnessed a crime."

They turned a corner and he stopped short.

"What?" She looked around him.

A stranger was coming out of Will's cabin.

"Do you recognize him?" she said.

"No." He motioned to a nearby tree. "Hide back there. I'll check it out."

"It could be dangerous."

"Or simply a hiker lost in the mountains. Kinda like you." Will smiled and nodded toward the tree. "Go on."

"Maybe you should take this." She offered him the gun.

An odd smile creased his lips. "Thanks, but you keep it."

She nodded and watched him walk away, shielding herself behind the tree. From this vantage point she could watch the scene unfold, not that she had a great escape plan.

Suddenly, a gunshot echoed across the property.

An eternal optimist, **Hope White** was born and raised in the Midwest. She and her college sweetheart have been married for thirty years and are blessed with two wonderful sons, two feisty cats and a bossy border collie. When not dreaming up inspirational tales, Hope enjoys hiking, sipping tea with friends and going to the movies. She loves to hear from readers, who can contact her at hopewhiteauthor@gmail.com.

Maggie K. Black is an award-winning journalist and romantic suspense author with an insatiable love of traveling the world. She has lived in the American South, Europe and the Middle East. She now makes her home in Canada with her history-teacher husband, their two beautiful girls and a small but mighty dog. Maggie enjoys connecting with her readers at maggiekblack.com.

Yuletide Secrets

Hope White

&

USA TODAY Bestselling Author

Maggie K. Black

2 Thrilling Stories

Christmas Undercover and *Undercover Holiday Fiancée*

LOVE INSPIRED
INSPIRATIONAL ROMANCE

LOVE INSPIRED®

INSPIRATIONAL ROMANCE

Recycling programs
for this product may
not exist in your area.

ISBN-13: 978-1-335-42992-6

Yuletide Secrets

Copyright © 2022 by Harlequin Enterprises ULC

Christmas Undercover
First published in 2015. This edition published in 2022.
Copyright © 2015 by Pat White

Undercover Holiday Fiancée
First published in 2017. This edition published in 2022.
Copyright © 2017 by Mags Storey

For questions and comments about the quality of this book, please contact us
at CustomerService@Harlequin.com.

Love Inspired
22 Adelaide St. West, 41st Floor
Toronto, Ontario M5H 4E3, Canada
www.LoveInspired.com

Printed in U.S.A.

CONTENTS

CHRISTMAS UNDERCOVER

Hope White

This book is dedicated to
Mark Jamieson of the Seattle PD,
who generously answers my many questions.

May the God of hope fill you with all joy and peace
as you trust in Him, so that you may overflow
with hope by the power of the Holy Spirit.
—*Romans* 15:13

Chapter One

FBI agent Sara Vaughn awoke with a start, her heart pounding against her chest. Darkness surrounded her and it took a second for her eyes to adjust.

Panic took hold. No, she was beyond that. She'd outgrown it.

She counted to three, taking a deep breath, then exhaled. She clicked on her headlamp. Tall, majestic evergreen trees stretched up toward the starlit sky.

The mountains. She was in the Cascade Mountains following a lead that her supervisor, Greg Bonner, said was a waste of time.

Sara knew better.

The sound of deep male voices echoed from beyond a cluster of trees to her left.

"Be reasonable, David!" a man shouted.

David Price was one of the three business partners who were on this mountain getaway. The other men were Victor LaRouche and Ted Harrington, and together they owned the drug company LHP, Inc.

Sara made her way toward the sound of raised voices. She was proud of herself for managing to get on the trail guide team hired to lead them up Echo Mountain. This isolated spot in the Cascade Mountains of Washington would surely give the men the privacy they needed to solidify their plan.

Getting a dangerous drug into the hands of unsuspecting consumers.

"Why do you have to make this so hard?"

She recognized Vic LaRouche's voice because of its Southern twang.

She stayed off the main trail, not wanting to alert them to her presence, and made her way through the brush. Edging around a large boulder, she stepped over a fallen branch in silence. She needed to stay invisible, hidden. Something she was good at.

The men were no doubt having this discussion a safe distance away from the lead guide, Ned, so as not to wake him. It didn't take much to wake Sara. Even in sleep, she was always on alert.

"It's not right and you both know it," David said.

"It was an anomaly, a mistake," Ted Harrington said.

"A mistake that could kill people."

"Don't be dramatic," LaRouche said.

This was it—the evidence she'd been looking for.

She pulled out her phone, hoping to record some of their conversation. If she could catch them admitting to their plan, it would go a long way to proving she was right, that she wasn't just an "overzealous" agent trying to prove something.

She crept closer, shielding herself behind a towering western hemlock. Digging her fingers into the bark, she peeked around the tree. The three men hovered beside a small campfire, the flames illuminating their faces.

LaRouche and Harrington were tall, middle-aged men, older than David Price by at least ten years.

"I'm not in business to hurt people," David said.

"We're helping people, sport," Harrington said, slapping David's shoulder. "Letting them sleep like they never have before."

"And they don't wake up."

"That hasn't been irrefutably proved," Harrington said.

"Even one death is too many."

LaRouche, a tall, regal-looking man, jumped into the conversation. It grew into a shouting match, giving Sara the chance to sneak even closer. She darted to another tree, only ten feet from the men.

She clicked off her headlamp.

Hit the video record button on her phone.

And held her breath.

"I didn't sign on for this!" David said.

"Majority rules," Harrington countered.

"Then, I'm out. I'll sell you my share of the company."

Harrington threw up his hands and paced a few steps away.

"If you leave, stock prices go down," LaRouche said calmly.

"I don't care. Some things are more important than money."

"Like your family?" LaRouche taunted.

"Is that a threat?" David said.

"Sure, why not?"

David lunged at LaRouche. Harrington dived in between them. "Enough!"

The two men split apart, David glaring at his partners.

"Calm down. Let's talk this through," Harrington said.

"Talk? You mean threaten me?" David said.

"I like to think of it as persuading you, David," La-Rouche countered.

"No, I'm done." David started to walk away.

It seemed as if the conversation was over.

Then LaRouche darted around the fire, grabbed David's arm and flung him...

Over the edge of the trail.

The chilling sound of a man crying out echoed across the mountains.

Sara gasped and took a step backward.

A twig snapped beneath her boot.

LaRouche and Harrington whipped their heads around and spotted her. They looked as stunned as she felt. The three of them stared at each other.

No one moved. She didn't breathe.

Heart racing, she watched the expression on La-Rouche's face change from stunned to something far worse: the look of a murderer who was hungry for more.

"It was an accident," Harrington said.

LaRouche reached into his jacket, no doubt for a weapon.

In that millisecond, her only conscious thought was survival.

Sara clicked on her headlamp and took off, retracing her steps over the rugged terrain. She was outnumbered and couldn't retrieve her off-duty piece quick enough. She had to get safe and preserve the video evidence against them.

Shoving the phone in her pocket, she hopped a fallen branch and dodged the boulder on the other side. As she picked up speed, she heard a man grunt as he tripped and hit the ground behind her.

"Where are you going? We need your help!" Harrington called.

Beating back the tentacles of fear, she searched for a trail, or at least a more even surface. She'd left everything at the campsite but the clothes on her back, so her odds for survival weren't great, especially considering the cold temperatures in the mountains this time of year.

Stop going to that dark place, she scolded herself. She had to figure out how to contact her boss and report the murder before the men reported it as an accident.

Call her boss, right, the man who'd ordered her to take time off. He didn't even know she was chasing a lead he'd proclaimed was a dead end.

"David fell and we need your help!" Harrington yelled.

David fell? Is that what you call it when you fling a man off a cliff?

She sucked in the cool mountain air, pumping her arms, trying to get a safe distance away where she could get a cell signal and call for help.

"Let's talk about this!" Harrington pressed.

Like they'd "talked" to David Price? The memory of his desperate cry sent shivers across her shoulders.

She found the trail, but if she found it, so would they. They were taller than her five foot three, their strides longer. It wouldn't take them long to catch her.

And kill her.

They'd probably fabricate a story about how she was responsible for David's death. That would wrap everything up in a neat bow—just in time for Christmas.

No. She wouldn't let them win.

A gunshot echoed across the mountain range.

She bit back a gasp. How would they explain her

body riddled with bullet holes? Unless they hoped wild animals would rip it apart, making cause of death that much harder to determine.

Suddenly she ran out of trail. She peered over the mountain's edge into the black abyss below.

"Think," she whispered.

She realized her rope was still hooked to her belt. She hadn't planned to drift off to sleep earlier, so she hadn't taken off her gear. She wrapped the rope around a tree root jutting out from the side of the mountain below the trail and pulled it tight.

For the first time in her life, she appreciated Uncle Matt's insistence that she take wilderness survival courses, along with self-defense. She used to think he'd forced her to take the classes because her small frame made her a target for bullies. She eventually realized it was because of the nightmares. He thought the classes would empower her, make her feel safe.

Sara had never felt safe.

She dropped to her stomach and shimmied over the edge. Clinging to the rope, she let herself down slowly, hoping to hit a ledge or plateau where she could wait it out. She clicked off her headlamp. At least if she could disappear for a few hours until sunrise, she might be able to make her way out of Echo Mountain State Park.

She calmed her breathing, questioning her decision to follow this lead on her own. Was her boss right? Was she too determined for her own good?

Sara gripped the rope with gloved hands and steadied herself against the mountainside with her boots.

"What do you want to do?" Harrington said.

His voice was close, right above her close. She held her breath.

"We'll send Bill to find her," LaRouche said. "He's got climbing experience."

"Wouldn't it be better if we—"

"No, we need answers, like who sent her and what she heard. Then she needs to disappear."

Disappear. They were determined to kill her. Sara's pulse raced against her throat.

As she hung there, suspended in midair, she searched her surroundings, trying to see something, trying to stay grounded.

All she could see was a wall of black, which reminded her of...

Stay in here and don't make a sound.

But, Daddy—

I mean it. Take care of your brother.

Suddenly someone tugged on the rope, yanking her out of the memory.

"Sara Long, is that you?" LaRouche said.

She was relieved they only knew her undercover name, Sara Long. That should keep them from discovering her true identity.

Then, suddenly, they started pulling her up. No, she wouldn't let them get away with it, killing people, innocent people.

Killing her.

She released the rope and grabbed the tree root, then edged her way down the side of the mountain, grabbing onto whatever felt solid.

She grabbed onto a branch...

It pulled loose from the earth and she started to slide. Flailing her arms, she reached for something, anything, to slow her descent.

But it was too dark, and the fall too steep.

It wouldn't surprise the guys in her field office if she died out here like this: alone, on some rogue assignment gone south.

She didn't care. At least this time she'd taken on the enemy instead of hiding from him.

I'm sorry, Daddy. I should have done something to save you.

She came to a sudden stop. Her head whipped back, slammed against something hard, and she was swallowed by darkness.

Will Rankin approached the end of the trail and made the final turn. His breath caught in his throat at the stunning view, sunlight sparkling off the calm, turquoise water at the base of Echo Mountain, with the Cascade Mountain range spanning the horizon behind the lake. This was it, the perfect place to open his heart to God, hoping for peace to ease the resentment lingering in his heart.

Intellectually Will knew it was time to let it go for so many reasons, not the least of which being his daughters. They needed a loving, gentle father, not a bitter, angry one.

Will thought he had coped with Megan's death pretty well over the past two years, but the dark emotions continued to have a stronghold over his heart. He was still angry with his wife for shutting him out as she battled cancer, and he struggled with resentment about his mother-in-law, who challenged nearly every decision Will made about Claire and Marissa.

I love my girls so much, Lord. Isn't that enough?

Apparently not to his mother-in-law.

No, he wouldn't think about that today. Today he'd commune with nature and pray: for his daughters, for emotional peace and for the strength to get him through the upcoming Christmas season, the girls' second Christmas without their mom.

It was unseasonably warm at the base of the mountain. Although a recent light snowfall dusted the area around the lake with a layer of white, it would probably melt off by noon. He smiled, thinking about how much the girls were looking forward to playing in the snow.

Then something else caught his eye across the lake.

A splash of red.

Curious, he pulled out his binoculars and peered through the lenses. It looked like a woman in a red jacket, jeans and hiking boots. Her long brown hair was strewn across her face.

She looked unconscious, or worse.

Will shoved the binoculars into his pack and took off. He had to get to her, had to save her. He glanced at his cell phone. No signal.

Please, Lord, let me save her.

As he sped toward the unconscious woman, he wondered how she'd ended up here. Was she a day hiker who hadn't brought enough hydration? He didn't see a backpack near her body, yet even day hikers knew better than to head into the mountains without supplies since the weather could change in a flash.

By the time he reached the unconscious woman, his heart was pounding against his chest. He shucked his pack and kneeled to administer first aid. "Ma'am?"

She was unresponsive.

"Ma'am, can you hear me?"

What had happened to this fragile-looking creature? He wondered if she got separated from her party or had fallen off a trail above.

He gently brushed jet-black hair away from her face. She had color in her cheeks, a good sign. He took off his glove and pressed his fingers against her wrist to check her pulse.

"No!" She swung her arm, nailing Will in the face with something hard.

He jerked backward, stars arcing across his vision. He pinched his eyes shut against the pain. Gripping his nose, he felt blood ooze through his fingers. He struggled to breathe.

"Don't touch me!" she cried.

"I'm trying to help."

"Liar."

He cracked open his eyes. She towered above him, aiming a gun at his chest.

"Please," he said, putting out one hand in a gesture of surrender. "I'm sorry if I upset you, but I really do want to help."

"Yeah, help them kill me."

He noticed a bruise forming above her right eye and lacerations crisscrossing her cheek.

"You're hurt," he said.

"I'm fine."

Will guessed she was frightened and confused. Maybe even dehydrated.

"I'm Will Rankin, a volunteer with Echo Mountain Search and Rescue."

"Sure, and I'm Amelia Earhart."

"Check my pack. My driver's license is in the side pocket."

It was worth a try, although he knew all the sensible conversation in the world may not get through to someone in her condition.

Narrowing her eyes, she grabbed his backpack and stepped a few feet away. Never lowering the gun, she unzipped the side pocket.

"May I sit up to stop my nosebleed?" he asked.

She nodded that he could.

He would continue to act submissive so she wouldn't see him as a threat. It was the best way to keep her from firing the gun by accident. He sensed she wasn't a killer, but rather she was disoriented and frightened.

Sitting up, he leaned forward and pinched his nose, just below the bridge. He'd have dual black eyes for sure and didn't know how he'd explain that to his girls, or their grandparents.

You've got bigger problems than a bloody nose. He had to talk this woman down from her precarious ledge.

She rifled through his wallet and hesitated, fingering a photograph of Claire and Marissa.

"My girls," he said. "They're in first and third grades."

She shot him a look of disbelief and shoved his wallet and the photos haphazardly into his pack.

"Did you fall from a trail above?" he asked.

"I'm asking the questions!" She straightened and pointed the gun at his chest again. "And you'd better give me the right answers."

"Please," he said. "My girls… I'm all they've got. Their mother…died."

He thought he'd gotten through to her.

She flicked the gun. "Get up."

He slowly stood, realizing how petite she was, barely coming up to his chest.

"Where are they?" she demanded.

"Who?"

"LaRouche and Harrington."

"I'm sorry, but I don't know what you're talking about."

"Right, you randomly happened to find me."

"I did."

"Uh-huh. And you're out here, in the middle of nowhere, why?"

"I'm spending a few days in the mountains for—" he hesitated "—solitude."

"You're lying. There's more to it."

"I'm not lying, but you're right, there is more to it."

She waited and narrowed her eyes, expectant.

"I come to this spot by the lake to find emotional peace—" he hesitated "—with God's help."

"Yeah, right. Great story, *Will*."

He didn't miss the sarcastic pronunciation of his name, nor the paranoid look in her eye.

She dug in her jacket pocket and pulled out her phone. She frowned.

"You have a phone?" she asked.

"I do."

She shoved hers back into her pocket. "Give it to me."

He pulled it out, dropped it between them and raised his hands. "You won't get a signal here, but there's a spot by my cabin where I can usually find service."

"Your cabin?"

"I'm renting a cabin about a quarter of a mile north."

She eyed his phone, must have seen there weren't any bars, and shoved it into her other pocket.

"Let's go." When she picked up his pack, a groan escaped her lips.

"Do you want me to—"

"Walk," she demanded, her eyes watering.

They were obviously tears of pain. He guessed from the rip in her jacket and strained look on her face, she might have cracked a rib or two.

With a nod, he turned and headed toward the cabin. She was hurt and confused, and the worst part was, she wouldn't accept his help.

He'd have to rely on patience, kindness and compassion to make her feel safe. That would go a long way to ease her worry and earn her trust.

Hopefully that would be enough.

Sara wasn't sure how far she'd get before passing out from the excruciating pain of her headache, but she'd fight until she dropped. She had somehow survived the fall, and wouldn't allow herself to die at the hand of a hired thug.

It figures LaRouche and Harrington would send a handsome, clean-cut guy to find her—a real charmer, this one. Will or Bill or whatever his name was, had to be over six feet tall, with chestnut brown hair and green eyes, and he spoke with such a gentle, calming tone. What a story he'd crafted for himself: he'd come out here to pray?

He'd laid it on thick, all right. Those were probably his little girls in the photograph, girls who had no idea what their daddy did for a living.

In her ten years with the FBI, Sara had learned plenty about sociopaths and how they used their cunning intelligence and polished charisma to convince an interrogating agent of their innocence.

Clutching the gun, she took her finger off the trigger in case she stumbled and pulled it by accident. He wouldn't know the difference. As long as Will thought she aimed a gun at his back, he'd do as she ordered.

The trees around her started drifting in and out of focus. She blinked to clear her vision, and stumbled on a rock jutting out of the ground.

Strong, firm hands gripped her arms, keeping her upright. Will's green eyes studied her face, as if assessing her head injury. He must have realized his mistake, that he was still holding on to her, because his hands sprung free and he raised them, as if to say, *please don't shoot me*.

She stepped back and dropped the backpack on the ground. "It's throwing me off balance."

He picked up the pack and adjusted it across his shoulders with ease. "That bruise above your eye—" He hesitated. "Are you experiencing blurred vision?"

"I'm fine." She flicked the gun barrel toward the trail.

He continued walking.

"I have ice packs at the cabin," he said. "And pain reliever."

She hated that he was being so polite. It was an act, his strategy to discover how much she knew. Those were LaRouche and Harrington's orders, right?

Much like her official orders had been to leave it alone, put aside the LHP, Inc., investigation due to lack of evidence. But she'd pushed and pushed until Bonner had had enough, and told her to take a couple of weeks off.

So she did, and spent her vacation going undercover and buying her way on to the trail guide team that LaRouche, Harrington and Price had hired to take them up the mountain. Her goal: watch and listen, glean whatever information she could from the men who were on vacation with their guards down.

"Would you like some water?" Will offered.

She ignored him. Sara might be hurting, but she wasn't stupid. It would be too easy for Will to slip something into her water, rendering her unconscious.

"Guess not," he said softly.

She took a deep breath and bit back a gasp at the stab of bruised ribs. She decided it was a good thing because the pain would keep her conscious and alert.

He slowed down, closing the distance between them.

"Keep walking," she said through clenched teeth.

"I thought you might need to rest."

"I don't."

With what seemed like a frustrated sigh, he continued. Sure, he was frustrated. He wanted to finish this job quickly and move on to his next high-paying assignment.

She focused on his backpack as she struggled to place one foot in front of the other without losing her balance. It wasn't easy when she felt as though she'd stepped off the Tilt-A-Whirl at the county fair.

They continued in silence, her pulse ricocheting off the inside of her skull with each step. She had to make it, had to put these arrogant criminals behind bars.

She hoped they could pull the video recording off her phone, even though she'd noticed it had been damaged in the fall.

Will's phone was working just fine. Maybe they were close to getting reception. She pulled his phone out of her pocket, but her trembling fingers dropped it. She snapped her gaze to Will, fearing he'd seen her weakness. He continued up the trail.

She waited until he was a good distance away and knelt down to retrieve the phone. When she stood, her vision blurred and she could barely make out Will's form. She squinted through the haze to see him.

He was no longer within sight.

She shoved the phone into her pocket and clutched the gun grip with both hands. Where did he go? Had he taken off up ahead, waiting to ambush her? She approached a sharp turn, blocked by a boulder.

Took a slow, shallow breath…

Darted around the corner.

And spotted Will, on his knees, with his hands interlaced behind his head.

"What are you doing?" she said.

"Waiting for you."

"Get up."

He stood, his back to her. "Are you all right?"

"Go on, keep moving."

He continued along the trail and she followed. He was waiting for her? More like he was messing with her head, and doing a good job of it.

"The cabin's not far," he said.

She ignored him, knowing how these guys worked. They insinuated themselves into your psyche and destroyed you from the inside out. This guy was luring her with his father-of-the-year, single-parent story. She'd seen the wallpaper on his phone of two adorable girls with strawberry blonde hair and big smiles. This guy was a master.

They trekked the rest of the way in silence, Sara focusing on breathing through the pain and shutting out the panic taunting her from the fringes of her mind. She was in the middle of nowhere with an assassin, and her next step could be her last.

No, she was tough. Even if others didn't believe it, she knew it in her heart.

If only she'd been tough when she was twelve.

They turned a corner to an open field with a cabin in the distance. Surely she'd be able to get a signal out there, in the middle of the field.

He marched in the direction of the cabin.

"Stop," she said. She'd be a fool to let him go inside with her. No doubt that was where he kept his tools of the trade—coercion tools.

"Sit down, over there." She jerked the gun barrel.

He sat down beside a fallen tree.

"You have rope in your pack?" she said.

"I do."

"Get it."

He unzipped his pack and pulled out what looked like parachute cord.

"Toss it over here. And put your hands behind your back," she said.

He did, not making eye contact. With a fortifying breath, she grabbed the rope off the ground and climbed over the downed tree.

"Lean forward."

He did as ordered. "I'm not going to hurt you."

"You're right, you won't."

She quickly bound his wrists behind his back, and secured him to a limb of the fallen tree. She stood and started walking.

"Drink some water," he said. "It will help with the headache."

"You can stop now."

"The best cell reception is over there, by that cluster of boulders." He nodded, ignoring her comment.

With determination and focus, she marched toward the field, on the other side of a narrow creek. That had to be the spot where she'd find a signal. It would also put her out in the open, making her vulnerable, an easy target. No, these guys usually worked alone. She checked his phone, hopeful and more than a little desperate, but she still had no bars.

She glanced up. A ray of sunlight bounced off the creek and pierced her vision. Pain seared through her brain. She snapped her eyes shut, but it was too late. A sudden migraine blinded her.

She stumbled forward. Had to get to…had to get service. Call her boss…

"What's wrong?" Will shouted.

She broke into a slow jog. Had to get away from him. Get help.

Breathing through the pain, she stepped onto the rocks to cross the creek. One foot in front of the other. She could do it.

But she slipped, jerking forward. She put out her hands to break her fall.

And landed in the water with a splash.

The man's shouts echoed in the distance.

She feared he would somehow free himself and finish her off.

She crawled through the creek, her soggy clothes weighing her down. Pain bounced through her head like a pinball.

With a gasp, she surrendered—to the pain, to her own failure—and collapsed into the cold, bubbling water.

Chapter Two

"**M**a'am!" Will shouted, pulling on the rope binding his wrists. She was down, unconscious in the creek. Was her head even above water?

"Hey!" He realized he didn't even know her name. "Ma'am, get up!"

She didn't move.

"Argh!" he groaned, pulling violently on his wrists. This was not going to happen. He was not going to sit here and watch a woman die in front of him.

"Get up!" he shouted.

She didn't move.

He yanked on his wrists and dug the heels of his boots into the ground, trying to get leverage. This craziness wasn't going to do him any good. He took a deep breath and forced himself to be calm.

"Think," he said. He remembered that his pocketknife was clipped to the side of his backpack.

He stretched out, making himself as long as possible, practically dislocating a shoulder in the process. With the toe of his boot, he caught the strap of his pack and dragged it across the soft earth. In a low crouch, he kicked it behind him until his fingers could reach the knife.

He flicked it open and sawed away at his bindings, unable to see what he was doing. A sharp pain made him hesitate when the blade cut his skin. He clenched his jaw and continued.

"Ma'am!" he called out. "Ma'am, answer me!"

She didn't move.

He continued to dig at the rope with the blade, and accidentally cut his skin again. Didn't matter, he had to get free and—

Snap! He jerked his wrists free, reached around and started working on the rope that bound him to the tree.

"Come on, come on," he muttered. The parachute cord he kept in his pack was meant to be strong, which was why it felt as if it was taking forever to cut himself loose.

Please, God, help me get to her in time.

He finally sliced through it, pocketed the knife and grabbed his pack. Racing across the property, he focused on the woman, who was only partially submerged in the creek. What if she'd swallowed water and it blocked her airway?

He rushed to her side, looped his forearms under her armpits and dragged her out of the creek.

He leaned close. She wasn't breathing.

"No," he whispered.

With one hand on her forehead, and the other on the tip of her chin, he tilted her head backward. He hoped it was only her tongue blocking the airway. He pinched her nose and administered two deep breaths.

She coughed and a rush of relief whipped through his chest. Will rolled her onto her side. "It's okay. You're okay now," he said, although his heart was still racing at breakneck speed.

He had to call for help, get Echo Mountain Search and Rescue up here and quick. He spotted his smartphone, partially submerged in the creek. He snatched it out of the cold water. It would dry out and be usable at some point, but until then Will was on his own.

The shiny glint of metal caught his eye. The woman's gun lay mere inches away from him. He wasn't a fan of guns, but couldn't leave it here for a random stranger to pick up. He shoved it into his pocket.

The woman coughed. "P-p-please don't hurt me."

He snapped his attention to her shivering body. She was clutching her jacket above her heart, terrified.

"You don't have to be afraid of me," he said. "I'm going to help you."

She closed her eyes, as if she didn't believe him. He wondered if she saw him pocket the gun and assumed the worst.

"Do you think you can get up?" he said.

"Yeah."

He extended his hand. She ignored it and shifted onto her hands and knees. A round of coughs burst from her chest. That didn't sound good. He feared the water in her lungs might lead to something worse.

She stood, but wavered. Her eyes rolled back and he caught her as she went down. Hoisting her over his shoulder, he marched to the cabin. He had to get her dry, tend to her head wound and then determine what other injuries she'd sustained. It was obvious she had a severe headache, and most likely suffered from dehydration. He could treat those easily enough, but didn't have the ability to treat internal bleeding from her fall, or other, more serious injuries.

He'd do his best. The rest was in God's hands.

Taking quick, steady steps, he made it to the cabin and laid her on the single bed. He grabbed logs and started a fire to warm the room. Once he got it lit, he refocused on the woman.

The woman. He wished he knew her name.

He pulled her into a sitting position, leaning her head against his shoulder to remove her jacket. He noticed it was water-resistant.

"Smart girl," he whispered.

Most of her clothes, except for her jeans, were dry thanks to the jacket. She could remove her jeans to dry out when she regained consciousness. He wouldn't do anything that would make her feel uncomfortable.

He adjusted her on the bed, covered her with a wool blanket and pulled the bed closer to the fire.

Rushing into the kitchen area, he grabbed more first-aid supplies from the cabinet. Her groan echoed across the small cabin. Cracking an ice pack a few times to release the chemicals, he grabbed a kitchen chair and slid it close to her.

"Let's get a better look." He analyzed the lacerations on her face, retrieved an antiseptic wipe from the first-aid kit, and pressed it against the scrapes scarring her adorable face.

Adorable, Will? Really?

Shaking off the thought, he cleansed the debris from her head wound, and then placed a bandage over the cut. He pressed the ice pack against a lump on her head that was sure to swell and probably leave her with at least one black eye, if not two.

"Uh," she groaned.

"I'm sorry, but this will reduce the inflammation."

She pinched her eyes shut as if in extreme pain, which indicated a concussion.

"Where else are you hurt?" he said.

She didn't answer. He noticed she gripped her left wrist against her stomach.

"Your wrist?" he said. "May I see it?"

She buried it deeper into her stomach. Yeah, it was injured, all right. Her reaction was similar to Marissa's when she'd broken her wrist after falling off her bike last spring.

The mystery woman wasn't making this easy, but he wouldn't force the issue. He suspected that dehydration intensified her confusion and fear, and he wouldn't risk making it worse.

He grabbed a water bottle out of his pack. "You need to hydrate."

Supporting her with his arm, he sat her up and offered the water. Slowly, her eyes blinked open.

"You really need to drink something," he encouraged.

She pursed her lips, and her blue eyes clouded with fear. Ah, she thought he'd put something in the water.

"It's filtered water, see?" He took a swig, and made sure to swallow so she could see him. "Delicious."

He sounded as though he was trying to convince five-year-old Marissa to eat her broccoli.

The woman nodded and he held the bottle to her lips. He tipped it and she sipped, but coughed. He pulled her against his chest and gently patted her back. How long had it been since he'd comforted a woman like this? Lord knew Megan wouldn't accept his comfort during the last months of her life.

The mystery woman leaned into Will and he held his breath. Maybe she'd decided to trust him?

"What's your name?" he said.

She pushed away from him.

He put up his hands. "I'm sorry."

Clutching her wrist to her stomach, her blue-gray eyes widened, her lower lip quivering.

"At least let me wrap your wrist?" he said.

She glared.

"The longer we wait, the more it will swell. I'll wrap it, then ice it to reduce the inflammation. It might hurt less once it's iced."

She didn't shake her head, so he thought she might be open to the idea. He pulled an elastic bandage out of his first-aid kit and extended his hand. "May I?"

She tentatively placed her wrist in his palm. It didn't look broken, but they wouldn't know for sure until she had it X-rayed.

"Did this happen when you fell in the creek?" he asked.

She nodded affirmative.

"It's probably a sprain." He slid his palm out from under her wrist. "I need you to hold this steady between your thumb and forefinger," he said, placing the bandage just right.

He wrapped the bandage down to her wrist and back up between her thumb and forefinger, noting how petite her fingers were.

"They'll obviously do this better at the hospital," he said, guiding the bandage to circle her wrist a few times. He secured it with a plastic clip. "I've got some pain reliever."

He dug in his backpack and found ibuprofen. When

he turned to her, she'd scooted away from him again, her eyes flaring at the sight of the bottle.

"What do I need to do to convince you I'm a friend, not an enemy?"

"Give me my gun."

"I'd rather not."

She clenched her jaw.

"You're dehydrated and not thinking clearly," he explained. "The gun could go off by accident."

She pulled her knees to her chest, her hands trembling.

He grabbed an extra blanket off the foot of the bed and shook it open. He started to drape it across her shoulders, but noticed she'd gone white. He hesitated. Yet he had to get her warm somehow.

Gently draping the blanket around her, he pulled it closed in front.

"Hold it together," he said, as softly as possible.

She reached up with her right hand and their fingers touched.

She burst into a more violent round of shivers.

It tore Will apart that she was having this kind of reaction to him. Maybe it was a physical reaction to near hypothermia.

"We need to warm you up. Let me try something." He rubbed her arms through the thick blanket.

He thought he was being gentle, but after a minute she pinched her eyes shut as if suffering severe pain. He snapped his hands from her body and stood abruptly.

"You can't get warm with those wet jeans soaking your skin. You can take them off, and wrap this around your waist." He pulled his spare blanket out of his pack and laid it on the bed. "And ice the wrist. I'll go try to get the phone working."

He shifted his backpack onto his shoulders and turned to leave.

"Wait," she said.

He hesitated, hopeful.

"My gun?"

His heart sank. He pulled the weapon out of his jacket pocket and slid it onto the kitchen table.

"I'll be outside if you need me." Will shut the door and strode away from the cabin, kicking himself for his last remark. Of course she wouldn't need him. She thought Will the enemy, a man out to kill her.

"She's dehydrated," he muttered. "And confused."

Which made him a complete idiot for leaving her alone with the gun. Although he'd removed the clip, there was still one bullet in the chamber.

Talk about not thinking straight—he'd been thrown off-kilter since he'd found her. What else would explain his behavior? She'd practically broken his nose, yet he still wanted to help her. She'd tied him to a tree, and he'd cut his own skin to free himself so he could save her life.

He glanced at his wrist. He should have bandaged it while he was in the cabin, but had completely forgotten about his own wounds, and he'd left the first-aid kit behind. The cuts weren't that bad. A good thing since the woman would probably lock him out of the cabin.

The woman. He still didn't know her name.

He took the phone out of his pocket and removed the battery. Trying to power it up while wet could cause more problems, so he'd try to dry it out. He sat on a rock and dug into his pack for the small can of compressed air. His friends often teased him about the random things he carried in his pack, but after Marissa had dropped his phone into the town's water fountain, he knew anything could happen where his girls were concerned, and he had to be ready.

Glancing at the cabin, he realized he hadn't been ready for today's events. He hadn't been prepared to stumble upon a wounded, vulnerable woman in the mountains, nor had he been prepared to have to fight so hard to help her.

He aimed the compressed air nozzle at his phone and squeezed. As it blew away the moisture, he considered that maybe he should accept the fact he would never win this woman over. Perhaps he should cut his losses and head back to town, leaving her to her own devices until SAR could make the save.

He stilled, removing his finger from the compressed air button. No, he was not his father. He did not abandon those who needed him. Wasn't that exactly why he'd gotten involved in Echo Mountain SAR?

A crack of thunder drew his attention to the sky. Clouds rolled in quickly from the south. Not good.

Although the compressed air might have helped, he knew he'd have to wait a few hours before reinserting the battery and trying it out. He pocketed the phone and battery, and headed back to the cabin.

He hoped she wouldn't shoot him on sight.

As soon as he left, Sara grabbed the gun and sneaked out of the cabin. Maybe not the smartest move, but then staying with this man, this very manipulative man, could prove much worse.

She was actually starting to believe him.

As she trudged up a trail, clutching a wool blanket around her shoulders, she realized how close she'd come to dying back there at the hands of her captor.

Dying because he was so good at his job.

He'd nearly convinced her of his sincerity as he'd gently tended her wounds and warmed her body with his strong hands. And to think, when their fingers touched, she'd felt a sense of calm she'd never felt with another man.

Dehydration. A concussion. General insanity. Check on all of the above. LaRouche and Harrington must have paid big bucks to send such a master manipulator out here to find her.

At least she still had her gun. She pulled it out of her pocket, only then realizing the clip was missing. "Great."

Her head ached, her ribs ached and now her wrist was throbbing thanks to breaking her fall when she went facedown in the creek.

The creek. Will the assassin had saved her life after pulling her from the water. He hadn't had to do that, had he?

She focused on the rugged trail ahead to avoid any missteps. There'd be no one to catch her this time.

A flash of Will's green eyes assessing her injury as he'd held her upright taunted her. A part of her wished he'd truly been the man he'd claimed to be: a single dad on a hiking trip to commune with God.

But then, Sara wasn't a fool. She knew how *that* relationship worked—people prayed and God ignored them.

She stuck her gun back into the waistband of her wet jeans. At least she had one bullet left in the chamber.

A deep roar echoed through the woods. She froze.

Another roar rattled the trees.

She snapped her gaze to the right…

And spotted a black bear headed her way.

Everything in her body shut down—her mind, her legs, even her lungs. She couldn't breathe. Frozen in place, she stared at the beast as it lumbered toward her.

Closer.

Don't stand here, idiot. Run!

Could she outrun a bear? Were you even supposed to try? She struggled to remember what she'd learned about bears, but her brain had completely shut down. One thing she did know was that she couldn't defend herself if he decided she'd make a good appetizer.

"Don't run or he'll attack," a deep male voice said from behind her.

Will.

"Wh-wh-what are you…doing here?" she whispered, unable to take her eyes off the bear.

"Listen to me carefully. Do not look into the bear's eyes. Okay?"

She nodded and redirected her attention to the ground.

"Now back away slowly. Toward the sound of my voice."

She hesitated.

"It's okay. Slow movements shouldn't spook her," he said.

Sara followed his directions and backed up, but the bear kept coming. Will stepped in front of her.

The bear roared, aggravating her headache.

"What does she want?" she said.

"Probably the same thing you want. To be left alone. Maybe she's got cubs nearby."

"I have the gun."

"That'll only make her angry. Back up slowly."

She took a step back, then another.

"That's it," he said.

As she and Will tried to distance themselves, the bear slowly followed.

"This isn't working," Sara said, panic gripping her chest.

"Easy now. Don't make eye contact. You're doing great."

Sara continued to step back. "What if she charges us?"

"We make ourselves big and threatening. I have a feeling you'll do great."

Was he teasing her? As they were both about to be torn apart by a bear?

They kept backing away and Sara was stunned when the bear hesitated.

"That's right, we're boring hikers, mama bear," he said in a hushed voice.

That smooth, sweet voice he'd used on Sara.

They backed away until they were out of sight. Will turned and gripped her arm. "Let's move."

"You think she'll follow us?"

"Doubtful, but we're safer in the cabin. What were you thinking, taking off with nothing but a blanket?"

"I was… That you were—"

"Enough. I don't want to hear any more about how I'm going to kill you. The dehydration is messing with your head." He stopped and looked deeply into her eyes. "If I wanted you dead, I would have let Smokey eat you for dinner, right?"

True. An assassin wouldn't have risked his own life to save a mark from a bear, only to kill her later. In La-

Rouche's and Harrington's minds, a dead witness was the best witness, yet Will have saved her twice.

Which meant she'd been abusing this innocent man, Good Samaritan.

Single father.

She sighed as they kept walking.

"Thanks," she said. "For the bear thing."

"You're welcome. I don't suppose that warrants me knowing your name?"

"Sara."

"Nice to meet you, Sara. I'd rather you not run off again and get eaten by wild animals on my watch."

"No promises," she half joked.

"Ah, you like pushing back for the fun of it," he teased.

But he'd nailed it. Sara was always pushing, although, not necessarily for fun.

"Why do you think someone wants to harm you?" he asked.

"I witnessed a crime."

They turned a corner and he stopped short.

"What?" She looked around him.

A man was coming out of the cabin.

"Do you recognize him?" she said.

"No." He motioned to a nearby tree. "Hide back there. I'll check it out."

"It could be dangerous."

"Or simply a hiker lost in the mountains. Kinda like you." Will smiled and nodded toward the tree. "Go on."

"Maybe you should take this." She offered him the gun.

An odd smile creased his lips. "Thanks, but you keep it."

She nodded and watched him walk away, shielding herself behind the tree. From this vantage point she could watch the scene unfold, not that she had a great escape plan. Hiking back up the trail meant crossing paths with the bear, but sticking around meant being interrogated by the real assassin, if that's who the stranger was.

If it was the man hired by LaRouche and Harrington, that meant Will, a single father of two girls, was walking into trouble.

For Sara.

"No," she whispered, and peered around the tree, wanting to go to him, to tell him not to take the chance.

A gunshot echoed across the property.

And Will dropped to the ground.

Chapter Three

Will hit the dirt, thinking Sara had come after him and took her best shot. But that didn't make sense. She was smart enough to know it was safer where he'd left her, camouflaged by the trees.

Sara might be confused, but she wasn't foolish.

He struggled to slow the adrenaline rush flooding his body.

"Hey, sorry about that," a man's voice said.

Will eyed a man's hiking boots as he approached.

"I saw a mountain lion and wanted to scare him off."

Will stood and brushed himself off, irritated both by the hiker's decision to discharge a firearm and by his own reaction to the gunshot. It was a defense response developed from growing up in a house with a volatile, and sometimes mean, drunk.

"I'm B. J. Masters." B.J. extended his gloved hand and Will shook it.

"Will Rankin."

B.J. was in his late thirties, wearing a top-quality jacket and expensive hiking boots. He didn't seem like an amateur hiker, nor did he seem like the type to be hunting a helpless woman.

"Whoa, what happened?" B.J. motioned to Will's face.

Bruising must have formed from Sara nailing him with the gun.

"Embarrassing hiking moment," Will said. "Would rather not go into the details. I noticed you were in my cabin."

"Yeah, sorry about that," B.J. said, glancing at the ground. "I thought maybe it was abandoned, but once I went inside I saw your things and the fire going. Didn't mean to trespass."

"No problem. You on a day hike or...?"

"Yeah, I'm scouting places to hold a retreat for guys at work. I'm with Zippster Technologies out of Seattle." He handed Will a business card. "I was surprised to see a cabin in this part of the park."

"A well-kept secret. Where are you headed today?"

"Squawk Point."

"That's a nice area," Will said.

He eyed Will's cabin. "You rent the cabin through the park website?"

"I do."

"I wonder how many guys could fit in there?"

"Probably eight to ten," Will said. "After that it might get a little crowded."

"Yeah, well, probably not big enough for our team." B.J. gazed across the field, then back at the cabin. "But a nice area, for sure. Well, thanks for not calling the cops on me for breaking and entering."

"Actually, I dropped my phone in the creek. Don't

suppose I could borrow yours to call my girls and let them know I'm okay?"

Will figured he'd call SAR.

"Wish I could help you out, but the battery's dead. This new-model smartphone is worthless."

"What if you run into trouble?"

"I've got a personal locator beacon. Besides, what trouble could I possibly get into out here?" He gazed longingly at the mountain range.

"You'd be surprised," Will muttered.

"Well, nice meeting you." B.J. extended his hand again.

"You, too. Have a good day."

With a nod, B.J. headed for the trail.

Will went to the side of the cabin and pretended to get wood for the fireplace. Once B.J. was out of sight, he'd retrieve Sara and bring her to the cabin. Made no sense letting B.J. know of her presence, especially if the men who were after her questioned random hikers about seeing her.

When he'd found Sara just now, he noted her pale skin and bloodshot eyes. At least she was walking around, and maybe even thinking a little more clearly than before.

That woman was tough, no doubt about it, tough and distrusting.

Will wandered to the side of the property to search for a cell signal. The sooner he could get Sara medical attention the better.

He pressed the power button, but the phone was still dead.

He gazed off into the distance. B.J. was turning the corner, about to disappear from view. Will waited until he could no longer see the hiker, then started for the trail where he'd left Sara. She was already on her way down, clutching the gun in her right hand.

"Who was that?" she said.

"A techie from Seattle scouting out retreat spots."

"And you believed him?" She scanned the area.

"Sara, it's okay." He reached out.

His mistake.

She jerked back as if his touch would sear her skin. "Get inside."

He put up his hands and prayed for patience. What more could he do to make her feel safe?

"Are you hungry?" he said, going into the cabin. "I thought I'd heat up some red beans and rice for supper."

She followed him inside and shut the door. "I'm fine."

"I didn't ask if you were fine. I asked if you were hungry."

"Stop being nice to me."

"Would you rather I be mean to you?" He pulled out supplies for dinner.

"He could have been working for Harrington and LaRouche," she said.

"Doubtful. He gave me his business card." Will offered it to her. She took it and sat on the bed, still clutching the gun.

He pulled out a pot and found a can opener in a drawer. "As soon as the phone dries off, I'll get a signal and call SAR, but it might not be until tomorrow morning."

"Go ahead. Ask me," she said.

"Ask you what?"

"What I'm doing out here, and why men from a tour group I was assisting with are after me."

"My goal is to get you back to town for medical attention. If you want to tell me what's going on, that's completely up to you."

He heard the bed creak and her soft groan drift across the cabin. She was hurting. The adrenaline rush from her encounter with the bear had probably masked her pain, and now that she considered herself relatively safe, she was feeling every ache, every pinch of pain.

"How about some pain reliever?" he asked.

"Yeah, probably a good idea."

"Check my backpack, side pocket," he said, pleased that she was accepting his help. "You'll find a small container with ibuprofen and vitamins. Probably wouldn't hurt for you to chew on a few vitamin Cs to boost your immune system."

Filling the pot with water, he went to the fireplace to warm it. He didn't look at her for fear he'd scare her again, that she'd retreat behind a wall of paranoia and fear.

"Wouldn't hurt to drink more water," he suggested. "To help the dehydration, and probably the headache."

She grabbed the water bottle off the bed and sipped.

"Why are you here?" she said.

"It's my cabin, at least for a few more days."

"Why don't you leave me alone?"

"That wouldn't be very gentlemanly of me."

"Gentlemanly, huh?" she said.

"You sound as if you've never heard the word before." He stirred their dinner.

"Or I haven't met many—" she paused "—gentlemen."

"That's unfortunate."

"It's life."

He dropped the subject, not wanting to antagonize her with a philosophical discussion on how men were supposed to be gentlemen, especially to women, that men weren't supposed to think solely of themselves.

And abandon their children to a volatile mother.

Whoa, shelve it, Will. This getaway was supposed to be about easing the resentment from his heart, not battling the scars from childhood.

Out of the corner of his eye, Will noticed Sara shivering as she popped off the top of the ibuprofen bottle.

"If you remove your wet jeans we can dry them by the fire," he offered.

"No, thanks."

"Okay."

"No offense, but I won't get very far without my pants."

"Nor will you get very far if you come down with pneumonia."

"Okay, Dad."

He sighed. "Sorry, guess I clicked into parent mode."

He refocused on the water heating in the pot. For whatever reason, she still couldn't completely trust him.

Understanding comes from walking in the other person's shoes. Reverend Charles's advice when Will struggled to understand Megan. No matter how hard he'd tried, he couldn't make sense of why she'd pushed him away.

Since he and Sara would be stuck in this one-room cabin for a while, he tried seeing the world from her point of view to better understand her reactions. She seemed clearheaded, not as delusional as before, and she feared someone was out to harm her. That was her reality. He had to respect that fact. She was also wounded and stuck in a remote cabin with a stranger who, in her eyes, was somewhat of an enigma because he considered himself a gentleman.

The fact that the thought of a good man was so foreign to Sara probably intensified her distrust.

Will realized that in order to take care of her, he needed to respect her space, and not act aggressive or domineering. He hoped she would open her mind to the possibility that he truly wanted to help.

Gripping the gun firmly in her hand, Sara found herself struggling to stay awake. Not good. Things happened when she slept.

Bad things.

"Do you have any coffee?" she asked.

"Sure."

Will went into the kitchen. She eyed the bottle of ibuprofen in her lap, then the chewable vitamin C tablets. She'd taken both, thanks to Will's suggestion.

Will. A stranger with really bad timing who'd happened upon a woman with a target on her back. A stranger who wouldn't leave her, even after she'd told him her life was in danger, that she could be putting his life in danger.

"It's instant," he said, returning to the fire to warm water.

"That's fine." She handed him the chewable vitamin bottle. "You could probably use some extra C, as well."

He popped one into his mouth. "Thanks."

She watched his jaw work and his Adam's apple slide up and down as he swallowed. He fascinated her, this gentle, strong and honorable man.

He scooped coffee into a mug and added water. "You can take up to five of those vitamin Cs if you want."

"What I want is to be home," she let slip.

"Which is where?" He handed her the mug.

She noticed blood smudging his skin. "What happened to your wrist?"

"Ah, nothing," he muttered. He dug into his pack and pulled out an antiseptic wipe. "I'll bet you're a city girl."

"That obvious, huh?"

"A good guess."

"What about you?" she said.

"I live in Echo Mountain," he said as he cleaned blood from his wrist.

"What's that like, living in a small town?"

"It's nice, actually." He opened a dehydrated packet of food, poured hot water into it, sealed the bag and set it aside. "Never thought I'd end up living in a small town, but I've been here for ten years and can't imagine living anywhere else."

"You moved here from...?"

"Denver," he said. "My wife was from here originally, but she wanted to live near the Rockies so she got a job in Denver after college. We met on a group hike and..." He glanced at the fire.

"What?" Sara asked.

Will stood and went to the kitchen. "I should find us something to eat on."

She sensed he regretted talking about his wife. Sara wondered what had happened to her but wouldn't ask.

"Tell me more about your girls," she said.

Walking back to the fire, he handed her a spoon. She used it to stir the instant coffee.

"Claire's my eldest daughter. Eight going on eighteen."

He shook his head and sat in a chair beside the fire. "I'm not sure how I'm going to make it through her teenage years without getting an ulcer."

"That's a ways away. Perhaps you'll remarry."

The flames danced in his green eyes as he stared at the fire. "Perhaps."

"How long were you married?" she pushed, sipping her coffee.

"Ten years. Claire was six when her mother died, and little Marissa was only three."

"It's hard for kids to lose a parent."

"So I've been told," he said.

There wasn't a day that went by that Sara didn't ache for her mom and dad.

She pulled the blanket tighter around her shoulders. They spent the next few minutes in silence. Will seemed temporarily lost in a memory about his wife, and Sara beat herself up for not getting enough evidence to put LaRouche and Harrington away sooner.

Sure she'd recorded their conversation and the murder, but when she'd checked her phone earlier, she'd noticed it had been damaged in the fall. Hopefully a tech could retrieve the file.

Will opened the packet of rice and beans, dumped it onto a metal plate and handed it to her.

"What about you?" she said.

"I'll eat whatever's left over."

She hesitated before taking it.

"Go on, it's not bad," he said.

"But it's your food."

"I've got more."

She took the plate, avoiding eye contact. The more

time she spent with Will, the more frustrated she became about her situation, and relying on his good nature.

Relying on anyone but herself was dangerous.

Since she hadn't eaten in nearly eighteen hours, she took the plate. "Thanks."

"Tell me more about the man who is after you," he said.

"Hired by two businessmen who killed their partner." She took a few bites of food and sighed. "I saw them toss the guy over a cliff."

"They killed their partner?" he said. "Why?"

"Who knows, money?" She didn't want to share too much with Will because it could put him in danger.

"I can see why you've been so frightened," he said. "I'm sorry if I haven't been patient enough."

Her jaw practically dropped to the floor. What was he talking about? He was apologizing after everything she'd done? Given him two black eyes and verbally abused him?

After a few minutes, she handed him the half-empty plate.

"You sure?" he said. "I can always heat up something else for myself."

"No, go ahead."

With a nod, he accepted the plate and started eating. She took a deep breath, then another, staring into the fire.

Maybe it was the flames dancing in the fireplace, or the sound of his spoon scraping against the plate. Whatever the case, she found herself relaxing, fighting to keep her eyes open.

Stay awake!

"Relax and I'll keep watch," he said, as if sensing her thoughts.

Will might think they were safe in the cabin, but Sara knew better. Danger was almost always on the other side of a closed door.

The warmth of the fire filled the cabin and she blinked, fighting to stay alert. Exhaustion took hold and she felt herself drift. She snapped her eyes open again, and spotted Will lying on the floor on top of his sleeping bag. He wore a headlamp and was reading a book.

He was definitely a trusting man, but was he really so naive to think they weren't in danger? He was a civilian determined to protect her. Yet she'd brought the danger to his doorstep.

For half a second, she wanted to believe there were quality men like Will Rankin who rescued failed FBI agents, and protected them from bears and assassins.

Comforted her with a gentle hand on her shoulder. She drifted again...

Don't make a sound...

She gasped and opened her eyes. Will was no longer on the floor beside the fire. She scanned the room. She was alone.

The door opened and she aimed the gun. Will paused in the threshold. "Needed more wood." He crossed the small cabin and stacked the wood beside the fireplace.

"What time is it?" she said.

"Nineish," he said.

"I've been out for..."

"A couple of hours. Your body needed it."

Her mind ran wild, panicked about what could have happened in the past two hours. How close the assassin was to finding her.

"Give me your phone."

He handed it to her. She stood and headed for the door.

"I don't think it will work yet," he said.

"I've got to try."

"Want me to come with?"

"No." She spun around and instinctively pointed the gun at him. The look on his face was a mixture of disbelief and hurt.

"Sorry." She lowered the gun. "Just...stay here."

"Try a few hundred feet that way." He pointed, and then turned back to the fire, his shoulders hunched.

The minute she stepped out of the cabin a chill rushed down her arms. She should have brought the blanket with her, but wasn't thinking clearly. Why else would she have pointed the gun at Will?

His hurt expression shouldn't bother her. She hardly knew the man. Yet shame settled low in her gut.

Focus! It was late, but she had to call her boss if she could get a signal.

The full moon illuminated the area around the cabin. She pressed the power button and practically jogged toward a cluster of trees up ahead.

"Come on, come on." She held the button for a few seconds. The screen flashed onto the picture of the two redheaded girls.

"Yes," she said.

But still, no signal.

She waved the phone above her head, eyeing the screen, looking for bars.

The click of a gun made her freeze.

"There you are."

Chapter Four

A firm hand gripped a fistful of Sara's hair. "Did you think you could outrun us?" a man's deep voice said.

Us? They'd sent more than one of them after her?

"Nice to meet you, Sara. I'm Bill." He snatched the gun from the waistband of her jeans and pushed her toward the cabin.

"What do you want?"

"Why'd you run off from the group?"

"I had a family emergency."

"Sure," he said, sarcastic. "Who sent you in the first place?"

"No one. I work for Whitman Mountain Adventures."

"Convenient how you showed up out of nowhere and worked your way onto LaRouche and Harrington's camping trip."

"I needed the job."

"Yeah, yeah. We're meeting up with them tomorrow so you can explain yourself. We'll sleep here tonight."

Sleep here? In the cabin? Where Will was innocently stoking a fire?

"No," she ground out.

"Yes." He shoved her forward.

She opened the door to the cabin, but Will was gone.

"Where's your friend?" the man asked.

"What friend?"

He pushed her down in a chair. "The guy I met earlier today. Before our pleasant chat, I noticed your torn jacket on the bed. I guessed you were close. Where'd he go?"

"I have no idea."

A thumping sound echoed from the front porch.

"You sit there and be quiet while I go hunting." Her attacker bound her wrists in front.

When she winced at the pressure against her sprained wrist he smiled as if taking pleasure in hurting her. He leaned close. So close she was tempted to head-butt him. Instead, she stared straight ahead, acting like the innocent victim she claimed to be. He tied another rope around her midsection, securing her to the chair.

"Behave," he threatened.

He turned and went outside in search of Will. Why had Will gotten himself involved in this? Why had he had to help her when he'd found her unconscious body next to the lake?

Silence rang in her ears as fear took hold. The assassin would kill Will, leaving two little girls without a father. No, she couldn't let that happen. Couldn't let those girls suffer through the kind of mind-numbing grief Sara had experienced, especially since Will's girls had already lost their mom.

"Never give up," she ground out. And she wouldn't, ever, unlike the cops who'd given up on finding Dad's killer.

She dragged the chair into the kitchen, awkwardly opening drawers in search of a weapon.

She found a multipurpose fork in a drawer. It would have to do.

The door swung open with a crash.

She spun around, aiming her weapon…

At Will.

"You're here," she gasped.

He rushed across the small cabin. "Are you okay? Did he hurt you?" Will untied her and searched her face, as if fearing she'd been beaten up.

Sara shook her head. "I'm sorry, I'm so sorry."

"It's not your fault." He led her back to the fireplace, removed his backpack and dug inside. "Let me find—"

The assailant charged into the cabin, wrapping his arm around Will's throat.

"Let him go!" she cried.

Will tried to elbow the guy in the ribs but the assassin was too strong. Digging his fingers into the guy's arm, Will gasped for air. Sara darted behind the guy and wrapped her arm around his neck. The guy slammed her back against the cabin wall, sending a shudder of pain through her body. She collapsed on the floor.

He dragged Will outside and Sara stumbled after them. "Stop! Let him go!"

He threw Will to the ground and stomped on his chest, over and over again. "You like that?"

"Leave him alone!" Sara charged the assassin. He flung her aside, but not before she ripped the gun from the waistband of his jeans.

He continued beating on Will, unaware she had his weapon.

Sara scrambled to her feet. Aimed the weapon. "Stop or I'll shoot!"

The assassin was drowning in his own adrenaline

rush, the rush of beating a man to death. She squeezed the trigger twice and the guy went down. She rushed to Will, who'd rolled onto his side clutching his stomach.

"Will? Will, open your eyes."

He coughed and cracked them open. "That was... the guy who was after you?"

"He was hired to find me, yes."

"So someone else will come—" he coughed a few times "—looking for you?"

"Not tonight. He was supposed to take me to meet up with them tomorrow."

"Is he dead?"

"I don't know."

Will groaned as he sat up, gripping his ribs. "We need to check. If he's not dead, we need to administer first aid."

She leaned back and stared at him, stunned by his comment. "He tried to kill you."

He pressed his fingers to the assassin's throat. A moment later he nodded at Sara. "He's gone."

Will coughed a few times as he scanned the area. "We can't leave him out here. Animals."

She didn't have a response for that, either, speechless that Will could show compassion for a man who most certainly would have beaten him to death if she hadn't shot him first.

She eyed the body.

The dead body.

She'd just killed a man.

Her fingers tightened around the grip of the gun and her hand trembled uncontrollably, sending a wave of shivers across her body.

"Whoa, whoa, whoa," Will said, rushing to her. "Let's get you inside."

She thought she nodded, but couldn't be sure.

"Relax your fingers," he said, trying to take the gun away.

Staring at her hand, she struggled to follow his order but couldn't seem to let go.

"Sara, look at me."

She took a quick breath, then another. With a gentle hand, he tipped her chin to focus on his green eyes. Green like the forest after a heavy rain.

"That's it," he said. "Everything's okay. You can let go now."

But she didn't feel okay. Her hands grew ice cold and thoughts raced across her mind in a random flurry: her boss's disappointed frown, her cousin Pepper's acceptance into med school, the look on her father's face when he savored a piece of coconut cream pie.

A long time ago. Before...before...

Her legs felt as if they were melting into the soft earth.

She gasped for air...

And was floating, her eyes fixed on the moon above before she drifted into the cabin.

It was warm inside. It smelled like burning wood, not death. She was placed on the bed in front of the fire, but she didn't lie down because she didn't want to sleep, to dream, to be held captive by the nightmares.

"Keep the blanket around your shoulders," Will said.

It was then that she realized he'd carried her inside. He pulled the blanket snugly around her, and poked at the fire. It flared back to life.

He kneeled in front of her. "You're probably going into shock, but you'll be fine."

Those green eyes, brimming with promise and sincerity, made her believe that things would actually be okay.

It only lasted for a second.

Because in Sara's life, things were never okay.

"I'll be right back." Will squeezed her shoulder and left.

That was when the terror of her life came crashing down on her.

If she were a religious person, she'd go as far as to say she'd sinned in the worst possible way.

She'd killed a man.

She'd become like the monsters she'd sworn to destroy.

Like the monster that killed her father.

Will clicked into overdrive. He tossed logs out of the wood container, rolled the body onto a tarp and dragged him across the property.

A part of him was shocked, both by the murder of a stranger, and by his own reaction. He found himself more worried about Sara than the ramifications of this man's death.

It should be justified in the eyes of the law, since she'd shot him to save Will's life. The guy would have surely beaten Will to death, leaving his children parentless. Will wasn't sure Sara had had another option. The man was about brutality and death, and that was how his life had ended.

But taking another man's life was a sin, so after Will placed the body and weapon into the wood container, he kneeled beside it and prayed. "Father, please forgive us. In our efforts to live, we took another man's life."

Guilt clenched his heart. He still couldn't believe what had happened. But he couldn't dwell on it, not while Sara was going into shock. He needed to tend to her.

As he went back to the cabin, he noticed the man's blood on his gloves. He took them off and dropped them outside the door. The sight of blood might upset her further. He stepped inside the cabin.

Sara was not on the bed where he'd left her. He snapped his head around. "Sara?" His heart slammed against his chest. Had she left again? Was she wandering aimlessly in the mountains in a state of shock?

"Sara!"

The echo of his own voice rang in his ears. He turned, about to race out into the dark night.

Then he heard a squeak. Hesitating, he waited to see if he'd imagined it. Another squeak drifted across the room. He slowly turned back. The sound was coming from under the bed.

Will went to the bed and checked beneath it. Sara's terrified blue eyes stared back at him.

"He won't see me in here," she said in a childlike whisper.

"No, he won't. That's a good hiding place." He stretched out on his back and extended his hand. She looked at it. "Your hands must be very cold," he said.

She nodded. "Like ice-cycles."

"My hand is warm. May I warm the chill from your fingers?"

Her eyes darted nervously beyond him. "What if he comes back?"

"He won't. He's…" Will hesitated. Reminding her she'd killed a man would not help her snap out of shock. "He's gone."

"Are you sure?"

"One hundred and ten percent." The number he used with his girls.

She eyed Will's hand. He motioned with his fingers to encourage her to come out.

"I'm only safe if I stay hidden," she whispered. "He won't see me in here."

That was the second time she used the phrase *in here*. Where did she think she was? Will suspected she might be drifting in and out of reality, the present reality mixed with a past trauma, perhaps? At any rate, he needed to keep an eye on her condition by making sure she was warm and comfortable. If she felt most comfortable under the bed, then that was where she'd stay.

"Are you warm enough?" he asked.

She shrugged.

"How about another blanket?" He snatched one off a chair and placed it on the floor.

Her trembling fingers reached out and pulled the blanket beneath the bed. "Thanks."

"Is there anything else I can do for you?" he said.

"No, thank you."

He positioned himself in front of the fire. A few minutes of silence passed as he stared into the flames. The adrenaline rush had certainly worn off, because he was feeling the aches and pains from the beating he'd survived.

Survived because of Sara. She'd saved him from an ugly, painful death.

As energy drained from his body, he struggled to stay alert. Will needed to protect Sara, take care of her.

He glanced left. Her hand was sticking out from beneath the bed. Was she trying to make a connection with him? He positioned himself on the floor and peered under the bed. She'd changed positions and was lying on her side, bundled up in the blankets.

Bending his elbow, he brushed his hand against her petite fingers. She curled her chilled fingers around his.

"Wow, you are warm," she said.

"Yeah," he said, barely able to speak. This connection, the fact that touching Will comforted her, filled his chest with pride.

"Do you have a fever?" she said.

"Nah. The warm body temperature is a family thing. My girls run hot, too."

"Your girls." She closed her eyes and started to pull away.

Will clung to her hand. "No, don't. I… I need the connection."

She opened her eyes. "You do?"

"Yes."

"But I've been horrible to you. Accusing you of being an assassin, tying you up." Her eyes widened. "Oh, my God, that's why your wrists were bleeding. You had to cut yourself free."

She snatched her hand from his and rolled away.

Well, good news was she'd returned to reality and was no longer caught up in some trauma from her past. The bad news was she blamed herself for whatever pain Will had suffered.

He went to the other side of the bed. The fire didn't

light this part of the room so he couldn't see her face, but he still tried to connect with her, there, in the dark.

"It's not your fault," he said. "You were terrified and confused, and most likely suffering from dehydration."

"I gave you a bloody nose."

"I startled you."

"You were trying to help me." She sighed. "I'm so ashamed."

"Why, because you were protecting yourself from men who wanted to harm you? You should be proud. You escaped. You survived."

"No, they were right. I don't belong out here."

"Where, in the mountains?"

She didn't answer him.

"Sara?"

She rolled over again and he went to the other side of the bed. He bit back a groan against the pain of bruised ribs as he stretched out on the floor next to her.

"Could you do me a favor and stay in one position so I don't have to get up and down again?" he teased.

"I'm sorry."

"It's not that bad. But the ribs are a little sore."

"I meant, I'm sorry for everything that's happened."

"Sara, it's not your fault."

"Yes, it really is."

Silence stretched between them, punctuated by the sound of the crackling fire. Will sensed there was more behind her words, but he wasn't going to challenge her. He tried another strategy.

"Thank you," he said.

"For what?"

"For saving my life out there."

"You saved mine first." She extended her hand again and he grasped it. Unfortunately it was still ice cold.

"Do you want to sit by the fire to warm up?" he offered.

"Maybe later."

He sensed she was still frightened and probably felt vulnerable. But the more he knew about her situation, the better he could help her.

"Are you up to talking about what's going on?" he asked.

"Sure."

"Men are after you because you witnessed a murder?"

"Yes. They want to know what I saw, and what I heard."

"Did you hear anything?"

"Yes."

He waited.

"I shouldn't involve you further," she said.

"How can I help you if I don't know what's going on?"

"I would never forgive myself if you, or your girls, were threatened because of your association with me," she said.

She was a strong, determined woman, and an honorable one, as well. He couldn't fault her for that.

She yawned and pulled the blanket tight around her shoulder. She hadn't coughed in the past few hours, so he felt hopeful she wouldn't come down with pneumonia.

"Perhaps we should sleep," he suggested. "To be fresh for tomorrow. We'll need to hike a bit to find a cell signal."

"Okay, sleep sounds…good." She yawned again.

Although he knew sleep would help him function tomorrow, he doubted he could relax enough to drift off. He decided to brainstorm the necessary steps to get them safely back to town.

As options whirled in his brain, exhaustion took hold, making his mind wander to other things like his girls, his latest work assignment, Megan's death and the gray cloud of grief that hung over his house for so many months afterward. Could he have done something differently to help his girls adjust? No, ruminating about the past wouldn't help him raise his girls with love and compassion.

Sara squeaked and squeezed his hand. She must have fallen asleep. Will focused on the feel of her cool skin clinging to him, and decided he'd been given another chance to help someone.

And he wasn't going to blow it this time.

When Sara awoke, it took her a minute to figure out where she was, and whose hand she clung to.

Will.

Embarrassed, she considered pulling abruptly away, but didn't. She wanted another moment of peace, and it felt so comforting to be holding on to him.

He slept on his back, breathing slow and steady. She envied him for such a peaceful sleep. Since childhood she'd struggled with nightmares that often left her feeling exhausted in the morning.

With a sigh, he blinked open his eyes as if he knew she was watching him. He turned his head toward her.

"Good morning," he said, his voice hoarse.

"Good morning."

"Did you sleep okay?"

It was then that she realized she hadn't been plagued by nightmares. "Yeah, actually, I did."

"Good." He eyed his watch. "It's eight. We must have needed the sleep." He stood and offered his hand.

"I'm good," she said.

"Want me to make coffee?"

"That would be great." Sara climbed out from beneath the bed and stretched. "Uhh," she moaned. Her body ached from her fingertips to her toes.

"Hey, easy there." He went to her, touching her arm to help her sit in the chair.

"I'm okay, just sore." She looked up into his eyes. "Coffee will make it better."

"You got it."

A sudden pounding on the door made her gasp.

Chapter Five

"**W**here's the gun?" Sara said, anxiety rolling through her stomach.

"Outside in the wood container."

The pounding continued.

Will grabbed a log from the woodpile by the fire-place and motioned for Sara to get behind him. But she was no weakling, and no matter what injuries she'd sustained, she wasn't going to let Will fight this battle for her. He'd done enough.

Ignoring the pain of her injured wrist, she also grabbed a log and got on the other side of the door. If someone broke it down, he was going to get an unpleasant welcome.

The muffled sound of men talking on the other side of the door echoed through the thick wood. There were more than one of them? Not good. How had they found the isolated cabin? Then again, Bill had found it easily enough.

Another knock made her squeeze the wood so tight a sliver edged its way into her forefinger.

"Will? Will, you in there?" a male voice called.

"Nate?" Will dropped the log and reached out for the door.

Sara darted in front of him.

"Nate's a friend of mine, a cop," Will said. "It's okay."

She didn't step out of his way. She trusted Will but didn't trust the situation. It was too much of a coincidence that Will's friend happened to be hiking nearby.

"Sara, it's okay," Will said, touching her shoulder. "Trust me."

Maybe it was his gentle tone, or the sincerity of his rich green eyes that eased her worry. With a nod, she stepped aside, but didn't drop the log.

Will opened the door and shook his friend's hand. "Man, am I glad to see you."

Nate was tall, like Will, with broad shoulders and black hair. He wore a heavy jacket and gloves. An older gentleman with gray hair stood beside Nate.

"Hey, Harvey," Will greeted. "What are you guys doing up here?"

"Got a SAR call," Nate said. "We knew you were up here and figured you might be bored so we decided to swing by and pick you up." Nate studied Sara with a raised eyebrow. "Obviously, not bored."

The older man snickered.

"Right, sorry," Will said. "Nate, Harvey, this is Sara. Sara, Nate's a detective with Echo Mountain PD."

Sara placed the log on the floor and shook hands with the men. "Nice to meet you."

Nate redirected his attention to Will. "I didn't know you were dating anyone."

"Dating? Wait, no, not dating," Will said.

She thought he blushed, but couldn't be sure.

"We met when…" Will glanced at her.

"Will saved my life," she explained to Nate. "I witnessed a murder, and I'm on the run from men who are out to kill me because of what I saw."

Nate narrowed his eyes at her. "Direct, aren't you?"

"We've had a long night," Will said. "A guy tried to kill me and Sara shot him. The body's in the wood container."

"Wait, you killed a man?" Nate said.

"I had no choice," Sara answered.

"We've gotta get her to the hospital," Will redirected. "She's got an injured wrist, possible head trauma and who knows what else. We need to move fast before they send someone else after her."

"Can you hike?" Nate asked her.

"Hiking's not good for her concussion," Will said.

"Let her speak." Nate studied Sara.

"Not far, and not very fast, unfortunately," she admitted.

"I'll stay with you two for protection and call dispatch to send another team with a litter. Shouldn't take more than an hour since they're already on their way. Harvey, go ahead and help with this morning's rescue."

"You got it. It was nice to meet you, ma'am," Harvey said.

"You, too."

Sara instantly liked Harvey. He reminded her of what her father might have been like had he lived.

She went back into the cabin and sat at the kitchen table. Why did she have to think about Dad today? She didn't need that guilt and sadness dragging her down while trying to puzzle her way out of this dangerous situation.

"Sara?" Will said.

She absently looked at him.

He studied her with a concerned expression. "You okay?"

How could he possibly know that she'd gone to that dark place again?

"Yes, I just want to get out of the mountains and go home."

Will sat beside her, and Nate leaned against the kitchen counter. "And where is home?"

She sensed him clicking into cop mode and she could understand why. If someone was out to get Sara, innocent civilians could be at risk.

"Seattle, but I'd taken a temporary job with Whitman Mountain Adventures out of Spokane Valley," she said. "They needed extra help with groups they were taking up into the mountains."

"So you're a tour guide?"

"A cook, mostly." It had been a good cover considering she'd cooked for her dad and brother after her mom had died. She felt it wise to maintain her cover for now.

"How long have you been with Whitman Mountain Adventures?"

"Nate," Will interrupted. "Can't you do this later? She's been through a lot."

"So you said," Nate studied her. "You shot a man."

"Because he was beating me to death," Will interjected. He yanked his shirt up to expose his bruised torso.

Sara had to look away, but noticed Nate's expression harden.

"Give it a rest," Will said. "I'll go get water to make coffee." He grabbed a metal bucket and headed for the door. Will hesitated and turned to Sara. "You'll be okay?"

"Sure."

Will shot one more cautionary nod at Nate, then left.

"You cold?" Nate said, wandering to the fireplace.

"A bit."

Nate stacked some wood in the fireplace and shoved kindling beneath it. It was awfully quiet all of a sudden, and Sara realized she missed Will's grounding presence.

Whoa, not good. She'd have to separate from him completely once they made it back to town because somehow she'd grown dependent on him.

"Ya know, Will's had a tough couple of years," Nate said, his back to her as he started the fire.

"He told me."

Nate snapped around. "What did he tell you?"

"That his wife died, that he has two little girls."

Nate refocused on the fire. "Then, you can understand why residents of Echo Mountain are protective of him."

"Yes, that would make sense."

"Very protective."

"I understand. You have nothing to worry about from me. I plan to distance myself from Will as soon as we get off this mountain."

An hour later, Will finally took a deep breath as they were headed down the trail toward town. Sara was secured to the litter carried by two SAR volunteers, while a second team handled the recovery mission of the dead body in the wood container.

It turned out they'd had an abundance of SAR volunteers for this morning's call, so they'd sent half of them to the cabin for Sara. Will, Sara and Nate hadn't waited long for a team, which was good because the tension in the cabin had been palpable.

Will wasn't sure what had transpired between Sara and Nate while he was getting water, but she didn't say much after Will's return. She stretched out on the bed and rested until the team arrived. Will asked Nate what had happened, but instead of answering, Nate fired off questions, asking Will what he really knew about this stranger. He went as far as to caution Will to keep his distance.

When they arrived at the hospital, SAR friends hovered around Will, worried about his condition. Surrounded by the group, he felt the love of family, even though they weren't blood relations. Then he spotted Sara, all alone, being wheeled into the ER. Will started to follow her but Breanna McBride, a member of the SAR K9 unit, blocked him.

"What happened to your face?" She eyed his bruises. "I thought you were on vacation."

"I was, but I went hiking and found an unconscious, wounded woman."

"Then, you should have called for help, not played hero," Grace Longfellow, another K9 SAR member scolded as she approached.

"I appreciate the concern," Will said. "I'd better find a doctor and have my ribs looked at."

"Your ribs, what happened to your ribs?" Breanna asked.

"And who gave you the black eyes?" Grace pushed.

"Ladies, I need to speak with Will," Nate interrupted, walking up to them.

"You can't. He has to see the doctor," Grace said.

"I'll make sure he does." Nate led Will away from Breanna and Grace.

"Thanks for the save," Will said.

"You're welcome, but I really do need to talk to you."

Will strained to see the ER examining room door. "I'd like to know how Sara's doing."

"Take care of yourself first."

"But—"

"Get looked at by a doctor. Then if Sara's story checks out, you can see her." Nate stopped and looked at Will. "Although, if someone's after her, wouldn't it be better to keep your distance?"

"But you're going to protect her, right?"

"We need to get all the facts."

"You don't believe that she's in trouble? Who do you think that guy was that she shot and killed? He would have killed her after he finished me off."

Nate planted his hands on his hips and sighed.

"What's wrong with you?" Will said, realizing his accusatory tone bordered on rudeness.

"I guess I'm a little more cautious than most," Nate said. "I don't necessarily believe people until I have proof. A man is dead—this is serious."

"You don't have to tell me that. Wait, are you thinking about arresting Sara? You can't. It was self-defense."

"I understand that, Will, but I still have to question her as soon as possible."

"I get it, but make no mistake that she's in danger. And she's all alone."

Nate put his hand on Will's shoulder. "Once they fix her up, I'll question her, confirm her story and we'll go from there, okay?"

Will nodded, but he wasn't totally satisfied. He didn't

like the way Nate was talking about Sara, as if she was the suspect, not the victim.

"You'll see a doctor?" Nate said.

"Sure."

Nate nodded that he was going to stand there and watch to make sure. With a sigh, Will went to the registration desk, described his injuries and was told to sit in the waiting area. He found a corner spot, away from people.

He closed his eyes and pressed his fingers to the bridge of his nose, needing to think, to pray. For Sara.

Please, God, keep her safe in your loving embrace.

"Am I intruding?" Breanna said.

Will opened his eyes. "No, but I'm not very good company right now."

She sat down next to him. "You look worried."

"I am."

"About that woman? The woman you met yesterday?"

"Stupid, huh?"

She glanced sideways at him. "Hey, are you calling me stupid?"

"What? No, I—"

"I'm the one who rescued a semiconscious man from the mountains, remember?"

Will cracked a half smile. "Oh, yeah, forgot about that."

"Then, you're the only one. My family still hasn't let me live that down."

"But they like Scott. We all like Scott."

"Not at the beginning they didn't. I rescued a wounded man with amnesia, who couldn't remember why men were shooting at him, and he had an unregistered gun in his hotel room. They thought I'd lost my mind."

"I have a feeling Nate shares that same opinion about me."

"Well, he didn't find her, did he? He didn't look into her eyes."

"Or comfort her," Will let slip.

"Or comfort her." Breanna leaned toward him. "Don't let anyone make you feel ashamed about that, okay?"

He nodded.

"William Rankin?" a nurse called.

"That's me." Will stood and nodded at his friend. "Thanks, Bree."

"Anytime."

The headache was the worst part of her physical injuries. Sara could tolerate pain from the sprained wrist and various aches whenever she moved, but the headache was nearly paralyzing.

Detective Nate Walsh's questions didn't help matters. His voice was starting to wear on her. She'd learned he'd been promoted to detective just last year, so he was probably trying to make a good impression on his superiors.

He was only doing his job by conducting his interview as soon as possible, but right now she was desperate to turn off the lights and sleep.

"So, Miss Long, you witnessed two men from your tour group, Mr. LaRouche and Mr. Harrington, throw a third man, Mr. Price, off the mountain. Why would they do that?"

"I don't know." It was the best she could come up

with considering she wasn't ready to expose herself as an FBI agent, make that a rogue FBI agent on leave, which complicated things even more.

"You must have overheard something…"

Oh, she had. She'd heard LaRouche and Harrington try to convince David Price to get on board with their plan.

A criminal plan to distribute the dangerous drug Abreivtas into the United States.

"Sara?" the detective pushed.

"I'm sorry, what was the question?"

"What did you hear before they supposedly pushed Mr. Price over the edge?"

Supposedly. Right. The detective didn't believe her.

"They were arguing about a business decision, I think. David said he was done and started to walk away. Mr. LaRouche grabbed him and…" She hesitated. "Hurled him over the edge."

"And Mr. Harrington did nothing?"

"No, sir. I think he might have been in shock."

"Then what?"

"They heard me and turned around…"

The memory shot adrenaline through her body as she recalled the predatory look on LaRouche's face.

"Did Mr. LaRouche say anything?" the detective asked.

"No, sir. But he looked—" she hesitated "—furious. So I ran."

"Is it possible they got into an argument and the fall was an accident?"

She eyed the detective. Was he on LaRouche and Harrington's payroll? No, that couldn't be possible. Nate seemed like a solid guy and he was Will's friend, which went a long way in her book.

Will. A man you barely know. Maybe she didn't know him all that well, but she trusted him. Will was what her father used to call "good people."

"Ma'am?" Nate said. "Could the fall have been an accident?"

"No, I don't think so." She studied her fingers interlaced in her lap.

"Okay, so you took off and left your gear behind?"

"Yes, sir."

"Did they chase you?"

"Yes. I tried to escape down the side of the mountain and fell. Will found me the next day."

"And the man who attacked you and Will? Did you know him?"

"No, sir."

"Then, how did you know he was an enemy?"

"The way he yanked on my hair and threatened me."

"What did he say specifically?"

"He said, did I really think I could outrun them, and that he was ordered to bring me to a meeting the next day so I could explain myself."

"And then?"

"He tied me up and went to find Will. They fought— the man was kicking Will to death, so I shot him." She eyed the detective. "Wouldn't you have done the same?"

Someone tapped at the hospital room door.

"Hey, Sara," Will said, joining them.

He went to the opposite side of the bed and gently placed his hand over hers. Although she sensed the gesture might be inappropriate in Nate's eyes, the contact instantly calmed her.

"How are you feeling?" Will asked, ignoring Nate, and searching her eyes.

"I'm okay. My head hurts, though."

"Want to buzz the nurse for a pain reliever?"

"No, I've already taken something. It should kick in soon."

Nate cleared his throat and raised an eyebrow at Will's hand, gently covering Sara's. She started to pull away, but Will wouldn't let her go. It wasn't a forceful grip; it was a comforting one.

Will looked at Nate. "I think she needs to rest."

"Is that right, Dr. Rankin?"

"She's not going anywhere. Can't you wait until she's feeling better to finish your interview?"

Nate directed his attention to Sara. "We're pretty much done, although I'd prefer you stay in town until we wrap this up."

"Of course," she said.

Nate directed his attention to Will. "I'll need to take your official statement, as well."

"I can swing by the station this afternoon."

"No, now. You can start with how you got the black eyes," Nate said.

"That was my fault," Sara said.

"A misunderstanding," Will offered.

"*She* gave you the black eyes?" Nate said.

"It was an accident," Will defended.

Nate raised an eyebrow.

"When I found Sara, she was unconscious," Will explained. "She regained consciousness and she thought I was one of the guys trying to hurt her. In an effort to defend herself, she nailed me with her weapon."

Sara didn't miss Nate's speculative frown.

"Continue," Nate said.

"I took her back to the cabin to tend to her injuries."

She appreciated that he didn't describe how horrible she'd been to him, verbally abusive and threatening, making snide remarks when all he wanted to do was help her.

"Last night she went outside to find a cell signal and I went to get more wood. I saw a man approach Sara from behind and force her into the cabin at gunpoint. I recognized him as a man I'd met earlier in the day. He seemed so innocuous. I've got bad instincts, I guess."

"Sociopaths can be charmers," Sara muttered, realizing the drugs might be loosening her lips a little too much.

"You saw him take Sara into the cabin. Then what?" Nate prompted.

"I tried luring him outside."

"Even though he had a gun and you didn't," Nate said disapprovingly.

Will seemed to ignore the tone of Nate's voice and continued, "He came outside, I knocked him out with a piece of wood and went to check on Sara," Will said. "I guess I didn't hit him hard enough because he came after me in the cabin, dragged me outside and kicked me until I nearly passed out. I heard two shots and he stopped kicking."

"As I said before in my statement, I shot him because I feared for Will's life, and my own," Sara added.

"You shot him with *your* gun?"

"No, the attacker's gun. I grabbed it when he was beating up Will and I was trying to pull him off."

"You shot him in self-defense?" Nate asked Sara.

"Yes."

"Then I put the body in the wood bin to keep it away from animals," Will said, directing the detective's attention away from Sara.

"Why didn't you call for help?" Nate asked Will.

"I couldn't get a signal at the cabin, and I didn't want to leave Sara alone in search of one. She was exhibiting symptoms of shock. I'd hoped she'd be better by morning, at which time we'd hike a short distance to find a signal. Then you showed up."

"We'll have the deceased fingerprinted, which might give us some answers. That is, if he's even in the system."

"Oh, he will be," Sara said, her cop instinct stating the obvious.

"You sound pretty sure," Nate said. "Had you ever met him before?"

"No, sir, but I know his type."

"What type is that?"

Nate and Will looked at her, expectant. Oh, boy. She'd better come up with a good answer.

"Bullies," she said. "They're usually not one-time offenders, are they, detective?"

He hesitated, as if puzzling over her answer. "No, they're not."

Sara closed her eyes, hoping the detective would take the hint and leave. She needed time alone, without doctors and medical staff poking at her, and without the local police's pointed questions.

"Sara, have you ever shot a man before?" Nate asked.

She snapped her eyes open. "Of course not."

It was the truth. In her tenure with the FBI, she'd never found herself in a situation where she had to shoot and kill someone.

Until last night.

In order to save Will's life.

He was only in danger because of you.

"If you don't mind, I could really use some sleep." She rolled onto her side away from Nate and slipped her fingers out from under Will's hand. The guilt of putting him in harm's way weighed heavy on her heart.

"Will, you and I can finish your interview in the lounge."

"Okay," Will said. "Sara, I'll be close if you need me."

She had to distance herself from this man before he was even more seriously hurt because of Sara and her quest to nail LaRouche and Harrington. More seriously hurt? He was almost killed last night. The bruising below his eyes and swollen nose made her stomach burn with regret.

"No, you can leave," she said.

"Excuse me?"

"Just go, Will. You've done your bit."

"My bit?"

She mustered as much false bitterness as possible in order to drive him away. "Yeah, saving the damsel in distress. You're relieved of your duties."

She closed her eyes, hypersensitive to the sounds in the room: the clicking of the blood pressure machine, a car horn echoing through the window...

Will's deep sigh as he hovered beside her bed.

She'd hurt him with her acerbic comment, but it was for his own good. So why did she feel like such a jerk about the silence that stretched between them?

"Come on," Nate said.

She felt Will brush his hand across her arm—a good-bye touch.

A ball of emotion rose in her throat. This shouldn't hurt; she shouldn't feel anything for a man she'd only met yesterday.

Her emotional pain was a side effect of her injuries, that was all, the trauma of the past twenty-four hours. It had nothing to do with Will and his gentle nature, or his caring green eyes. She sighed, and drifted to sleep.

Sara awakened with a start.

Where was she? She sat up in bed and searched her surroundings. Right, she was in the hospital. It was dark outside; dark in her room. Someone had turned off the lights, probably to help her sleep.

"You're okay," she whispered.

But then why was her heart pounding against her chest?

She flopped back on the bed, remembering the nightmare that had awakened her—running down the middle of a deserted street, LaRouche and Harrington chasing her in a black limousine. Even as she slept, the corrupt businessmen were terrorizing her.

The intensity of her nightmare drove home how much danger she was in—even here, in a hospital. She was a target and she would continue to be a target until she put them behind bars.

Holding onto her IV pole, she went to the closet and found her now dry jeans. Although she favored her sprained wrist, she dressed herself, remembering how Will had offered to dry her jeans by the fire.

How he'd taken care of her.

Talk about a weak moment. After the shooting, she'd completely fallen apart, sucked into the black emotional hole of her past, remembering the sound of her father fighting for his life downstairs.

The sound of the gunshot that had taken his life.

If Will hadn't been there last night to talk her down from her traumatic shock, to offer her a blanket and a warm hand to hold on to, she would have spun herself into a blinding panic attack.

"You can't keep relying on him," she reminded herself. "You've got to do this on your own."

On her own. By herself. That had been Sara's mantra since childhood, even after her aunt and uncle had taken her into their home.

Today was no different. She had to protect herself, call in and update SSA Bonner about what had happened. He was going to be furious that she'd pursued this case against his orders, and she might even lose her job.

She hesitated and gripped the IV pole. Maybe she should wait to contact him until after she retrieved the recorded argument between the men—proof that there was truth to her claims about LHP, Inc.

Unless she had firm evidence in the death of David Price, it would be her word against LaRouche's and Harrington's. The word of two slick businessmen against Sara's, a rogue FBI agent with a chip on her shoulder who couldn't follow orders and took extreme measures to prove her point.

Maybe she should have dropped this case months ago and kept her mouth shut instead of hounding Bonner. But she couldn't watch the corporate hacks at LHP, Inc., get away with introducing a dangerous drug into the United States and promoting it as a safe and effective sleep aid. She'd uncovered solid evidence, buried reports from the pharmaceutical testing, even if Bonner thought them innocuous. She knew what Abreivtas could really do.

It could kill. She had to stop them.

She went into the bathroom and splashed water on her face. It wouldn't look good to local authorities if she left the hospital, but staying here made her a target. Detective Walsh didn't seem to be taking her story seriously, and even if he did, the local cops couldn't protect her from the likes of LaRouche's and Harrington's hired goons.

Drying her face with a paper towel, the image of Will being kicked, over and over again, flashed across her thoughts. She hated that she'd been responsible for such a violent act on a gentle man.

A widower and single parent. Hadn't he suffered enough?

Slipping into her jacket, she felt for her wallet and phone. They were both tucked into her inside zippered pocket. Good. She took a deep breath and pulled the IV out of her hand.

She peeked around the corner. All clear. She was far enough away from the nurse's station that they wouldn't see her leave, and even if they did, they couldn't stop her, right?

She hurried to the elevator, but decided it was too risky. She didn't want to take the chance Nate Walsh had come back with more questions or, more likely, Will had returned to check on her.

She ducked into the stairwell and headed down. Gripping the handrail, she took her time. No need to rush and pass out before she got safely away.

Her head ached from the emotional tension and physical movement. She focused on taking slow and steady breaths.

A door opened and clicked shut from a floor above. She hesitated.

"Sa-ra?" a man called in a singsong voice.

Her blood ran cold.

"I need to talk to you," he said.

She stumbled down the last few steps, tripping and slamming into the door to the first level. Whipping it open, she shuffled away from the stairwell. Eyes downcast, she wandered through the ER waiting area toward the exit.

And spotted a tall, broad-shouldered man coming into the hospital and heading toward her.

Don't be paranoid.

In his midthirties, he wore jeans, a fatigue jacket and military-grade boots.

Their eyes locked.

"Sara?" he said, reaching into his jacket.

She spun around and took off.

Chapter Six

Will wasn't sure why he'd returned to the hospital. Sara had been pretty clear that she didn't want him around.

But something felt off. Her voice said one thing, but he read something else in her eyes. It was almost as if she thought sending him away was the right thing to do, yet she desperately wanted him to stay.

"Or you're losing it," he muttered as he parked the car.

At any rate, he'd decided to check on her. Maybe she'd be asleep, which would be the best scenario. He needed to see her and know she was safe, then he could leave.

Yeah, who was he kidding?

"What are you doing here?" Nate said from a few cars away. Apparently he'd had a similar thought, only a different motivation.

"Don't bust my chops," Will said. "I want to make sure she's okay."

"She's fine."

"I'd like to see for myself." Will continued toward the hospital entrance.

"Do I have to get a restraining order against you?"

Will snapped his attention to Nate. The cop's wry smile indicated he was teasing.

"Sara and I have been through a lot," Will said. "And last night…" He shook his head.

"Last night, what?" Nate challenged.

"I know it's your job to be suspicious, especially because she shot a man, but trust me, it was not something she enjoyed doing. She was traumatized afterward."

"She's not your responsibility."

"I didn't say she was."

"But you're coming here at—" Nate checked his watch "—nine fifteen to check on her?"

They entered the hospital and went to the elevators. "I've got nothing better to do. The girls are spending another night with their grandparents."

"Uh-huh."

"Hey, don't give me a hard time for being a good guy."

"Good guys finish last, remember?"

"I didn't know it was a race," Will countered.

"Just…be careful."

Will nodded his appreciation for his friend's concern. A lot of folks in town seemed concerned about Will since Megan had died. Did they all think him that fragile? Or incapable of making good choices?

As Nate and Will stepped out of the elevator onto Sara's floor, a frantic-looking officer named Spike Duggins rushed up to them.

"I went to grab a coffee," Spike said. "She was sound asleep. The nurse was going to keep an eye out."

A chill arced across Will's shoulders. "Sara's gone?"

"I notified security," Spike said, directing his answer to Nate.

"How long?" Nate said.

"I don't know, five, ten minutes?"

"You had her under surveillance?" Will asked Nate.

"Spike, you start at the north end," Nate said, ignoring Will's question.

"Spike, this is security, over," a voice on Spike's radio interrupted. "I think I spotted her in the lobby."

Nate grabbed Spike's radio. "Keep her there."

"She's already gone. I must have scared her off."

"Which direction?" Nate asked.

"Toward the cafeteria," the security officer said.

"Head to the south exit," Nate ordered him. "Spike will go north and I'll check out the cafeteria."

"Roger that," the security officer responded.

"What about—"

"You stay here in case she returns," Nate ordered Will.

The two men jogged off and disappeared into the stairwell.

Will couldn't stand here and do nothing. The security guard said he'd scared her off, so what made Nate think he and Spike would have better luck?

Was she having another flashback, like the one she'd had last night? If so, she wouldn't trust a stranger, or even a cop.

But she'd trust Will.

He went into her room and checked the closet. Everything was gone. She definitely hadn't planned to come back.

He took the stairs closest to the cafeteria and headed down.

Will had to find her, had to make her feel safe so she

wouldn't run away. Perhaps if Nate had told her he'd left a police officer to guard her, she wouldn't have felt so vulnerable.

But Will sensed Nate's motivation had been to keep her under surveillance, not protect her from a violent offender. Will never should have left the hospital, even after she'd asked him to.

What was the matter with him? Why did he feel such a deep need to protect this woman?

Because of the look in her eyes and the sound of her voice when she'd hidden under the bed. He'd seen that look before on his sister's face when they'd hid from their raging mother. Will had perfected the role of protector at an early age.

He got to the ground floor and headed to the cafeteria, readying himself for the lecture he'd surely get from Nate. Will entered the empty dining area as Nate stormed out of the kitchen.

"I told you to stay upstairs," he snapped.

"She's frightened and she trusts me."

"Whatever. I'm going to check the security feed." Nate continued down the hall. "Go home, Will," he called over his shoulder. "You don't belong here."

Nate disappeared around the corner. His words stung, but only for a moment. Will knew Nate's comment was born of concern for Will.

As Will scanned the cafeteria, he considered the extent of Sara's injuries. She had winced if she moved too quickly, or put pressure on her wrist by accident. A woman in that kind of pain couldn't run for long. More likely she would hide until she saw an opportunity to quietly slip away.

He wandered through the cafeteria. The tables were

empty, but a few visitors were standing at the coffee station filling up, probably in anticipation of a long wait ahead of them tonight.

His gaze drifted to a cluster of office plants in the opposite corner of the cafeteria, and he remembered what she'd said last night.

He won't see me in here.

Hiding meant safety to Sara. He approached the plants, fearing he was wrong and she wouldn't be there, in which case, she might be wandering the property somewhere, completely vulnerable. He clenched his jaw, fighting back his worry.

As he got closer, he saw the reflection of a woman hugging her knees to her chest against the glass window. With a relieved sigh, he devised a plan to ease her out of hiding. He wanted this to be her idea; he wanted Sara to feel in control.

He went to the hot drink station and plopped teabags into two cups, poured hot water and gave the cashier a few singles. He carried the hot beverages across the cafeteria and sat down near the plants.

"Sara, it's Will," he said. "I thought you might still be cold." He slid a cup toward her.

She didn't take it.

"Sorry it couldn't be something better, like a scone or a muffin, but food service pretty much shuts down at this time of night. That's herbal tea. It's orange blossom," he said. "The girls like that one, and I like it because it's caffeine-free and won't keep them awake."

"You shouldn't be here."

"I came back to check on you."

"No, you really shouldn't be here. It's dangerous."

"What do you mean?"

"I heard a man behind me in the stairwell. He said my name—they sent him to get me. I ran, and another man was blocking the exit."

"I think that was actually a hospital security officer."

"No, he was wearing military-grade boots. He also knew my name and was…was…"

"It's okay. You're safe now, and I'm not leaving until you believe that."

She reached out and took the cup. At least her fingers weren't trembling like they had been last night.

"How did you know I'd be here, behind the plants?" she asked.

"It seemed like a logical spot to hide out." He finally glanced at her. She looked tired, worn down and still frightened. "Did the man threaten you?"

"He said he needed to talk to me."

"But nothing else?"

"No, why? You think I'm crazy, too?" she snapped.

"Sara." He hesitated. "I'm on your side, remember?"

She tipped her head back against the glass and sighed.

"Here's a thought—why don't you work *with* the police instead of shutting them out?" Will said. "Detective Walsh can protect you."

"Detective Walsh doesn't even believe me."

"Don't be put off by his tone. He's a big-city detective turned small-town cop. He's got an edge to his voice, sure, but you want a tough guy like that on your side, don't you?"

"What I want is to get out of here, without putting anyone else in danger."

"Let me call Nate and have him escort you back to your room."

"Where I'm a sitting duck."

"Not if he offers twenty-four-hour police protection." He wasn't about to say that he would also stay close, because he knew she'd fight him on that decision.

"Okay, I guess that's the best choice, if you can get him to believe me."

"I'll talk to Nate. If he doesn't believe you, I'll talk to the chief. I've got some pull in this town."

"Yeah, I noticed how everyone surrounded you when we first arrived at the hospital. You have a great support system."

"I am blessed. For sure." He remembered how friends from church and SAR had rallied around him after Megan's death. How they wouldn't let him wallow, brought him meals and offered to entertain the girls.

But that was two years ago. He'd mostly healed and was a strong man, and a good father, even if his in-laws didn't always think so. Sure he'd stumbled a few times along the way, but today Will felt confident in his abilities to raise his girls with love and compassion.

"Okay, let's head back to my room," Sara said.

Will stood and offered his hand.

"Can you hold my tea?" she said.

"Of course." He'd wanted to take her hand, but would not force the issue. Taking her cup, he restrained himself as he watched her stand. It was frustrating to see her struggle against the pain. He tossed his cup into the garbage can behind him, and reached for her again.

"No, I can do it," she said.

He should respect her determination, not be hurt by it. The rejection wasn't a criticism of his abilities, but he sensed her need to rely on herself.

She straightened. "Thanks." She stepped out from behind the plants and started across the cafeteria.

Will noticed a slight waver in her step and he reached out to steady her. His hand gripped her upper arm, and she snapped her gaze to meet his.

"It's okay to accept help," he said. "I won't expect anything in return, promise." He smiled, hoping to lighten the moment.

"No, you wouldn't, would you?" she said in a soft, almost hushed voice.

For a moment, he couldn't breathe. It was as if she saw right through him, into his wounded heart.

"We found her, sir," a man's voice said.

Sara ripped her attention from Will and paled at the sight of a man heading toward them. He was in his thirties, wearing jeans and a fatigue jacket. Will assumed it was the security guard, since he held a radio in his hand. Then Will noticed his boots—military grade.

"Are you the security officer?" Will clarified, to ease Sara's worry.

"Yes, sir, Jim Banks, hospital security. Are you taking her back to her room?"

"I am," Will said.

"Why aren't you wearing a security uniform?" Sara pointedly asked.

"I'd already changed into street clothes when I heard the call go out that you were missing, so I thought I'd help find you before I left," Jim said. "I'm sorry if I frightened you."

She nodded, but didn't look convinced.

"I'll accompany you both to her room," Jim said.

"Thanks," Will said.

Sara didn't look happy. For whatever reason, the security officer intimidated her. Will wasn't sure why. The guy seemed okay to Will, but then Will hadn't been the best judge of character or he would have figured out the friendly hiker from yesterday was really a hired thug.

They walked in silence to the elevator. As the doors opened, Nate came rushing around the corner.

"Someone was after her, here in the hospital," Will blurted out.

Nate nodded at Jim. "Thanks, I've got this."

Jim hesitated for a second, then with a nod, he said, "Have a good night."

"You, too," Will offered.

Will, Nate and Sara got into the elevator. Nate pressed the third-floor button. Sara leaned against the elevator wall, and Will shifted himself between her and Nate. It was an instinctive, protective gesture.

"When you disappear like that it makes you look as if you're hiding something," Nate said, eyeing the elevator floor numbers.

Sara didn't answer at first. Will knew if he answered for her, Nate would only criticize him and come down harder on Sara. She needed to explain her actions.

Will squeezed her hand and nodded, encouraging her to respond.

"I'm sorry. I was scared," she said. "I had a nightmare that reminded me how much danger I was in. I freaked out and took off, and some guy was stalking me."

"What did he say?" Nate said.

"That he needed to talk."

"Did you recognize him?"

"I didn't see him. I heard him."

"Where did this happen?"

"The stairs at the end of my hallway."

Nate sighed. "I'll post a uniform outside your room."

Will squeezed her hand.

"Thanks," she said.

They reached her floor. Will and Nate escorted Sara to her room, where Spike waited.

"I'm so sorry, ma'am," Spike said. "I stepped away for a minute and—"

"Officer Duggins will be relieved by Officer Pete Franklin in about half an hour," Nate said, narrowing his eyes at the young cop. "I'll also hang around for a while."

"No one's going to hurt you here," Will said, looking at Nate for confirmation. "Right?"

Nate nodded.

"Thanks." She glanced at Will as if she was going to say something. Instead, she offered a grateful smile, turned and went into her room.

Nate narrowed his eyes at Will. "I'll be here and Pete will show up soon."

"I'm still here," Spike offered.

"Don't push it," Nate warned, and then looked at Will. "You can really go now."

"I know." Will didn't move.

"But you're not going anywhere, are you?"

Will shrugged.

The next day Sara convinced doctors that her minor concussion and sprained wrist didn't warrant her staying in the hospital any longer, although once they released her she wasn't sure where she'd go. Nate had requested she stay in town until they finished their investigation of David Price's death.

There was still no word from LaRouche and Harrington. She wondered how they'd talk their way out of this one.

It didn't matter. At this moment what mattered was finding a safe place to stay, a place where her mystery stalker wouldn't torment her further.

She put on her torn jacket and left her hospital room where she found Will, camped on the floor, working on a laptop.

"Will?"

"Hey, Sara," he said, shoving his laptop into a briefcase and standing to greet her.

"What are you doing here?"

"I thought you might need a ride."

His wavy chestnut hair fell across his face, and he was wearing the same clothes he wore last night.

"You never left the hospital?" she said.

"Didn't have any place to be."

"What about your girls?"

"They're with their grandparents. I wasn't supposed to be home until the day after tomorrow anyway. I thought I'd let Nanny and Papa spoil them one more day."

"Where is—"

"Your protective detail? Officer Franklin's shift just ended and Nate left earlier this morning. He figured you'd be released today and apologized about not having the manpower to offer you protection 24/7. He was going to send an officer to drop you off wherever you needed to go, but I said I was already here. I could do it."

"Oh, he must have loved that," she said sarcastically.

"Yeah, well, I think he gave in because he knew it was a losing battle. So where can I drop you?"

"Really, that's not necessary. I can get a cab."

"What, do I smell that bad?" He sniffed his armpit teasingly.

"Stop," she said, almost smiling. "I appreciate the offer, but I think you've done enough."

"Miss Long?"

She turned and saw a police officer headed toward her. "Yes?"

"I'm Officer Petrellis. I was sent to give you a ride."

"Officer, I'm Will Rankin." They shook hands. "Did Nate Walsh send you?"

"Yes, sir."

"Guess I lost that argument after all," Will said, frowning.

"Where can I drop you, ma'am?" Petrellis asked.

She looked reticent to tell him, so Will stepped in. "No, really, Officer, I insist."

"Detective Walsh said it's fine if you want to drive her, but I need to follow to make sure she gets safely settled." He turned to Sara. "Ma'am, are you okay if Mr. Rankin gives you a ride?"

"Of course she is." Will turned to Sara. "Aren't you?"

She could tell from the expression on Will's kind face that it was important for him to do this, to help her. After everything she'd put him through, she didn't have it in her heart to disappoint him.

"Sure, that would be fine," she said.

Will motioned Sara toward the elevator.

She put on her emotional mask, needing to embody her undercover identity—Sara Long, tour guide assistant.

"We'll start by finding you a comfortable place to stay," Will said. "Nate suggested we book you a room at Echo Mountain Resort."

"Right, so he'll know where I am."

"No, because it's a very secure facility." They stepped into the elevator. Officer Petrellis joined them, but didn't participate in the conversation.

"They've had some experience protecting people at the resort," Will continued.

"Oh, really?" she said with a raised eyebrow.

"Long story. You hungry? We could stop for something to eat first."

"Actually, I desperately need a cell phone."

He pulled his smartphone out of his pocket and offered it to her. "It's working again."

"Thanks, but I need my own."

"Ah, calling your boyfriend, huh?"

She shrugged and decided not to answer, letting him draw his own conclusions. Having a boyfriend would certainly discourage Will from continuing to help her.

They stepped out of the elevator onto the main floor.

"What type of vehicle are you driving, sir?" Officer Petrellis asked Will. "In case we get separated."

"A gray Jeep."

"Plate number? Again, in case we get separated."

Will gave the plate number and the officer wrote it down. He was being awfully accommodating, Sara mused, especially since she was under the impression Nate didn't have the manpower to spare. But then this was small-town law enforcement. They were about building relationships and protecting their community.

"We can swing by the Super Shopper and get you a phone, some clothes and whatever else you need since you left your backpack up in the mountains," Will said.

She fingered the rip in her jacket. "That's probably a good idea. Tell me more about Echo Mountain Resort."

"It's on the outskirts of town," Will said. "I know a few people who work there, and the manager, as well. I'll give them a call to see what's available."

They went outside and headed for his Jeep.

"I feel bad that you're still involved in this, in my drama," she said.

"No worries. I want to see this through to the end."

Sara knew Will Rankin had no clue what he was signing on for.

Will called the resort. "Hi, Nia, it's Will. I have a friend who needs a room….Wait, that's *this* weekend? I completely forgot…" He shot Sara a defeated look. "Okay, I'll try something in town….I hope you're wrong about that….Sure, I'll bring the girls by." He ended the call as they approached his truck.

"Bad news?" Sara asked.

"I forgot about the resort's big festival this weekend. It's booked solid. We'll try a B and B in town. How about we get you set up with a phone, and we'll make calls while we eat lunch? Sound good?"

"Sure."

He opened the door for her and she got into his Jeep. She noticed how he was careful to make sure she was settled before closing the door. He was the true definition of a gentleman, she thought, as she watched him walk around the front of the vehicle. What other kind of man would invest himself in a stranger's dangerous situation like Sara's?

One who, no doubt, had white knight syndrome tendencies. Well, she'd accept a ride from him, and buy him lunch to thank him for everything he'd done. Then, after he dropped her off at a B and B or wherever she ended up staying, she'd offer a firm goodbye.

* * *

They picked up supplies at the Super Shopper, and Sara made her call, but didn't look happy about the outcome. Will decided not to ask too many questions. He didn't want to push her away by being nosy.

Something still felt off, as if she acted a good game, but felt utterly alone, maybe even abandoned. Will decided he would not abandon Sara, then he cautioned himself not to feel so responsible for her.

He couldn't help it.

As they stood by his Jeep, she slipped on her new blue winter jacket and smiled at her reflection in the window. The smile lit her face, and he forced himself to look away. His gaze landed on the police officer's car a few parking spots away, reminding Will that Sara was still in danger.

"Well, I kinda like it," she said.

He snapped his attention to her. "I do, too."

"Then, why'd you look away?"

"Sorry, got distracted. Is it warm?"

"Yeah." She half chuckled.

"What's so funny?"

"You're such a dad."

"Is that a bad thing?" He opened the car door and she slid onto the front seat.

"No, but be warned, at some point with your girls it's going to be about looking good, not being warm."

"Don't remind me." He shut the door and went to the driver's side of the Jeep. He got behind the wheel and said, "You ready for lunch? There's this great new spot a few minutes away. My girls love it."

"What, is the menu all candy?" Sara teased.

Will pulled out of the lot. "Actually, it's called

Healthy Eats." He smiled. "Don't let the name scare you."

"You're assuming I'm a junk-food person." She shifted in her seat and winced.

"Bad, huh?" he said.

"No, I'm fine. Looking forward to a nice room with a soft bed, and no police officers questioning me."

He understood her frustration, but she had killed a man in the mountains—to save Will's life. The primary reason he would not abandon her.

"There are three B and B's in town," Will started. "Annabelle's, Cedar Inn and The White Dove. Maybe you should give one of them a call?"

"Okay."

With each call, he could tell she grew more frustrated. A few minutes later they pulled into the lot at Healthy Eats.

"Don't worry," he said. "I know Lucy, the owner at The White Dove. They keep a spare room open in case her daughter shows up in town unexpectedly. I'll talk to her."

"Thanks."

Will sensed she was starting to fade. Food would definitely help renew her energy.

A few minutes later, they were seated in a booth ordering tea, scones and sandwiches from the owner of the restaurant, Catherine, who was Nate's sister.

"Shouldn't take long," Catherine said. "You two look as if you could use some of my healing broth. I'll bring some out, on the house."

"We really appreciate it, Catherine," Will said.

"Anything for you, Will." She winked and walked into the back.

"Someone's got a crush on you," Sara said.

"Who, Catherine? Nah, she's on the 'help Will' team."

"Help you what?"

"At first, it was to help me recover from my wife's death."

Sara reached across the table and touched the hand gripping his tea mug. "I'm so sorry, I did not mean to bring that up."

"It's okay. I've been grieving long enough. A lot of the folks in town, and especially from church, can't stop looking out for me. I'm blessed with good friends, yet sometimes…" His voice trailed off.

"Sometimes what?"

"All the attention can be suffocating. It makes me feel as if they think I'm incompetent." He didn't know why he said it, and wanted to take it back.

"You're the opposite of incompetent, Will," she offered. "Look at everything you've done for me."

"Thanks. I wasn't fishing for a compliment, honest."

She cracked a smile.

Again, he had to look away. That adorable smile of hers was enchanting. "I'll call Lucy about her daughter's room at The White Dove Inn."

"That would be great, thanks."

He pulled out his phone.

"Will? What are you doing here?"

Will looked up and spotted his in-laws crossing the restaurant toward him.

"And what happened to your eyes?" his mother-in-law, Mary, asked.

He got out of the booth to greet them. "Hiking accident," he said. Will shook hands with his father-in-law, Ed, who then went to the register to pick up their order.

"Where are the girls?" Will asked.

"Susanna Baker called and invited Claire and Marissa to join her and the twins for a movie." Mary studied Sara with judgment in her eyes.

"What movie?" Will asked. "Is it PG? Because the last PG-13 movie Marissa watched gave her nightmares."

"It's fine." Mary waved him off. "They were going to an animated film. Why are you back early? And who's this?"

He wouldn't sugarcoat it, nor would he go into great detail, either.

"Mary, this is Sara. I assisted Sara when she was injured in the mountains."

Sara offered Mary a smile. "Nice to meet you."

"Search and rescue...so that's what cut your vacation short," Mary said disapprovingly. "Are you expecting to pick up the girls tonight? Because we'd planned a trip to the children's museum tomorrow, and they were looking forward to tea at Queen Margaret tea shop."

"That's fine," Will said. "What time will you be dropping them home?"

"Between seven and seven-thirty."

"Sounds good. I'll be ready."

Mary cast one last look at Sara. "I most certainly hope so."

Ed joined them, gripping a to-go bag in his hand. "What'd I miss?"

"Will cut his trip short to save this young lady."

"Sara," she introduced herself.

"Ed, nice to meet you." He nodded at the bag. "I've worked up an appetite. Those girls never stop, do they?" He smiled at Will.

"No, they surely don't. Thanks again for watching them."

"Don't be silly," Mary said. "They're our grand-daughters. We love them. You'll be home by seven to-morrow to greet the girls?"

"Of course," Will said.

"Goodbye, then." She turned and left.

Ed shrugged at Will and nodded at Sara. "Good to meet you."

"You, too."

Will watched them leave. Only after they'd pulled out of the lot did the tightening in his chest ease.

"Are you going to sit down?" Sara asked, with a question in her eyes.

"Yeah." He slid into the booth.

"What was that about?" Sara said.

"What?"

"She seemed awfully—"

"Judgmental? Critical? Close-minded?"

"Something like that." Sara smiled again.

The tension in his shoulders uncoiled. He shrugged. "It's complicated."

Catherine approached their table with soup. Good timing. He didn't want to get into the ugly story about how his in-laws had grown resentful of Will after Megan lost her battle with cancer, and how they questioned his abilities as a father.

"This is amazing," Sara said, spooning a second taste of soup.

They spent the next hour enjoying delicious food and natural conversation. He wasn't sure how that was possible, since he'd only known her for a day, yet he felt comfortable chatting about whatever topic drifted into their discussion.

He wondered if she also enjoyed their companionship. Then she offered to pay for his lunch and he wondered if this was her way of thanking him for saving her in the mountains, nothing more.

He called Lucy at The White Dove Inn and was able to secure Sara the room reserved for Lucy's daughter.

They finished their meal and he drove her across town to the inn, pointing out highlights of Echo Mountain, including the Christmas tree in the town square.

"We'll light it next weekend at the Town Lights Festival, not to be confused with the Echo Mountain Resort Festival," he said.

"Wow, there's a lot of celebrating going on for such a small town."

"There's a lot to celebrate this time of year," he offered.

She turned to look out the side window, as if she wasn't so sure. In that moment, he pictured himself showing her how beautiful Christmas could be: drinking hot cider in the town square amongst friends and neighbors, attending Christmas church services and singing songs praising the Lord.

But Sara seemed lost in a dark memory, one he wished he could replace with new ones.

A few minutes later he pulled up in front of The White Dove Inn and Sara's eyes rounded with appreciation. "It's lovely."

He reached for his door.

"Don't."

He turned to her.

"Your journey ends here," she said.

"I'm confused. Did I somehow offend you?"

"No, nothing like that." She hesitated. "Let's face it, Will, it's in your best interest to steer clear of me."

"How do you figure?"

"I saw the way your mother-in-law looked at me, at this—" She motioned at the space between them. "I mean, I really appreciate everything you've done."

"But?"

"I need to ask you not to seek me out anymore."

"Seek you out? You make me sound like a stalker. I thought I was helping a friend."

"We don't know each other well enough to be friends. Maybe we could have been, if the situation were different."

"This has something to do with the call you made earlier, doesn't it?"

She didn't answer, glancing at him with sadness in her eyes. "You're a good man, Will. I wish you all the best." She leaned across the seat and kissed him on the cheek.

He couldn't breathe for a second, stunned by the kiss. She quickly grabbed her bag of supplies and hopped out of the Jeep, slamming the door and hurrying up the steps to the B and B.

She hesitated as she reached the door.

Turn around. Come on, change your mind, turn around and let me help you.

She didn't. She knocked on the door and a moment later it swung open. Lucy waved at Will over Sara's shoulder. He offered a halfhearted wave and Lucy shut the door.

Will glanced through his front windshield at the neighboring houses decorated in green, red and gold lights. Sara was right, of course, yet it still stung.

At first he thought he was drawn to her because she needed him, needed someone to take care of her, which was dysfunctional on so many levels. As he sat in his Jeep after being told to keep his distance, he realized it was something else that made him want to stay close.

He had connected with this stranger on a level he hadn't experienced with another woman since Megan. How was that possible?

"You're sleep deprived," he muttered, and pulled away from the curb.

He'd better catch up on his sleep if he wanted to be fresh and energized for the girls tomorrow. As he drove away from the B and B, he spotted the unmarked police car across the street. Officer Petrellis was on the phone, and nodded at Will as he passed.

Will was grateful that Nate had changed his mind about offering Sara protection, and decided to call him using his hands-free device.

"Will," Nate answered. "Was about to call you. Turns out the man Sara shot and killed had a rap sheet for assault and battery, and attempted murder, which he skated on thanks to high-priced attorneys he couldn't afford."

"You think LaRouche and Harrington paid the bill?"

"That'd be my guess. The DA doesn't see any reason to press charges against Sara for killing him in self-defense."

"That's great news. Listen, I wanted to thank you."

"For what?"

"For putting protective surveillance on Sara."

"Yeah, Spike's been sending me text updates all day."

"Spike? You mean Officer Petrellis."

"What are you talking about? Officer Petrellis took early retirement last spring."

Chapter Seven

A chill shot across Will's shoulders. "Petrellis said you sent him to protect Sara."

"No, Spike offered to give her a ride from the hospital to make up for messing up last night."

"I've gotta get back to Sara." Will spun the Jeep around. "I just dropped her off at The White Dove Inn."

"I'm on my way."

"How long will it take you to get there?"

"Five, maybe ten minutes."

"Hurry."

"Will, wait for me."

"I'll see you when you get there." Will ended the call, unable to agree to wait for Nate. It wasn't in Will's DNA to sit by and do nothing while someone stalked her.

He pulled up to the inn, a safe distance behind the unmarked cruiser. Drumming his fingers against the steering wheel, he peered into Officer Petrellis's car.

His empty car.

Will gripped the steering wheel with unusual force. Five minutes—he tried talking himself into waiting five minutes for Nate to arrive. He scanned the inn, study-

ing every window for signs of trouble, then realized he
wouldn't be able to see Sara from here since her room
was by the dining room.

In the back where it was dark, where an intruder
could easily sneak in unnoticed.

He was driving himself crazy sitting here, waiting
for something to happen.

Worrying about what could happen.

Worrying about being too late.

He whipped open his door and took off toward the
house. Would Petrellis harm Sara in front of an inn full
of guests? No, he wouldn't be that bold. Besides, Will
doubted the cop had been hired to hurt Sara. More likely
he'd been ordered to get information and report back to
the men who were after her.

Will decided to bypass the front entrance and enter
through the back. As he walked along the dark side of
the house, he saw a shadow up ahead, lit by a floodlight.

"Hey!" he called out.

The person turned around...

It was Lucy, owner of the inn.

"Hi, Will. What are you doing back here?"

"I wanted to check on Sara."

Lucy, in her late thirties, with short dark hair, planted
her hands on her hips. "And you decided not to use the
front door?"

"Sorry, I heard someone back here and thought I'd
check it out."

"Just me, composting dinner scraps."

"Did a police officer stop by?"

"No, why? Am I in trouble?" she teased.

"Did you see anyone else out here tonight?"

"No, but then I wasn't looking." Her smile faded. "What's going on?"

"Let's go inside." He motioned her toward the house, hoping that Sara was okay.

As Will and Lucy climbed the back stairs, he scanned the property one last time before they went inside.

What if Petrellis had sneaked inside while Lucy was disposing of the dinner scraps?

"Maybe I should go in first," he offered.

Without argument, Lucy stepped aside and let him enter the kitchen. Pots and pans were stacked in the sink, and plates were lined up on the countertop.

No sign of Officer Petrellis.

"Sara's room is where?" he asked.

"Over here." Lucy led him through the dining room to a door off a small hallway.

He took a deep breath and tapped on her door. "Sara?"

No response.

"She said she was exhausted," Lucy offered.

He looked down at the soft glow reflecting from beneath the door.

Tapping harder, he called out, "Sara, it's Will. Are you all right?"

Again, silence.

"Please open the door," he said to Lucy.

"I don't feel right going into a guest's room while she's inside."

If she was still inside.

"It's an emergency," Will said. "I think she's in danger. While you were out back, someone could have made his way into her room."

The front doorbell rang repeatedly.

"That's probably Detective Walsh," Will said. "Go ahead and let him in. He'll explain the urgency."

With a worried nod, she went to greet Nate. Will continued to tap on the door. Maybe there was a simple explanation. Yeah, like she didn't want to talk to him. She'd said as much when she'd left his Jeep, right?

"Sara, please open the door," Will said.

Nate marched up to Will. "I told you to wait for me."

"Officer Petrellis wasn't in his car," Will said. "I couldn't wait, and now Sara's not answering her door."

Nate nodded at Lucy. "Please open it."

She pulled a master key out of her pocket. "Sara? We're sorry to intrude." She opened the door.

The room was empty.

Will noticed open French doors leading outside. "He took her."

Nate went to the doors, and turned to Lucy. "Where does this lead?"

"The driveway."

Nate checked the door. "Someone messed with the lock." Nate went outside to investigate.

Will couldn't move. The walls seemed to close in around him. His fault; this was his fault.

"Lucy, are you down here?" a guest called from the living room.

Lucy placed her hand on Will's shoulder. "I have to take care of my guest."

Maybe Will nodded, maybe he didn't. He couldn't be sure of anything right now, except for the fact he'd failed Sara.

As he struggled to calm his panicked thoughts, he noticed the backpack she'd bought at the Super Shopper beside the bed, plus the sneakers she'd worn out of the store. She'd been so happy to get out of the stiff, dirt-covered boots and into a pair of comfortable shoes.

She'd taken them off, and wore what out of here? The uncomfortable boots again? No, he didn't see that happening. Will snapped his attention to the armoire. He approached it and tapped gently with his knuckles.

"Sara, you in there?"

There was no response. He held his breath and cracked one of the doors open.

It was empty except for wood hangers and an ironing board.

"No one's outside." Nate came back into the room and shut the doors behind him. "And the sedan you described is gone. Spike's not answering my texts. I have to assume he wasn't sending the messages. Petrellis must have somehow gotten his phone. Hope Spike's okay." Nate patted Will's shoulder. "Hang in there, buddy. We'll find her."

"Okay." Will's mind raced with worst-case scenarios.

Nate hesitated before stepping out of the room. "This was not your fault, Will."

"Yeah, okay."

"I mean it." Nate left the room, his voice echoing across the first floor of the inn. "Base, this is Detective Walsh. I need you to ping Officer Spike Duggins's cruiser and get me that location. Also, send an officer to Stuart Petrellis's house, over."

As Will shut the doors to the armoire, he considered what could have happened. If Petrellis had broken into her room she wouldn't have gone willingly with him, and Will hadn't been gone that long, maybe five minutes, tops. He surely would have heard her protests.

Her cries for help.

His gaze drifted to her newly bought sneakers. Convinced she was still in the house, he went into the living area. Voices drifted from the kitchen, Lucy's voice, and another woman's—not Sara's.

Sara was hiding. He could feel it.

As he wandered through the living room, he noticed a door built into the wall beneath the stairs. His girls would definitely consider that the perfect hiding spot. Could Sara be in there? Or was he kidding himself, denying the reality of the situation?

The possibility that she'd been taken, and might be dead by morning.

Will went to the door and tapped gently.

"What are you doing?" Nate said, gripping his radio.

Will knocked again. "Sara, it's Will. You okay in there?"

A few tense moments of silence passed.

Please, Lord, give her the courage to open the door.

"I'm brewing tea," Lucy said from the kitchen doorway. "And warming scones."

"I needed a snack," her female guest said from the kitchen.

"Tea and scones, how about it, Sara?" Will tried again.

Either she was scared and hiding, or Will was making a complete fool of himself.

"Nate's here. You're safe," Will encouraged.

With a soft click, the closet door opened. Will offered his hand and Sara took it. As she stepped out, she glanced at Nate then at Lucy.

"Sorry," Sara said. She slipped her hand out of Will's and went to her room. Will and Nate followed.

"I'm so embarrassed," she said.

"What happened, and why were you in the closet?" Nate asked.

"I thought I saw a man outside my window. I was being paranoid."

"No, you're being careful," Will said. "And that's a good thing, right, Nate?"

"Yes. Especially given the circumstances."

"What circumstances?" Sara said, worry coloring her blue eyes.

"We'll explain on the way," Nate said.

"Where are we going?" she asked.

"We need to find you another safe house. Better yet, we've got an open cell at the station."

"No, you're not locking her up," Will said.

"For her own good," Nate argued.

"I've got a better idea."

It felt wrong on so many levels, Sara thought as she looked out the loft window to the parking area below. Will and Nate were outside having a heated discussion, probably about Sara, and why Will needed to stop helping her. Nate had been clear—Sara could remain free as long as she promised to stay in Echo Mountain until they finished investigating the stranger's death, and the supposed death of David Price.

Supposed, right.

To think that without Will's help Sara would be locked in a cell right now. Her gaze roamed the loft that his deceased wife had used as her art studio. It had a peaked ceiling with wood support beams, and lace curtains covering the rectangular windows. It was a peaceful place, a place where one could dream, imagine and create.

The loft wasn't meant to be used as a fortress.

It felt wrong to be here, not only because of the danger Sara brought with her, but also because of the lie she had to hide behind. Would Will see her differently if he knew the truth, that she was an FBI agent who'd failed miserably as she'd watched a man being murdered?

She didn't like lying to Will or the local authorities, but she wasn't ready to go public, not until she spoke with her supervisor. Unfortunately Bonner wasn't answering her calls. She wondered if it was a tough love thing, that he thought if he ignored her she'd get back to relaxing on a beach somewhere. Then she realized he wouldn't recognize the new phone number. She'd been hesitant to leave a message regarding the situation, she wasn't sure why. So she decided to keep trying until he picked up.

The last thing she wanted was to blow her cover and expose herself as FBI to LaRouche and Harrington. They'd surely destroy evidence that could be used to build a case against them.

Evidence. She felt in her pocket for her broken phone. She had to get it to a tech person and retrieve the recorded murder of David Price.

"How do I find one of those?" she whispered to herself.

Maybe she'd ask Will, since he seemed to know most everyone in town. Yes, she'd tell him she wanted to retrieve photos from her ruined phone.

She sighed, eyeing Will's commanding presence through the window as he spoke with Nate. She wanted to stop lying to Will, to the man who had continually offered support and encouragement. No man, besides her uncle, had ever done that for her. Most of the men she'd dated had seemed too self-absorbed, and the male agents at work were focused solely on their careers.

There was no room in the FBI for weakness. She thought she'd covered hers pretty well with sheer grit and determination to nail criminals. Instead, Bonner criticized her for her tenacity, saying it had gotten her into trouble, that she saw crimes where there were none. He even insinuated she was overcompensating for something, like her small stature or even…

A past failure.

That seemed like a low blow, considering Bonner knew about her father's death.

She stepped away from the window and unzipped her backpack, still frustrated with herself for hiding when she felt the threat looming outside her room at the inn. She should have stood up for herself and taken the guy down. Any other FBI agent would have detained him for questioning.

"Yeah, with bruised ribs and a sprained wrist?"

The sound of footsteps echoed against the stairs. Putting distance between her and Will was getting more and more difficult, especially since she was staying in his wife's art studio.

That's not the only reason, Sara.

She felt herself opening up to him, allowing herself to be vulnerable for the first time since…

Had she ever really been vulnerable to a man before?

"It's not a five-star hotel, but it's pretty nice, huh?" Will said, stepping up to the top floor.

"It's charming." She glanced at him. "But I don't like putting you or your family in danger."

"You aren't. This place is a few blocks from my

house, and isn't in my name, so no one will be able to make the connection between us."

"Who owns it?"

"A couple that travels ten months out of the year. I'd agreed to maintain things around here in exchange for Megan's use of the loft. I kept doing it, you know, as a favor."

Sara suspected it was more than that. She suspected he liked being around his wife's former space.

"The daybed isn't bad," he said. "Megan spent her share of nights here." He looked away, as if he hadn't meant to admit that.

"I'm sorry," she said.

He frowned. "Why?"

"You two were having trouble?"

"No, it wasn't that…well, not initially. It was the cancer. She wanted to spend the last few months here with the caregiver so I could get used to raising the girls alone. At least that's what she said."

"That must have been rough."

"Yeah, well, we had the loft cleaned out, so no cancer germs," he joked. He closed his eyes and sighed. "I don't know where that came from. I'm sorry."

"You don't need to apologize. You've been through a lot, and you have a right to react any way you want."

"Yeah, but that made me sound like a heartless jerk."

"Not even on your worst day could anyone think of you as a heartless jerk."

Will snapped his gaze to hers. Sara felt her heartbeat tapping against her chest.

Don't do this, Sara. He's a man still grieving for his wife, and you happen to be standing in her space.

"Hopefully a room will open up at the resort in the

next day or two and I can move over there." She refocused on emptying her backpack of clothes and setting them on a wooden bench. "Oh, I meant to ask if you knew of a place in town where I could get my phone looked at?"

"The new one?"

"No, my original phone. It was damaged in the fall and I'd like to retrieve things from it, like pictures."

"I know a techie who could help."

"Great, thanks."

"Nate has assigned a police officer to keep watch."

"What about Spike, the one who Nate thought was looking after me?"

"They found him wandering by the highway, disoriented, and took him to the hospital."

"Officer Petrellis did that to him?"

"Nate suspects so, yes, and that Petrellis took Spike's phone and was texting updates to Nate."

"Is Spike okay?"

"He'll be fine. He's a tough kid who came on the force a few months ago. He's probably wondering if that was such a good idea right about now."

"Did they track down Petrellis?"

"No one was home when they checked his house. No car in the driveway, and the blinds were all closed. They've got a bulletin out on him. Anyway, a police officer should be arriving shortly to keep an eye on things here."

"I thought Nate didn't have the resources, or are they worried I'll flee the county?"

"Nate is concerned about your safety."

She nodded, hoping the detective truly believed her.

"Sara?"

"I'm fine. You don't have to stay."

"Okay, well…" He ran an anxious hand through thick chestnut hair. "There are fresh towels in the bathroom, and you bought toiletries at the store so you should be all set."

"Yep, looking forward to a good night's sleep."

"Okay, well, until tomorrow."

"Will, you don't have to—"

"Don't tell me not to check on you, Sara."

"You're awfully determined."

"Sometimes not determined enough. I won't make that mistake again."

She frowned, trying to figure out what he meant.

"Have a good night," he said in a firm voice. "The door automatically locks when I shut it. You can flip the deadbolt if you want, as well."

"Okay, thanks."

With a nod, he went downstairs and shut the door with a click.

She felt so alone in this strange place, a place where Will's wife had withdrawn from the world, which was kind of what Sara felt as though she was doing.

She could neither withdraw from the world, nor her current situation. There was a case to solve, two men to put away for murder, at the very least.

She pulled out her newly purchased cell phone and called her boss, this time deciding to leave a message.

"This is Agent Bonner. Leave a message."

"It's Agent Vaughn. There's been a development in the LHP case and I need to speak with you immediately. Here is my new number." She rattled it off. "The suspected drug case is now first-degree murder. I witnessed LaRouche kill David Price."

She ended the call and stared at the phone. That should get him to call her back.

Exhaustion took hold, and she flopped down on the daybed. The echo of car doors slammed outside, and she figured the new surveillance officer had arrived.

Sara took a deep breath and relaxed, knowing she'd think more clearly after a decent night's sleep. She felt safe for now. No one knew where she was. LaRouche and Harrington couldn't find her here.

She sighed and drifted off to sleep.

Sara awoke with a start. She wasn't sure how long she'd been asleep, perhaps not long because it was still dark outside. She grabbed her phone. It was nearly ten.

Then she heard what had awakened her: the creak of wooden floorboards. Someone was coming up the steps.

Sara sat up, her heart racing. She'd left the desk lamp on, which she often did, so she wouldn't be disoriented if she awakened. She searched the room for a closet, a place to hide.

No, she wouldn't keep hiding like a coward, a weak and fragile woman who didn't belong in the field. But she needed a better position from which to defend herself.

She noticed a rock candleholder on the desk across the room. She grabbed it and crouched beside a set of file cabinets.

Her attacker was pretty smart to have eluded the police officer outside. Was Petrellis coming up the stairs? She bit her lower lip with worry, remembering he was at least six feet tall. Sure, she could call 911, only they wouldn't get here in time to prevent the assault. They'd arrive after the fact, after she'd been taken, or beaten up, or worse.

She focused on the sound. Silence rang in her ears. Was she was imagining things?

No, she wouldn't be swayed by her boss's comment that, at times, her overzealousness bordered on irrational.

Another creak of floorboards echoed across the loft.

Focus, Sara. Breathe.

Creak, creak.

Now it sounded as though the creak was coming from the other side of the loft.

The intruder was up here, with Sara. Coming closer.

Closer.

Weapon in hand, Sara waited…

Chapter Eight

Will had drifted off to sleep on the sofa when the phone awakened him.

"Yeah?" he said.

"Is Claire with you?" his mother-in-law said.

"What?" He sat up.

"Susanna can't find her. She thinks she might have gone home."

The phone pressed to his ear, Will searched the house. The beds were neatly made. No Claire. "She's not here. What happened?"

"Claire got upset and Susanna thought she went into the bedroom, but now she can't find her. One of the girls thought she heard her go out the back."

"I'll go look for her. She shouldn't be walking around at night."

"You're preaching to the choir. That girl should be grounded for life."

"I'll call when I find her." He pocketed his phone, grabbed his house keys and headed outside, figuring he'd walk to Susanna's house and hopefully run into his daughter making her way home.

He tamped down the panic, knowing it was a sense-less emotion, yet a natural one. What happened that upset Claire? She'd been moody lately, and he wondered if something was happening with her friends or at school, and she couldn't bring herself to talk to Will about it. Listening and giving advice had always been Megan's role.

He walked a few blocks and automatically glanced to his right, across the park at the house with the up-stairs loft that his wife, and now Sara, used as a refuge.

A shriek echoed across the park.

More lights popped on in the loft.

And a little person sprinted out of the house, past the patrol car parked out front.

Claire?

He took off toward her. What was she doing at the loft? Unless...

She missed her mom.

And found a stranger in her mother's space.

That must have been confusing, not to mention frightening for his daughter.

Will caught up to her on the lake path.

"Daddy! Daddy!" she sobbed.

Will whisked her into his arms. "Hey, baby girl. It's okay. I'm here."

"There was a...ghost in the loft!"

"No, honey, there's no such thing as a ghost."

"I saw her!"

She continued to sob against his shoulder and he debated taking her home, or going back to the loft to clear this up. A uniformed police officer headed toward them. The one thing Will did not want was for Sara's protective detail to leave his post.

Carrying Claire in his arms, Will headed toward the loft.

"Where are we going?" Claire said.

"To show you it wasn't a ghost, then I'll take you home. What were you doing at the loft anyway?"

"Nothing."

"Claire Renee Rankin."

A few seconds passed, then she said, "I go there sometimes, that's all."

"You go inside?"

"Yeah. I found a secret way inside."

He approached the police officer and recognized Officer Ryan McBride, Bree's cousin. "Hi, Ryan," Will said.

"I didn't even see her until she came racing out of the house. Is she okay?"

"Yeah, just scared. What about Sara?"

They both turned to look at the house. Sara stood in the doorway on the first floor, gripping a blanket around her shoulders.

"See, that's the ghost!" Claire cried into Will's shoulder.

"No, honey. That's Sara, a friend of mine," Will said. "I'm sure she feels badly about scaring you. Let's go talk to her."

Claire shook her head no.

"Look, you weren't supposed to be at the loft in the first place, were you?"

She shook her head again.

"Okay, then, let's face the consequences of your actions and sort this out." He nodded at Officer McBride and continued to the house.

"Will, I'm so sorry. I thought it was an intruder,"

Sara said, pulling the blanket tight around her shoulders with one hand.

"Let's go inside."

The three of them went upstairs. Will sat on a gray wingback chair and adjusted Claire on his lap. His little girl buried her face against his shoulder.

Sara sat on the daybed across the room. "I'm so sorry," she repeated.

"So is Claire, aren't you, baby girl?" Will said.

"I'm not a baby anymore, Daddy."

"No? So you're a big girl, and big girls can run off without telling anyone where they're going?"

She didn't answer.

"What happened, sweetheart?" he said, softening his voice.

"Nothing."

"Claire?" he pushed.

"We were making cookies."

"And…?"

"Olivia wanted to make snicker doodles, and Marissa said, you mean snicker poodles."

"That upset you because…?"

She leaned back and looked at him. "Those are Mommy's special cookies."

"Right. And it made you miss your mom?"

She buried her face against his neck. "It made me sad, so I went for a walk. Don't be mad, Daddy."

"I'm not angry. I was worried. So was your grandmother, Mrs. Baker, and what about your little sister? Remember the buddy system? You're never supposed to leave her alone."

"She was eating cookie dough. She didn't care."

"Of course she did. As a matter of fact, I'd better

call over there. First, let me introduce you to my friend, Miss Sara. She was hurt in a hiking accident and SAR rescued her. I offered to let her stay here."

"This is Mommy's place," Claire's muffled voice said.

"I know, but Mommy's not using it right now, and Miss Sara needs a place to sleep." He shot a half smile across the room at Sara.

Sara's gaze was intent on the back of Claire's head.

"How about it?" Will said. "Can we show Miss Sara our gracious hospitality by letting her stay here for a few days?"

"I guess." Claire leaned back and looked at Will. "What happened to your face, Daddy?"

"I had a hiking accident, too."

"Did they have to rescue you?"

"No, I walked down on my own."

"You look like you were in a fight."

"Do I look like I won?" he teased.

"Yeah." Claire giggled.

"Good answer," he said. "Now, I'd better call your grandmother before she sends out the National Guard." Will shifted Claire off his lap and made the call.

By holding the blanket loosely around her body, Sara managed to hide the fact that she was still trembling. The adrenaline rush hadn't worn off from the past few minutes.

Will's daughter studied her with fascination and fear coloring her eyes. To think Sara had nearly conked the girl on the head with the rock candle.

Yet she hadn't because as Sara had been about to

jump out of her hiding spot, the little girl had whis-pered, "Mommy, where are you?"

Sara had put down her weapon and stepped out from behind the file cabinet. Unfortunately revealing herself had terrified little Claire.

Mommy, where are you?

Hadn't Sara asked the same question a hundred times as a child? Wondering why her mom had had to go live at the hospital, and then why she'd never come home.

Sara's heart ached for Claire.

"It's fine. She's fine," Will said into the phone.

Sara noticed how he inadvertently stroked Claire's hair while speaking to his mother-in-law.

Claire hadn't taken her eyes off Sara.

"I'm sorry if I frightened you," Sara said.

"Why were you hiding?"

"I was scared."

"Of me?" Claire said, incredulously.

"I didn't know it was you," Sara explained. "All I heard was someone coming up the steps."

"Oh," Claire said, thinking for a minute on that one. "Can you draw?"

Sara bit back a smile at the random nature of her question. "No, not really."

"Mommy says everyone can draw."

"She created wonderful things." Sara eyed the sketches pinned to the walls.

"No, I'll take her home and pick up Marissa on the way," Will said into the phone. "I think she should be grounded, don't you?" He glanced at Claire.

His daughter shook her head no, that she didn't want to be grounded.

"Nonrefundable, huh?" Will continued. "Okay, I

guess you can swing by in the morning and pick them up... See you then." Will pocketed his phone and looked at Claire. "Nanny and Papa spent a lot of money on tickets to the museum, so I'm going to let you go with them tomorrow, and then tomorrow night we'll talk about the consequences of your actions."

"Don't ground me next week, please, Daddy. It's after-school art camp."

"We'll talk about it later."

The little girl looked as if she was going to burst into another round of tears. Sara did not envy Will's job of being a single parent.

"Let's go," he said, reaching out for Claire. "Sara needs to get some sleep."

Claire ignored her father's hand and studied her shoes.

"Claire?" Will prompted.

"Whenever I come here—" she hesitated "—I usually say a prayer for Mommy."

Will's expression softened. "Good idea."

Claire pressed her fingers together in prayer, as did Will.

Sara hadn't prayed since...well, she couldn't remember the last time she'd prayed. She figured, why bother? It hadn't helped when Mom was sick, and what kind of God would take Sara's father away from her?

"Don't you know how to pray?" Claire asked Sara with a frown. "It's easy. You put your hands together, see?" She nodded at her own fingers.

Sara had to stop thinking about her own pain and consider little Claire's emotional recovery. Sara pressed her hands together, the feeling so awkward and uncomfortable. "Like this?"

"Yes, then close your eyes."

Sara did as requested. How could anyone deny such a sweet little girl who was still grieving for her mom?

"Dear Lord," Claire began. "Take good care of my Mommy because she always took good care of us. I hope she's helping you in Heaven, and I hope she'll never forget us. I love you, Mommy. Amen."

"Amen," Sara and Will said in unison.

She didn't know about Will, but Sara could hardly speak past the ball of emotion in her throat.

"Good," Will said in a rough voice. "Good prayer."

"You did good, too, Miss Sara," Claire offered.

"Thank you."

Claire went to take her father's hand.

"Hopefully there won't be any more excitement," Will said to Sara. "I'll see you tomorrow."

"You don't—"

"I'll bring breakfast by after my in-laws pick up the girls."

"We want to come for breakfast," Claire said. "Please, Daddy, please?"

"Enough, sweetheart. Let's get your sister and go home. We'll figure out the rest tomorrow."

Claire grinned. Sara wondered if the little girl had Will wrapped around her finger.

"Until tomorrow, then." Will escorted Claire to the top of the stairs.

"Good night, Will," Sara said. "Sweet dreams, Claire."

Claire smiled at Sara. "I'll say a prayer for you to-night so you won't be scared anymore."

Claire started down the stairs and Will glanced at Sara.

"She's adorable," Sara said.

"Yeah."

With an odd, almost sad smile, Will disappeared down the stairs with his daughter.

After everything that had happened today and this evening, Sara realized spending time with Will and his girls for breakfast tomorrow was a horrible idea. She'd be hiding behind a shield of lies, and that was starting to feel terribly wrong.

As she stretched out on the bed, she heard Claire's prayer: *Take good care of my Mommy because she always took good care of us.*

That was what Will and his girls needed most: someone to take care of them. Sara was a dangerous diversion from that goal, although Will didn't know how dangerous.

She felt something brewing between she and Will: a closeness, a connection. She couldn't let that happen.

"Stop thinking about them."

No matter how much a part of her enjoyed watching Will interact with Claire, listening to Claire pray for her mother and taking refuge in the loft, the reality was, Sara had a job to do. If only her boss would call her back.

Until then, she had to stop involving innocents like Will and his girls, for their own good.

Sara got up early the next morning and tried to leave, but Officer McBride asked her to wait until Nate arrived. Asked? More like ordered her to stay put, up in her tower.

Sara could have argued, but she wasn't an idiot. Making enemies with the local cops wasn't a great idea, especially since she'd need their support, not their suspicions.

As she gazed out the window, she imagined what it would be like to live in a small town like Echo Mountain. Sara had hopped from one place to another after high school, first switching colleges to get the best criminal justice degree, then taking jobs to support her goal of becoming an FBI agent.

Yet life seemed so peaceful in Echo Mountain.

She sighed. Things always looked different from the outside. Like the bureau, and how it was nothing like she'd imagined. They didn't rush out and nail the bad guys. They had to follow protocol and procedure, and sometimes that meant a criminal wouldn't be prosecuted.

As she gazed at the mountain range in the distance, she wondered if LaRouche and Harrington had come down from the mountain, and what story they'd tell.

She spotted Will's Jeep cross the property. He parked and got out, with both little girls in tow.

"Will, no," she said. Bringing the girls here would only make things harder.

He carried what looked like a pastry box. Sara couldn't believe he'd awakened his daughters this early to bring her breakfast.

"Sara?" Will called from the bottom of the stairs.

"Come on up!" It's not as if she could turn them away. She wouldn't be that cruel, especially not to two little ones.

Will, Claire and her little sister came up to the loft. "Marissa, this is Miss Sara," Will introduced.

"You look like Mommy," Marissa said matter-of-factly.

"She does not," Claire argued.

"Girls," Will said. "Show Miss Sara what we brought her."

Claire shook her head disapprovingly at her little sister, then placed a box on the desk. She opened it slowly, reverently, as if she was showing off the crown jewels instead of creatively designed pastries. "These are Maple Bars, these are Chocolate Chipmunk Bars and these are Penelope's Pink Pansies."

Marissa leaned over the box, her green eyes widening. She looked a lot like her father. "Pansies are my favorite."

"I'm guessing these didn't come from Healthy Eats," Sara said.

"You'd guess right." Will smiled.

"We only get these on special occasions," Claire explained.

"Yeah, special occasions," Marissa echoed.

Was that what this was, a special occasion? Sara was in deeper trouble than she thought.

"Wow, how do I rate?" she asked Will.

"Thought it might help your aches and pains. Here." He pulled napkins out of his pocket and put them on the desk. "We're calling this first breakfast."

"Yeah, because Papa likes to eat breakfast out so we'll have second breakfast with him," Marissa said, licking the frosting off her Pink Pansy pastry.

For a brief second, Sara enjoyed the warmth of family, of children. In that moment, she shoved aside all thoughts of LaRouche and Harrington.

She reminded herself that this, the smiles of little girls licking frosting off their lips, was only an illusion, one that would evaporate soon enough.

Claire lifted a doughnut out of the box and raised it to her lips, eyes rounding with delight.

"It's terrifying, isn't it?" Will said.

Sara looked at him. "What?"

"The expression on her face when she's about to eat copious amounts of sugar and fat."

"If you think that's terrifying, how about this?" Sara grabbed a Maple Bar, took a bite and rolled her eyes from side to side, and up and down.

The girls giggled.

"You look crazy," little Marissa said.

"She looks happy," Claire countered.

"Happy doesn't look like this." Marissa imitated Sara. "It looks like this." Marissa cracked a broad grin, exposing frosting on her teeth.

"Gross. You are so immature," Claire said.

"I'm not manure."

"I didn't say…" Claire sighed. "Oh, never mind."

Will and Sara shared a smile.

"Tell Miss Sara where you're going today," Will said, plucking a chocolate doughnut for himself.

"A doll museum," Claire said with awe in her voice. "They have dolls from all over the world. Even Russia."

"Is that far away?" Marissa said.

"Of course it is," Claire countered.

"How do you know? Have you been there?"

"You know I haven't been there."

"Then, how do you know it's far away?"

"I learned it in school, silly."

"Oh." Marissa thought for a second, then looked at Sara. "Do you draw?"

"No, not really."

Marissa looked at her sister. "Mommy said—"

"Miss Sara hasn't learned yet," Claire explained.

"Let's teach her." Marissa scrambled off her chair and rushed to the other side of the room. She grabbed a sketch pad and dashed back to her sister.

"Pencils?" Claire said.

Again, Marissa raced across the room, went to a shelf and snatched a few pencils.

"Good." Claire cracked her knuckles.

This was quite the operation, Sara mused.

Claire nodded at the doughnut in Sara's hand. "You'll have to put down the doughnut."

"Right." Sara laid it on a napkin and brushed off her hands.

"Hold the pencil between your fingers like this." Claire demonstrated. "Watch me."

Marissa studied her sister and mimicked her every move.

Sara caught Will's expression, a mixture of pride and sadness, punctuated with a thoughtful smile. Drawing obviously reminded him of his wife.

"Then you draw a *t* in the middle of the page."

"Why are you drawing a *t*?" Sara said.

"It's how you draw a face. You connect the corners." Claire nibbled her lower lip. Marissa imitated the motion of drawing a circle. "And there you have the outline of the lady's head." Claire held up the sketchpad.

"Why are you drawing a lady?" Marissa asked.

"Men are boring. Ladies have hair and makeup and fun stuff like that," she answered her sister. She pointed to her drawing. "Then you'll draw the eyes here." Claire pointed. "See, the eyes are above the cross line, like on a real face. You try." Claire handed Sara a pencil.

Sara made a *t* and drew an oval shape by connecting the tips of the letter.

"That's good, now make the eyes," Claire said.

Will's phone buzzed.

"Whoops, that's Nanny and Papa. They're wondering where you are. Let's go, girls."

The girls grabbed their doughnuts and headed for the stairs. Claire turned to Sara. "Don't eat all the Pink Pansies or you'll get a tummy ache."

"Okay, I won't." Sara smiled.

"I'll be back in twenty," Will said.

"I'll be here, practicing my drawing."

Marissa ran up and hugged Sara's legs. "Don't worry. You'll be able to draw someday."

So stunned by the display of affection, Sara didn't immediately return the hug. Her heart sank. She never realized what she'd been missing. Just as she wrapped her arms around the little girl, Marissa sprung free and skipped up to her dad and sister.

"Dolls, dolls, dolls!" Marissa chanted.

Will cast one last smile at Sara and led the girls downstairs. Sara went to the window. She watched them get into Will's Jeep and pull away.

An ache permeated her chest. They were such a lovely family: a protective, gentle father and two sweet, albeit precocious little girls. Will's family seemed so perfect, so…

She turned back to the room. How could they be so grounded and at peace after having lost a mother, a wife?

Sara wandered to the table where they had practiced drawing. A day hadn't gone by since her father's murder that Sara hadn't felt the burn of anger.

The Rankin family had suffered a great loss, but didn't seem to let the grief shadow their conversations.

Their every thought.

All of Sara's decisions since Dad's death had been motivated by anger and the need for justice. Get a criminal justice degree, work her way into a job with the FBI and hunt down bad guys and put them behind bars.

Make them pay.

Because her dad's killer was never caught, never served his time.

Now, in her thirties, Sara was all about her career. She had no personal life, no boyfriend or even close friends for that matter. She never had time to nurture those kinds of relationships.

Being with Will and his girls, seeing how the community rallied around him and protected him, triggered an ache in Sara's chest for that which she would never have.

"One more reason you need to get out of here." She grabbed her backpack and considered her options. If Officer McBride wouldn't allow her to leave until she spoke with Nate, perhaps she could talk him into taking her to the police station to wait this out. One thing was for sure—staying here, in Will's deceased wife's studio, was messing with Sara's head. Big-time.

She glanced around the loft to make sure she hadn't forgotten anything. Her gaze landed on a photo of Will's wife with an arm around each of her little girls. Sara had a photo a lot like that one, of Sara, her dad and little brother, Kenny. It was taken at the beach. They were happy, laughing.

A perfect moment lost in the chaos of murder.

You and your brother hide in the closet. Do not come out until I say it's okay.

The slamming of a car door outside ripped her out of the memory. Time to distance herself from Will and his girls. It was stirring up too many memories and buried grief.

Grief she'd been able to neutralize with determination to get justice.

She headed downstairs, deciding she'd sleep in a cell if she had to. She'd be safe at the police station, and a lot safer emotionally than if she continued to stay here.

As she headed for the patrol car, she saw Detective Walsh talking on his phone. He didn't look happy. Then he shot her a look, and she slowed her step. Something was very wrong.

"I understand. Text me the coordinates and I'll pass them along to SAR. We'll send a team. Once they're down I'll want to interview each of them individually.... Yes, I have her in custody."

In custody? Sara dug her fingers into the strap of her backpack.

Nate ended the call and turned to Sara. "Mr. La-Rouche and Mr. Harrington finally called in. They said David Price disappeared after he got into an argument with you."

Chapter Nine

"What?" Sara said in disbelief.

"They claim the last time they saw Mr. Price, you two were arguing over money."

"Unbelievable," she muttered.

"Is it true? You were arguing about money and, what, he fell?"

"Absolutely not."

"Just the same, I need you to come with me to the station."

Her heartbeat sped up. "Are you arresting me?"

"I'm bringing you in for questioning."

"They're lying. I don't care about money," she ground out. "I only care about…"

Don't say it. Not yet.

"Ma'am?" Detective Walsh prompted.

"Forget it." Of course they'd pin the murder on her. It was an easy solution to fix their problems. And they'd get away with it. They'd discredit Sara and make her a viable suspect.

"Is there anything you want to tell me?" Nate asked.

She clenched her jaw, wanting to tell the detective

who she really was. Sara feared losing traction with this case if word got out and LaRouche and Harrington discovered she was FBI.

She noticed Will's Jeep heading toward them. Perfect. This would drive him away, Will and his adorable girls, girls who didn't need to be exposed to the ugliness of Sara's life.

"Do what you have to do," she said to Nate.

Nate studied her with creased eyebrows. "Let's go." He motioned for her to get into his unmarked squad car.

Will pulled up beside them and hopped out. "Hey, what's going on?"

"I've been accused of murder," Sara said. "Okay? I'm dangerous. Stay away from me."

She climbed into the car and Nate shut the door. She couldn't hear what they were saying because they'd stepped away from the car, but she could tell Will argued fiercely with the detective.

Finally, Nate shook his head in frustration and got into the car.

She stared at the headrest of the seat in front of her, trying to block out Will's presence. He tapped on her window and she glanced out at his confused face. He looked as if he wanted answers.

As if he deserved answers.

She ripped her gaze from his emerald eyes. "Are we going or what?"

As Nate pulled away, Sara's eyes watered. *Goodbye, Will.*

She felt utterly alone. She wasn't working in an official capacity for the FBI, her supervisor hadn't returned her calls and now she'd pushed away the one person who truly wanted to help her.

"He deserves the truth."

She snapped her eyes to the back of Nate's head. "Meaning what?"

"Will saved your life and put himself at risk by protecting you. Don't you think that deserves complete honesty?"

"It doesn't matter."

"Oh, yes, ma'am, it does. Will Rankin is one of the most honorable men I know. For some strange reason he's decided you're worthy of his protection. He's usually got good instincts about people."

She gazed out the window as they passed a park filled with children.

"So? Were his instincts right about you?" Nate pushed.

She sighed. If LaRouche and Harrington were going to frame her, she'd better get ahead of this thing and confide in the local police.

"Yes, his instincts are good."

"And?"

"I'm FBI."

"Really," he said, disbelief in his voice.

"Yes."

"And you didn't bother to tell me or Will that before now because…?"

"I'm undercover."

"Then, you should have brought me into your investigation." Nate got a call and answered his radio. "Detective Walsh, go ahead, over."

"Someone saw Petrellis at the Super Shopper, about half an hour ago, over."

"He's still in town?" Nate muttered to himself, then responded into the radio, "Send a unit to check it out.

If the officer sees Petrellis, he needs to call for backup. Do not approach him alone, over."

"Ten-four."

He clicked off the radio and eyed her in the rearview. "We'll finish our discussion at the station."

Nate focused on driving, visibly frustrated by the call.

"You think he should have left town?" she said.

"Wouldn't you? I mean, we suspect that he drugged Spike, and was following you around all day for some nefarious reason."

"What happened with Spike, exactly?"

"Petrellis saw him outside the hospital and approached him, acting as though they're buddies. He congratulated Spike on the new job with Echo Mountain PD and slapped him on the shoulder. Hard. Spike says he thought he felt a pinch, like a bee sting. That's pretty much all he remembers." Nate shook his head. "What is happening to my town?"

Sara gazed out the window, feeling even guiltier that she brought trouble to the community of Echo Mountain.

Within minutes Will was on the phone calling Royce Burnside, the best lawyer in Echo County. Will had done search engine optimization marketing work for Royce's law firm and knew of their stellar reputation.

As a favor to Will, Royce said he'd meet him at the police station right after lunch. Will stopped himself from marching into the station alone, all fired up. He worked on marketing projects for the next few hours in his home office. Unfortunately, the image of a bruised and fragile Sara being aggressively interrogated kept seeping into his thoughts, distracting him.

Will leaned back in his chair and pulled his fingers off the keyboard. What was Nate thinking? Sara wasn't a criminal or a violent woman. She'd gone into shock after shooting a man, and had experienced traumatic flashbacks.

Although he sensed that Sara wanted to go this alone, the more she pushed Will away, the more determined he was to help. Sure, he knew once this case was resolved and she was given her freedom, she'd probably leave town and he'd never see her again. It didn't matter. She needed help and he wanted to be the one to give it to her.

He warmed up butternut-squash soup from Healthy Eats for lunch, hoping Nate at least had the decency to feed Sara. Maybe Will would bring some soup just in case. He had plenty.

Minutes stretched like hours as he waited for one o'clock.

"This is ridiculous." Although it was only twelve fifteen, he packed up a container of soup, grabbed a small bag of crackers and headed for the station. He brought his laptop as well, figuring he'd get some work done while waiting for Royce.

Will wasn't even sure Sara needed an attorney, but it wouldn't hurt to have one in her corner.

He parked in the lot, pulled out his laptop and moved his seat back so he could open it up and work. The whole work thing lasted about five minutes. Glancing at the building and knowing she was inside being questioned about a murder she didn't commit drove Will nuts.

Some folks would call him nuts for believing in a complete stranger.

But they weren't strangers. She'd exposed herself to him in a way he suspected she hadn't with many, if anyone. When she'd hidden under the bed, clutching the blanket to her chest, she'd seemed like a child, fearing for her life.

Something terrible had happened to Sara in her past, and it had all come rushing back after the shooting.

Will tucked the laptop into his backpack and grabbed the soup bag. He didn't care if he was early. He'd text Royce to meet him inside.

As he headed for the building, he spotted a familiar car parked across the street from the police station.

Officer Petrellis's unmarked sedan.

Surprised and concerned, Will glanced away, so as not to be obvious. He pulled out his phone and texted Nate about the car. They were looking for the retired officer to question him about yesterday, about drugging Spike and stalking Sara.

"Hello, Mr. Rankin."

Will glanced up. Petrellis was heading toward him.

"Officer," Will greeted, then hit Send on the text to Nate.

"What brings you to the station?" Petrellis said.

"Visiting my friend Nate."

"And what about your other friend Sara? How is she doing?"

"I wouldn't know. I've been busy with work."

"How well do you know her, if you don't mind my asking?"

"I don't know her at all, actually. I helped rescue her after a nasty fall. That's it." He glanced at his watch. "Whoa, I'm late. Excuse me."

Will turned to walk away, to put distance between

him and the retired officer with questionable motivations.

Something stabbed Will in the arm and he instinctively jerked back. "Hey!"

"You need to come with me."

"Excuse me?"

"I need to ask you some questions."

"I don't have time. I've got to get inside and…and…" Ringing started in his ears, and his surroundings went in and out of focus.

"Here, let me help you." A firm hand gripped Will's arm and led him away from the police station, away from Sara.

"No." Will yanked his arm away. "I have to talk to her."

"Her? You mean Sara?"

A part of Will knew he'd said too much. His brain was floating on some kind of wave, pulling him away from the shoreline of reality.

They found Spike wandering the highway, Nate had told Will.

That must be what was happening to Will.

"Relax," Petrellis said as they approached his car. "It will be over soon."

Over? As in…

Was Petrellis going to kill him? Leaving the girls with no parents, and judgmental grandparents to raise them?

"No!" Will shouldered Petrellis against the car and fired off punches.

"Will!" Nate called from across the street.

Petrellis yanked Will forward, kneed him in the gut

and cast him aside. Will collapsed on the pavement and watched Petrellis's car speed off.

"No," Will croaked, wanting Petrellis to come back, to tell them why he was after Sara.

Sara. The beautiful woman with the big blue eyes.

"Will." It was Sara's voice.

He looked up, into her worried eyes.

"No, I want all patrols to be on the lookout," Nate's voice said from behind her. "He's headed south on Main Street toward the interstate, over."

"Will?" Nate said.

All Will could see were Sara's blue eyes.

"Nate didn't arrest you, did he?" Will asked her.

"No." She placed a comforting hand on his chest. "What happened?"

"Dispatch, I need an ambulance," Nate's voice said.

"No," Will said. "No ambulance."

"Will, you're hurt," Nate argued.

"Drugged like Spike. Felt him stick my arm."

"Then, an ambulance can take you to the hospital."

"Everyone will know. My in-laws—"

"This wasn't your fault," Sara said.

"Stop worrying about them, Will," Nate said. "The ambulance will be here shortly."

"Have to get home… The girls."

"They're not coming home until seven, remember?" Sara offered. "It's only twelve-thirty."

"Oh, yeah." He closed his eyes, then opened them again. "Are you okay?"

"I'm fine." She frowned. "I'm worried about you."

"What's going on?" Royce said, joining them.

"Who are you?" Sara said.

"Your attorney," Royce said. "Will hired me."

"Ambulance is here," Nate said.

Will stood, Sara holding onto one arm for support, while Nate gripped the other. He flopped down onto a stretcher, but wouldn't let go of Sara's hand.

"I need to—"

"Go find Petrellis," Sara interrupted Nate. "I'll ride with Will."

As Will was being examined by medical staff, he worried what his in-laws would think, what they would say. This would be the second time he'd been examined by doctors at the hospital in the past few days. In Mary's and Ed's minds, he probably threw himself onto the path of danger yet again by interacting with a suspected…what? What was Officer Petrellis, exactly? Will still didn't know.

Once they reached the hospital, Will was given a medication to counteract the drug. His brain fog began to clear and he was able to focus again. Sara said she'd be in the waiting room speaking with Royce, who had followed them from the police station.

Will puzzled over Nate's sudden turnaround from almost arresting her to letting her accompany Will to the hospital.

"How's your vision?" the nurse asked.

"Good, excellent," Will answered.

"Are you nauseous or dizzy?"

"No, ma'am. I'm much better now, thanks. Can I go?"

"Where's the fire?" Dr. Kyle Spencer, a member of SAR asked, coming into the ER. "Hey, buddy, I heard you were brought in."

"Hey, Spence," Will said.

"How's the head?"

"Fine."

"No headache?"

"No."

"Blurred vision?"

"Not now."

"So…when?" Spence studied him with concern.

"After I got stuck with the drug."

Spence pulled out a penlight and checked Will's eyes. "Did you fall and hit your head again?"

"Not that I know of."

Spence was referring to an altercation in the mountains last year. That injury had left Will with temporary, selective amnesia. At the time Will didn't remember that Megan had passed away. Once his memory returned, reliving that grief had left him gutted, as if she'd just died.

"The medical team identified elements of the drug we found in Spike's system and were able to give him, and now you, something to counteract the effects," Spence said.

"Yeah, so they told me."

"It wouldn't hurt to rest this afternoon."

"Okay, doc." Will shifted off the gurney and planted his feet on the floor.

Spence studied him. "A-OK?"

"Solid as a rock, thanks."

"Excellent." They shook hands. "Until our next mission, then."

"Yep." Will left the examining room and found Sara in the waiting area with Royce.

"Hey, how are you?" Sara went in for a hug.

It was a brief embrace that shocked Will. He didn't want to let go.

"I'm okay," Will said. "Was Royce able to help you?"

"Turns out it wasn't necessary," Royce said. "In case

you do need me, you've got my card." Royce smiled at Will. "Glad you're okay. Take care."

"You, too."

Royce left the ER waiting area and that was when Will noticed a uniformed officer by the door.

"Okay, someone's going to have to draw me a map here," Will started. "This morning Nate was arresting you, then he did a one-eighty and let you accompany me in the ambulance and now he's posted a police officer, I'm assuming for your protection?"

"Yeah, you and I need to talk. It's rather crowded here. Officer Carrington will take us to the station, unless you need to go home and rest?"

"No, I'm okay."

Will and Sara left the hospital with Officer Carrington, Sara's eyes constantly scanning their surroundings. She seemed different today, stronger, more sure of herself.

He almost wondered if she was the same person he'd found in the mountains. Of course she was, yet something had definitely changed.

And he liked it, especially the hugging part.

The ride back to the station was somewhat quiet. Will was desperate to know what was going on, but didn't dare ask in front of a third party.

Officer Carrington escorted them into a conference room at the station. Sara wandered to the window and looked outside.

"First, I need to apologize for bringing this danger to Echo Mountain—" she turned "—and into your life."

"I don't see a need to apologize. Go on." He pulled out a chair at the table and sat, hoping she'd join him.

She leaned against the wall and crossed her arms over her chest.

"The truth is, I'm FBI. I was on an undercover mission to find evidence against a company called LHP, Inc.—LaRouche, Harrington and Price's company. I suspect they plan to distribute a sleep medication that will make them millions, and potentially put lives at risk."

"You followed them on a hiking trip?"

"I bought my way onto the guide team, hoping they'd let their guard down and I'd find evidence of their plan. Then I saw Vic LaRouche throw David Price to his death. Wasn't expecting that."

"Have you told Nate this?"

"This morning, when he picked me up. He kind of—" she hesitated "—guilted it out of me."

"Yeah, I could see him doing that."

"Now I feel even more guilty because of what happened to you this afternoon."

"You didn't stick me with the drug."

"Don't be so literal here, Will. This is my fault. Maybe if I would have made a different choice."

"What choice? You've been in survival mode ever since you witnessed the murder."

She cocked her head slightly. "How do you do that?"

"What?"

"Offer so much compassion for someone who has been making your life a mess."

"What mess? I don't see a mess."

"Will, Petrellis knows you and I are connected, so now you're a target. The smartest thing for me to do is leave town and somehow draw them away from Echo Mountain."

"Why did Nate take you in this morning?"

She pulled out a chair and sat at the table. Good, she was getting closer.

"LaRouche and Harrington reported David Price missing this morning," she said. "They claim he disappeared after he and I got into an argument."

"So they're turning this around on you?"

"Looks that way."

"But you're FBI."

"They don't know that, and they can't." She reached across the table and placed her hand on Will's. "Only you and Nate know who I really am," she said. "It has to stay that way. If these guys find out the FBI is on their trail, they'll bury evidence so deep we'll never find it."

His gaze drifted to her hand, and she slid it off.

"You seem different," he said, glancing into her eyes. "More grounded and confident."

"It feels better to have people know the truth, people I trust." She cracked a slight smile.

The door opened and Nate joined them wearing a frown. He planted his hand on Will's shoulder. "Doing okay?"

"Yeah, I'm good. How's Spike?"

"Embarrassed, but otherwise good."

"And Petrellis?" Sara said.

"In the wind. For now."

"What's his motivation?" she asked Nate.

"Have no clue. Yet."

"Why did he take early retirement?" she said.

"He had issues at home and it interfered with his work."

"What kind of issues?"

"Not sure. He was a private guy." Nate slapped a folder onto the table. "We've got a bigger problem."

Will and Sara shared a worried look.

"One, your investigation has made Will a target," Nate said.

"Hey, Nate—"

Nate put up his hand to silence Will. "And, two, according to your supervisor, there is no case. Officially, you're on vacation, so that makes you a rogue agent with a vendetta."

Chapter Ten

"That's not true," Sara said, her face heating with anger. Why couldn't Bonner support her and admit she had been working on a case?

"Sara, what's going on?" Will said with a puzzled frown.

"It's easy, Will," Nate said. "Your friend here has been lying to us and manipulating us this whole time."

Will studied her with such pain in his eyes. "You've been lying to me?"

Regret coursed through her. No, she had good intentions, even if her execution was off.

"Will." She leaned forward. "I'm sorry, truly. But I'm doing the right thing here. My boss probably threw me under the bus because he's tired of me hounding him about tough cases, the criminals that get away." She glanced over her shoulder at Nate. "You worked in a big city—you know what I'm talking about."

Nate didn't answer, so she continued, redirecting her attention to Will, wanting him to know everything.

"LaRouche and Harrington were trying to convince David Price to go along with their plan to distribute a dangerous drug that could kill people. Because of who they are and their influence and who knows what else, they're going to get away with it. That's why LaRouche shoved David Price off the cliff—because he was going to walk away from the company, which would have raised suspicion and tanked their stock. So yes, I came out here because I didn't have enough evidence, and I decided to find more. Call me nuts, call me rogue, I don't care, as long as I put these guys away before they kill anybody." She glanced at Nate once more. "Didn't you ever watch a suspect walk away with a cocky smirk on his face when he should have been in cuffs?"

Nate tapped a pen against his open palm and studied her. "How do you know the drug is dangerous?"

At least he was listening to her. Now if she could get Will to forgive her for lying.

"They were arguing about an anomaly in the test results," she explained to Nate. "David Price said it wasn't right, that it could kill people. I recorded it on my phone, which was damaged in my fall. I was hoping a tech could still retrieve the video. That's my nail in their coffin."

"What motivated you to follow them into the mountains?" Nate asked.

"An email exchange between LaRouche and the drug testing company. I printed them out. My supervisor said it wasn't enough."

"Why not?" Nate said.

"It was too—" she made quote marks with her fingers "—vague."

She glanced at Will, who still looked like a man who'd just met her for the first time. As if he didn't recognize her. Shame burned her insides, both for having lied to him, and for putting him in danger.

She shifted in her chair and waited for more questions from Nate.

"He said once you got your teeth into something, you weren't giving it up," Nate said. "Even if there was no basis for an investigation."

"Nice," she muttered.

"He told you to let this one go," Nate continued.

"Well, I couldn't."

"You ignored a direct order."

"He ordered me to take vacation time—"

"Because you hadn't taken time off in five years."

"I didn't have any reason to."

"But you had reason to go against a direct order and pursue this case?"

"If it could save lives, yes," she countered. "I can't believe you've never done the same."

"We're not talking about me. We're talking about you, and why you're so tenacious. Your boss said—"

"What, that I'm an aggressive head case because I hid in a closet while a random home invader broke in, killed my father and made me and my little brother orphans? As if we hadn't been through enough after Mom died."

Sara shook her head in frustration and stared at the gray laminate table. Silence filled the room. There, she'd said it, what everyone who knew her, and knew about her past, thought whenever she did anything off book.

Someone knocked on the door and a secretary poked her head inside. "The chief wants to see you, Nate. It's important."

"I'll be right back." Nate followed the secretary out of the room and shut the door, leaving Sara and Will alone.

With her shame spread out on the table, exposed for him to see.

She clenched her jaw, wishing she could be anywhere else, be anyone else at this moment. Will's opinion of her mattered more than it should.

"Sara?" he said.

She couldn't look at him. He pushed back his chair and came to her side of the table. He knelt beside her, reached for one of her hands and gently clasped it between his.

"I am so sorry about your father," he said.

She nodded.

"How old were you?"

"Twelve."

"Oh, honey." He pulled her against his chest and stroked her back.

She almost started crying and stopped herself. It would only prove that they were right about her: that she was weak and fragile, and had no business in law enforcement.

"Don't." She pushed away and stood, pacing to the opposite side of the room. "I appreciate your compassion, but it only makes me feel worse."

"Why?"

She hesitated. Never in her life had she confided in anyone about Dad's death, not even her uncle. Right now, in this conference room, she ached to talk about it with Will. He wouldn't think her weak or damaged, would he? Knowing Will, he'd offer to hug her again.

She'd gone a lot of years without hugs. Maybe she

should appreciate them while she could. Besides, once this case was done she'd leave town and never see Will again, never see the look of pity on his face because he knew the truth about Sara failing her dad.

"I guess," she started, "I don't deserve your compassion."

"Don't say that."

"Why not? I lied to you."

"You thought you were doing the right thing."

"Oh, Will. I'm not worthy of your compassion. I failed Dad and I keep failing victims who depend on me to protect them."

He took a few steps closer. "What victims?"

"People like the Williamsons, whose daughter was killed by members of a drug gang. She went missing and we were called in to find her. I was this close." She pinched her fingers. "Bonner, my supervisor, took me off the case. He said we'd invested too many man-hours in the investigation. Local police in Detroit found the girl's dead body a week later. I could have found her, Will. I know I could have."

"I'm sorry," he said.

"Yeah, well, sorry is for losers." She snapped her attention to him, afraid she'd hurt his feelings again. Surprisingly, he shared a look of understanding.

"No," he said. "Being sorry is a way to share a friend's burden. I'd like to share yours."

"Why?"

"I feel as if we've become friends. I wish you'd stop trying to push me away."

"But I lied to you about who I was."

"Because you were working a case. I get it, even if

I'm disappointed that you felt you couldn't completely trust me."

"Stop being nice to me."

Will leaned against the wall and crossed his arms over his chest. The corner of his mouth turned up in a slight smile. "That's the second time you've said that. Now it's my turn to counter—toss that chip off your shoulder and get on with your life."

"What life?" she muttered.

"So it's really all about work for you?" Will said.

"You wouldn't understand. You have a family."

"And friends, and a church community," he added.

"Rub it in, why don't ya," she said teasingly.

He didn't smile. "My point is, there are many dimensions to life, not just work or family. Maybe, while you're in Echo Mountain, you could experience some of those other things."

"My goal is to not only nail LaRouche and Harrington, but also to keep my distance from people so I don't put them in jeopardy."

People, meaning Will. From the disappointed look on his face, he obviously got the message.

The door popped open and Nate came into the room. "I spoke with our chief. We think it best if you stay undercover for the time being to continue the investigation of LaRouche and Harrington."

"You believe me?"

"Yes, I do," Nate said. "Although I don't appreciate you lying to me. The chief and I also realize we have a bigger problem." He looked at Will. "You've become a target, my friend."

"Because Petrellis came after me?" Will said. "No,

I happened to be at the wrong place at the wrong time. That's all."

"Let's assume Petrellis is working for LaRouche and Harrington, that they hired him to find Sara, find out what she told authorities. He knows the two of you are connected, which means he can get to her through you. And possibly get to you through your girls."

Sara's heart ached. She'd done this. She'd dragged two adorable little girls into the ugliness of her work.

"Will, I'm so—"

"What do you recommend, Nate?" He cut Sara off.

"We'll put police protection on the house tonight while we look for a place to relocate you and the girls," Nate said.

"Where to?" Will asked.

"How about the resort?"

"They were booked last time I checked," Will said.

"Maybe the resort's had some no-shows," Sara offered, trying to be both helpful and hopeful.

An emotion so foreign to her, yet she'd embrace hope if it might help the girls. Help Will.

"How about Bree's cottage at Echo Mountain Resort?" Nate suggested. "She's got an extra room upstairs, and a state-of-the-art security system. Plus, with everyone around for the festival, Petrellis wouldn't be foolish enough to try anything."

"I'd hate to impose on her like that," Will said.

"Come on, buddy, you know Bree. She'd be offended if we didn't ask for her help."

Will nodded. "True."

"Why don't you call her, Will?" Sara said.

"It's settled," Nate said. "You call Bree and I'll send

Sara's phone to the lab in Seattle to see if they can pull the recording off it."

"How long will that take?" she said.

"Depends how backed up they are."

"Or we could take it to Zack Carter at the resort," Will said. "He's an amazing tech specialist."

"Can't. It's a chain of evidence thing," Nate explained. "I take it from Sara and it goes directly to the lab. Otherwise, once this goes to court they could challenge the third-party intervention."

"Oh, right," Will said.

Nate extended his hand for Sara's phone. She hesitated. "No offense, but this is not just a recording. It's my life."

"I understand," Nate said. "I'll make sure it gets into the right hands. I'll put a rush on it."

Will shot her an encouraging nod.

Sara handed Nate the phone, trying to process this new feeling—this feeling of genuine trust.

"I'll set up police protection for tonight," Nate said. "Tomorrow we'll covertly relocate you and the girls."

"We have church in the morning," Will said.

"I'll assign myself to that detail and keep watch outside. Sara, I'd advise you to stay in the loft until further notice."

"I can't do that."

"Excuse me?" Nate said.

"I'm responsible for Will and his girls being in danger. I want to be close enough that I can be part of your protective detail."

"Absolutely not," Nate said. "You're a trouble magnet."

"Nate," Will admonished.

Sara didn't let the comment affect her. "No one will

know I'm there. I'll change my appearance, whatever is necessary, but I won't abandon Will and his girls."

"Even if that could prove dangerous for them?" Nate said.

"Then, we find Petrellis first. We'll use me as bait to catch him."

"Sara, no," Will said.

"I will not keep looking over my shoulder," Sara said. "And I certainly don't want him terrorizing your family, Will." She redirected her attention to Nate. "How about it?"

"Okay, let's get Will and the girls settled, then we'll cast a line for Petrellis."

"I wish you wouldn't do this," Will said to Sara.

"This is my job. On a normal day I'm pretty good at it."

"But you're hurt—"

"I'll be fine."

She'd do whatever was necessary to make sure Will and his girls were out of danger.

Sara sipped her hot tea as she sat at the counter in the town's most popular diner. It was a long shot, but the best plan they could come up with on short notice.

Nate waited outside with another officer in an unmarked car. The agreement was Sara would text them when Petrellis showed up. Surely someone in this crowded restaurant knew Petrellis, and many of them had heard of her—the strange woman who'd been rescued from the mountains. She could tell from their expressions, from their curious frowns as they passed by.

But somehow she was going to disguise herself when she joined the protective detail for Will and the girls?

Who was she kidding? She was probably the town's biggest celebrity.

Which she hoped worked in her favor right now. Hopefully her diner visit would start a buzz about the mysterious lady who fell off the mountain and had been rescued by the local bachelor. Sara was under the impression locals were not only protective of Will, but also wanted to find him a suitable mate.

Sara was not at the top of that list, even on her best day. Will was about compassion and raising his girls in a healthy environment. Sara was about…well, you wouldn't call her lifestyle necessarily healthy.

For the first time in years, she caught a glimpse of her obsessive nature, a nature that turned people off, especially her superiors at work. And now she was so obsessed with keeping Will and his girls safe that she was putting herself in danger. Yeah, *obsessive* was a good word to describe her current decision. It was part of the job, a job Will would never truly understand.

The restaurant wall clock read nine fifteen. She wondered what Will was serving his girls for dinner. Probably something healthier than the cheeseburger and fries sitting on the counter in front of her. Would Will read Claire and Marissa a bedtime story? Work on their Christmas lists?

The waitress, a middle-aged woman with black hair pulled back, came by with a water pitcher. "How was the burger?"

"Good, thanks."

"Need more water?"

"No, I'm good."

"Can I ask you something? I mean, if I'm being rude just tell me."

"Go for it."

"Are you her? The woman who fell off the mountain and was rescued by Will Rankin?"

Success! Word had spread. They knew who she was.

"Yes, that's me."

"Where are you from?"

"Seattle."

"Ah, so hiking was a new experience for you."

Sara shrugged. She'd hiked plenty as a kid.

"Good thing Will happened to be out there," the waitress offered.

"Yep."

But not so good in Sara's book. Finding Sara had sent Will's life into a tailspin of trouble.

"Will's a nice man," the waitress said.

"Exceptionally nice."

"He's been through a lot."

"Yes, he has."

"So you know about his wife?"

"Yes, Will and I have become friends."

"Oh," she said, disappointed. A customer caught her eye and she walked away.

Sara's phone buzzed with a text. It was from Will.

You okay?

She responded.

All is well. How are the girls?

She glanced over her shoulder toward the door. The waitress stood beside a table of customers, three elderly couples who seemed to be glaring at Sara.

Oh, boy. Her friendship with Will was causing her to be the most disliked person in town. She redirected her attention to her phone. Will hadn't responded. She didn't want to look back at the locals in the corner. Their message was clear. "You should be ashamed of yourself for involving Will."

Oh, she was very ashamed of herself for putting him in danger. Yet, she kept hearing Will's voice: *I wish you'd stop trying to push me away.*

He appreciated their friendship, or whatever you could call what was developing between them. Every time she tried drawing a boundary line, he'd reach right across and hold on tighter. What kind of man did that?

A compassionate, generous man.

One who deserved better than a damaged friend like Sara Vaughn in his life.

The waitress returned and placed the check on the counter. A hint that Sara had overstayed her welcome?

"Thanks," Sara said.

With a nod, the waitress walked away. Sara flipped over the check, and noticed a message written in ink: "Meet me out back."

She scanned the restaurant. A few people still stared at her, but chances were none of them had written the message. She placed cash in the bill sleeve and shifted off the barstool. Cradling her sprained wrist against her stomach, she went down the hall leading to the bathroom. At the end of the hall was a bright red exit sign over a back door.

This could be it. Either Petrellis waited outside for her, or it was a local wanting to give her a lecture about staying away from Will. She pulled out her phone to text Nate, and hesitated.

Once Petrellis was brought in for questioning, he'd clam up like his kind usually did, hiding behind his lawyer.

She couldn't let that happen.

Pocketing her phone, she pushed the door open. A gust of wind sent a chill across her shoulders.

"Hello?" she called down the dark alley.

Her voice echoed back at her. Anxiety skittered across her nerve endings.

She knew what she was doing, she told herself. She was a smart agent who was going to get information out of Petrellis.

Suddenly someone gripped her shoulders hard, and shoved her forward.

"You don't have to restrain me," she said. "It's not as if I'm in any shape to fight back."

He led her to his car and pushed her into the driver's seat, then across into the passenger seat. She hit the record button on her new phone, hoping maybe this time the evidence wouldn't be destroyed.

Aiming the gun at her chest with one hand, Petrellis started the car and pulled out of the alley.

"Where are we going?" she said.

"Someplace we can talk."

"About?"

"Who you really are."

She stilled. Did he know? Had her cover been blown?

He shot her a side-eye glare as he headed out of town. "Because you're not some random trail assistant or you'd be terrified of this." He waved his gun. "But you're not. Which means you have experience with guns."

"I was taught to shoot as a kid."

"Let's cut to the truth. Who sent you and what did you hear out there in the mountains?"

"So they did hire you to find me."

"What are you after?" he demanded.

"It was a job, that's all."

"You killed David Price, why?"

Whoa, so LaRouche and Harrington were telling their own people that Sara had killed him?

"I didn't kill him. LaRouche did."

"Stop lying. I need the truth!"

"I told you the truth."

"No, you didn't, but you will."

He turned onto a farm road and hit the accelerator. The car sped up, the speedometer needle reaching sixty miles per hour.

"Why are you doing this?" she cried.

"I have nothing to lose. My life is over."

The car sped toward an abandoned barn in the distance. Faster. Faster.

"Slow down!"

"Either I get answers from you or we both die. Makes no difference to me."

Chapter Eleven

$\smile$

Great, Sara had been kidnapped by a man with a death wish? No, there was more to this.

"What have they got on you?" she said.

"Tell me who hired you!" he countered.

"Are they blackmailing you? What? I know you're a cop—"

"Not anymore I'm not."

"I heard you had to retire early because of family issues. Have they offered you money?"

He sped up. Seventy miles per hour.

"Okay! I'm FBI!" she cried.

He shot her a look of disbelief.

"LaRouche and Harrington are the enemy here, not me," she protested.

The flash of police lights lit the car from behind.

He eyed the rearview, then refocused on the barn in the distance.

"You might want to die, but don't be a coward and take me with you. And what about the people who will die because of a faulty drug?"

He looked at her again.

"They didn't tell you about that, did they?" she said.

His foot eased up on the gas.

"You were a cop, a good cop," she said. "Getting the bad guys is in your blood. Help me stop them."

"I can't."

"Then, don't stop me from putting them away!"

She was grasping at the wind, but she had to try to get through to him. As the sirens wailed louder behind them, her heartbeat pounded against her chest. She didn't want to die this way.

Use your training. Talk him down.

"Innocent people will die. Do you want to be remembered as a murderer by your family? Your wife and kids?"

An ironic chuckle escaped his lips. "My kids don't care about me."

Okay, she'd hit a nerve. She was getting through to him.

"I don't believe that. They're going to be devastated when their father dies and is branded a criminal. There's still a chance to save yourself, Petrellis. Help us nail these guys."

A tear trailed down his cheek.

"Remember why you put on your uniform in the first place," she continued. "I could really use your help here, Stuart," she said, remembering his first name from the file she'd read at the police station.

He eased his foot off the accelerator. The barn loomed in the distance. He pressed down on the brake. The car came to a stop.

"I'm sorry," he said, and started to raise his gun.

To his own head.

She lunged, wrestling the gun away.

It went off, shattering the front windshield. Officer McBride whipped open the driver's door and pulled Petrellis from the car. Nate opened Sara's door. She shoved the gun at him and stumbled away from the car, trying to catch her breath, trying not to throw up.

She'd almost been killed. Twice. First by the suicide crash into the barn, then when she'd disarmed him.

What was she thinking?

That she couldn't watch a man die because of criminal jerks LaRouche and Harrington.

"Take a deep breath," Nate said.

"I'm fine, I'm fine." Her face felt hot and cold at the same time.

"Why didn't you text me when you saw him?" Nate said.

"Didn't want him lawyering up."

"You could have—"

"Don't leave him alone. He's suicidal. He tried shooting himself in the head. They've got something on him, Nate. Find out what it is. I think he'll help us if you can destroy whatever they've got on him."

"Okay, okay, breathe. You're going to hyperventilate."

"How's Will? Is he okay?"

"He's fine. Let's get you out of here."

As Will fed the girls dinner, he tried to stay present and engaged in their stories about the museum, and their grandpa ordering monster hash for lunch.

Thoughts about what was happening with Sara's plan to draw out Officer Petrellis kept taunting him.

A few hours later, as he tucked them into bed, little Marissa asked, "Are you mad at us?"

Both girls looked at him with round green eyes.

"No, why would I be upset with you?" he said, glancing across the room at Claire.

"Because you've got that grandma look on your face," Claire said.

"What look?"

"You know, like this." Claire scrunched up her nose and pursed her lips in the patented grandma, disapproving frown.

Will smiled. "I look like that?"

Marissa nodded that he did.

"I'm sorry, girls. The fact is, I'm distracted because I'm worried about a friend."

"Miss Sara?" Claire asked.

"Yes. She's having a tough time and I think she could use a friend or two right about now."

"Doesn't she have any friends?" Marissa asked.

"I don't think so. She works so much and has no time for friends."

"That's sad," Claire said.

"But God's her friend," Marissa offered.

"Let's say a prayer for her." Claire climbed out of bed and kneeled, interlacing her fingers. Marissa followed suit, and Will's heart warmed. They were such good, loving girls.

He interlaced his fingers. "Who wants to lead?"

"I do, I do!" Marissa said.

The room quieted.

"Give us this day our daily bread—"

"Wrong one," Claire corrected.

"Oh, yeah." Marissa cleared her throat. "Dear God in Heaven, we are praying for our friend Miss Sara, who can't draw, and has no friends, but she's really nice and we like her anyway. We pray that she…" Marissa hesitated and looked at Will.

"Is safe," Will said.

"Is safe," the girls echoed.

"Is at peace," Will said.

"Is at peace."

"And will open her heart to the wonder of grace. Amen."

"Amen," the girls said.

"Okay, back into bed. I've got a surprise for you tomorrow after church."

"What kind of surprise?" Claire said.

"It wouldn't be a surprise if I told you." He tucked her in and kissed her forehead. "I think you're going to like it."

He went to Marissa's bed and tucked her in, as well.

"Love you, Daddy."

"Love you, pumpkin."

Will went to the door and switched off the light; the ceiling lit up with the twinkling of glow-in-the-dark stars.

He shut the door, appreciating the moment, realizing in a few years Claire wouldn't want to share a room with her little sister.

Will had plenty of work to catch up on, which he hoped would keep his mind off Sara. He fixed himself a cup of tea and went into the living room to enjoy the colorful lights on the Christmas tree while he worked.

He opened his laptop and forced himself to focus. One of his best clients, Master Printing, had had their website hacked and taken down by search engines. He'd rewritten the code and corrected the problem, so he signed on to check if their website was back online.

There wasn't much an SEO specialist like Will could do to force the search engines to reupload the pages. Still, he let them know the situation had been rectified.

A soft knock sounded from the door. He wondered if he'd imagined it. He stood and peeked through the window. Sara stood there with Nate behind her.

Will opened the door. "Thank God you're okay."

Sara wrapped her arms around Will and squeezed. Tight.

"Let's go inside," Nate said, looking over his shoulder.

"Sorry," Sara said, releasing Will.

"Why? I was thinking of doing the same thing." He put his arm around her and led her to the sofa.

"Actually, could I use the bathroom?" Sara asked.

"Sure, at the end of the hall on the right," Will said, and offered a smile.

It looked as if Sara tried to smile, but couldn't get her lips to work. She disappeared around the corner.

"You got Petrellis?" Will asked Nate.

"We got him."

"You don't sound happy about it."

"She went rogue on me, Will," Nate said, frustration coloring his voice. "I told her to text me when she saw Petrellis. Instead, she got into his car, and he…" Nate shook his head.

"He what?" Will fisted his hand.

"He almost killed them both, then tried to shoot himself in front of her."

"Oh, Sara," he whispered.

"She disarmed him, but she shouldn't have been there in the first place," Nate said, frustrated. "I apologize for bringing her here. She was insistent."

"No, it's okay," Will said. "I would have been up all night worrying about her anyway. At least I can see she's okay, sort of."

"The chief is trying to get Petrellis to work with us. The guy's pretty messed up. I guess his wife's in bad shape."

"How so?"

"She's got multiple sclerosis. Living in a nursing home in Bellingham, very expensive. LHP's security chief tracked Petrellis down and offered him a boatload of money to find Sara and figure out what she was up to. Petrellis needed the money to keep his wife in the Bellingham facility." Nate hesitated. "I had no idea she was so sick."

"How did LaRouche and Harrington track him down so quickly?"

"Companies like LHP employ top-notch IT specialists who probably went through bank records and personal histories to identify someone they could manipulate. I wonder who else they targeted in town."

"And no one knew about Petrellis's wife?"

"Nope. I feel bad about that. Why didn't he talk to the chief?"

"Sometimes if you don't talk about it, you can pretend it's not happening," Will offered, speaking from personal experience. "What I still don't understand is how LaRouche and Harrington discovered Sara was in Echo Mountain."

"The whole town knew she'd been rescued by SAR. Wouldn't be hard for them to figure it out."

"What happens next?"

"Waiting to hear from the chief," Nate said. "I still

want to move you and the girls to the resort. Did you speak with Bree?"

"She graciously invited us to move into her cottage."

"And Aiden's holding a private room for Sara at the resort."

"So you'll set her up there, as well?"

"That's the plan, not that she'll take orders." Nate's phone buzzed.

"You get that. I'm going to check on Sara," Will said.

"Detective Walsh." Nate wandered to the front window.

As Will headed for the hall, he heard the echo of little girl voices.

"I like those the best," Marissa said.

"That's because they're little, like you," Claire said.

"You make that sound like a bad thing."

It was Sara's voice. Will hesitated, not wanting to interrupt the moment.

"She always teases me about being little," Marissa said.

"I was little when I was a kid," Sara offered.

"You were?" Marissa said.

"Yep. Sometimes kids made fun of me, but my dad used to call me his little darling, which made it all okay."

"Does he still call you that?" Claire asked.

Will took a step toward the bedroom, wanting to intervene.

"My dad's in Heaven," Sara said.

"With Mommy." Marissa hushed.

The room fell silent. Will stepped into the room and froze. Sara was lying on the floor between the girls' beds, her hands folded across her chest.

"Hey girls," Will said.

Marissa jackknifed in bed. "Sara was little, too, Daddy."

"No kidding?"

Sara sat up and hugged her knees to her chest. "Sorry, they spotted me when I was walking by and asked me to come say good-night."

"I'm glad they did."

"Will you be here tomorrow, Miss Sara?" Claire asked.

"Maybe. We'll see. I'd better go so you can get some sleep."

"Daddy has a surprise for us tomorrow." Marissa clapped her hands in excitement.

Sara reached for Will, and he extended his hand to help her up. When she stood, they were only inches apart.

"Be careful of the mistletoe in the hallway," Claire said in a singsong voice.

Marissa giggled.

"Okay, girls, bedtime. For real," Will said. He motioned Sara out of the room and shut the door so adult voices wouldn't disturb them.

"They're so…" Sara started. "Precious."

"You sure you don't mean precocious?"

She stopped in the hallway, inches from the dreaded mistletoe, and placed an open palm against his chest.

"You're right, you are so—" she hesitated as if she struggled to form the word "—blessed."

In that moment, everything seemed to disappear: the danger, his anxiety about his in-laws and the fact that his best friend stood in the next room.

Will leaned forward and kissed Sara on the lips—a brief, loving kiss.

When he pulled back, her blue eyes widened and she pressed her fingertips to her lips.

Giggling echoed behind him. He turned and spotted his girls watching from a crack in their door.

"Bed," he ordered.

They slammed the door. When he turned around, Sara was walking into the living room.

Will sighed. Had he upset her?

He followed her into the living room where Nate continued his phone call.

Will sat next to Sara on the couch. She studied her fingers in her lap.

"So...am I in trouble?" Will asked.

She snapped her gaze to meet his. "No, but I am."

He studied her blue eyes, trying to discern the meaning of her words. Had something happened with the case, or was she referring to the kiss? Did she share the strong feelings he was developing for her, and decided that was unprofessional?

"Okay, I'll figure it out. Thanks, Chief." Nate ended his call and turned to Will and Sara. "Petrellis has been medicated for now. He went nuts on the way to lockup and they rushed him to the hospital. The chief likes our plan about relocating you at the resort, but suggested Sara head back to the station with me and spend the night in a cell."

"Nate, come on, why can't she stay at the loft?" Will said. "No one knows about it."

"The station is harder to breach, plus someone is always there. I can't put twenty-four-hour guard on both your house and the loft."

"Then, let Sara stay here, at the house."

"Will—"

"My home office doubles as a guest room." He interrupted Sara's protest, and looked at Nate. "You've got us under police protection anyway. This makes the most sense."

"Not to me, it doesn't," Sara said.

Nate sighed. "He's got a point. Keeping you all in one spot will make our job easier. I'll call the chief and let him know. I'll take the first shift. Better get my overnight bag from the truck." Nate went outside.

"I shouldn't be staying here, Will," Sara said.

"You don't belong in a jail cell." He stood and extended his hand. "Come on, I'll show you to your room."

She took his hand and he gently held on, anticipating her wanting to pull away.

She didn't.

He led her down the hallway and flipped on the light. Papers were scattered across the daybed.

"Sorry." He rushed over and collected them and then placed them on his desk. "The bed's only been slept in a few times, when Megan's sister came to visit. Clean towels are in the guest bathroom, which we rarely use. What else?" He looked around the room.

She reached out and touched his cheek. "Thank you."

"Of course."

"For so many things."

The walls felt as if they were closing in, and he could hardly breathe. Her gorgeous blue eyes studied him, as if she was trying to tell him something, something important, and intimate.

"Whatever happens, please know how much I appreciate you..." She hesitated. "Your generosity and your strength. You amaze me."

"My ego thanks you."

His gaze drifted to her lips. He wanted to kiss her again.

"I... I could use a glass of water," she said, her voice soft.

"We've got that here," he teased. "In the kitchen."

She didn't move. Neither did he.

Will's heart pounded against his chest. He sensed she needed to put distance between them, and he understood why. It was important they stayed focused on remaining safe, and not get distracted by their attraction to one another, or the promise of...did he dare say love?

Two loud cracks echoed from outside the window.

Followed by a crash.

And the house went dark.

Chapter Twelve

Sara protectively yanked Will away from the window and pulled him into a crouch.

"Daddy! Daddy!" the girls cried.

"Go to the girls," Sara said calmly. "And stay down."

They both felt their way into the dark hallway.

"Where do you keep flashlights?" she asked.

"Everywhere. Kids are afraid of the dark. Got one in here." He opened a hall closet and fumbled for a second, then handed her a flashlight.

"What about you?"

A light winked from inside the girls' bedroom. "Claire's on it."

"Daddy!" Claire called.

"Go." Sara pointed the flashlight so he could make his way down the hall.

"You aren't going outside, are you?"

"No. Go on, they need you." She gave him a gentle shove. Once he was in the room with his girls, Sara went into the living room and peered through the curtain. The entire block was dark.

Neighbors opened their doors. She spotted a neighbor across the street starting down his front steps to investigate.

"What is going on?" she whispered.

She watched a few more neighbors wander outside, then head toward the end of the block. She went to another window to search the dark street. Someone flipped on their car headlights, illuminating a vehicle that had collided into an electrical pole. It must have damaged the transformer.

"Yikes." She wondered if the driver had been under the influence, or if he'd hit the gas instead of the brake by accident.

Another set of headlights clicked on, illuminating the street in front of Will's house. She snapped her attention to Nate's car and spotted someone kneeling beside Nate, who was on the ground.

"Oh, no," she said in a hushed tone.

She wanted to check on him, but figured he'd be furious if she left the house. She called 911, but they'd already been alerted about the accident and downed police officer.

"What happened?" Will said coming into the room.

Little Marissa dashed to Sara and wrapped her arms around her from behind. Tense from the past hour, Sara fought the urge to untangle the girl's arms from her waist. *Stop thinking about yourself and consider how much this little girl needs female comfort.*

"Looks as if a car hit the transformer," Sara said, stroking Marissa's hair. "Your neighbors are taking care of things."

"Can I see?" Claire said.

"No," Sara said.

Claire stopped dead in her tracks. Will looked at Sara in question.

"The car is pretty smashed up, and the driver is probably…" She hesitated. "Well, images like that can give you nightmares for weeks. Trust me, I've had my share of those."

"You have?" Marissa said, looking up at her.

"Yup. Better idea, let's light some candles and have a party."

"A party, cool." Claire started for the kitchen, where Sara assumed they kept the candles.

"Me, too," Marissa said, chasing after her sister.

As they rooted around in drawers, Sara motioned Will to come closer.

"Was it really a transformer?" he said in a soft voice.

"Yes, but there might be more to it. Nate is hurt."

"Where, outside?"

"Yes."

Will started for the front door. "I've gotta help him."

"Will, your girls—"

He whipped open the door just as Nate came stumbling into the house with help from Will's neighbor.

"I tried keeping him down until the ambulance came. He wasn't having any of it," the elderly neighbor said.

"What happened?" Will asked.

"I'm fine." Nate collapsed on the couch.

"I'm Sara," she said, extending her hand to the neighbor.

"Oscar Lewis, nice to meet you." They shook hands.

"Yay, more people for the party!" Marissa said, coming out of the kitchen.

Claire took one look at Nate and said, "What happened to Detective Nate?"

"Car clipped me," Nate said.

"Marissa, take the candles. I'll get some ice." Claire

unloaded the candles into her sister's arms and disappeared into the kitchen. Sara marveled at how mature the eight-year-old Claire acted in the face of a crisis.

Sirens wailed from the street.

"Oscar, can you tell them I'm in here?" Nate said.

"Sure, police and EMTs?"

"I don't need an ambulance, but the driver of that sedan will."

Oscar left and Sara shut the door. Marissa stood in the corner, lining up candles.

"Hey, baby M, can you help your sister?" Will asked. "We need ice, and warm, wet towels for detective Nate's cuts and bruises."

"Okay, Daddy." Marissa danced off to join her sister in the kitchen.

Sara sat on a coffee table in front of Nate, Will hovering close by. "What really happened?" Sara said to Nate.

"I'm not totally sure. One minute I was texting, the next, a sedan was speeding toward me. I dived out of the way, but he clipped me. I went down, shot at his back tire and he crashed."

"Why would he run you down?" Sara said.

Nate shook his head. "This case is getting stranger by the minute."

A knock sounded at the front door. Will went to open it.

A cute blond woman in her twenties rushed into the living room, spotted Nate and froze. "You're hurt."

"I'm fine," Nate said.

"I heard the call go out and came to see—"

"I'll answer questions for the blog tomorrow, Cassie. This isn't the time."

Sara read more than curiosity on Cassie's face. Sara read true concern.

And Nate was oblivious.

"What happened?" Cassie said, taking a step toward him.

Claire rushed into the room carrying an ice bag wrapped in a towel. "Here's the ice."

"He needs ice?" Cassie said.

"Where do you need it?" Claire asked.

"My knee would be great."

Claire held the ice pack to his knee, and an odd expression crossed Nate's face. "You'll probably get a better story by interviewing the neighbors."

"Really?" Cassie said, her voice laced with sarcasm. Shaking her head, she muttered, "Turkey." She stormed out of the house.

Sara and Will shared a look.

"I saw that," Nate said.

"Who was she?" Sara asked.

"She writes a community blog. I'm her source."

"Yeah, that's one word for it," Will said.

"Focus, guys," Nate said. "Obviously you're not safe here."

"Not a problem," Will said. "I'll call Bree and we'll head over there tonight."

"Head where, Daddy?" Claire said.

"Echo Mountain Resort. We're going to stay there for a while."

Another knock sounded at the door and Will answered. Chief Washburn joined them in the living room. "You okay?" he asked Nate.

"Yeah, but seriously frustrated."

"Well, you're gonna be more frustrated," the chief said. "The driver ran off."

"How is that possible?" Nate said.

"Neighbors saw where he headed. We'll do a search."

"Unbelievable," Nate said. "We lost another one."

"Let's focus on what we do have control over," Will said. "I'll help the girls pack."

Will and the girls were situated at Bree's cottage and fast asleep a few hours later. The girls shared an upstairs bedroom. Sara decided to stay upstairs as well, wanting to be close to protect Will, Claire and Marissa. Will and Nate bunked in the living room for the night.

Even with all the excitement, the girls were up bright and early the next day, ready for church. He asked them to be as quiet as possible so as not to wake Sara, yet she came down for breakfast. Will invited her to church, but she said she needed to focus on changing her looks. He suspected something else kept her from surrendering her troubles to God. That was a discussion for another time.

Officer Ryan McBride escorted Will and the girls to church, and stood guard outside. Nate hung back at the cottage to help Sara and brainstorm angles about the case.

During the service, Will said an extra prayer of thanks that Nate wasn't seriously injured last night.

The theme of the service was having faith during troubling times. Will embraced the message, needing the extra encouragement. He held firm to his faith regarding his abilities to be a good father, and he had faith things would work out for Sara.

Maybe even for Sara and Will?

From a practical standpoint, this relationship wasn't real. It was formed by tense emotions during dangerous circumstances. Sometimes love and practicality had little to do with one another. He was drawn to Sara, without question. Hopefully, after her case was solved, he could share his feelings. To what end? Her job, her life, was back in Seattle; sure, only three hours away, but it might as well be three thousand miles away. The next woman he married would have to be a good mom for the girls. Parenting wasn't a part-time job.

Parenting? Marriage? Between the excitement of yesterday and his clients' needs, Will was obviously sleep deprived, apparent in his random thoughts today.

"Go in peace and serve the Lord," Pastor Charles said. "Amen."

"Amen," the congregation repeated.

Will helped the girls on with their jackets, and waited while they buttoned up. Friends smiled and greeted him as they passed down the center aisle. Will offered greetings in return, exchanging pleasantries and a brief story or two.

With his girls on either side of him, Will clung to their hands and they made their way toward the exit. Once outside, he spotted Nate. Beside Nate stood a blond woman wearing a red ski cap and sunglasses. She looked like a teenager, and it took him a minute to realize it was Sara. She certainly had changed her looks.

Will led the girls toward Nate and Sara.

"You guys ready to head back to the resort?" Nate said.

"Yeah, they have an indoor pool," Claire said.

"Who's got a pool?" Will's mother-in-law, Mary, said over his shoulder.

"The resort," Claire said.

"Will, may I have a word with you?" Mary said.

"Sure, Mary, what's up?"

"Over here, please." She motioned for Will to join her a few feet away, while his father-in-law entertained the girls with a story.

"Mary?" he questioned.

She stopped, turned around and waved an envelope between them. "It's our official request for custody of the girls."

Will's heart dropped to his knees. "I don't understand."

"I haven't filed these papers, and I won't. Unless you continue to put the girls in harm's way."

"I would never—"

"You're not thinking straight, Will. I heard about last night, about how someone tried to run down Detective Walsh in front of your house. Why was the detective there anyway? Because he was keeping watch over the woman you rescued. Why was she at your house?"

"She was checking to see if I was okay."

"Why wouldn't you be okay?"

He didn't answer.

"Because something else happened that I don't know about." Mary sighed. "I stopped by the house last night and you and the girls were gone. Where did you stay?"

"At the resort."

"In hotel rooms?"

"No, at a friend's cottage."

"Because you were too frightened to stay in your own home. Do you see why I'm concerned?"

"We've got it under control."

"Look—" she hesitated "—you and I often don't see

things the same way, but we agree on one thing, and that's the welfare of your girls."

"And?"

"Whatever trouble this woman is in, she's brought it into your life, correct?"

He didn't answer, he couldn't answer. She was right.

"I don't want a court battle, and I don't want to upset Claire and Marissa, but I can't stand the thought of them being put in harm's way because you played the Good Samaritan."

He couldn't believe she was making him feel ashamed about helping a person in trouble.

"Let the girls stay with us until this situation is resolved, and we'll forget about this." Mary slipped the envelope into her purse.

"Will? Everything all right?" Sara said, approaching them.

His mother-in-law narrowed her eyes at Sara, and then glanced at Will. "Please call me by the end of the day and let me know your decision." She passed by Sara and motioned to Ed that they were leaving.

"What was that about?" Sara said.

"She's worried about the girls." He gazed across the parking lot at his daughters, under the protective eye of both Nate and Officer McBride.

"Because of me and the case," Sara said in a flat tone.

"Mary came to the house last night after hearing about the accident. We were gone. She figured out we didn't feel safe at the house. She threatened to take the girls away."

Sara touched his arm. "Will, no."

"Threatened, but she won't. She loves them too

much. It would crush them to have us embroiled in a court battle over their welfare."

Marissa started to run off and visit with her friend Addy. Nate blocked her and shifted her closer to the car.

In that moment, looking at his baby girl's disappointed frown as she waved goodbye to her friend, Will realized this was no way for the girls to live—under the watchful eye of an overprotective father and police officers—until the case was solved and Will was out of danger.

It would break his heart to be away from them again, but he had to think of their well-being over his emotional needs.

"I need to talk to Nate."

As he headed toward Nate, Sara walked beside him. "You're a good dad," she said. "Don't ever forget that."

"Thanks." Will nodded at Nate. "Got a sec?"

Sara asked Claire a question about drawing, and both girls offered their advice. Will pulled Nate aside. "I'm thinking it might be easier on all of us, and safer for the girls, if they went away for a few days with their grandparents."

"Are you sure?"

"Yes. I should have suggested it sooner, but was missing them something fierce when I got home from my hiking trip."

"Setting them up at the resort—"

"Doesn't remove them from the potential danger. How safe do you think they'd be with my in-laws?"

"Safer than staying with you, especially if they take them out of town. Also, we could ask Harvey to tag along and play bodyguard. His cop instincts are razor sharp and he's got plenty of time on his hands since he retired from the resort."

"Good idea, thanks." Will gazed at his adorable girls. "I did the right thing by helping Sara, and now I have to do the right thing by keeping Claire and Marissa safe."

"Your in-laws might still be here." Nate craned his neck.

"No, not yet. I want to spend the day with the girls, then if you don't mind, could you take them over to Mary and Ed's?"

"Sounds good. Let's get you back to the resort."

Sara, Will and the girls hung out in Breanna McBride's cottage, drawing, baking and playing games. Sara had tried to isolate herself upstairs in the bedroom, but the girls were having none of it. They demanded she come downstairs and *visit*, as Marissa put it.

They made Christmas cookies, drank hot cocoa and laughed at silly jokes. Sara couldn't remember the last time she'd felt like a part of a family. Then Will told the girls his surprise was that Claire and Marissa were going on an adventure with their grandparents for a few days.

They were excited at first, then disappointed when they found out Will wasn't going. They moaned about missing their dad, and Sara's family moment shattered before her eyes. Rather than blame herself for the situation, Sara was more motivated than ever to wrap up this case so Will could get back to his life, his family.

And Sara could get back to…what?

She wasn't sure anymore. Was there even a job waiting for her back at the bureau? She didn't know. Oddly, she felt resentment toward her job. All of her determination, all of her drive to get the bad guys, had caused Will and his girls to be in danger, and now to be split up for their own protection.

The girls packed their things shortly after dinner and brought their bags down into the main entryway of the cottage.

"You just got home," Claire complained, hugging Will.

Sara looked away, the child's voice ripping at her heart. Marissa watched her big sister's reaction with curiosity, as if she was deciding if she was supposed to complain, as well.

"You girls are going to have fun with Nanny and Papa, okay?" he said to Claire.

"Okay," Claire said. "But no more adventures without you."

Marissa wrapped her arms around Sara's legs. "Bye, Sara."

"Bye, sweetie." She stroked the little girl's hair.

"Practice your drawing," Claire said. She looked at her dad. "Make sure she practices."

Will smiled. "Come on, I'll walk you girls to the car," he said, his voice raspy. "I'll be right back." Will nodded at Sara and escorted his girls out front.

Frustration burned low, and Sara marched into the kitchen. She started to pour herself a cup of coffee. Probably not a good idea to have caffeine at night, then again she wouldn't be able to get much sleep anyway, not until she could guarantee the safety of Will and the girls by putting LaRouche and Harrington away.

How was she going to do that? She wasn't even involved with the investigation, other than being a witness to the murder of David Price. She should be tracking down leads, helping Nate somehow, instead of baking cookies and playing board games with the girls.

She eyed the Christmas cookies, spread out on cooling racks. Little girls' laughter echoed in her mind as her gaze landed on a snowman cookie with green candy eyes and a red nose. Marissa had giggled uncontrollably when her dad had sprinkled powdered sugar on the cookie and called him Rudolph Frosty.

Sara wandered across the kitchen to the cookies and tried remembering a time when she'd made cookies with her dad, yet there was no memory of making Christmas cookies or telling jokes. Sara, her dad and Kenny had seemed to live under a cloud after her mom had randomly gotten sick and died.

"Shake it off," Sara scolded herself.

She left the kitchen and decided to check email in the living room. As she adjusted herself at Breanna's desk, she glanced out the window and spotted Will saying goodbye to the girls. He gave them each a big hug, and had to pry Claire's arms loose from his neck. A ball lodged in Sara's throat.

The girls finally got in the squad car and Will shut the door. When he turned, she saw him swipe at his eyes, and she felt even worse about dragging him into this mess.

There had to be a way to make it up to him.

Sure there was. Remove the threat. She reconsidered distancing herself from him, only they'd established that it wouldn't make a difference. They could get to Sara through Will.

Somehow word had gotten back to LaRouche and Harrington that Sara and Will had grown close, or maybe they knew that he'd saved her life and vice versa. Whatever the case may be, the only way to keep Will safe was to prove LaRouche and Harrington were the criminals she knew them to be: men who didn't care about killing innocent people for profit.

She refocused on the computer and checked her email. One caught her eye, an email from her boss demanding she call him ASAP. She pulled out her phone and called his cell. It went into voice mail.

"It's Agent Vaughn returning your call. The local police are being very helpful. I look forward to speaking with you." She ended the call, not feeling all that grateful to the man who didn't support her quest to nail LaRouche and Harrington, the man who insinuated to Nate that she'd lost her perspective and maybe, even, was off the rails.

"Bonner," she muttered, and paced the living room. Why did he have to make things so hard? Why didn't he believe her when she showed him the proof of tampering with test results?

This train of thought wasn't going to help her move forward. She'd been stuck in the past on so many levels, that it had almost become habit for her: dig her heels in and hold on like a pit bull with its teeth around an intruder's leg.

She made a mental list of things to discuss with Nate once he returned. In the meantime, the least she could do was be there to support Will. He must feel horrible about separating from his girls again. She wondered what was taking him so long to come back inside.

She went to the front door and hesitated before opening it. Would she find him crying on the front porch? She wasn't sure if she could handle that, nor could she handle the look of resentment in his eyes—resentment toward Sara for causing his life to be turned upside down and sideways.

A car door slammed outside. Nate had already left to take the girls to their grandparents' house, so it couldn't be his car. She opened the door and spotted Officer Carrington headed for the cottage. She scanned the area for Will.

"Wait, did Will end up going with the girls?" she asked, partly hopeful and partly disappointed.

"No, ma'am."

Her heart raced up into her throat. "Then, where is he?"

Chapter Thirteen

"Will!" Sara called out. She rushed past Officer Carrington to get a better look at the property.

"Ma'am, please get back in the house where it's safe."

"Not until we find him. Will!"

What could have happened? In those few minutes while Sara had been away from the window feeling sorry for herself, had another one of LaRouche and Harrington's men swung by and snatched Will?

"Ma'am, I insist you go inside where it's safe."

Of course, standing here in the open made her a target. If LaRouche and Harrington's men were using Will to lure her out, they had succeeded. She rushed past Officer Carrington, went back into the cottage and called Nate.

"Detective Walsh."

"It's Sara. Are you on speakerphone?"

"Yes."

"Call me after you drop off the girls." She ended the call. The last thing she wanted was to upset Claire and Marissa by announcing their father had gone missing.

She paced the kitchen and eyed the wall phone.

Posted beside it was a list of numbers, including one that read Security. She used Bree's house line to call it.

"Hey, sweet Bree," a man's voice said. "I thought you were helping with the—"

"It's not Breanna. It's Sara, I'm staying in Bree's cottage. Who's this?"

"Scott Becket, security manager for the resort."

"Have you been briefed about my situation?" she asked.

"Yes, Nate told me you're undercover FBI. Is there a problem?"

"Will is missing," she said, trying to sound calm, but failing miserably.

"When did this happen?"

"A few minutes ago. He was saying goodbye to the girls, and then he was gone."

"I'm on it. Stay put."

The line went dead.

"Argh!" she cried. Sliding down the wall, she wrapped her arms around her bent knees, feeling utterly helpless. She buried her face in her arms, brainstorming a way to help them find Will without putting herself in danger.

Suddenly a wet nose nudged her ear. She looked up, and got a big, wet kiss on the cheek from Bree's golden retriever, Fiona.

"What's wrong?" Bree placed a bag of groceries on the kitchen table and kneeled beside Sara.

"It's Will" was all she could get out.

"What about him?"

"He's gone. I don't know where. He disappeared."

"I've got to call Scott."

"Already did."

"Good, then everything will be fine. Scott was an

exceptional cop before becoming our security manager. Did you call Nate?"

"He's with the girls. He'll call after he drops them off."

"Then, there's only one thing left to do while we wait." Bree reached out and placed a comforting hand on Sara's shoulder.

And said a prayer.

Sara didn't fight it this time; she was so desperate for Will's safety that she bowed her head and opened her heart. She hoped that God was truly forgiving, that he'd hear Sara's heartfelt prayer and keep Will safe.

"Stop!" Will called.

He'd seen the man hovering on the grounds near the cottage, thanks to the resort's property lights, and Will had called out, demanding the stranger identify himself. Instead, he'd run.

And Will had taken off after him. Maybe not the smartest idea, but the burn of frustration had driven Will out into the night. Frustration about his girls being forced to go away with their grandparents, frustration about Sara being constantly threatened.

"What do you want?" Will called after the guy, who turned a corner. Great, a blind spot. What if he had a gun and was waiting for Will? He stopped and searched the ground for a weapon, a rock or tree branch, something.

This was not Will. He wasn't a violent man by nature.

Yet this stranger might have information to help the authorities with this case. Will couldn't let him get away. He'd do anything to help Nate prove Sara's innocence and the businessmen's culpability in the death of David Price.

He grabbed a rather large branch and hesitated before making the turn.

Took a deep breath.

And flung the branch around the corner. No reaction. Surely the man would have fired off a shot.

Will clicked on the flashlight app on his phone, took a deep breath and peered around the corner. He aimed the light up the trail. The man was gone. Vanished.

How was that possible? The trail took a sharp incline five hundred feet. There was no way the man would have made it to the top, and to the next switchback so quickly.

Then Will noticed something on the ground. He approached a discoloration and kneeled for a better look.

Fresh blood.

The man was wounded, which meant he wouldn't be able to fight very hard against Will once he caught up to him.

Will straightened and started up the trail, using the flashlight to scan left, then right. The blood trail led straight up, then disappeared.

Will pulled out his phone and called Nate.

"Where are you?" Nate said before Will could get off a greeting.

"Are the girls—"

"Just dropped them off. Sara said you disappeared. What happened?"

"I saw a man watching the house so I followed him."

"You what? Get back to the house."

"I'm on a trail leading from the back of the cottage into the mountains. The guy's hurt."

"You found him?"

"Not yet. I found fresh blood and—"

Something slammed against Will's shoulders and he went down, breaking his fall with his hands. He collapsed against the damp earth, the wind knocked from his lungs. The guy would have already shot him if he had a gun, so Will figured he'd stay down and pretend to be unconscious. Depending on how badly the stranger was hurt, Will could detain him until help arrived.

"I've got him," the man said into his phone. "You'll have to come get him. I'm injured."

By the time this man's associates came to get Will, Nate and the local police would be swarming the area. Good, then maybe they'd catch these guys and one of them would confess to working for LaRouche and Harrington.

"Aw, come on, that wasn't the deal," the guy argued.

Will cracked his eyes open and spotted the man's black military boots pacing back and forth. Will also spotted his phone a few inches away. Will snatched it.

The man, clearly agitated, didn't notice Will retrieving his phone. The assailant seemed anxious and frustrated, and definitely not on board with the orders coming from the other end of the phone.

"No, I never signed on for that....Fine, I'll call my brother to help."

A few seconds of silence passed. Will figured they wanted his attacker to move Will's body. To where?

"Bobby, it's Jim. Get out here to Echo Mountain Resort, the trail behind Bree McBride's cottage. I've got a guy I have to keep hidden....Will Rankin....I know. I know! They threatened to tell the police about the morphine I stole from the hospital....I had no choice. She's in a lot of pain....You'd know if you bothered to stop by, big brother."

As the conversation continued, Will figured out that the criminal businessmen were blackmailing his assailant. Will suddenly remembered where he'd seen those boots before: at the hospital. This was Jim Banks, the security officer who'd helped them look for Sara.

Apparently LaRouche and Harrington were able to get to anyone in town.

"I can't go to jail!" Jim yelled at his brother on the phone.

He had paced a good twenty feet away, as if Jim didn't like to look at what he'd done to Will. Will took the opportunity to flip the situation around. He took a deep breath, stood and aimed the flashlight at his attacker.

"Jim?"

Jim spun around, whipped a knife out of his pocket and pointed it at Will with a trembling hand. Abrasions reddened his cheek, and his right jacket sleeve was soaked with blood.

"I have first-aid training," Will said. "I can help you."

"No, you can't. Come on." He flicked the knife sideways, motioning for Will to lead the way back down.

Which meant they'd be passing right by Bree's cottage. How could this guy think he'd get very far in public? The guy had obviously stopped thinking once he found himself working for LaRouche and Harrington.

Kind of like how Will had stopped thinking clearly when he'd taken off in pursuit of this man.

"I sense you don't want to do this," Will said.

"Stop the psychobabble and walk."

Will realized he'd had enough: enough of hiding out and enough being bullied. He was definitely done surrendering to violent situations without a fight. It was time to protect the people he cared about.

As he approached Jim, he glanced up ahead at the trail. "You're here!"

Jim instinctively looked to his right.

Will kicked Jim in the side and he fell to his knees. Will grabbed Jim's wrist and twisted until Jim let go of the knife. Will yanked Jim's arm behind his back and the man cried out in pain.

Will shoved him to the ground, pinning him with a knee to his back. "I don't want to hurt you."

Jim groaned in surrender.

"What happened to your arm?" Will said.

"Car accident."

"The accident outside my house last night?"

The guy nodded.

"Will!" Nate called.

Will spotted Nate and Scott jogging toward him, both wearing headlamps.

"How many guys?" Nate called.

"One guy. Jim Banks from the hospital," Will said.

"Found him," Scott said into his cell phone. "He's fine. We'll be back shortly."

"You've obviously got this under control." Nate raised a brow as he motioned for Will to move aside.

Will pushed off the guy, struggling to calm the adrenaline rush. Nate and Scott helped Jim up and he groaned.

"He's bleeding pretty badly," Will offered.

Nate and Scott looked at Will, as if shocked that Will had drawn blood.

"He was the driver who crashed into the pole last night," Will clarified.

"Whoa, okay. I was afraid you lost your temper," Nate said, then looked at Jim. "So what's this about?"

Jim studied the ground.

"Someone's blackmailing him," Will explained. "Something about stealing drugs from the hospital."

"Is that right?" Nate pressed, eyeing his suspect.

"Lawyer," Jim said.

"Sure thing. Right after we book you for attempted murder."

"What! I didn't attempt to kill anyone."

"Did he threaten you with a weapon?" Nate asked Will.

"A knife." He aimed his flashlight at the ground, and went to pick it up.

"I got it." Scott picked up the knife with gloved hands and analyzed it. "Yeah, this could definitely kill someone."

"No, that wasn't the plan. I needed him to come with me."

"Where?" Nate pushed.

"They said...they said to bring him to the water tower on the north side of town."

"For what purpose?" Nate asked.

"I don't know."

"Will!" Sara came racing around the corner, Officer Carrington right behind her.

"I'm sorry, sir," Carrington said to Nate. "Once she heard you'd secured the scene, I couldn't get her to stay put."

"How did she—"

"I called Bree," Scott interrupted Nate.

Sara spotted the knife in Scott's hand and snapped her gaze to Will. Her eyes widened with horror.

"I'm fine," Will said.

"He didn't..."

"He didn't. Let's go." He reached out for her and she hesitated, then took his hand. He didn't like her hesitation, wondering what was behind it.

They headed back down the trail toward the cottage, where two more squad cars were parked.

"Officer Carrington, take Will and Sara inside and keep them there," Nate said. "I'll swing by the hospital with Jim for medical attention." Nate put Jim in the backseat of a patrol car, and pointed at Will and Sara. "Stay inside, hear me?"

"Yes," Will said.

Bree bolted out of the house, her dog right beside her. The golden retriever rushed up to Scott.

"It's okay, girl. We're all okay." Scott scanned the property with a concerned frown, then forced a smile when he looked at Bree. "Let's get inside before Nate locks us up for disobeying orders."

Sara released Will's hand. He wasn't going to let her push him away. He cared about her. A lot.

Will put his arm around Sara's shoulder and pulled her close, whispering in her ear, "Don't push me away."

She shook her head in frustration.

Once they got into the cottage, Bree and Scott headed for the kitchen. "I've got cookies," Bree announced.

"We'll join you in a minute," Will said, leading Sara into a secluded corner of the living room.

He motioned her to a Queen Anne chair, and he shifted onto the footstool in front of her. Her gaze drifted to the hardwood floor.

"What's going on?" He tipped her chin to look at him.

"You could have been killed."

He took her hands in his. "Hey, you didn't make me follow Jim up the trail. That was my decision."

"I'm always involving people in my violent life and they get hurt and I can't seem to fix anything."

"Hold on a second. This isn't about what just happened, is it?"

She didn't answer, but she didn't pull her hands from his, so he pressed on.

"This is about your father?"

Silence stretched between them.

"Sara, you didn't do anything wrong, and you were certainly not responsible for what happened to him. He made the decision to protect you by hiding you in the closet."

Her gaze held his, her eyes tearing. "Why? Why did he do that?"

Will pulled her into a hug and stroked her back. "Because he loved you so very much. It's hard to understand until you have children of your own. You'd literally jump in front of a moving bus to save them. Your dad hid you in a closet so that you would live, and become this strong, tenacious woman who fights for justice."

She sighed against him. "You make that sound like a good thing."

"It *is* a good thing. Think of all the people you've protected. You have sacrificed your life, your happiness to fight for those who can't defend themselves because they're either ignorant of the danger, or don't have the skills to stop the violence. You've become a strong, dedicated woman thanks to your life experiences. God has been watching out for you, Sara, watching you choose the tough cases and fight the hard battles. Embrace what you are instead of thinking it should be different or somehow better. This is better. Here, being here with me."

"You should be holding on to your girls."

"I will, once we resolve this case and everyone is safe. I ache for them, sure, yet as a father I must sacrifice my own needs for theirs. So we're a lot alike, you and I, which is probably why we've connected this way." He continued to stroke her back, liking how it felt when she leaned into him, almost as if…

She needed him.

"I… I don't know what *this* is," she said.

"You don't have to define it, but answer me this. How do you feel, in this moment, here with me?"

"At peace, maybe even…blessed."

"Hold on to that and have faith the rest will work itself out."

Faith. Sara was pretty sure she'd given up on having faith a long time ago. She went to sleep that night with a curious sense of peace, dreaming about possibilities for the future. She'd never really thought about the future before, at least not beyond the next few weeks anyway.

Somehow, through the crises of the past few days, something had awakened inside of her, something akin to hope. Did she dare embrace it?

They had set Will up in a private apartment at the resort for the night, while Sara stayed in Bree's cottage. The resort's security manager, who was Bree's boyfriend, Scott, and Officer Carrington took turns keeping watch over the cottage. They parked two squad cars out front, the strategy being that the police presence would discourage another direct attack.

Sara hated feeling helpless to resolve this situation— her mess of a case—and still felt utterly responsible for bringing the danger to this charming town.

For bringing the danger into Will's life.

Today she would dedicate herself to helping the local authorities with their investigation any way she could.

She went downstairs and spotted Officer Carrington napping on the sofa, while Scott stood guard at the window. Not wanting to awaken the officer, she continued down the hallway into the kitchen.

Will sipped coffee at the kitchen table. He must have sensed her presence because he looked up and cracked a natural smile. "Did you sleep okay?"

He automatically stood and greeted her with a hug.

"Sure, pretty good considering the circumstances."

"Bree left you some scones, and I made a fresh pot of coffee." He turned to grab a mug off the counter.

"I'll get it, thanks."

Her phone vibrated with a call and she answered. "Vaughn."

"It's SSA Bonner, returning your call."

"Good morning, sir." She straightened. "I thought you'd want an update—"

"You're supposed to be on vacation, not chasing a lead I specifically told you was off-limits."

"Sir, I—"

"Do you have any idea what you've done, Agent Vaughn? You've screwed up an eighteen-month investigation."

"I don't understand."

"Another team at the bureau had been working the David Price angle, trying to get enough leverage on him to make him roll on his partners."

"I had no idea."

"It was above your pay grade. And now Price is dead, and potentially so is your career."

"Wait, what?"

"It isn't always about you and your crusades, Agent Vaughn. I've told you that over and over again. We can't have agents who won't take orders. Therefore, you're suspended until further notice."

The room seemed to close in around her. She glanced at Will, his remarkable green eyes studying her with concern. She wanted to go to him again, be held in his strong, comforting arms. He believed in her. He believed she was an honorable crusader with an altruistic mission to protect people.

And that gave her strength.

"I disagree with this course of action," she said to her boss.

"You can appeal with personnel. But consider what your supervisors will say when asked about working with you, about how you've constantly challenged their authority. I'm not sure you were ever meant to be a part of our team, Agent Vaughn."

"Because I don't give up?" she said, her voice rising in pitch.

Bonner sighed heavily into the phone. "No, Sara." He hesitated. "Because of your tunnel vision. You only see what you're looking at, not anything else, or anyone else around you. If you'd been more aware of the people around you, you would have picked up on the cues that there was something else in the works regarding LHP. Other agents did, and they backed off, but you couldn't, because you shut out everything else."

"I thought focus made me a good agent."

"It does, to a point. You also have to trust your co-
ers and the system, and that's where you discon-

nect. You don't trust anyone or anything besides your own instincts."

"Which were right in this case. Once I get my phone back, I'll have proof."

"I hope so, for your sake. If there's evidence on the phone and we're able to use it to build a case against LHP, my superiors might reconsider your suspension. Until then, you cannot act on the authority of our office, and I need to ask you to turn in your ID and firearm when you return."

It felt as if she'd been slugged in the gut. He was stripping away her identity.

"I… I'm not sure when I'm coming back," she said, her voice sounding foreign to her.

"Do what's necessary to help the local authorities in the Price homicide as a witness only, not as an agent." Bonner paused. "For what it's worth, I am sorry, and I wish you the best of luck. Goodbye, Sara."

She stared blindly at her phone.

"What is it?" Will touched her arm.

"I've been suspended."

"Oh, honey. I am so sorry."

"He accused me of only thinking about myself, of only seeing what I'm focused on, nothing else around me." She sighed. "He said I can't work with a team."

"Then, he doesn't know you very well."

"It sounds as if the only chance I have of keeping my job is the evidence on my phone."

"Come here." Will pulled her into an embrace.

She felt broken, betrayed, a complete failure. If only they would have told her about the other team investigating LHP she would have dropped it as ordered. But she hadn't because she'd thought they were giving up too easily.

A man cleared his throat, and Will released Sara. Nate hesitated in the doorway of the kitchen.

"She got some bad news," Will said.

"Unfortunately, I've got more bad news." Nate held up Sara's phone as he stepped into the kitchen. Scott also joined them.

"The video file is not retrievable," Nate said. "We can't use it to prove who killed David Price."

There went her job, plus LaRouche and Harrington would get away with murder and pin suspicion on Sara.

"That's unacceptable," she said.

Maybe Bonner thought her determination was a bad thing, yet in this case, it was her best defense.

"Didn't you say you knew a tech?" she asked Will.

"Yes, Zack Carter. He works here at the resort."

"I could get it to him," Scott offered.

"Let's try it, Nate," Will said. "I mean, what have we got to lose?"

"Even if Zack somehow gets the file, we couldn't use that in a court of law," Nate countered.

"LaRouche and Harrington wouldn't need to know that, at least not when you initially question them, right?" Sara offered.

Nate raised an eyebrow. "I suppose not."

"We could still use the recording to our advantage," she said.

The back door opened and Bree came inside with Fiona. "Oh, hey, everybody. Text alert went out. They're sending K9 teams to search for David Price's body on the east side of Granite Ridge."

"On the east side?" Will questioned.

"Yeah, why?"

"Because I found Sara on the west side of Echo Mountain. You have a map?"

"Sure." Bree went to her pack across the room and pulled a map out of a side pocket.

"What are you thinking?" Nate asked.

"That they're sending SAR teams to the wrong location."

Will spread the map out on the table and pointed to a small lake. "When this is where I found Sara."

"Sara, do you know where you camped the night you and David fell?" Nate questioned.

"We hiked up to Flatrock Overlook, then went west another two miles, so right about here." She pointed. "I fell down this side, and David was hurled off the trail toward the north."

"Which makes sense, because she ended up by the lake," Will said. "But Nate, look at how far away that campsite is from Granite Ridge."

"LaRouche and Harrington are sending search teams on a wild goose chase," Sara said.

"Because they don't want anyone finding the body," Nate offered.

"Which means there might be evidence on the body implicating LaRouche and Harrington," Sara said.

"Or they think David is still alive down there," Nate said.

They all shared a concerned look.

"It's happened before," Bree said. "A hiker has survived a nasty fall."

Nate's phone buzzed on his belt. He ripped it off, studied the message and looked at Sara. "It's my chief. LaRouche and Harrington are in town. They're demanding I lock you up."

Chapter Fourteen

Instead of locking Sara up, Nate scheduled a meeting with the chief and LaRouche and Harrington.

Then Nate made a call to the search and rescue command officer. "I have a witness who claims David Price fell off the north side of Echo Mountain."

Sara, Will, Bree and Scott anxiously listened in.

"I understand....Uh-huh. Thanks." Nate ended the call with a frustrated groan. "They won't change their plan to search the east side of Granite Ridge."

"Then, they'll never find David Price," Sara protested.

"I'll talk to the chief. Maybe he's got more influence with SAR."

"What about LaRouche and Harrington's demands to lock me up?" Sara asked.

Nate looked at Sara, then Will. "I have no choice."

"Nate, think about this," Will argued.

"No, he's right," Sara said, putting her hand on Will's arm. "Bringing me in for questioning is proper procedure."

"Why do I feel like there's a 'but' at the end of that sentence?" Nate said, crossing his arms over his chest.

"But if you arrest me, and they find out I'm FBI, they'll bury any evidence of wrongdoing. If they cover their tracks, more people will die from the release of their drug, and if SAR searches the wrong area, David Price, our best chance at stopping them, will never be found, and what if he's alive?"

"That's a lot of ifs," Nate said.

Sara released a sigh. "I messed up by going after this on my own, I get it. Let me help you make it right."

"What do you think?" Nate asked Scott, a former cop.

"I guess it depends how badly you want to keep your job versus putting away the elitist jerks."

"You up for a search mission?" Nate asked Will.

"You bet."

"I'm coming," Sara said.

"No, it's not safe—"

"I can show you exactly where David fell," she interrupted Will.

"We need Sara on the team," Nate said. "Scott, you keep an eye on things back here."

"Fiona and I could help if we had something of David Price's so she could catch his scent," Bree offered.

"They have some items at the command center," Nate said. "We'll swing by, then head up into the mountains." Nate glanced at Scott. "If that's okay with you."

"Wait a minute, you're asking his permission to let me go on the mission?" Bree planted her hands on her hips and narrowed her eyes at Nate.

Scott went to her and brushed hair back away from her face in a sweet gesture. "He knows I lie awake nights worrying about you when you're on a mission, and this one has an added element of danger. I have total confidence in your abilities, love, but I don't trust these guys."

"Yeah, and LaRouche and Harrington might have their own guys searching the mountains, too," Sara said.

"Then, we'd better get going and find him first," Bree said with a lift of her chin.

Scott kissed her and looked at Nate. "You heard the woman. You guys better get going."

Three hours later, Sara, Will, Nate and Bree, along with her golden retriever, were closing in on the spot where David Price should have landed after being flung over the mountainside by Victor LaRouche. Sara had taped her ribs so they didn't hurt too much, and kept her wrist close to her stomach for added protection. Nothing was going to stop her from going on this mission— a dangerous mission that might cost Nate his job, and worse. An encounter with thugs out here in the wilderness could be disastrous.

Nate said they had today to work with, then it would be over. He'd have to officially question Sara about David's death, taking into account LaRouche and Harrington's false accusations.

And the chances of finding David Price in one day? Well, she didn't want to think about that. She needed to stay focused.

"Your boss is wrong," Will suddenly said.

Sara eyed him. "Excuse me?"

"You're working with a team right now." He winked.

Warmth filled her chest at the sight of his smile, the teasing wink and the adorable knit hat he wore that made him look young and untouched by the grief she knew he'd survived.

"Stop flirting," Nate said over his shoulder.

"That obvious, huh?" Will answered.

"Nah," Nate said sarcastically.

"Wait, she's got something," Bree said as they approached a thick mass of brush. "Okay, girl, go find him."

Bree released her and the dog took off. The four of them followed.

Will hung back, probably to make sure Sara was okay. As she eyed Nate and Bree in front of them, and Will beside her, she realized the truth to his words: she was part of a team. She liked the feeling.

"I see something!" Bree called.

Nate put out his hand, indicating he'd go first to investigate. The dog barked excitedly and Bree commanded her to heel.

Sara, Will and Bree approached Nate, who stood beside a small cave.

"You think he's in there?" Will asked.

"One way to find out." Nate clicked on his flashlight and headed into the cave. Sara and Will followed, and Bree waited beside the entrance with Fiona.

Heart pounding, Sara hoped, she prayed, that David was still alive. A part of her felt guilty for not being able to stop Vic LaRouche from throwing him off the cliff.

"David? David Price, this is the police," Nate called. "We're here to help."

Nate hesitated and turned to Will and Sara. "That's far enough for you two. Wait here." Nate continued into the cave while Sara and Will waited anxiously for news about David's condition.

Will interlaced his fingers with Sara's. They waited, the passing seconds feeling like hours.

"Get away from me!" a man shouted.

"No, wait—" They heard a grunt and a thud.

Then silence.

"Out, now." Will pushed Sara toward the exit.

She got safely outside and Bree peered around Sara. "Where's Will?"

Sara spun around. "I thought he was right behind me. He must still be in there." Sara instinctively started back inside. Bree grabbed her arm.

"Wait." Bree dug in her pack and pulled out a small black canister. "To defend yourself."

"Pepper spray?"

"Long story."

Sara turned back to the cave.

"We got him!" Will called out.

A minute later, Will and Nate exited the cave, propping up a disoriented David Price.

"He's okay?" Sara said, shocked.

"Dehydrated and out of it," Nate said, rubbing his forehead where a gash dripped blood. "Bree can you get me some gauze or something? And get David some water."

"Sure."

"He hit you?" Sara asked.

"Probably thought I was a bear."

She studied Will.

"I'm fine," he said. "Talked him down so we could bring him out."

They led David out of the cave to a small clearing and sat him on a boulder. "David Price, I'm Detective Walsh of the Echo Mountain PD. Can you tell us what happened?"

Sara remained silent, not wanting to influence David's recollection.

"They came at me." He looked at Nate with wide eyes. "Huge bees!"

Will offered the guy some water and he drank.

"Do you remember how you ended up down here?" Nate asked as he pressed gauze against his own head wound.

"Do you remember going on a mountain excursion?" Sara said, then eyed Nate, hoping she hadn't crossed a line. He was still focused on David.

"You went on a hiking trip with your partners," Nate offered.

"No!" David stood abruptly and swung his arms. Will got behind him and put him in a hold that rendered him immobile.

"Calm down, sir," Nate said. "We're your search and rescue team, remember?"

"Search and rescue," David repeated, and stopped struggling. "Oh, yeah, sorry."

Will released him and David sat on the boulder again.

"Nice hold," Sara said to Will.

He winked. "Gotta be ready for when the girls bring their boyfriends home."

It amazed her that Will could find humor while embroiled in this intense situation.

"Tell us what you remember about your fall," Nate asked David.

"He threw me… My business partner threw me over the edge." He looked at Sara and scrunched his eyebrows. "I know you, don't I?"

"I was on the trail guide team that led you into the mountains."

David nodded, his gaze drifting to his hands.

"She helped us find you, Mr. Price," Nate offered.

David nodded at Sara. "Thank you. I wouldn't have survived another night."

"Can you walk?" Nate asked.

"I think so."

"If not, we've got a litter," Nate offered.

"No, no, I can walk."

"Did you injure yourself in the fall?" Will asked.

"My arm. I may have broken my arm."

Will examined David's arm. "We can splint it temporarily. Should we call for another team to help bring him back?"

"I'd rather do this on our own for now," Nate said.

David suddenly slumped over. Will eased him down to lie the ground.

"You okay to help me carry him down?" Will asked Nate.

"Yeah, I'm fine." Nate rubbed his head.

"Not so fine if you've got a concussion," Will countered. "Call for another team. There aren't enough of us to carry you down if you pass out."

Nate nodded. "I'll call for backup."

"LaRouche and Harrington will find out where we are," Sara said.

"Unofficial backup," Nate explained. "Friends of mine." He yanked his radio off his belt and squinted to see it.

"Blurred vision?" Will asked.

"Take care of David," Nate ordered.

Will and Sara shared a frustrated look as Will continued splinting David's arm.

"It's Nate," he said into his phone. "We found him where I marked it on the map. He's wounded and we need help carrying him down. Yep....What?... Okay, will do." He looked back at the group. "They'll be here as soon as possible."

David moaned and opened his eyes, blinking as he focused on the towering trees. "I'm still here. I can't be here." He struggled to sit up.

"Hang on, buddy," Will said.

"I have to get back to my family. It's Christmas," he said.

"You've got time. Christmas is two weeks away," Bree offered.

"If you're up to it we can start down," Nate said. "Help is on its way. Chances are we'll run into them and they can carry you the rest of the way."

"I can do it. I can walk," David said.

Will and Nate helped David stand up, and they stayed close, probably worried he'd collapse again. As they hiked down, Bree tried making conversation with Sara, but Sara was more focused on her surroundings. The slightest sound could indicate a potential threat. They were far from safe, and wouldn't be until David had given his official statement.

My business partner threw me over the edge.

Mitigated relief drifted across Sara's shoulders as she considered the significance of David's declaration. It was the proof she needed to clear her name and put an end to LaRouche and Harrington's sinister plan.

And maybe, just maybe, she'd be able to keep her job.

An hour later, a prickling sensation tickled the back of Sara's neck. She'd learned to never question that instinct.

"Everybody down," she ordered, and shoved Will

and David down on the ground behind a fallen tree trunk.

A gunshot rang out across the mountain range.

"No!" David cried.

Bree stood there, motionless, the dog barking by her side. Sara dived at Bree, yanking her behind a boulder.

"Tell Fiona to be quiet," Sara said, not wanting the innocent dog to become a target.

Bree looked at Sara with a confused, terrified expression.

"Bree, you're okay," Sara said, squeezing her arm. "Tell the dog to be quiet."

"Fiona, no bark," Bree said.

Fiona nudged Sara's hand so she'd release her grip on Bree. "She's fine, Fiona," Sara said. "Bree, tell her you're fine."

"Good girl," Bree said. "Mama's okay. Right here, honey." The dog settled down beside Bree, who still looked shell-shocked.

"Will, are you okay?" Bree called out.

"David and I are good."

"Nate?" Sara said.

Silence.

"Detective Walsh!" she called out with more force. "Nate!"

Nothing. Sara peered around the boulder and saw Nate's blue jacket. He was down. She took a step to go to him…

Another shot rang out. She darted behind the boulder.

"Sara!" Will shouted.

"I'm fine."

Sara wasn't anxious or panicked. Instead, she suddenly grew calm. She had to protect this group of people who a week ago were strangers, and today meant much more.

Especially Will.

"Everyone stay where you are." Sara turned to Bree. "You're safe back here. Keep Fiona close and quiet, okay?"

Bree nodded.

Sara darted between trees and bushes to get closer to Nate. He lay facedown on the trail. Exposed. "Nate?"

He groaned. "Yeah."

"You need to move. Stay low," she coached from the bushes.

He shifted onto hands and knees, rather one hand, because his other hand clutched his shoulder.

"Come on," she urged.

Nate crouch-ran across the trail to Sara.

A third shot rang out.

Nate ducked, kept running and collapsed beside Sara. He winced as he gripped his shoulder. "Unbelievable."

"How bad?"

"I think through and through."

She pulled a scarf from around her neck. "Move your hand so I can put pressure against the wound."

"Don't worry about me. Take care of the others."

Sara ignored him, pried his hand away from the wound and shoved the scarf in place.

"You have to protect…" Nate's voice trailed off and his head lolled to the side.

Between his head injury and the bullet wound, he was out of it.

"Bree?" she called.

"Yes?"

"I need you to come over here and help Nate."

"Won't they shoot at me?"

"You've got good cover if you stay behind trees and bushes. And stay low."

Bree and Fiona darted to where Sara was tending to Nate. No shots were fired, which confirmed Sara's suspicion that the shooter didn't want to kill all of them, probably just David and Sara.

"Keep pressure on the wound," Sara directed Bree.

"Okay."

Sara grabbed Nate's radio and called in. "Base, this is Sara Vaughn. We have an officer down and we're taking fire. We need backup. Our location is—" She paused. "Will, best guess where we are?"

"About one and a half kilometers north of the resort on Cedar Grove Trail."

She repeated the information into the radio. There was no response.

"Base, do you read me, over?" she said.

When no one responded, she decided to take action.

"Bree, stay with Nate." Sara grabbed Nate's gun and went to check on Will, again staying low. As she scrambled across the damp terrain, a shot cracked through the air.

She dived over the fallen tree trunk and landed beside Will and David. "How's it going over here?"

Will narrowed his eyes. "Just peachy."

"David?" she said, sitting up.

A blank expression creased his features. "We're all going to die."

"Nope, not today."

"What's the plan?" Will asked.

"I'll draw his fire, then you're going to have to use this." She handed Will the gun.

He looked at it. "I don't do guns, and I'm not letting you run out there like a duck at a shooting gallery."

"It's our best option."

"There's got to be another one."

"I'm open for ideas." She placed the gun beside Will and turned to ready herself for the hundred-yard sprint. She wasn't even sure where she was going, yet she had to draw the guy out of hiding.

She felt a hand on her shoulder and she turned to look into Will's warm green eyes.

"Be careful," he said. And he brushed a kiss against her lips.

It was all so surreal: the smell of fresh pine, the kiss and the incredible warmth from his lips that drifted across her shoulders. How could something so beautiful be happening at the same time as something so ugly?

Ugly? She'd never thought of her work as ugly before.

Will broke the kiss. "Try calling for backup again, please?"

She looked beyond him at David, who stared straight ahead at nothing in particular. He looked to be in shock.

She tried the radio again. "Base, we have an officer down, over."

Sara and Will held each other's gazes.

"Base, come in, over." Another few seconds passed. "They can't hear us."

With a sigh, Will closed his eyes. She guessed he was praying. A few seconds later he leaned forward and kissed her cheek, as if to say goodbye.

As if he feared she would be shot and killed.

"Do what you think is best," he said, his voice hoarse.

She hesitated, realizing how deeply he cared about her, and she him.

"This is Chief Washburn. We're sending a team, over."

Sara snapped her gaze from Will's and eyed the radio in shock. "Thanks, Chief," she said. "Nate called for a SAR team to carry down David Price. I'm worried about them being in harm's way, over."

"There are two police officers on that team. We estimate they're only ten minutes out from your location. How bad is Nate hit, over?"

"Shoulder wound. He also suffered a head injury and is currently unconscious, over."

"Doc Spencer is with that first team, plus we have another team of cops headed your way. Stay put and stay safe, over."

"You got it, over."

Another shot rang out. Bree shrieked in fear.

"This is ridiculous." Sara grabbed the gun, ready to go out there and shoot blindly at their tormentor.

Will placed his hand over hers. She hesitated and looked into his eyes.

"Help is on the way," he said. "There's no need for you to put yourself at risk."

"I can't sit here and do nothing while they terrorize us. I refuse to hide anymore." She peered around the tree trunk.

"Sara?" Will said.

Irritated, she turned to him.

"Staying here is not the dishonorable thing to do," he said. "His goal is to draw you out. If you go after him, he wins. He will have taken away the only person in our group with the skills to defend us. We need you, Sara." He hesitated. "I need you."

His emerald eyes, so sincere and compassionate, pinned her in place. She couldn't move if she tried.

"Okay?" he said. "Will you stay and protect us?"

"I… Sure."

He motioned for her to sit beside him.

"No, I'll keep watch, in case he advances on us," she said.

Another shot rang out.

"Really?" she snapped.

Fiona burst into a frantic round of barks.

"What's he shooting at? He can't see us," Will said.

"It's called intimidation," Sara said. "Bree, it's okay, he can't see you. You're safe!"

"I don't feel very safe," she called back.

"I hate this," Sara muttered.

"Then, let's change it," Will offered.

"What are you talking about?"

"If there's one thing I've learned in my thirty-four years, it's that in any given situation we have a choice," Will said. "A choice to be fearful or to feel loved."

"Uh… I know you're religious and all that, but even Jesus wouldn't feel loved if someone was shooting at him."

He cracked a smile. "Probably not. Since we're stuck here until help arrives, and this man's goal is to paralyze us with fear, let's make the choice to feel something else."

And then, Will started singing.

"Joy to the world, the Lord is come!" his deep voice rang out.

Sara felt her jaw drop as she stared at this man with the peaceful demeanor and beautiful voice, and wondered how she'd ended up here, in the company of such an amazing human being. They were being used as target practice, yet he sang instead of panicking.

Then Bree's voice chimed in, and even David croaked out a few words here and there.

Sara shook her head with wonder. She could only guess what their assailant was thinking—probably that they were all crazy.

"Repeat the sounding joy," Will sang, encouraging her to sing along.

She did, but kept her focus glued to the rugged terrain where the shooter hid, waiting for an opportunity to take one of them out.

"Repeat the sounding joy," she sang softly, her eyes scanning the area.

"This is Officer McBride. We hear you, over," his voice said through the radio.

"Officer McBride, this is Sara Vaughn. Nate's been shot and is unconscious. The shooter is still out there, over."

"Ten-four."

"Who's with you?" she asked.

"Officer Duggins, Doc Spencer and Scott Becket."

She withdrew behind the tree trunk and spoke in a low voice. "We need to flush this guy out of hiding, over."

"We're on it. Keep singing to distract him, over."

She nodded at Will. "You heard them. They want us to keep singing."

Will started "Joy to the World" from the beginning, and the group chimed in. Adjusting her fingers on the gun grip, she aimed around the tree trunk in case the shooter planned one final suicide move to kill David Price.

"Police, put your weapon down!" a voice shouted.

Three shots rang out.

She hoped they didn't kill the attacker, because he could provide more evidence against LaRouche and Harrington if he rolled on them.

She spotted movement behind Bree and Nate.

Sara aimed Nate's weapon…

Scott darted up and over shrubbery and landed beside Bree. He held her in his arms. Sara eased her finger off the trigger.

"Breathe," Will said.

She took a slow breath in.

"I've got to get out of here!" David shouted.

Out of the corner of her eye, Sara spotted David take off.

"No!" Will went after him.

"Will!" Sara shouted.

A shot rang out.

Sara sprung out of their hiding spot.

All she could think was *Will was shot!*

The shooter was heading her way. Totally focused on Will and David, both on the ground.

She aimed her weapon. "Hey!"

The guy turned.

Gotta keep him alive.

She fired, hitting him in the shoulder. He kept coming. She fired again, hitting him in the thigh.

He went down and kept crawling toward David and Will.

She sprinted to the shooter and stepped on his firing hand. Officer McBride and his team raced up to Sara.

Oh, God, Will can't die. You can't let him die.

"Doctor Spencer," Sara said. "Will and David… I think one of them was shot…" She could hear herself stumbling, not making much sense.

"What about Detective Walsh?" Officer McBride asked.

"Over here!" Scott called out.

"Spike, go help Nate." Officer McBride stepped closer to Sara. She couldn't take her eyes off the shooter, or her hand still aiming the gun at his back.

"Agent Vaughn?"

Sara glanced at Officer McBride.

With a nod of respect, he said, "Well-placed shots."

She nodded her thanks. "Was he the only one?"

"Yes, ma'am. We searched the immediate area. It's clear. Do you recognize him?"

"No," Sara said.

The shooter attempted to crawl away.

"Yeah?" Officer McBride dropped and kneeled on his back. He pulled his arms behind his back to cuff him. "Where do you think you're going?"

Sara blinked, seeing the gun still at the end of her extended arm. She was okay. They got the shooter.

But Will… Was he…? She lowered her arm and closed her eyes.

"Sara?"

She opened her eyes to Will's tentative smile. They went into each other's arms.

"Was David Price shot?" Officer McBride asked.

"No. He's suffering from dehydration, a possible concussion and a broken arm," Will said.

"Well put, Doctor Rankin," Dr. Spencer said as he examined David.

"Command, this is Officer McBride," he spoke into his radio. "We've located the injured parties, over." He clicked off the radio. "Scott, how's Nate?"

"I'm fine," Nate called back.

"He needs a litter," Scott countered.

"What are you, my mother?" Nate said.

"And he's belligerent from the head injury," Bree said.

"This is Chief Washburn. Have the assailants been neutralized, over?"

"Yes sir, just one, over," Officer McBride answered.

"Is Will Rankin okay, over?" the chief asked through the radio.

Everyone looked at Will.

"I'm fine," Will said.

"He's fine, over," Officer McBride said.

"A SAR team is on the way to assist. Send Will Rankin down ASAP."

"What, why?" Will said.

"Chief, is there a problem?" Officer McBride prompted.

"His mother-in-law is missing."

Chapter Fifteen

Will paled. "My girls," he muttered, and headed down the trail.

Sara glanced at Nate for permission to follow Will. After all, she'd shot a man with Nate's gun, and perhaps he wanted her to stay at the scene.

"Go," Nate said.

She took off after Will, but didn't crowd him. She didn't want him to feel smothered.

More like, she didn't want to see his face twisted with panic and emotional turmoil. She wasn't sure she could handle that.

Coward, she scolded herself. He'd spent the past few hours keeping everyone sane and calm, and she didn't have the guts to do the same for him?

If she offered comfort and he pushed her away, she'd ignore the rejection and keep on trying.

"Will," she said, close enough to touch him.

He shook his head. "I can't believe I've put her in danger."

"Hey, hey, let's not assume anything here." She finally touched his arm.

He acted as if he didn't even feel her. She let her hand fall to her side.

"Even if it is related to the case, this is not your fault. You did not willingly put your family in danger. La-Rouche and Harrington are the ones who deserve the blame."

She thought he might have nodded. She'd never seen him like this, so lost and closed off.

"I'm not sure…" His voice trailed off. "I'm not sure how I could live without them."

She darted in front of him and placed her hand against his chest. "Don't talk like that. There's no reason to hurt the girls, even if they have them, which I highly doubt."

He stepped around her. "Didn't know you had an optimistic streak, Agent Vaughn."

"Yeah, I'm full of surprises. Now stop going to those dark places and show me how to pray."

He snapped his attention to her. "What?"

"You heard me. So do I need to fold my hands together or do anything special? Look up to heaven or what?"

"You don't have to do this," he said.

"I want to."

His frown eased a bit. "We could recite the Lord's Prayer, I suppose."

As they made their way back to the resort, they repeated the Lord's Prayer, the words feeling unusually natural as they rolled off her tongue. Color had come back to Will's cheeks, and he had stopped clenching his jaw every few minutes.

For the first time in her life, Sara felt a connection to God as she helped Will avoid the pitfalls of fear and focus on the guiding light of hope.

* * *

Mary's heart raced, pounding against her chest like a jackhammer. Where was she? She slowly blinked her eyes open. White surrounded her. Was she dead?

I'm coming, Megan, I'm coming.

No, Mary couldn't die. Who would take care of the girls? Will was always off on his dangerous adventures, putting his own needs first, before the girls'. And while Edward was a fun grandpa, he wasn't a disciplinarian. Without Mary's influence in their lives, the girls would grow up wild and lost.

She fingered a trail of warm blood trickling down her forehead. No, she wasn't dead. Yet.

She pushed at the billowy white material—the airbag that had saved her life. That was right, she had gone out to get construction paper for Marissa's art project, a project that her father should have helped her finish. But he was too busy saving some strange woman's life— a woman who brought trouble to Echo Mountain. Because of Sara, Mary and Ed were taking the girls out of town tomorrow for a few days.

On the way home from getting construction paper, Mary's tires had lost their grip on the slick road, and she had skidded over an embankment.

She looked left, then right. Surrounded by greenery, trees and bushes, she started to panic.

Then heavy white snow started to fall.

She unbuckled herself and looked over her shoulder. She'd landed at the bottom of a ravine.

In a few hours the car would be covered with snow and no one would even know she was down here. She pushed on the door. It wouldn't budge. She reached across the seat to the other side.

Shoved open the door.

It would only open so far. Not far enough to get her body out. Even if she did, how would she climb up to the street level without help?

Her phone—she had to call for help. Then she remembered leaving it behind because she didn't think she'd be gone that long.

"Somebody help! Help me!" she wailed.

She slammed her blood-smudged palm against the horn three times. Waited. Punched three more times.

She couldn't die this way, withering away, probably starving to death.

Alone.

Mama, I love you, but you're going to die a lonely old woman if you don't start softening your edges with the girls, Megan had lectured.

Mary couldn't help herself. She worried about everything and everyone, especially the girls, since their father seemed to let them do whatever they wanted. That was no way to raise a family.

Yet they adored him. Mary saw it in their eyes every time Claire and Marissa saw their dad after being apart for even a few hours.

Suddenly Mary wondered if all this anger she felt toward Will was really coming from somewhere other than worry. No, she was dizzy from the accident, that was all.

Be honest with yourself, Mary.

She finally admitted that her resentment and anger were born of fear, fear that the girls would forget their mother, Mary's pride and joy. Mary feared Will would bring another woman into their lives, they'd forget about their mom and Grandma would be cast aside like a used paper towel.

"No!" she shouted, gasping for breath as fear smothered her.

She slammed her palms on the horn again, desperate to stay alive, to see her granddaughters, to hold them, to show them she did, in fact, have softer edges.

"I can't die!" she cried, slamming her hands on the horn.

Something thudded against the passenger door. She shrieked.

Will shot her a smile and a casual wave. "Looks as if you took a wrong turn, Nanny."

"Oh, Will!" she sobbed with relief.

Another man came up beside Will, about Will's age with a full beard and jet-black hair. Mary didn't recognize him.

"Is she okay?" the bearded fellow asked.

"She'll be better when we get this door open."

They managed to get the door open. Will reached in and touched her shoulder.

Which only made her cry more.

"Hey, it's okay, Mary," Will said in a gentle voice.

She couldn't stop crying. With relief, with gratitude and maybe even with shame.

Will, of all people, had found her. He'd saved her. She'd been so nasty to him since Megan's death, so judgmental.

"We've located her," Will said into a radio. "She seems okay, a little banged up." He hesitated. "Mary, where are you hurt?"

"Everywhere." She sighed.

"Can you be a little more specific?"

"My head's bleeding and my chest aches. That's about it."

"That's plenty." Will clicked on his radio. "We need a litter and two more guys." He nodded at Mary. "You're going to be fine."

"I can't believe you found me."

"Of course I found you. My girls would be lost without their Nanny. Griff here has got more medical training than me, so we're going to switch spots, okay?"

She squeezed his hand, not wanting to let go. "Could you… Would you be able to… Never mind." She didn't have the gall to ask him to stay close considering the way she'd treated him.

She released Will's hand and he backed out. His partner climbed into the car. "Hi, Mary, I'm Griffin Keane. I'm going to examine your head wound to see how serious it is, okay?"

"Sure." As he reached out to remove hair from the wound, she closed her eyes.

A moment later, she felt Will's hand settle on her shoulder from behind. He'd climbed into the backseat.

She reached up and placed her hand over his. "I get it now," she said. "This is what you do with your time off, rescue little old ladies."

"Little, big, old, young, we don't discriminate," Will said. "We make sure we're ready to go when and where we're needed."

"On call for others," Griffin muttered as he placed a bandage on Mary's forehead.

As understanding opened her heart to compassion, Mary felt more alive than she ever had. She looked over her shoulder at Will. "I'm so sorry."

"Aw, don't worry about it. Ed never liked this car anyway."

"That's not what I meant."

He winked. "I know."

Two hours later, Will waited at the hospital for news about Mary. He had truly felt God's presence when he'd rescued her from the car. It was the first time he'd felt a connection to Mary: a positive, healthy connection.

As they had waited for the second team to assist, Mary had confessed her fears about Will and the girls forgetting Megan. He'd assured her that would *never* happen because he and Mary would remind the girls what a wonderful mother Megan had been.

Will closed his eyes and sighed. Through all the danger and threat of violence over the past few days, he'd come to accept that Megan hadn't pushed Will away because she hadn't had confidence in him as a husband to take care of her. Rather, she had feared for him as a father, a challenging position for even the strongest person. Megan had wanted Will to practice being a single parent while she was still around to advise.

So much sacrifice. So much love.

"How about some tea?"

He opened his eyes to Sara, the determined federal agent he'd somehow fallen in love with.

"Sure," he said, and she handed him the paper cup. He clenched his jaw against the awareness that sparked between them every time they touched.

She sat down next to him. "What aren't you telling me?"

"Excuse me?" He snapped his attention to her.

"That jaw-clench thing usually means trouble."

"No, Mary's good, pretty minor injuries considering. When I first saw the car at the bottom of that ravine…" His voice trailed off.

Sara touched his arm. "But she's okay."

"She is, and I think narrowly escaping death has changed her a bit."

"It usually does." Sara studied her teacup. "Not always for the better."

He guessed she was referring to her father's death.

"Daddy! Daddy!" Claire and Marissa sprinted across the hospital lobby. He put the teacup on the table beside him and opened his arms. They launched themselves at him and he held them close.

"How are my girls?"

"Hey, Will. Thank-you doesn't seem like enough," his father-in-law said.

"I should be thanking you for taking care of my rascals."

Marissa leaned back. "Daddy, I'm not a rascal. Did you really rescue Nanny from a car wreck?"

"I did."

"Does she have a broken nose?" Marissa asked.

"No, what makes you ask that?" Will realized Claire's face was still buried against his shoulder.

"Because Olivia's mother got in a car wreck and her nose was broken, and she wore this big white bandage here." She pressed little-girl fingers on her nose.

"Well, Nanny's nose is fine. She's got some scratches and bruises. She'll be A-OK."

"Hi, Miss Sara." Marissa went in for a hug and Sara hugged back.

Will turned his attention to Claire. "Baby doll?"

She tipped her head and whispered into his ear. "I

know about the guy in the mountains trying to shoot you. I didn't tell Marissa. She'd have nightmares."

His heart sank. He didn't want either of his daughters knowing about the danger. "I'm okay, sweetie," he whispered back. "Miss Sara protected us."

"Mr. Varney," a nurse called from the ER doorway. "Your wife can see you now."

"I'm going, I'm going!" Marissa rushed to her grandfather's side.

"What about you, Claire bear?" Ed asked.

"I need to stay with Daddy," her muffled voice said against his neck.

Ed took Marissa into the examining area.

"I should give you some privacy," Sara said.

"No, wait." Will reached out and grabbed her hand. "Don't leave."

Sara nodded and clung to Will's hand.

Claire sniffled against his neck. She was crying.

Compassion colored Sara's blue eyes as she studied his little girl. She'd make such a great mother some day, a fierce protector. He suspected she would brush off such a suggestion.

She slipped her hand from his and reached out to stroke the back of Claire's head. "Your daddy was so brave. He was never frightened, and he made us all feel safe."

Claire turned her head to look at Sara. "He did?"

"I did?" Will said.

"Yep, and you know how?"

Claire shook her head that she didn't.

"He sang."

"He's a good singer."

When Sara looked at Will, his heart warmed in his chest.

"He's good at many things," Sara said softly.

He sensed someone approach from the left. "Will, where is he? Where's Nate?"

Cassie McBride towered over him.

"He's being patched up in the ER," Will said.

"I'm fine, thank you very much," Bree said, walking up to them.

"Bree, Bree, you're here, too!" Cassie threw her arms around her sister and hugged her tight.

"Yeah, I thought you heard about—"

"Where's Nate?" Cassie broke the hold and looked into her sister's eyes.

"In there." She pointed.

Cassie dashed toward the examining area as Nate was being wheeled out.

"Are you okay?" Cassie said. "Where were you shot? Does it hurt? Where are they taking you?"

"Yes… The shoulder… No, thanks to the pain meds, and I don't know." Nate tipped his head toward the orderly. "Where are you taking me? To Hawaii, I hope."

Cassie narrowed her eyes at Nate. "How much pain medication?"

"I dunno, enough?"

With Claire in his arms, Will walked over to Nate, and Sara followed.

Nate extended his hand and they shook. "Hey, buddy. Hey, Claire. Your daddy's a hero, did you know that?"

Claire nodded. "Miss Sara told me."

Nate nodded at Sara. "You talk to the chief?"

"Not yet. He's taking David's statement."

"I need to get him upstairs so he can rest," the orderly said.

"I'm coming with," Cassie said, tagging alongside the stretcher.

"He said rest, Cassie, not answer twenty-seven questions," Nate said.

"I've never asked that many."

"I'll tell ya what, I'll start counting."

"Why are you being such a wise guy? Do you have a concussion? Have they done an MRI? How'd you get that cut on your forehead?" Her voice softened as they turned the corner.

"She talks too much," Claire said.

"She only talks like that when she's nervous," Will said.

"Why's she nervous?" Claire asked.

"Because she was so worried about Detective Nate."

"Ooh," Claire said. "I get it." She giggled.

"Yeah? What do you get, huh?" Will tickled her tummy as the three of them wandered back to the lounge.

"Sara Vaughn?" Chief Washburn said coming down the hall.

"You ready for my statement?" she asked.

"Yes. I need you to come to the station with me."

Two men turned the corner behind the chief. From Sara's tense reaction, Will assumed they were La-Rouche and Harrington.

"Can't she give it to you here, chief?" Will said.

Chief Washburn approached Sara and Will. "I'm afraid not. David Price has given his statement. He claims Sara shoved him off the trail."

Chapter Sixteen

Will stood there in shock, devastated by the false accusation. A few hours ago David Price had admitted that Mr. LaRouche shoved him off the mountain, and now he was blaming Sara?

The only thing keeping Will from blowing a gasket was the fact he held Claire in his arms.

Sara touched his shoulder, and Will ripped his attention from LaRouche and Harrington's victorious smirks.

With a resigned expression she said, "It's okay. I'll figure things out from here. Take care of your family." She reached out and brushed her thumb across Claire's cheek. "It was nice seeing you again, sweetie."

"You, too, Miss Sara."

With a sad smile, Sara turned and the chief handcuffed her. Will walked away so that wouldn't be the last image Claire would see of Sara: being led away in cuffs by the chief of police.

Will sensed LaRouche's and Harrington's arrogance, their satisfaction. Somehow they'd convinced David to change his story and accuse Sara of attempted murder. But how?

His father-in-law came out of the examining area with Marissa in tow.

"How's Mary?" Will asked.

"She'll be fine once they get her to a room. She was a little cranky and didn't want the girls seeing her like that—" he squeezed Marissa's hand "—so she asked us to wait out here."

"Would you mind watching the girls for a few minutes? I need to talk to Nate."

"Sure, sure."

Will put Claire down. "Stay close to your sister. I'll be right back."

"Okay, Daddy."

He hugged both his girls and went to see Nate. When he got into the elevator, he wondered if Nate was the right guy to be talking to right now. Will changed his mind and made his way to David Price's room.

Will was unsure what he'd say or how he'd persuade the man to admit the truth. Even if he could, David had given his official statement to the chief about Sara.

As he stepped into David's room, he heard a woman's voice behind the privacy curtain. Will hesitated.

"Send them away? Why would I send them away, David? They were so worried about you when you didn't come home. We all were."

"Listen to me, Beth. It's best for everyone if they spend a little time with their cousins over break. I'm also going to hire security to be with them 24/7."

"Security? Why?"

"Our business is dangerous. I know that now."

"That woman's going to jail. She can't hurt you anymore."

"It's not her I'm worried about," he croaked. "It's my criminal partners."

"David," she said, shocked. "What are you talking about?"

"Abreivtas is dangerous. They knew it and pushed it through anyway. I found out and confronted them. That's when LaRouche shoved me over the cliff."

Will ripped the curtain back. "Then, why are you sending an innocent woman to jail?"

"Who are you and what are you doing here?" David's wife said. "I'm calling security." She reached for the phone.

David grabbed her wrist. "Don't."

She released the phone and waited.

"I owe this man my life," David said, nodding his thanks to Will.

"Then, tell the truth," Will countered.

David sighed. "I can't." He squeezed his wife's hand and shook his head.

"David?" she said.

"I can't risk you having a car accident on the way to Pete's soccer practice, or Julianna's skating lessons or…or someone breaking into the house when I'm out of town," he croaked.

His wife's face paled with shock.

David narrowed his eyes at Will. "Do you have a family, Mr. Rankin?"

"Two girls."

"What would you do if someone threatened them?"

Will remembered the visceral panic that had coursed through him when he'd heard Mary had disappeared and he'd feared the girls were with her.

Will had feared the girls had been taken because of his involvement with Sara.

"Mr. Rankin?" David pushed.

"I'd do whatever was necessary to protect them."

"Then, don't judge me for trying to protect my family."

With a nod, Will left the couple alone. What now? Find Nate? Tell the chief what was going on? Who would believe Will, the man who'd fallen in love with a rogue FBI agent accused of attempted murder?

Will would contact Royce, one of the best attorneys in the county, to make sure she didn't go to jail for a crime she didn't commit. Perhaps Royce could leak damaging information to the proper authorities about Abreivtas.

"Don't get ahead of yourself," he said.

He'd get the girls settled at home and make his calls. Will did whatever was necessary to protect the people he loved, and Sara was now on that list.

Sara flung her arm over her eyes as she stretched out on a cot in Echo Mountain PD lockup.

She hadn't seen Will since the hospital last night. She wondered if he'd given up on her, not that she'd blame him. Anyone involved with Sara would be sucked into a melee of problems, staring with her own traumatic childhood, and violent career. Make that her former career.

She'd failed. Miserably.

It didn't surprise her that David Price had changed his story. LaRouche and Harrington had obviously gotten to him, probably threatening David's kids and lovely wife.

Still, Sara hadn't thought she'd end up being arrested and going to jail. Being an FBI agent had to carry some weight with a jury, and once Nate testified that David had, in fact, claimed LaRouche threw him over the mountainside, well, that should be enough for reasonable doubt.

Unless LaRouche and Harrington were able to buy off the jury. No, she couldn't go there, nor did she want to give up on preventing Abreivtas from being distributed. How was she going to do that from a jail cell?

She had to stop her mind from spinning, and rely on others for help. Nate had stopped by earlier and praised her for how she'd handled herself in the mountains. He'd said he was determined to clear her name, as was Will, although Nate had asked Will to keep his distance from Sara. She agreed with that decision, of course, but missed him all the same.

The door to the cell area creaked open.

"Hello, Sara," Vic LaRouche said.

She sat up and glared at him. Ted Harrington stood right beside him. "You've won," Sara said. "Leave me alone."

"Not quite," LaRouche said. "Proving your innocence can be problematic for us. And we know you don't like problems."

"Neither do you, apparently. What did you do to David, threaten his kids or what?"

"We don't threaten. Threats are a bullying tactic, and infer you never mean to follow through." LaRouche leaned into the bars. "We leverage."

"Don't waste your time on me. I'm not fighting the charges."

"No, but your boyfriend is."

She sighed. "Don't have a boyfriend."

"Will Rankin."

She forced a disinterested look on her face. Psychopaths like LaRouche saw right through it.

"He's already contacted a top defense attorney. We can't have that kind of publicity, can we, Ted?"

"Wouldn't be good for business," Ted Harrington agreed.

"Right, the business of killing people," she snapped.

"We don't kill anyone. We offer approved medications to help people cope with the stresses of life," LaRouche said.

"Whatever. I'm going to jail. What more do you want from me?" she said.

With a maniacal smile, he slipped a photograph through the bars. It dropped to the floor. She glanced down at the smiling faces of Will, Claire and Marissa.

"Since you've been unable to convince Mr. Rankin to distance himself from all this, you leave us no choice. It will be a shame to orphan those adorable girls."

She charged the bars to grab him, but he leaned back, out of reach. "Leave that family alone!"

"Tell you what, we'll do just that on one condition."

She waited, clenching her jaw, wondering how much of this she had to endure.

"You'll take our lovely medication and go to sleep with the comfort of knowing the Rankin family will be safe, and the girls will grow up to live long and happy lives."

She eyed the pill in his hand. Now what? If she didn't take it, they'd probably send another assassin, this time to kill Will. The thought of a world without Will's smiling face and warmhearted laugh was not a world worth living in.

She had no choice. She'd take the pill, and bury it in the side of her mouth.

This was going to be a tough sell, yet she had to do it. If she took the pill and something went wrong...

It would be her last sacrifice.

To save Will and the girls.

"Fine." She motioned with her fingers.

"Oh, no, lovely. Open your mouth."

She hesitated. There was no going back now.

"Or were you going to trick us?" LaRouche raised an eyebrow.

She cracked her mouth open. He reached into the cell and grabbed her hair. With a yank, he tossed the pill down her throat and slammed her jaw shut. Her eyes watered. She had no choice but to swallow.

And she did.

He released her with a jerk and she stumbled back. Her gaze drifted to the photo on the floor. She kneeled and picked it up. This was why she'd taken the risk and set herself up as bait: to protect Will and the girls.

"How long were you hunting us?" LaRouche asked.

She snapped her attention to him and straightened. "What?"

"We know you're FBI. We also know you're unstable, which makes this whole—" he motioned with his hand "—overmedication work seamlessly into our plans."

She swayed, gripping the bars. "You can't—"

"We already have. The drug will be released to the general public next month."

It was having a quicker effect on Sara than she'd expected. She struggled to find her words, make sense of the thoughts going through her brain.

"How did you get it…get it through testing?" she asked.

Her eyelids felt heavy and her legs weakened.

"There she goes," Harrington said.

Collapsing on the floor, she stared up at the bright ceiling lights. A low hum filled her ears. She held the photograph so she could see it.

Will. Will and his emerald eyes.

She would die without telling him she loved him. And more innocent people would die because Sara had failed.

"People will die!" she gasp-shouted.

"Well, you will anyway."

She closed her eyes, wanting them gone, wanting her last few moments on earth to be filled with the image of Will and his girls.

"Sa-ra, oh, Sa-ra," LaRouche said.

"Let's go," Harrington said.

"Wait, I've got to leave this."

"Come on, come on, already," Harrington said.

Sara had no idea what LaRouche had put in the cell and didn't care. She wanted them to leave so she could open her eyes and gaze upon the photograph of a smiling father and his two precious girls.

A door slammed and she opened her eyes. They were gone.

She crawled to the toilet, hoping to make herself throw up. Gray fog blurred her vision. She gasped, gripping the photograph in her hand. Willing herself to focus, she held the photograph close, struggled to see.

"Will," she whispered.

Will couldn't wait any longer. He tracked Nate down at Healthy Eats, where Will demanded to see Sara. Nate seemed worn down, probably from the gunshot wound, and he finally gave in. Will felt bad about pressuring his friend, but he needed to see Sara.

When Will and Nate arrived at the police station, the front office was empty.

"Spike?" Nate said.

Will started toward the cell area and Nate yanked him back. "Hang on a second."

Nate went to the computer and punched a couple of keys. A visual of the cell came up on the screen.

Sara was passed out on the floor.

"We've got to—"

Nate put up his hand to silence Will. Then he rewound the video feed and played it back. There, on the screen, they watched Victor LaRouche shove something into Sara's mouth.

Nate pushed Will aside and went to unlock the door to the cell area.

"Sara," Will said. "Sara, wake up."

Nate unlocked the cell door and called for an ambulance.

"This is Detective Walsh. Send an ambulance to Echo Mountain Police Station immediately. I've got an unconscious female."

Will rushed to Sara's side and felt for a pulse. "Nate, we can't wait for an ambulance." He noticed a pill bottle on the cell floor. "Grab that and follow me," Will ordered.

He picked her up and marched out of the cell. When they got into the front office, Spike came in from the back. He was covered in dirt and carried a fire extinguisher.

"Where were you?" Nate said.

"A car fire out back. I locked up."

"Sit behind this desk and don't move until I tell you to."

"Yes, sir."

Nate opened the door for Will. "Let's get her to the hospital."

Will squeezed his hands together in prayer. *Please, God, please let her wake up. Let her be okay.*

They'd given her a drug to counteract the pill La-Rouche had shoved down her throat, and the doctor said the next twenty-four hours were critical.

So Will sat beside her bed. And prayed.

She'd been still all night, hardly stirring, barely breathing.

He closed his eyes and continued to pray. Will couldn't lose her this way. He couldn't lose her, period. He hadn't felt this kind of connection since Megan.

Who would have thought he'd fall in love with a woman like Sara? The FBI agent was determined first and foremost, and had a protective instinct that would scare off a hardened criminal. Such instincts would come in handy with his precocious daughters. That was, *if* Sara had any interest in a future with Will and the girls.

Was he assuming too much? Was he the only one who felt the dynamic pull between them, the trust growing each and every day they spent together? He hoped he wasn't imagining things.

"You're praying."

He snapped his eyes open. Sara stared at him with a confused frown.

"And you're awake," he said, reaching out to take her hand.

"I'm not dead?" she said, with surprise in her voice.

"We got you to the hospital in time."

"LaRouche and Harrington?"

"The truth is out. Nate's got LaRouche on video, forcing you to take the pill. They thought they'd destroyed it, but Nate had a second feed going to another server, courtesy of Zack Carter, who also retrieved the video off your phone."

"That's great news."

"There's more. David Price decided to tell the truth. He gave the feds evidence against LaRouche and Harrington."

"Wow, all this while I was asleep. Did Nate ever figure out how they got to Petrellis?"

"LaRouche and Harrington tracked him down through employee records and bribed him to kidnap you."

"That poor guy. He was collateral damage."

"The ladies at Echo Mountain Church are planning a fund-raiser to support his wife's care."

"That's awfully nice. Think he'll go to jail?"

"Nate's pushing for community service. But be assured, LaRouche and Harrington are going to jail for a very long time."

"It's over." She sighed. "Finally."

Silence stretched between them. The case may be over, but there was more to discuss.

"Sara—"

"Thanks for stopping by." She pulled her hand from his.

"That sounds like a dismissal."

"You should go."

"Excuse me?"

"Will, I'm in the hospital because I was given an overdose of a medication that could have killed me. This is what I do for a living. I pursue violent offenders. That kind of ugliness has no place in your life."

"You're going back to the FBI? I thought you were suspended."

"After everything that's happened, especially the lengths I went to to nail LaRouche and Harrington, I think Bonner will offer me my position back."

"Sara, there are other ways to fight for justice that don't involve throwing yourself into the line of fire."

She interlaced her hands together, making it impossible for Will to hold them again. "You don't really know me, Will. You know only a fragment of what I am—the fragile woman who needed to be rescued from the mountains. But I know you. I see the wonderful life you have with two precious girls, and a community that cares about you. You need a woman who will stay home and bake cookies and draw pictures with your daughters. That's not me."

He took a chance. He had to. "How do you know if you've never tried?"

Sara sighed and shook her head. "You should go home, be with your family."

"After you answer me one last question, and I need to know so I don't keep messing things up."

"Okay."

"I wasn't imagining it, was I?" he said, his voice hoarse. "This thing between us?"

"Adrenaline. We were swimming in it most of the

time we were together. It's to be expected that you'd confuse it with something else."

"You never felt anything—" he hesitated "—when I did this?"

Leaning forward, he pressed a gentle kiss on her lips. When he pulled back, her eyes watered with unshed tears.

"Of course I felt something," she said. "That's why you need to leave." She turned her back to him. "I wish you and the girls the very best."

Will started to reach out and stopped himself. He couldn't force her to open her heart to the glorious possibilities of love, of making a life with Will and the girls. Yet she'd admitted to feeling something, which meant she loved him, right?

Determined. Wasn't that one of her finest qualities? In this case he sensed she was determined that Will find a better woman than Sara.

There was no better woman than Sara, not for Will anyway. How could he convince her of that?

He pressed a light kiss against her head. "I love you, Sara Vaughn. God bless."

Chapter Seventeen

Two days later, Sara was released from the hospital and moved into the Echo Mountain Resort at the request of Detective Walsh. Although the case against LaRouche and Harrington seemed solid, Nate wanted Sara to stay in town until they resolved some issues.

The longer she stayed, the harder it would be to leave, especially because of the gifts Will and the girls dropped off at the front desk for her: chocolates, home-made cookies she assumed were snicker poodles and drawings. There were drawings of Will and the girls, drawings of the mountains and drawings of Will and Sara holding hands.

She sighed. If only...

And why not? Why couldn't you be happy here with Will and the girls?

She grabbed her phone and pressed the number for her boss at the FBI, but didn't hit Send. He'd left her a few messages asking her to call him back and discuss her situation.

A part of her had no interest in whatever he had to say, even if he offered an apology and her job back.

After spending the week with the people of Echo Mountain, she saw what true loyalty looked like, loyalty and trust. For whatever reason, she'd never developed that kind of relationship with her peers or supervisors at work. They hadn't even trusted her enough to share critical information about their investigation of David Price—which would have prevented this entire disaster.

The lack of trust was partially her fault. Up to this point in life she rarely trusted anyone, yet if you didn't trust, you couldn't expect people to trust you in return.

Then there was Will.

She placed her phone on the table and gazed out the window.

Who would have thought a man like Will would have helped her see the world differently, taught her to trust and work as a team? She could take that lesson back with her to the FBI, which would make her a better agent.

For some reason, she couldn't make the call.

"What is wrong with you?" she muttered.

A knock sounded at the door. She crossed the hotel room and welcomed Nate. "Hey, come on in."

Nate, arm in a sling, entered her room.

"How's the shoulder?" she asked.

"Less irritating than yesterday."

"And the shooter?"

"Alive, and talking once he heard LaRouche and Harrington had been arrested. He'd been on their payroll for years as an enforcer."

"A drug company needing an enforcer. That says it all." She shook her head. "How's the investigation going?"

Nate noticed her neatly folded clothes in an open suitcase. "Why, you in a hurry to leave town?"

"I guess." She went back to the window. Bree and a young man were putting up Christmas lights along the split rail fence.

Christmas, the holiday she never celebrated because she was alone, because she thought spending it with her little brother would only remind him of everything they'd lost.

"It doesn't work, ya know," Nate said.

She turned to him. "I'm sorry?"

"Running."

"Not sure what you mean."

"I recognize that look in your eye. I used to see it when I looked in the mirror. So I ran, thinking it would go away." He shrugged. "It didn't."

"I'm not sure I know what—"

"Will Rankin."

"What about him?"

"You'll regret it."

She tore her gaze from Nate's and changed the subject. "You think the case is solid against LaRouche and Harrington?"

"One hundred percent. I've gotta ask—what were you thinking swallowing that pill?"

"I'd hoped to fake it, but well, you saw the video. LaRouche got hold of me."

"Why agree to take it in the first place?"

"They threatened to hurt Will and the girls."

"Ah, right, go after the people you love as leverage." Her gaze shot up to meet his.

"I'm a detective, remember?" He winked. "I know Will fell fast and hard, but I wasn't as sure about you—" he hesitated "—until just now. Wish you'd reconsider abandoning him. The guy's been through a lot."

"It's better this way."

"Better for whom?" he challenged.

Her phone rang and she eyed the caller ID. "My boss," she said, to put an end to her conversation with Nate.

"I'll see what I can do about letting you leave town," he said. He opened the door and turned. "Too bad, though. Chief Washburn is retiring and they've offered me his job. I could use a seasoned detective on my team."

"I'm sure you'll have plenty of officers fighting for that spot."

"None with the experience of a federal agent."

Nate left and she went back to the window. Light snow dusted the grounds with the spirit of Christmas. Bree looked up and waved at Sara. Sara waved back and smiled. Then Sara glanced at Claire's and Marissa's drawings on the dining table. Another smile tugged at the corner of her lips. She wasn't used to all this smiling.

Sara fingered one of the drawings and noticed writing on the backside. She turned it over...

And read a Bible quote written in Will's hand: "Hope deferred makes the heart sick, but a longing fulfilled is a tree of life." Proverbs 13:12.

Sara's phone beeped, indicating another missed call. Her boss. Rather than call him back and make a rash decision that would affect the rest of her life, she decided to try something radical, for her anyway.

She kneeled beside the bed, clasped her hands together and opened her heart to God's love, praying for guidance, and maybe even...forgiveness.

Will hadn't seen Sara in the past few days, but he knew she was staying at the resort. His friend, resort manager Aiden McBride, told Will that she rarely left her room.

Will had to stop thinking about her and let nature take its course. Sara must come to peace in her own way, in her own time. When she did, Will hoped, he prayed, she'd find her way back to him.

Tonight, as they waited for the town's Christmas tree to light up, as it would every Saturday through Christmas, he ached for Sara to be here with him and the girls.

"What time is it, Daddy?" Marissa said, smiling as she stared at the tree.

"Almost time, sweetie pie," he said.

Claire squeezed his other hand. "Can we get cider after the tree lighting?"

"Sounds like a great idea."

"And roasted checker nuts?" Marissa asked.

"They're called chestnuts, not checker nuts," Claire said, rolling her eyes.

"I like checker nuts." Marissa pouted.

"So do I," his mother-in-law said, stepping up beside them.

She smiled at Will, actually smiled.

"Hi, Mary," Will said, giving her a hug.

"I like chocolate more than checker—I mean, chestnuts," Claire said.

"We'll get you some of that, too, if you'd like," Mary said.

"Really? You said sugar makes us hyper," Claire said.

"A little sugar at Christmastime won't hurt." Mary smiled at her granddaughters.

"She came, she came to the tree lighting!" Marissa took off into the crowd.

"Wait, Marissa, hang on." Will ran after her, while Mary hung back with Claire.

Eyes on his daughter's bright pink jacket, he didn't even notice what had gotten her all excited until he was face-to-face with Sara.

"Hi, Miss Sara! Merry Christmas!" Marissa said, hugging her. Sara kneeled and hugged Marissa back.

Will was speechless, unsure what to think. She'd kept to herself, locked in her hotel room for the past five days, yet she was here, standing right in front of him.

Sara stood. "Hi," she said to Will.

"Hello."

"Give her a hug, Daddy," Marissa encouraged.

Before he could reach for her, Sara wrapped her arms around his waist and leaned against his chest. He held her then, squeezed her tight so that he could remember this moment forever, because it could be just that, a moment.

He breathed in her scent, a mix of vanilla and cinnamon, and realized he'd always think of Sara at the holidays.

"Claire, Claire, look!" Marissa motioned to her sister.

Will released Sara, who greeted his eldest daughter. "Hi, Claire, it's so good to see you."

"You, too, Miss Sara," Claire said.

"Merry Christmas, Sara," Mary said. "Girls, how about we find Papa at the hot-cocoa table."

"Cocoa! Cocoa! Cocoa!" Marissa clapped, jumping up and down.

"Calm down." Claire rolled her eyes again.

The girls grabbed on to their grandmother's hands and waded through the crowd.

"Wow, your mother-in-law actually wished me a Merry Christmas," Sara said.

"I guess she was impressed that you were willing to die to protect me and the girls."

She looked at him in question.

"Nate told us why you took the drug in the first place."

"Wow, word really gets around."

He shrugged. "Small town."

A moment of uncomfortable silence passed between them, then he asked the question he dreaded hearing the answer to. "When do you go back?"

"To work?"

He nodded.

"I'm not going back."

Could this mean…?

"Why not?" he asked.

"I'm leaving the FBI."

Hope swelled in his chest. "What about catching the bad guys?"

"I can do that from anywhere." She hesitated. "Like here, maybe?"

"You mean…?"

She shrugged. "Echo Mountain, if that's okay with you."

"Really?" he said in disbelief.

"Unless you think it's a bad idea."

"No, it's a great idea. What changed your mind?"

She slipped her hand into his. "A very wise man told me I could fight for justice in ways other than throwing myself into the line of fire."

"Sounds like a brilliant man," he teased.

"I guess that's why I fell in love with him, huh?" She offered a tender smile.

"Aw, honey, I am blessed beyond words," he said,

and kissed her, right there, in front of the entire community of Echo Mountain.

Applause broke out around them, and they both
smiled, breaking the kiss. Friends patted him on the
back, offering congratulations and warm wishes.

All he could see was Sara, the woman he loved.

The Christmas tree suddenly lit up, bathing the
crowd in an array of color. The group burst into song—
"Joy to the World."

Will and Sara shared a knowing smile.

"They're playing your song," she teased.

"No, sweetheart, it's our song."

* * * * *

UNDERCOVER
HOLIDAY FIANCÉE

Maggie K. Black

In memory of my grandfather,
who taught me how to tell stories,
and my grandmother, who taught me how to laugh.
I miss you and I hope I made you proud.

Thanks as always to my agent, Melissa Jeglinski;
my editor, Emily Rodmell; and the rest of the
Love Inspired team, who encourage authors like me
and bring stories like these to life.

"Come now, let us settle the matter," says the Lord.
"Though your sins are like scarlet,
they shall be as white as snow."
—*Isaiah* 1:18

Chapter One

The crash of exploding glass echoed up through the empty halls of the Bobcaygeon Sports Center, shattering the early morning peace and drowning out the melody of Christmas carols. Moments earlier, Ontario Provincial Police Detective Chloe Brant had been running in place as a treadmill cycled endlessly beneath her. Now she heard shouting. She yanked the treadmill's emergency cord and grabbed the handles for stability as the belt shuddered to a stop beneath her feet. Her steady green eyes looked through the interior window of the sports center's second-floor exercise room down at the lobby below, just in time to see a skinny figure in a rubber elf mask knock over the Christmas tree with the wild swing of a baseball bat.

What's happening, Lord? What do I do to help?

The large window that had encased the front desk had been bashed in and was now a cobweb of shards held together by nothing but safety-glass coating. The first elf was joined by a second, who was holding a knife and seemed equally intent on mindless destruction, stomping on tree ornaments as they rolled across the floor.

At five thirty in the morning, the center was so deserted that the front desk and the coffee counter hadn't even been staffed when she'd headed up to the exercise room. Hopefully that just meant destruction and chaos—not actual casualties.

If gossip around her police division was true, local Trillium Community College—where Chloe herself had spent a year over a decade ago—had a major drug problem the Bobcaygeon police were completely failing to deal with. Accidental overdoses had spiked last spring. A baggie containing thousands of dollars' worth of a new designer pill, nicknamed "payara," had turned up in the sports center locker room. Now, vice units across the country were hearing about payara being trafficked, in small amounts, through their own communities' criminal networks. Seemed whoever was creating it was testing Canada's appetite for a new illegal way to get high.

Some said local staff sergeant, Frank Butler, was going to find himself facing a major internal investigation if he didn't figure out where the drugs were coming from, and fast. Butler had been Chloe's first training officer. He was in his late sixties and, while they'd never been close, she had attended his wife's funeral two years earlier and now hated the thought of a dedicated officer's reputation being destroyed so close to the end of his career. Even if he had made a mistake, he deserved an opportunity to get help and fix it. Not to mention that if he was embroiled in a scandal, it could tarnish her own career and sabotage the promotion to detective sergeant she'd been striving for. She had a week off for Christmas and a house less than an hour away. She'd emailed Butler, asking if there was anything she could do to help. He hadn't answered.

Chloe was the kind of person who took action while praying. So, for the past three days, she'd been scouting the sports center, just exercising, observing and asking God for guidance—never expecting the first hint of trouble she'd spot would come in the form of masked elves brazenly destroying the place.

Gang violence, probably. Especially considering the drug connection. Most ordinary criminals weren't that brazen.

She glanced back toward the exercise room. There were two other people in there and both seemed to be college students. The blond jock on the treadmill was wearing a jersey from nearby rival college: Haliburton. He'd introduced himself as Johnny when he'd first walked in and made a cocky attempt at impressing her with some tale of being a tech genius and entrepreneur before quickly moving on to flirting with the dark-haired young woman on the rowing machine. Now both of them were staring in her direction.

She yanked her badge out of her sweatshirt and held it up on its lanyard. "Stay there. Don't move."

Before they could answer, she slipped off the treadmill and crept along the window for a better view of what was happening below. The faint outline of her reflection mirrored back at her. Six feet tall and lithe, she might've been mistaken for some kind of athlete. But with her long, flaming red hair often scraped back into a bun, she knew the overall impression she usually gave was more of a librarian, especially since she'd reached her midthirties.

The scene shifted below her. She saw a third, bulky elf shove the elderly security guard up against a wall as the shape of a young woman cowered behind Nanny's Coffee counter. There was a gun in the elf's hand. Chloe turned back to the students.

"I'm Detective Chloe Brant, OPP." Her voice rang with authority. "There's a disturbance on the main floor. At least three armed intruders wearing elf masks. I'm going to check it out. You're both going to stay here and lock the door." She pointed to the young woman, making the snap judgment she'd be the more responsible of the two. "What's your name?"

"Poppy." Her dark eyes were filled with fear but her voice was strong. "Did you say elves?"

"Yes, elves." If this was somebody's idea of a sick holiday joke, Chloe wasn't laughing. "Poppy, please call 9-1-1. Johnny, look for ways to barricade the door."

But the young woman was staring at her. "I know you, right? You're dating one of my teachers. I think I saw your picture at the college."

"Focus, Poppy!" Chloe ignored the ridiculous question. She'd assumed Poppy would be the better choice. It never ceased to amaze her how people's brains seized up in shock. Relationships might be top of the mind for these young people but they were the last thing on hers. "I need you to call 9-1-1. Hand me the phone when they answer." She held out her hand and waited while Poppy dialed.

She took the phone, gave Dispatch her name, badge number, cell phone number and a concise description of the situation. Then she handed the phone back to Poppy. "Stay on the line with them and answer their questions. They'll tell you what to do."

"But my boyfriend's on the Trillium hockey team," Poppy said. "He's at the rink setting up the Christmas toy mountain with the coach and Third Line."

Chloe took a deep breath. Okay, so that potentially meant even more people in danger. She'd spotted the dark hair and rather hunky broad shoulders of the bearded college coach pass by with a handful of players yesterday, but he'd left before she'd made her way downstairs or gotten a good look at him. "Don't worry. I'll make sure they get out okay. What's Third Line?"

"It's the group of guys on a hockey team who hit the ice third," Johnny said. "If they get to play at all, because they're not as good as first-or second-line players. I play first line for Haliburton." His tone implied he'd never be caught dead playing anything else. He stepped off the treadmill. "I'll go with you."

"No, you won't," she said. "Not unless you're a cop or military. Are you?"

"No, but a friend of mine is." His chin rose.

Right, and her sister was a journalist and her father was a con man.

"Stay here with Poppy," she told him. "Lock the door behind me and stay away from the windows."

She slipped out of the exercise room. The door clicked shut behind her. Her feet moved silently down the hallway, her fingers aching for her service weapon. But this was Canada and so, because she was off duty, her gun was in her car, safely unloaded and locked away.

She paused at the top of the stairs and looked down at the shards of red and gold glass spread across the floor below. She pulled out her phone, turned it on and made sure the ringer was on silent. It buzzed with a Missed

Call notification. She glanced at it. Apparently she'd missed a call almost an hour ago. It was from a blocked number, but she was so sure she knew who it was from, his name might as well have filled the screen. *Trent*.

Detective Trent Henry of the Royal Canadian Mounted Police was one of the nation's finest undercover detectives. Strong and rugged, with the kind of heart-melting blue eyes that hinted at a familiarity with danger, they'd worked together three times so far. They always clicked so well, she'd expected they'd stay in touch. But each time he'd dropped out of her life without even saying goodbye.

Then, suddenly, he'd called her a handful of times in the past two weeks, with the same curt and blunt demand. "Call me. We should get coffee." No, thanks. She didn't take orders from men like Trent, no matter how rugged their jawlines or how stellar their reputations. Not that she didn't wish Trent was with her now. When she'd met him, he'd been undercover with the province's most notorious gang, the Wolfspiders. Nobody knew more about Canada's drug and gang operations than Trent Henry.

She reached the bottom of the stairs. The hallway was empty. She crept over to the coffee counter and crouched down. A pair of huge and frightened brown eyes looked up at her. The girl was wearing a black shirt and an apron that advertised Nanny's Diner and Coffee. Her face was vaguely familiar in a way Chloe couldn't immediately place. Her name tag read Lucy.

Chloe raised her badge. "I'm Detective Chloe Brant and it's going to be okay. Where are the elves?"

"The ice rink." Lucy's voice barely rose above a

whisper. "They asked the security guard where it was. The guard escaped. But I stayed hidden."

"Probably smart," Chloe said. "How about the players and the coach?"

"They're hiding outside the rink, including my brother." Lucy held up her phone. It showed a string of messages from someone named Brandon. The contact picture was a slender young man with a nervous smile. "But the elves have their coach. They're going to kill him."

"Not if I can help it," Chloe said. If the elves were hunting hockey players, she hoped Johnny had done what he was told and stayed in the exercise room. She could hear footsteps in the distance now. Sounded like one of the elves was on his way back. "I need you to run out of here as fast as you can and don't look back."

Lucy hesitated.

"Hey!" A voice filled the air to her right. Chloe turned. It was the hefty elf. A knife flashed in his hand.

"Run!" Chloe sprang to her feet. "Don't stop until you're safe!"

The elf charged. Lucy ran. Chloe threw herself between them. She dodged as the knife slashed through the air inches from her stomach. She grabbed his wrist to wrench the knife from his grasp, but his wet boots slipped on the tiled floor. He fell backward. Chloe landed on top of him. The knife flashed in front of her eyes. She leveled a blow to his jaw, snapping his head back against the floor. As she twisted the knife from his hand, she noticed his tattooed wrist read GGB. It was a gang sign for the Gulo Gulo Boys.

The Gulo wrenched himself from her grasp, leaped up and ran after Lucy.

Chloe sprinted after him, ready to tackle him if that's what it took to help the young woman escape.

She heard a clatter and watched as his cell phone bounced across the floor behind him. *Gotcha!* She scooped up the phone, spun around and ran for the stairs. A roar of anger left his throat as he realized what she'd done. She almost smiled. A gang member was nothing without his phone. She sprinted up the stairs to the second floor, hearing his footsteps pound after her.

"Give me back my phone!" he bellowed, his voice echoing through the stairwell. "Or I'll kill you!"

She lead him in the opposite direction of the exercise room, dodged behind a pillar and then turned sharply to head down a side hall toward the hockey rink. Had he seen where she'd gone? She didn't know if he had another weapon on him and didn't much want to find out. She ducked behind a Christmas tree and gasped in a breath, just long enough to look over the railing. The round foyer in front of the hockey rink lay beneath her, complete with a wooden platform stage and a giant mountain of stuffed animals towering almost all the way up to the second floor.

Four figures lay flat on their stomachs under the stage, their shadowy outlines barely visible through the slats below. But, even at a distance, she could recognize the Trillium College hockey jerseys. The two Gulos she'd seen earlier stood between them and freedom. One was swinging his bat at anything he could break. The other stood stock-still, his back to her and a gun in his hand.

Then he shifted and her gaze fell to the man kneeling on the ground in front of him.

It was the coach. The sweet-looking, bearded man

was kneeling, his head bowed and hands outstretched, as he placed his life between the hidden students and the gang members. Something about his courage made it impossible for Chloe to look away. She could hear the other Gulo coming down the hallway toward her now. She had to run. She had to fight.

The gang member pressed the barrel of his gun between the coach's eyes, execution style. The coach's chin rose. Then his gaze turned toward her. Keen, piercing blue eyes met hers. Her heart leaped into her throat, stealing a breath from her parted lips.

It was Detective Trent Henry.

Trent's heart sank as his eyes latched onto Chloe's form crouched at the railing above. The feeling of dread in his gut was matched only by the frustration burning at the back of his throat. What was she doing here? First she ignored his calls and then she stumbled into his investigation? He'd called her to get some advice on his undercover assignment over a quick cup of coffee. Getting threatened by weapon-wielding Gulos had never been part of the plan.

Help me, God. This whole drug investigation has been a mess from the start and now it's falling apart around my ears. Help me figure out how to get everyone out of here alive.

If Chloe got killed, or even hurt, he'd never forgive himself. The gun currently pointed between his eyes didn't help matters much. He'd taken out quite a few Gulo operations over the years and the memories were especially vicious. He shuddered to think what it meant that they were staging something so blatant.

Seconds earlier he'd been praying for a diversion.

Something simple and straightforward that would enable him to take out two gang members at once in a way that didn't blow either his cover or risk the lives of his hockey players. Now, here the strongest, toughest and most infuriating cop he'd ever known had somehow materialized on the floor above him, making his job that much harder.

Her eyes were now locked on his face. She'd recognized him. He watched as shouts and footsteps suddenly sounded from above, giving Chloe barely moments to leap to her feet before a third Gulo pelted down the hall toward her. Chloe threw her shoulder into the Christmas tree and tossed it at the gang member like a football tackle. The Gulo grunted and fell under the force of pine needles and branches. Trent nearly whistled.

It was a gutsy move and impressive—not that he didn't wish she'd run instead. But he could tell she'd also seen his players in their hiding place. Had he been right to tell them to hide instead of fight? Hard to know. The four young men weren't the best athletes or experienced fighters. Hodge had gotten a text from his girlfriend, Poppy, saying there were heavily armed criminals swarming the building.

When Trent had heard the chaos and destruction moving through the halls toward them, he'd ordered his players to hide and not a single one had argued. Instead they'd all dived for the narrow crawl space below the platform. Later, he could worry about whether that meant anything to his case. He'd gotten used to thinking of the four of them as his suspects. So it was pretty ironic that a Gulo was now pointing a gun at his face and threatening to kill him if he didn't spill the exact same information he'd spent the last three months completely failing to figure out for himself.

The Gulos wanted to know who was manufacturing the new designer drug and the location of their lab. So did Trent.

After three months of painstaking undercover work as the interim Trillium College hockey coach and sports education teacher, he was absolutely positive that the only people who could've possibly hidden that baggie stuffed with payara pills in the garbage can was one of the four third-line players now hiding under the platform behind him.

He had little doubt that the other three players might very well have coordinated their stories to protect whoever it was. Breaking through their wall of silence and finding out who was his core mission and would be the key to finding the manufacturer and unraveling the entire drug operation. He also knew, without a doubt, that none of the players—whatever their crimes—deserved the vicious evil the Gulos would mete out.

And as of right now, the only two things standing in the way of that was him and the magnificent, glorious, red-haired cop now fighting an armed criminal on the floor above. He watched, with his knees pressed into the floor and his hands raised, as Chloe spun toward the masked Gulo. The thug yanked a knife from his boot and lunged. Her leg shot out hard with a flying roundhouse to kick the weapon from his hand. It slid across the floor and wedged in the railing. The Gulo threw himself at her and then it was a battle of limbs as Chloe and the gang member struggled for dominance.

The masked man standing in front of Trent jabbed

the barrel of his weapon into Trent's forehead. "Who's she?"

Now that was a complicated question and a pretty long story. Chloe was a stunning, difficult and complicated woman. The kind that would drive a man crazy if he let her, until he found himself lying awake at night, staring at the cracks in his hotel room ceiling, counting all the ways he wasn't good enough for her.

The gun dug even deeper. "Is she with you?"

"She's not with me," Trent said. "I honestly don't know what she's doing here."

Yes, he'd called her several times, including earlier that very morning. When he'd first taken this case, he hadn't expected it to take more than a few weeks. He'd get the young men to confide in him, find out where the payara had come from, determine if it had a link to the local police division and then an official task force would be formed to take over and investigate further.

In fact, he was supposed to launch into prep for another much larger and longer investigation way up in the Arctic after Christmas. The substitute teacher cover story had seemed ideal. After all, he'd gotten violent gang members and criminals to spill their deepest secrets. How hard could gaining the trust of four college students be? But the real Trillium sports professor and hockey coach was supposed to return from paternity leave after Christmas. Trent's excuse for being in Bobcaygeon and in these players' lives was rapidly ending, and he was no closer to finding the source of the payara.

He'd needed help. He'd needed advice. School had never been his scene. But Chloe had lived in Bobcaygeon. She'd gone to Trillium College. She was book smart. Plus, she'd trained under the very same local staff sergeant who'd either bungled the case or was corrupt enough to be bribed. Trent wasn't sure which it was, all he knew was that there was something off about Frank Butler. The staff sergeant had an agitation that rubbed him the wrong way. Not to mention that one of the third-line players was Butler's grandson, Brandon. Chloe could help, if they all made it out of there alive.

He watched as Chloe tossed the Gulo off and rolled away, out of sight. Her attacker lunged after her. He stared at the empty space above, willing for some kind of sign that Chloe was okay. Sweat formed at his hairline. *Lord God, please don't let her get hurt! Help me get this gun out of my face so I can rescue her and the players!*

A flash of brilliant red filled his view as he watched the Gulo grab Chloe and throw her against the railing. Her hair tumbled free from its bun in long loose waves that trailed down her back. Visceral pain pierced his chest as Chloe's head snapped back. The Gulo lifted her by the throat and tried to force her backward over the railing. Every muscle in Trent's limbs tensed to fight even as he felt the barrel of a gun holding him in place. If he got shot in the head, he was no use to her. But he couldn't just kneel there and watch as she got hurt. He'd learned when he was thirteen what could happen if he let somebody down. The death of his only sister had been a very high price to pay.

That was it. He'd risk the bullet. He pushed to his feet.

"Get back down!" the Gulo in front of him ordered.

Trent stared into the bland, lifeless eyes behind the mask.

"You think I won't kill you? You think you're gonna

save your own skin by not telling me where your players are? You know one of them is dealing payara?"

Well, Trent knew one of them had tossed the pills in the trash. But he wasn't convinced that meant they were an actual drug dealer. Sure the third-line players each had their problems but none had struck him as gang potential. He'd know. He'd been fourteen and still angrily grieving the murder of his sister when the Wolfspiders had tried to tangle him into their web. And that was a secret about himself he'd keep to his grave.

"We're here looking for payara!" The Gulo holding Trent hostage raised his voice. "Tell us where the lab is and who's been making it. Or I'm gonna shoot your coach between the eyes."

Trent gritted his teeth and prayed. Chloe's feet kicked futilely in the air as her attacker lifted her higher over the railing. If only he'd solved this case earlier, none of this would've ever happened and Chloe wouldn't be in this position.

God, please, don't let Chloe die because of my failure.

Then a scream, bordering on a warrior yell, filled the air above him as Chloe flew backward over the railing.

Chapter Two

Chloe's body tumbled through the air. She tucked her head into her knees, braced herself for impact and aimed for the huge mountain of stuffed toys. The second she'd felt herself about to go over the railing she'd kicked the gang member in the chest with both feet and launched herself out of his hands. If that criminal had been so determined to force her backward, she was going to take charge of the moment. Life had taught her that much. She couldn't always control whether or not she was going to fall. But she could control how she landed.

Her body hit the mound of fluffy stuffed animals, just like a kid cannonballing into a ball pit, sending toys flying. She gasped a prayer. Then she reached for her pocket and breathed a sigh of relief. She still had the Gulo's cell phone.

She pushed her way up through the mound and looked at Trent. He was still down on his knees, with the barrel of a gun against his skin, and his face pale as he scanned for her. Her gaze met his and a visible wave of relief swept over him.

But still she could read the question floating in his blue eyes.

She nodded, feeling the sliver of a smile brush her lips.

He grinned and turned back to the Gulo, who was staring at Chloe in shock. Trent struck. With one quick motion, Trent snapped the gun out of his hand so quickly the gang member gasped in shock.

Chloe grinned. Yeah, there was nothing quite like seeing Trent in fighter mode. Too bad she couldn't afford the time to stick around and watch. She tumbled from the stuffed animals. Toys cascaded across the floor. She allowed herself just one more glimpse of Trent's strong form now fighting for all their lives against not one but two Gulos. Her fighting style was precise and tactical, based on an understanding of anatomy and physics. But Trent was a blistering force, all power and instinct.

She rolled to the platform and peered under. Four pairs of stunned eyes met hers.

"Come on!" she said. "We've got to get you guys out of here."

"You're Coach's fiancée, right?" The whispered question came from a young man with curly brown hair and a composure that implied this wasn't his first crisis. Under any other circumstances she would've laughed.

"No, I'm a cop." She pulled her badge out and pushed it in front of his face. "You are?"

"Aidan. I'm the center for Third Line."

So, the hockey equivalent of a third-string quarterback then.

"Okay, Aidan. I'm going to crawl around to the other side of this platform, and you four are going to meet me there. We're all going to stay really low and head down the hallway. Once I give the word, you're going to jump to your feet and sprint to the exit as fast as you can. Nice and simple. Got it? Now let's go."

She turned to crawl away but felt a hand grab her ankle. It had to be Lucy's brother, Brandon. Dark hair falling over an angular face, his earnest eyes were deep with worry. "I have to find my sister, miss. She works at the coffee counter."

Being called "miss" grated. She preferred Detective or Officer. But she couldn't begin to imagine how he must be feeling and now was no time to quibble. "You're Brandon, right?"

He nodded. "Brandon. Brandon Butler."

She blinked. Frank Butler's grandson? She vaguely remembered seeing his grandchildren from a distance at their grandmother's funeral. "Your sister's okay. She made it out safely."

"Thank you." He let out a long breath and closed his eyes for a split second as he whispered a prayer. But the anxiety in his face didn't fade. "What about Coach Henri?"

He pronounced the French version of "Henry" like the letter *H* was silent, so it almost sounded like "Enry." Seemed Trent hadn't strayed too far from his real last name on this cover. But as Trent liked to say the best covers always contained a hint of truth.

"Don't worry. Your coach is going to be okay." Now, to hurry up and get them all out of there before they noticed just how okay he was doing.

Trent was still battling two Gulos at once. He was such a strong fighter he seemed almost invincible, except that she happened to know he'd dislocated his shoulder once or twice in the past. She prayed it wouldn't happen this time, and would come back to assist him once she got the civilians out.

She crawled flat on her stomach around the side of the stage, where the students were already making their way out from under the platform. The second-floor Gulo was nowhere to be seen. She waved a hand at the hockey players and started toward the wall, her body low as she moved across the floor on her forearms. The players followed. They reached the wall and she waved them on, putting herself between the young men and the gang members, praying the Gulos wouldn't see them.

The sport center's main hallway lay long and empty ahead of them in a maze of destruction and broken glass. The doors shone at the end as headlights blazed in the darkened parking lot, sending a blinding white glow against the glass, punctuated by dashes of moving red and blue. Emergency services had arrived.

Gunfire and vile shouts sounded from above. A huge decorative snowflake crashed to the floor ahead of them and shattered. They'd been spotted.

"Run!" She leaped to her feet and ran forward, pausing just long enough to make sure each and every member of the team had made it to their feet and was moving. Bullets rang behind her. The youths sprinted down the hallway. Chloe ran behind them, taking up the rear and urging the boys on.

The doors in front of them opened. Cops leaned in, reaching out for them. The young men ran through, guided by police. One by one they disappeared into the parking lot. *Thank You, God!* They were going to make it. Every single civilian Trent had been protecting was going to be okay.

Footsteps pounded down the hall behind her as the last player tumbled through the door. A hand grabbed her neck and yanked her backward so suddenly she felt her feet slip out from under her. A plastic mask pressed against her cheek. A rough voice barked past her ear, "Stay back! This pretty little thing is mine!"

The cops stepped back. The door closed. For one quick moment her eyes searched the hallway behind her. Two Gulos lay on the floor where Trent had been fighting just moments before. Trent was gone. Her body was pulled backward into an office. She looked up into the cold, plastic stare of an old-fashioned goalie mask.

She'd been taken hostage and Trent had left her to fight for her life alone.

Trent watched through the eyeholes of the vintage goalie mask as fear filled Chloe's face. A gasp slipped through her lips. He winced. Didn't she know it was him? Didn't she understand that he just needed to grab one quick moment to tell her what she needed to know about his undercover investigation before she ran into a mob of local cops? The security cameras in the center might be so bad they were practically nonexistent, but that didn't mean he wanted a phalanx of officers—let alone Butler—seeing the local hockey coach yanking a provincial detective away for a private chat.

"Hey, it's okay." He let go of her body and reached up to pull his mask off. He didn't get the opportunity. Chloe's strikes came hard and fast, beating him around the head and sending the mask spinning until he could barely see through the eyeholes. "Chloe! Stop! It's me—"

A strong, precise and determined kick caught him

in the gut and sent him flying back against the wall. She'd knocked the air right out of his lungs. He could barely make himself heard in this stupid mask. Or she was so determined to fight she wasn't even listening.

Her fists flew toward him again. Enough! He could hardly get this stupid mask off if she kept attacking him. He ducked her blow, swung her around and pressed her back up against the wall. He braced his forearm across her chest, pinning her, and yanked the mask off his face. "Chloe! Stop! It's me!"

"Trent?" The fear and the fight fell from her face. Her eyes went wide.

They were standing so close his arm was the only thing keeping her chest from touching his, and he could feel her heartbeat radiating through it. For a moment he couldn't tell if she was tempted to slap him or to hug him. He stepped back and raised both hands in front of him before either could happen. "I can't believe you didn't know it was me! Don't you remember when we first worked together undercover, I called you a 'pretty little thing' and then you pretended to be mad at me."

"That wasn't pretend." She blew out a long breath. "Not that I expect you to understand that."

He didn't know what she meant by that, but now was hardly the time for arguments. "Are there any casualties?"

"Not that I know of," she said. "There are two college students in the upstairs exercise room—a young woman named Poppy and a hockey player from Haliburton named Johnny. They're on the phone with 9-1-1 and barricaded themselves in. I also helped Brandon's sister, Lucy, escape. She told me the security guard had gotten out, too."

"And hostiles?" he asked. "I disarmed three."

"I only saw three, too." She touched her right sweatshirt pocket with the back of her hand, like she was checking to make sure something was still there. "Look, I don't know what you're playing at, Henry, but you have exactly sixty seconds to explain what's going on. Because now, thanks to you, there's probably a whole parking lot full of cops thinking that one of their own is being held hostage by a goof in a goalie mask."

A goof?

"What are you even doing here?" he asked. Trust Chloe to barge into the middle of his undercover investigation and start demanding answers. "You just happened to be hanging out in a random, small-town sports center when gang violence broke out?"

"I've been popping by here to work out," she said, without meeting his eyes. "I have the week off work, and I own a house in the country about half an hour from here. This is the closest gym that has a pool and equipment room."

He didn't doubt she was telling the truth. The Chloe he knew would never lie to him, and it wasn't unheard of for people in rural parts of Ontario to drive even farther for a grocery store or bank. Other college athletes and teams came from all over the area to use the facilities and rink. But, he also knew her well enough to know that there was more to it than just that. Fine, if she wanted to keep things to herself, so could he. His eyes traced down her slender throat to the lanyard she wore with her detective's badge.

"You identified yourself as a cop," he said.

"Of course I did. I had to rescue multiple people, report a crime in progress to the authorities and fight for my life against a Gulo gang member. So, yeah, I was going to pull on everything I could to get through." Her arms crossed over her badge. "And your minute is down to thirty seconds."

He let out a long breath and ran one hand through his hair. It was a lot shaggier than he liked, not to mention a bit of white had started to creep in at the temples right before he'd turned thirty-six. Then he ran his hand over his beard. That had taken some getting used to, too.

"I'm undercover—"

"I got that. You're Coach Henri."

"And a teacher at Trillium College," he said. "And you're here because of the payara investigation, aren't you?"

"Not officially," she said. "But I won't deny I've been very curious. Gossip's running pretty thick that Butler's botched the investigation so badly so far that some people think he's corrupt." Her tone implied she wasn't one of them. He wasn't sure what Butler had done to earn such loyalty from her.

"And you've been hanging out here because you thought he could use your help?"

Something flashed in the depths of her eyes. "Well, I'm guessing you think you could, too, considering you kept calling me."

"Maybe," he said. He crossed his arms, too. "I'm undercover, trying to find who's been making payara. Yes, I wanted your input. But, no, that doesn't mean I wanted you to barge in and snoop around. All I wanted was to go out for a simple coffee—"

"Because you're so good at showing up for coffee."

Yikes! She was still upset about that? Yes, he knew last time they'd spoken, months ago, he'd made plans to meet up with her at a diner. But then he'd gotten a new, immediate assignment and it had seemed easier just to leave than to go through the messiness of explaining he didn't know when he'd be able to talk to her again. Looks like he'd made the wrong decision.

"I apologize for that. Standing you up was a mistake." Asking her out in the first place had been an even bigger one. What had he been thinking? A woman like her was way out of his league, and the nature of his work made it all but impossible to form real relationships. "I could give you a long explanation, but it would all come down to the fact that I had a new case to start and had to disappear. If you want a longer explanation it will have to wait for another time. You're a cop. I'm a cop. All that matters now is dealing with the mess we're in."

She didn't answer, but she also didn't argue. He took that as a signal to keep going.

"Yes, a baggie of payara was found in the hockey team locker room garbage can a few months ago," he went on, talking as quickly as he could. "It contained thousands of dollars' worth of pills. It's like nothing our drug guys have ever seen before. And, as you know, a drug can't be properly banned until its exact chemical compounds are analyzed and made illegal, which means anyone arrested for dealing it is at risk of bouncing. I'm told it feels like a superhigh burst of adrenaline and endorphins without a crash afterward, which makes it popular with students and athletes. Also makes people aggressive, highly suggestible and wrecks their impulse control."

"So, it's your job to figure out how the drugs ended up in a small little town like Bobcaygeon?" she asked.

"The opposite. Bobcaygeon is the source. We've never busted anyone with more than a few pills on them. So a great, big baggie-full turning up in a sports center locker room is the biggest break we've had in the case. We suspect one of the third-line players you rescued left it there. The assistant coach had them skating laps the night the drugs were found. There was no payara in the locker room when they walked into it and thousands of dollars of it in a baggie in the garbage can when they walked out—"

"By who?" she interjected.

"I don't know," he admitted. And he should. He'd cracked much harder cases in much shorter periods of time. "Either nobody knows but the one guy who threw it there, or the others have chosen to keep it secret to protect each other. I don't know which. Police apparently couldn't get them to crack, so I went in undercover to try to build a relationship with them."

Light dawned in her eyes. "No wonder people think Butler is corrupt if there're only four possible leads and one of them is his grandson Brandon."

He almost smiled. This was the Chloe he'd missed. The one whose brain was so quick and sharp he could almost feel it sharpening his. "I've spent a lot of time with Third Line and none of them strike me as criminal material. Not to mention I still have no idea where in town the drug lab is or who's making the drugs."

"Why do I get the impression this is urgent?" she asked.

"One way or the other, my cover job finishes after Christmas. I'm supposed to start a much larger gang-related investigation in the new year."

"Wow. Ticktock." Chloe slid past him, filling his

senses with lavender and wood smoke. She always smelled far better than any cop had business smelling. "So, what's the plan?"

"The fact that everyone knows you're a cop is going to complicate matters if we're seen together." He ran his hand over the back of his neck. Further complicating matters was the fact that he had a picture of them together, smiling and hugging like the happy couple they sometimes pretended to be, displayed prominently on the desk in his office at Trillium. Fictional relationship ties were an important addition to an undercover persona, and he'd happened to still have the photo around from an undercover case they'd worked together. Thankfully she didn't know about that. "You go out there and do what you do. I'll wait a few minutes and come out after you. Then hopefully we can meet up later and talk further."

A smile curled at the corner of her lips. "And what exactly do I do?"

"You know. You say the right things. You make everything work the way it's supposed to. You fix things." He didn't know how to explain it, let alone define it. She was just smart about seeing the bigger picture stuff. He tended to fight in the moment.

"And how do you expect me to explain to the police how a mild-mannered teacher and hockey coach took out three Gulos?" she asked.

"One has a dislocated shoulder and mild concussion from trying to throw a bad punch that didn't land quite where he expected."

"You should be thankful you didn't dislocate your shoulder again," she said.

Despite himself, Trent chuckled. "Another was accidentally shot by his buddy whose aim was off, and a hockey coach kindly checked his wound and told him to put pressure on it. The third was already pretty badly roughed up in a fight with a brave and beautiful lady cop. All I did was make sure he tripped while running down the stairs after her. They were all very clumsy."

"Real cute, Trent." Her lips pursed and he could tell she was impressed, despite herself. "But if you ever call me that again, I'm decking you for real."

His face paled as his brain caught up with what his mouth had said. He'd called her beautiful. She had to know she could make a guy's tongue forget how to form words just by walking into a room. But why had he said it? "Sorry."

"Fine. But don't ever let me hear you call me Lady Cop again. It's Detective Brant. Got it?"

"Got it." Relief swept over him. Her hand slid back to her pocket. It was that move people made when trying to check something was still in their pocket, and it was the second time she'd done it. He could feel his detective instincts buzzing at the back of his brain.

"You were right," she said. "I was here working out because I'd heard about the payara and I wanted in on the investigation.

"When I trained under Butler, he was so sharp. I can't begin to imagine why he hasn't solved the payara case yet. But I'm putting my name in for a detective sergeant's job this spring and don't want the fact that I trained under Butler wrecking that for me. Hopefully, I can help clear him. If not, maybe I can confront him in a way that's respectful of his long career.

"Either way, I'm asking you, Trent, cop to cop, to find me an official role on the case. Nothing undercover or in your way. I can chase leads, conduct interviews or review evidence. Whatever you need. Just let's call our bosses and get me officially assigned to assist you from behind the scenes."

He laughed. It was a reflexive, defensive move and one he immediately regretted. Hadn't she heard him? He was down to his last week before this entire assignment had to end. And now he was supposed to ask for a provincial officer to be assigned to his federal case and find something for her to do? "No. Sorry. I'm not bringing someone else in officially at this stage. I want unofficial advice from you, nothing more."

Chloe took a step back and pulled out a cell phone. "I took this off one of the Gulos."

Trent felt his heart stop. She was holding a drug dealer's cell phone right out in front of his nose, and he needed it. They both knew how easily he could slide his hand around her slender wrist and take it from her, and that if she were a hostile, or a civilian, or someone other than Chloe Brant, he just might. Instead he watched as her fingers tightened around it.

"You know as well as I do, I'm under no obligation to hand this over to you," she said. "I could log it through the OPP and let you make an official request for the data, which we both know could take a while to go through. After all, I haven't received official confirmation of anything you've told me. All I've got to go on right now is trust. Nothing more—"

There was the crash of glass doors shattering. Loud voices shouted in the hall behind him, announcing police presence. Chloe slid the phone back into her pocket. "I'll find you and we can talk later."

She stepped out into the hallway, her badge held high.

Trent counted slowly backward from a hundred. Then he stepped out into the hallway. A cop stood in front of him. She was young, blonde and wearing a bulletproof vest. She pointed her weapon at Trent. "Hands up! You're under arrest!"

Chapter Three

Trent raised both hands above his head.

"I'm Coach Travis Henri," he said, giving his undercover name. "I'm the Trillium College hockey coach. Who are you?"

"Constable Nicole Docker." She didn't even blink. "Hands behind your head."

Trent held his tongue and complied, letting her cuff his hands behind his back and then lead him into the main foyer. With each step he fought the urge to remind her that she hadn't told him what he was being charged with or informed him of his rights. It was his job to figure out where the drugs were coming from. Incompetent cops weren't his problem. Not unless they were making or selling payara.

"Constable, let him go!" an authoritative voice barked to their right, accompanied by the sharp sound of footsteps. Trent looked up. A tall, uniformed man in his late sixties was striding down the hallway. It was Staff Sergeant Frank Butler. "And get those ridiculous handcuffs off him!"

Trent watched the staff sergeant approach as the female officer removed his cuffs. Butler was an elder by cop standards, with short-cropped white hair, a healthy outdoor tan and the kind of athletic build that looked like he could easily take on men a third of his age and win. But he was jittery, too, with a slight but telltale shake to his limbs that Trent usually associated with people who had something to hide. "It's Coach Henri, from Trillium, right?" he said.

Trent nodded. "That's me."

"I'm Frank Butler, Brandon's grandfather," the staff sergeant said. He stretched out his hand. "I'm sorry, I don't think we've ever been properly introduced."

The handshake was a little too firm and Trent couldn't help but notice that Constable Nicole Docker had seemingly evaporated.

"It's nice to finally meet you," Trent said. Despite nodding to each other at hockey games, Trent and the staff sergeant had never actually had much of a conversation. That was on purpose. Trent had learned long ago that when he was trying to maintain a cover, the less time he spent talking to local cops the better.

"I apologize for all that." Butler frowned. "I imagine that was your first time in handcuffs. Must've been quite the shock to the system."

Trent laughed. It was a safe, noncommittal response. He'd been handcuffed and arrested more times than he could count. It had usually been as part of his undercover work. But the first couple of times he'd been an out-of-control teen, just on the edge of the Wolfspiders gang's grasp and dealing with the fact that his twelve-year-old sister had been killed when he'd failed to show up to walk her home from school.

"They were under orders to be on the lookout for

someone matching your description," Butler continued. "We saw someone in a mask and mistakenly thought it was a threat. But Detective Brant explained that it was all just a silly misunderstanding and that you'd been trying to help. Next time, keep your head down, stay out of trouble and leave matters to the professionals, all right?"

"Understood," Trent said. He wondered if there was a reason Butler was pushing him away from the case, beside the fact that he presumed he was a civilian. "Brandon and the other third-line players got out okay?"

"They did, thankfully," Butler said. "Thank you for telling them to hide."

"You must've been worried sick," Trent said.

"To be honest, I had no idea he was even in there until he came running out the front door. The young men are saying you stayed behind to fight the gang members?"

"Well, they jumped me, so I fought them off the best I could." Trent chuckled self-consciously. "Guess my inner hockey brawler came out. I was a bit of a fighter in my youth. Not the kind of stuff I'd ever tolerate from my players, but handy in a situation like that. My dad always said I was all instinct and no common sense. Told me I'd get myself killed one day."

That was more truth than he liked admitting, but he'd always believed truth made the best cover. His dad was a farmer who hadn't quite known how to handle his second eldest son. What he'd actually told him, more times than Trent could count, was that if he didn't learn to take a breath instead of flying off the handle, he'd get himself or somebody else killed. Then, a teenaged Trent would come within an inch of shouting back, "You mean like I killed my sister?" before running off and doing something stupid like punching a hole in the barn wall.

He shook off the ugly memory.

"One of the masked men asked me if I knew where he could score some drugs," Trent added. "The name sounded a bit like 'pariah' or 'piranha.' But, like I told him, I honestly have no idea what that stuff is made of, let alone where to get it."

"Just remember to leave things like that to the police in the future," Butler said again. "The last thing we need is civilians running around the place trying to be heroes. Now, if you can please head outside, somebody will take your statement."

Dismissed, Trent walked outside. Cold, wet air hit him like a wave. The sun would be rising soon, but snow was now pelting down in sheets. Emergency vehicles and camera crews filled the parking lot. People huddled together in pockets around a tall fir tree decked in Christmas lights. They were so shrouded by winter gear and emergency blankets he could barely tell who was who. More specifically, he couldn't see Chloe anywhere.

A slender hand came out of nowhere, grabbing him firmly by the arm and pulling him under an overhang. He blinked. Chloe had pulled the furry hood of a jacket up over her head. It framed her face perfectly and made her look years younger. Wisps of red hair flew around her face. The overall effect was kind of adorable.

"You infuriate me, Henry," Chloe said. "You really do. You've been calling me for days and you didn't once think to mention what you were calling me about? Why were you even calling me if you didn't want me involved with this investigation?"

He was beginning to think it might actually have been because he'd missed her.

"I told you," he said. "I'm undercover at your old college. Bobcaygeon is your hometown. You worked with Butler and you live half an hour from here."

"Trillium is not my college." She frowned. "It's just a community college I happened to go to, before getting into the police academy. Bobcaygeon is not my hometown and owning a house somewhere I crash at between cases isn't the same as living there."

Well, obviously that bothered her. But he had no idea why. "So, you're not from here, then?"

"I thought you knew me better than that, Cop Boy. I'm not from anywhere."

"Cop Boy? I can't call you Lady Cop, but you can call me Cop Boy?" Despite himself, she'd just made him laugh. Yeah, he had missed her. He'd missed this. The light teasing. The verbal sparring. The sense that he always had to be on his toes around her. "How can you possibly be from nowhere? Everyone's from somewhere."

"Not me. My little sister, Olivia, and I grew up in the back of a station wagon, squished between suitcases. I don't know if our dad's intentionally a con artist, or just the kind of man who's really good at temporarily hiding the fact that he's a jerk and convincing people he's good at things he's not. But he has the kind of attitude problem that makes him think that nobody is ever treating him well enough. His charm makes him great at landing jobs. But his sense of entitlement makes him terrible at keeping them.

"So we'd land somewhere new, get settled in, live there for a few months, and then he'd get into an argument with someone and back into the station wagon we'd go. Bobcaygeon happened to be where I was for the last three months of high school and I entered Trillium because moving twice in grade twelve had killed my ability to get a student loan for university. That doesn't mean I belonged here."

That had been a defensive monologue he hadn't expected. What had gotten under her skin? "Then why do you own a house half an hour from here?"

"When my mother finally decided she'd had enough of my father, she had no bank account of her own and a divorce lawyer wasn't much help in taking half of my father's nothing. She begged me to cosign on a mortgage for her. So I did. I was twenty-two." She crossed her arms. "A few years ago, she decided she wanted to move into a retirement building in Southern Ontario, so I took over the mortgage. I tend to rent a place wherever I'm working, so I just use it as a place to crash and leave my stuff. I'm sure you know exactly what I'm talking about and expect you're in the same boat."

The huge warm Henry family farmhouse where he'd be celebrating Christmas dinner swept into his mind unbidden. He could almost feel the warmth of the fire in the living room, smell the hay in the barn and hear the rattle of cutlery and the babble of voices in the dining room as his parents and three brothers passed dishes around. No, he knew exactly what it was like to be from somewhere. He also knew what it was like to feel like he didn't really belong there. He blinked and the thought was gone, replaced with the pale light, snow and Chloe's eyes on his face.

"I hear you," he said, waiting for his mind to catch up with his words. "But, like I told you, I'm on borrowed time. My cover was never supposed to drag out this long and is now nearing its expiration date. I have to figure out who's making the stuff. That means finding who's selling it, and I've spent three months completely failing to make the kind of inroads I need to with these students."

"Hey, Officer Brant!" a female voice shouted. They turned. It was Poppy, an outspoken and dark-haired student he vaguely knew from one of his classes. She was running across the parking lot, dragging Hodge, one of his third-line players, after her.

"Poppy!" A smile filled Chloe's face. "Glad to see you got out okay."

"Yeah. Johnny and I piled some weights up against the door, and we stayed low until the police came for us." She propelled Hodge forward.

Trent couldn't help but notice that the young man wasn't exactly smiling. Jeremy Hodgekins, better known as "Hodge," was a giant, with a sturdy six-foot-three frame and a bright future, if he could figure out how to stay out of trouble long enough to make it through college. As far as Trent knew, he was the only member of Third Line to ever find himself in the back of a police cruiser, but only for throwing punches and nothing that had earned him more than a warning. "This is Hodge."

"Hey," the young man said. "Thanks for your help."

"No problem," Chloe said. "It was a team effort. Your coach really saved our lives and had our backs."

Hodge didn't look convinced.

See, this was Trent's problem. He could walk into any dangerous and dingy bar in the country and demand immediate respect because people knew in a glance what he was capable of. But these students? He'd never give them a reason to fear him and they'd never have a reason to trust him. Poppy whispered something in Hodge's ear. He ran his eyes over Chloe.

"Yeah, maybe," Hodge said. He nodded to Trent. "That's your fiancée, right? The one whose picture you showed us. Aidan thinks so, anyway. Why didn't you tell us you were marrying a cop?"

Heat rose to the back of Trent's neck. He forced a grin on his face and didn't meet Chloe's eye.

"Well, like I told you guys, she works in northern Ontario," Trent said. "But she came through when I needed her."

Hodge nodded like that was enough of an explanation. The students wandered back into the crowd. Trent turned to Chloe. "I can explain—"

"You don't need to," Chloe said quickly. "You're undercover. You used an old picture of me as a prop for your cover identity. It makes perfect sense."

Did it? There was something he couldn't quite place in her tone. Then again, something about being this close to Chloe threw his radar off.

"I just hope the fact that they now know I'm a cop won't hurt your cover," she added.

So did he. He took a deep breath and prayed. *Lord, You've been the one consistent presence through everyone I've ever been or pretended to be. I asked You for help. Is Chloe showing up Your answer?*

"We can work with it," he said. "I need that cell phone, and I could honestly use a second brain on this case. I used that old fake-engagement picture of us taken on the gondola at Blue Mountain to bolster my cover. It was an impulse more than a grand plan, but now that you're here, we can use it to our advantage.

"You'll go undercover for one day as my fiancée. Tomorrow's the twenty-third and the last day of school before the holidays. It's the last hockey game before Christmas, too. I'll take you to the college with me, then we can do the team dinner and you can come to the game. Maybe you'll spot something I've missed. Coach Henri is a big softy, so you'll probably want to play your cover as sweet, cute and kind of gushing. It's not ideal, but it's the only option I can think of and I'm not up for complications right now. So, how about it, Detective? You willing to pretend to be crazily into me in exchange for an official assist on this case?"

Her lips parted. A look floated in her eyes that was so raw the only word he could think to describe it was *personal*. She looked at him like they weren't just two cops—one provincial and one federal—who sometimes worked together on joint assignments. No, she was looking at him like they were close friends or even former sweethearts, and like he'd once done something to hurt her. Then she blinked. The look was gone. "Thanks, but no. I appreciate why you used my picture for your cover. But I'm not looking to go undercover with you like that again."

What? He thought she'd wanted in on this case. All she had to do was to pretend to be in a relationship with him for a day.

"I know it's not ideal. But my cover is already set and there's only so much I can change at this point. Plus, we've pretended to be a couple before. We play those roles well."

Maybe even a little too well. There'd been a moment at the end of the last case where he'd almost wished he'd had an excuse to drag it out a little longer, which is what had led to him asking her out for coffee. "It will only be for a day. Just one day. After that, you'll take the ring off your finger again and we'll go our separate ways."

But Chloe was still shaking her head. Then she reached into her pocket, pulled out the cell phone and pressed it into his hand. "Here. Take it. I'm off duty and you identified yourself as the lead officer on the scene. If you need me to write a report about what happened tonight, get someone to contact my superior officer."

This was unbelievable. The Chloe he knew was tenacious. But here she was just handing him her only leverage and leaving. "But I thought you wanted to be in on this case!"

"So did I." Her hand brushed his shoulder, sending odd and unexpected shivers up his spine. "But I think I was wrong. Take care of yourself, Trent. I really hope this works out well for you."

His mouth opened but he couldn't think of any words to fill it. Chloe was walking away and he didn't know what to say or how to stop her. The phone was in his possession. He'd just won the argument. So why did it feel like he'd just lost something much more important than that?

Chloe's cell rang. Headlights shone against her living room window, filling it with a brief flash of light. Then the glass went dark again. She sat up and looked out. Snow beat against the pane. Wind shook the glass. The clock read a quarter to seven in the morning. She picked up her cell and glanced at it to see a missed a call from a blocked number. It had to be Trent. But he was the last person she wanted to talk to right now. It was bad enough she'd just turned down the opportunity to work on the payara case and mitigate the damage an investigation into Butler could do to her career, the last thing she wanted was to try to explain to him why.

He'd asked her to pretend she had feelings for him.

Chloe sighed and lay back on the couch. She'd been wired after leaving the sports center. She hadn't spotted Butler at all after walking away from Trent, so she hadn't had the opportunity to really talk to him except for the few rushed words they'd exchanged in the moments after she'd first run out the sports center. The brief conversation she'd had at the scene with a rookie female officer named Nicole Docker hadn't told her much of anything. So she'd gone for a drive, then shopping and finally a long walk through the woods surrounding her rural, country house.

All the while she'd felt the problem of Trent and the payara investigation moving through her mind like the tumblers of a lock she couldn't quite open. When she'd told him she wanted in on the investigation, she'd envisioned something strictly professional—something that wouldn't involve staring longingly into his eyes while he pretended he had feelings for her.

But something about standing there with him in the early morning light as he'd asked her to act like she was crazy about him had sent her heart pounding like she was cresting the top of a roller coaster without knowing how big the drop was on the other side. She was done with chaos and the men who caused it. Working undercover with Trent was like eating a six-scoop ice-cream sundae with whipped cream, bananas, caramel and chocolate drizzle. It was an incredible thrill, which made her feel like she was working at the very top of her game. That was, until he'd left her sitting alone in a coffee shop wondering how she'd fooled herself into thinking he actually cared.

Her fake engagement ring from their last undercover mission lay on the coffee table. She'd dug it out of her jewelry box when she'd gotten home and wasn't quite sure why she'd bothered keeping it, considering it was probably only worth a few dollars and she'd never be able to wear it without thinking of Trent. She picked it up and twirled it around in her fingers. It was a heavy, solid ring inlaid with intricate strands of imitation diamonds and emeralds. It felt expensive. Not that she believed for a moment it was anything more than a good piece of costume jewelry. When Trent had given it to her at the start of their last assignment, he told her he'd fished it out of a mud puddle at a truck stop.

Headlights moved past her window for a second time. She looked out. It was a dark pickup. Was it the same driver passing twice or just a coincidence? Her cell phone buzzed again, and this time her sister's contact picture flashed on the screen. She dropped the ring and answered it. "Olivia! Hi!"

"Chloe!" Her sister's voice was breathless, almost flustered. "Hi! I hope this isn't too early. Abby's been teething. Molars, I think. So time has lost all meaning."

"No problem. Now is perfect." Besides, she was thankful to have something to replace the dangerously attractive picture of Trent that still floated at the edges of her mind. Instead she thought about Olivia. Five years younger and almost a foot shorter, both Olivia and her one-year-old Abigail had the same startling green eyes and red hair that Chloe had. A journalist, Olivia lived with her bodyguard husband, Daniel, two hours away. "Everything okay?"

"You asked me to let you know if I heard anything about Staff Sergeant Butler's OPP division in Bobcaygeon. There was a major gang shooting there yesterday—"

"I know." Chloe cut her off. "I was there. I'm sorry. I should've told you."

Olivia's voice froze midstream as it switched tone between journalist and sister. "Are you okay?"

"I'm fine," Chloe said. "I'm sorry I didn't call you earlier. Can we talk off the record?"

"Okay. But just so you know, the newspaper will be launching a major investigation into rumors that Butler botched a drug investigation. We'll be starting it the first week of January. We've been hearing it from several sources and this gang violence has given us a pretty strong hook."

"Got it." Chloe blew out a long breath. *Torchlight News* would be thorough and fair. And Chloe could no more ask Olivia not to run a news story than Olivia could ask her not to investigate a crime. "I saw Trent Henry."

"Wow," Olivia said. "And?"

"He asked me to help him out on an undercover case."

"You said yes, didn't you?" Olivia sighed. "Clo, you've got a rescue complex."

"No, I don't." True, there'd been a time when a simple phone call from her sister would be enough to make her drop everything and rush to help her, because her sister wasn't as strong and steady as she was. But Olivia had Daniel now, plus a whole team of bodyguards who worked for him.

"So says the woman trying to save her former training officer's career," Olivia countered.

"That's different. Butler trained me. I owe him some loyalty for that. Not to mention it won't exactly be great for my career if he's thrown under the bus."

Although seeing how little faith Trent apparently had in Butler was worrying.

"I told Trent no. I don't need the headache of Trent Henry right now. I mean, I'd like in on the specific investigation. I can't go into any details on what it's about, obviously. It would be great for helping me land that promotion. But Trent said it would mean posing as his fiancée and when he said that something inside me just balked. Something about pretending to be dating Trent wrecks me emotionally every time. Plus, I don't want him thinking he can just sweep into my life, disrupting everything, whenever he thinks he needs me and then just disappear again." She liked order. Trent was chaos. And, if she did have a rescue complex, it was clear Trent didn't want to be rescued.

"But you like him," Olivia said. "And he likes you."

"So? We're not teenagers. I'm not picking a buddy to do a book report with. And even if I was, Trent's the kind of guy who'd ditch class the day the report was due because he suddenly had something else come up."

"You could bring him for Christmas dinner," Olivia said. "It's going to be a big shindig. We're inviting all of Daniel's Ash Security colleagues and their partners. Both Josh and Alex are newlyweds. Zoe's fiancé has two amazing daughters. Abby adores them."

Was her sister even listening to what she was saying? It was like she was having a completely different conversation.

"Trent Henry is the last person I can imagine sitting around a table at Christmas dinner," Chloe said. "He doesn't want a relationship with me. He wants to pretend to have a relationship with me when it suits him, and then walk out of my life without saying goodbye."

She couldn't begin to get her head around why that was so much trouble for her heart. She just knew that it was.

"What do you want?" Olivia pressed.

"A cast-iron heart that he can't even dent," she said. Headlights flickered past her window for a third time. She tossed the blanket off and stood. It was the same truck. "I've got to go. Just pray for me, okay? And I'll see you at Christmas."

"Will do."

The call ended. Chloe shoved her feet into boots and yanked her arms through the sleeves of her jacket. It was probably nothing. But she'd slip through the woods by the road and watch for the truck to drive by again, just in case, and then search the plates.

She opened the door. It flew back instantly, knocking her hard in the chest and throwing her off balance. A large man—huge, bald and shrouded in winter clothes—shoved his way into her living room, kicking the door closed behind him. Her hands rose to protect herself. But it was too late.

He pushed her down onto the couch, tossing her like a rag doll. One hand clenched her throat. The other held a handgun to her cheek.

"I don't know what your game is," the man hissed. "But you took a cell phone off a Gulo yesterday, and you're going to give it to me."

Chapter Four

❧

She was pinned down helplessly on her own couch, in her own home, watching as a criminal waved a gun before her eyes. *Lord, help me! Please!*

She didn't regret giving Trent the cell phone. It had been the right thing to do. But as she felt the squeeze tighten on her throat, she knew without a doubt that it was a decision she might now die for.

In all the years she'd been on the job, nobody had ever entered her home or breached her sanctuary. No matter how vile and terrible the investigation, she'd always been able to draw a firm line behind it and walk away. Now the danger had followed her home.

He tightened his grip on her throat. "I'll ask you again. Where is that cell phone?"

"I gave it to a police officer." Her voice rasped. If only she could get some leverage, she might be able to defend herself. But she was on her back and sinking deep into the cushions, her legs bent awkwardly beneath her and the weight of her attacker on top of her.

"What police officer?" His voice was a deep snarl.

His eyes were two bloodshot circles of black. "Give me a name!"

She couldn't. She couldn't risk Trent's cover. Tears filled her eyes. She was about to be killed—or worse— to protect Trent, unless she found a way out.

Come on, Chloe. Focus! Don't let fear win! Her rational brain spun. The face was that of a stranger and the fact that he wasn't wearing a mask meant he probably wasn't planning on leaving her alive. The bulging muscles implied steroid use. He was bald and a tattoo on his neck looked like some kind of spider's web made of fangs. Her words came out staccato through shallow gasps. "One of the cops…who was at the sports center… He was plainclothes… I didn't see a badge…"

Vile swear words flowed from his lips. The barrel of the gun dug into the soft flesh under her chin, tilting her head all the way back. His hand moved from her neck to his pocket. He pulled out a pair of zip-tie handcuffs.

She grabbed the gun with both hands and yanked it high above her head while she arched, freeing her legs and pulling them into her chest. Then she kicked up hard with both feet, sending him flying forward, over her head and off the end of the couch, wrenching the gun from his hand as he went. He hit the floor head-first, with a thud so loud the room seemed to shake. She leaped up and spun around, weapon at the ready. "Don't move. Stay down."

He lunged at her. She pulled the trigger. The gun jammed. Again, her fingers squeezed the trigger. Another futile click, followed by a roar as the brute's body launched into hers. He tossed her backward again.

She hit the corner of the coffee table. The gun fell from her hand and pain shot through her spine. *Lord, please give me strength.* She leveled a strong blow to his jaw. He stumbled back.

She turned and ran for the door, burst outside and into the deep gray of an early winter morning. Bitter wind whipped against her. Her skin stung with the threat of frostbite.

There was a truck parked on the road. She looked up. Trent was sauntering up the gravel driveway, toward her, a takeout coffee cup in each hand.

"Trent!" she gasped.

"Chloe?" His clear blue eyes met hers and worry filled their depths. In a quick, almost seamless motion, he set the coffee cups down and ran for her, and it took all the strength left in her body not to crumple into his outstretched arms. "Tell me."

"There's a man…in my house… He wants the cell phone…"

"You're hurt." Trent's fingers gingerly brushed along the side of her throat.

Something she'd never seen before pooled in the depths of his eyes. Something protective. Something comforting.

"He choked you."

"He tried to strangle me." Her limbs were shaking. She wanted to fall into the strength of Trent's arms and let him hold her. Instead she pushed him. "I'm okay. Go! Stop him!"

"Wait in my truck." He pushed a set of car keys into her hand. "Just to be safe. It's already warmed up and, unlike your car, isn't buried in snow. Stay there. Stay safe." Trent's hand touched her shoulder for one fleeting moment. Then he pelted toward the house.

Her limbs shook from the cold and from shock.

She picked up the closest coffee cup and took a sip. It was thick with both cream and sugar, neither of which she usually took. But it was soothing in her throat and she was thankful for that. This was all wrong. Danger wasn't supposed to follow her home. Trent wasn't supposed to show up to her rescue. For the first time, since she'd lived under her father's roof she didn't feel in control of her life. Instead, she felt like a player in somebody else's story, and the thought of that tightened her throat so painfully she could almost feel the hands of the intruder clenched around them again.

An engine roared. A snowmobile shot out from behind the house and disappeared into the forest.

Her attacker had gotten away.

Trent stood in Chloe's living room. Signs of a struggle surrounded him on all sides. The coffee table was cracked. Shelves were knocked over. Frustration burned at the back of his throat. Chloe's attacker had burst out of the house and gone to his snowmobile so quickly that Trent had never even gotten a glimpse of his face. He could've gone after him. He could've leaped into his truck, raced down the back roads, cut him off, run him into a ditch and yanked him from the snowmobile.

Instead, seeing the ugly red marks on her pale skin had stalled something in his brain and kept him from leaving Chloe. His sister had been strangled to death when she'd been twelve and he was thirteen, because he'd made her walk home from school alone. And while he'd gotten so adept at his job that he'd long stopped viewing strangulation victims as different from any other, with Chloe it was different. Somehow everything with Chloe had always been different.

A floorboard creaked behind him. He spun. It was Chloe. She was standing in the open doorway of her home with the two coffee cups in her hand.

"Stand back," he said. "I've done a preliminary scan and there doesn't seem to be a second attacker, but it's probably safer if you wait in the truck until I'm absolutely sure."

"This is my house." Chloe stepped over the threshold into the living room and set the coffee cups down on the dining table. Her eyes scanned the room and something in him ached. There was a look in them. It was jaded—sadness, mixed with bitter resignation—as if this wasn't the first time she'd seen her home in disarray. He'd seen a lot of different looks in her eyes, most often focus and determination. But he'd never seen this one before. It was the look of seeing an old enemy return wearing a new face. "So, he's gone?"

"From as far as I can tell. What did he look like?"

"Huge." She hugged herself. "Bald, with bloodshot eyes, a wide nose and bulging muscles. He wore gloves, so we won't be able to pull prints, and he didn't touch anything we could use to get DNA. There was an unusual spiderweb tattoo on his neck. It was like it was made of teeth."

Royd from the Wolfspiders? No, it couldn't be.

There had to be dozens of other men who matched that description besides the former high school friend who'd tried to lure Trent into a life of gang crime when he'd been a teenaged ball of pain and anger. Royd and Royd's sister, Savannah, were like echoes from an ugly past that Trent desperately wished he could forget. Instead, he'd found himself revisiting that old version of himself, time and again, because convincing gang members to trust him was vital to his undercover work, and that meant letting them think he'd never changed.

Lord, You know how much I hate it when my undercover work takes me back to the parts of my past that I'm desperate to forget. Please, help me one day shut down the Wolfspiders for good. Please set me free from my past.

"Are you okay?" Chloe said. "You look like you're about to faint."

"I never faint," he said. He also wasn't about to start opening up ugly chapters of his life and sharing them with her. "It sounds like a Wolfspiders' tattoo. I wouldn't want to guess which particular gang member it is, because there are dozens of them. But it means we've potentially got two different gangs after the payara."

As if the stakes weren't already high enough.

"How would a Wolfspider know that I had a Gulo's phone?" she asked.

"I honestly have no idea," he said. "Everything the Wolfspiders do is coordinated through their leader. He owns a barbecue restaurant near Huntsville that basically acts as a cover. His real name is Stephen Point, but everybody calls him Uncle. The real question is why Uncle told someone to break into your home to retrieve it."

Trent had been waiting more years than he liked admitting to take Uncle down. But the old man kept his hands clean by authorizing crimes and never committing them himself, which had left the crime lord and Trent in an odd cat-and-mouse standoff, where neither risked tipping his hand enough to try to destroy the other. Trent had spent years biding his time, collecting evidence, coordinating arrests of lower level Wolfspiders in ways that didn't lead back to him. One day, Uncle would slip up, commit a crime and get caught red-handed. That day Trent would be waiting. "Walk me through what happened. Take it from the top."

"I saw headlights pass outside my window three times and got up to investigate. I'm guessing now that was you?" she asked. He nodded. She sat on the very edge of the couch, and he noticed the thick smears of mud on the cushions from where someone in boots had climbed on it. "When I opened the door, he forced his way in, grabbed my throat, pushed himself on top of me and demanded I tell him where the phone was."

"You told him I had it, right?" he asked.

"Of course not!" She tossed her hair defiantly. He'd almost never seen it loose. But now it rose and fell in a big swoop around her shoulders, hiding the stark imprint bruises of a thumb and fingers on her neck. "I told him the bare minimum without lying. I told him that I'd given it to a cop at the sports center."

"But he choked you!" Something rose hot and protective at the back of his neck. Why was he arguing with her? She was a cop. She'd done her job. She'd protected the cover of a fellow officer. But someone had tried to strangle her and it was because of him! "He could've killed you!"

"You think I don't know that? I'm a detective with the Special Victims Unit, Trent. Strangulation is pretty much one of the most common ways men attack women in this province. I've had more calls about that type of attack than any other."

Yeah, he knew that. Of course he did. He knew her undercover work usually involved rescuing women and girls from violence, trafficking and other situations so desperate and vile they made his chest ache. He could also rattle off crime stats almost as well as she could. But knowing it in his brain was different from feeling the visceral gut punch of seeing what someone from his former gang had done to Chloe's neck.

"You should have told him that I had it!" He heard his own voice rise.

"Why?" Her voice rose, too. "Because you think that would've stopped him from hurting me? I'd never give up your cover!"

"I know! Chloe, I know what kind of cop you are. I know you'd have let some criminal kill you to protect me. Just like I would for you. But I still wish you'd just told him I had it!"

"Why?" Frustration curled at her lips. "Give me one good reason why I should've thrown your life to the wolves to save mine?"

He couldn't. His heart was pounding in his chest. He was standing there arguing that she should've risked his life and wrecked his current cover, not to mention potentially cutting the knees out from his huge upcoming assignment at a remote diamond mine that he hoped would lead to crippling the Wolfspiders, Gulos and countless other gang operations. He was arguing that she should've wrecked all that for him to save herself. He didn't know why. He closed his eyes. *What's wrong with me? Why am I acting this way?*

Suddenly he saw himself as a different type of man. He pictured himself crossing the floor, gently brushing his fingers along her delicate skin and softly telling her how very sorry he was that this had happened to her. He imagined his fingers brushing tenderly along her bruised skin and wiping away the tears of fear he could see forming in the corner of her eyes. He saw his lips finding hers and kissing her with a kiss that promised protection. It was the kind of kiss he'd never imagined giving anyone before. Yet he could see it in his mind as clearly as a memory.

"Chloe, I'm sorry he hurt you." Trent opened his eyes. His hands reached out toward her and he wasn't even sure what they were reaching out to do.

"It's okay." She shrugged without really looking at him. Then she picked up one of the coffee cups and took a sip. "At least you knew to be here."

He pulled his arms back. Is that what she thought? That he'd had some heroic inkling she was in danger? No. If anything it was his fault she had seen headlights and opened the door.

"I never dreamed this would happen," he said. "I just dropped by to tell you that when I sent the phone to the tech unit, I made sure you were listed on the report as the officer who'd retrieved it."

He'd decided to tell her that in person, with coffee, because something had seemed off about how they'd parted ways yesterday and he hadn't been able to get her out of his mind. Then he'd driven past her house three times because he'd doubted his decision. He walked over to the table, picked up the full cup and drank. He grimaced. It was black. "I think you drank my coffee. This one is yours."

"Are you sure?" she asked.

"Of course I'm sure." He set the cup down. "I take sugar and cream, you don't."

"You remembered." She stood there a moment, holding the mostly empty cup that had contained his coffee.

"It's hard to forget a coffee order as boring as yours,"

he said. "You know, they make lots of different interesting coffees these days, with all kinds of milks and weird sugary syrups. You don't have to deprive yourself."

He was trying to be funny. But she frowned and then disappeared into the kitchen, and immediately he regretted saying something that flippant. The truth was he would've remembered her coffee order no matter how complicated it was. She reappeared with a tray, containing two types of milk and three types of sugar. His eyebrow rose as he reached for the plain, white, granular stuff.

"I take it with maple syrup when I'm at home," she said. "I have six different types of coffee in the freezer, and my sister bought me a cappuccino maker last year. But when someone else is pouring it for me, I like to keep it simple. Why cause extra hassle for a barista or waiter by requesting three sugars added to the cup before the coffee is poured and two and a half creams added after?"

His hand jerked so quickly he spilled sugar on the table. That was his usual coffee order. "Because coffee is a universal conversation starter. It's a way of connecting with people. I can't imagine why someone who faces down killers for a living, like you do, would be worried about inconveniencing a waiter."

Her phone rang loud and insistent. She set the coffee down, picked up her cell and held the screen for him to see. It was a blocked number. "This happened earlier. I thought the call was from you."

He shook his head. She answered the phone, turned the speaker volume to maximum and held it a few inches from her ear so that he could listen in.

"Hello?"

"Hello, Officer Brant?" The caller's voice was female. "I know who's making payara."

Chapter Five

"**Y**es, this is Detective Brant," Chloe said. Trent felt her reach out, grab his hand and pull him to her side. She led him to the couch and they sat. "Who's this?"

There was a pause. "You can call me Trilly."

Chloe waved her hand toward the pen and pad of paper on the floor. "Nice to meet you, Trilly. Have we met before?"

"No, I don't think so," the voice said.

He grabbed the pad and pushed it into her hands.

Chloe wrote quickly. *Trilly is the Trillium College mascot, right?*

He nodded. Trilly was a cartoon flower with three petals and huge eyes who appeared on things like notice boards.

"Well, I'm happy to help and listen to anything you want to tell me," Chloe said.

There was a long pause on the other end. Chloe waited. Good interrogation was all about knowing when to wait for the other person to talk.

He wrote, *Any guess who she really is?*

She shook her head. *Met three women yesterday. Poppy, Lucy and Nicole.*

He took the pen and wrote, *Nicole tried to arrest me.*

Chloe rolled her eyes.

"You said you were calling about payara?" she prompted.

"Yeah," Trilly said. "It's a drug. They're pills. They're yellowy-orange and make your brain go really fast. Like adrenaline but with no crash."

Not a bad description, but Trent noticed she'd left off the negative side effects like aggression and suggestibility.

"Do you know who's making them?" Chloe asked.

"I do. But I need to make a deal or something. If I give you information, I need some kind of money or plea deal or guarantee that I'm not going to get in trouble for this."

"I want to help," Chloe said. "But I can't help if I don't know what's going on."

"Well, there's a guy involved and it's kind of complicated."

Chloe nodded at Trent as if she'd been expecting it. What was it they said at the academy? Where there were drugs, there was money. Where there was money, there was violence. Where there was violence, there were women in trouble. "Is he your boyfriend?"

"I can't tell you, and he can't know I called you."

This was the part of interrogation he knew well. An informant would get in touch, claiming they wanted to spill information, only to suddenly hold back, make demands or try to force the detective to pry the information out of them. It was infuriating. But Chloe had a knack for it.

Trent's eyes drifted around the room. Something glinted under the broken table. He knelt, felt for it and pulled it out. His heart smacked against his rib cage. It was the ring he'd given her for their fake engagement.

Last winter he'd seen it glittering in a puddle of mud and slush in a truck stop parking lot in northern Ontario. He'd nearly frozen his fingers to the point of numbness trying to fish it out. It had been a gorgeous and valuable thing, lost and forgotten in a terrible place. Immediately, Chloe's face had filled his mind. It was both substantial and beautiful at the same time, which he'd figured was a rare quality in a piece of jewelry, so he'd saved it specifically for her. The fact that their next undercover assignment had required an engagement ring had just been a happy coincidence.

Her hand grabbed his shoulder and squeezed. Chloe was staring down at the ring. He felt his face redden to realize he was literally down on one knee with it in front of her. He sat back up on the couch.

"How about we meet up in person, Trilly?" Chloe said. "Would that help? We could sit down quietly, just you and I, and see if we can work something out."

"Yeah, that could work," Trilly said. "Do you know the hiking path by the gorge? There's a parking lot there."

Trent grabbed Chloe's free hand and squeezed. The parking lot of an isolated gorge in winter? She might as well as be showing up for an actual ambush. He opened his mouth.

Chloe pulled her hand from his grasp. Then she slid a finger over his lips and firmly pushed them shut, as if to say she didn't need his help.

"I don't think that's a good idea," Chloe said. "The

roads are terrible. Let's come up with somewhere private enough we can talk alone, but still safe enough it'll be easy for you to leave if you're not happy and want to go."

A bang sounded on the phone. It was like a door opening so quickly it smashed back against a wall. Then he heard footsteps echoing down a hallway.

"Come to the sports center," Trilly said quickly. "Tonight, during the hockey game. I'll meet you in the alley out back, by the garbage cans, during the third period."

"Third period by the garbage cans," Chloe repeated. "I'll be there."

The sound of footsteps grew louder.

"You can't talk to anyone about this and you can't let anybody see you at the game, okay?" Trilly said. "My guy has eyes everywhere. If he sees you around, he'll know you're a detective and get suspicious about why you're hanging around. If I see you around town, anywhere, talking to anyone, I'm bailing."

Chloe closed her eyes for a long moment. A deal like that would be hard to talk her way out of. Trent watched as her lips moved in what looked like silent prayer. Then her eyes opened again and he felt her fingers brush against his skin as she pulled the ring from his grasp.

"Well, I'm going to be at Trillium College, around town and at the hockey game with Coach Henri, today. I'll be everywhere. Your guy, whoever he is, will see me talking to all kinds of people. I might even talk to your guy, considering I don't know who he is and Coach might introduce me."

She slid the ring over the very tip of her third finger on her left hand and let it hover there.

What was she doing? A weird, unsettled feeling

filled the pit of his stomach, like she'd grabbed his hand just as she was about to leap off a cliff.

"You can't talk to him," Trilly said. "You can't talk to anyone!"

"It will look a lot more suspicious if I don't." Chloe still didn't meet his eye. Instead, as Trent watched, she slid the ring firmly and smoothly onto her finger. "I'm in town today specifically to spend time with Coach Henri. So I'll be going everywhere he goes and talking to anyone he introduces me to. He's my fiancé."

Chloe held her breath and waited. It was a calculated risk. Refusing to meet Trilly at some remote and unsafe location had been a no-brainer. Only a total amateur would agree to something like that. But announcing she was going to be seen around town with Trent all day talking to whoever she pleased had the potential to be a deal-breaker. Chloe closed her eyes and prayed. Silence dragged on the phone, punctuated by the sound of footsteps coming down a hallway.

"Fine," Trilly said. "Whatever. But you come meet me alone and don't tell anyone about any of this. If I think something's up, I'm bailing."

"Okay." The line went dead. Chloe let out a long breath then set the phone on the table and stood. "I'm guessing you caught most of that? We have an informant who gave us a fake name and claims to know where the payara is coming from."

Trent pushed himself to standing. "You made a snap decision about my cover without consulting me."

"It was your plan!" Her hand waved through the air. The ring felt heavy on her finger. "I thought this is what you'd wanted."

"I thought this is what you didn't want!" he countered.

"I needed to come up with something quickly. Your idea was solid. So I went for it."

He ran his hand over the back of his neck. Why was he being so difficult about this? Sure, she hadn't liked the idea of pretending to be Trent's fiancée. But that didn't exactly matter now. She'd been attacked in her own home and she had no way of knowing if the attacker would try again. Someone had contacted her claiming to have information about payara. Her life had tumbled into this chaos whether she wanted it to or not. The least she could do was take charge of how it all landed.

"I want you to tell me why you said no before," Trent said. "Tell me, point-blank, why you didn't like this cover plan."

She turned to the window and watched the mixture of early morning sun and snow flurries outside. "It doesn't matter anymore."

"It does to me, because this is my case and I'm the one who has to call my boss to explain what's happening and make an official request for your presence on it. Yesterday, I was looking at an entire day to sort that. Now, I've got an hour or less. Not to mention the fact that I've got to prep a partner who made it very clear yesterday that she didn't believe in this assignment and who I have reason to believe doesn't have her head in the game."

She could feel a soft but determined growl building in the back of her throat. "Oh, my head is plenty in the game."

"Then prove it to me," he said. "Convince me that this cover you've now committed us to is the way to go."

"Prove it to you?" she asked. "What is this, high school?"

"No, this is work," he said. Now the growl in her voice was overtaken by the deep rumble in his. "This is the superior officer on a hastily assembled, joint RCMP/OPP operation, calling rank and asking my colleague to take two minutes to tell me why she objected to my plan, so that everything is aired before we begin."

"Okay, then, *Sir*, if that's the way it's going to be." She spun back, feeling her thick, long mane settle around her shoulders. His eyebrows shot up into his shaggy hairline, as if her use of the word *Sir* had prompted something between alarm and panic. She crossed her arms. "Professionally speaking, I think your plan that I go undercover as Coach Henri's fiancée makes perfect sense. It creates a very easy in-and-out scenario with the minimum amount of suspicion raised. The fact that you already used a photo of me for your cover is a huge bonus. So, professionally speaking, I have no problem at all with the plan. It's a good plan. *Sir*."

This time, the second "Sir" made his lips turn into a wry smile. "But you shot down the assignment when I first pitched the mission, *Detective*."

"For personal reasons, not professional ones. You're not my supervising officer, we're not in the same branch of law enforcement and I'm on holiday. Turning down a suggested joint mission for personal reasons is completely acceptable."

Was it her imagination or did he just chuckle under his breath? "What were those personal reasons?"

"With all due respect, I don't have to tell you."

"I know you don't, but I'm asking you to, anyway. Chloe, we're friends. Or at least I think we are. I genuinely do care about you." There was something so raw in his voice that she felt something catch in her own throat. "Is there something I'm not getting about pretending to be my fiancée?"

She took a deep breath. "Honestly, I don't like playing the girlfriend role. I never do. You always get to be the strong man. I get to be the arm candy, the doting admirer, the damsel in distress or the pretty little thing under your shoulder."

"Except in this case I'm the mild-mannered hockey coach and you're the daring detective," he said.

A slight smile crossed her lips. Only Trent could manage to be adorable and frustrating at the same time.

"True," she said. "But, still, you command respect just by walking into a room. People always look at you and see a big, handsome guy, oozing with authority. They look at you and see a leader. Nobody thinks you need to be rescued. You do the rescuing.

"All too often, people look at me and underestimate me because I'm a woman. I'm not taken as seriously, and that seems to happen even more when it's my job to play a girlfriend role. It pushes my buttons.

"Growing up, my father used my sister and me like props to bolster his image. I hated it. Do I see the potential, as a detective, in pretending to be Coach Henri's fiancée? Absolutely. But that doesn't mean I'm always going to like it." She took another deep breath and let it out again. "Sir."

"If you call me 'sir' one more time, I'm going back to calling you Lady Cop." Trent ran his hand through his shaggy hair. "You're some piece of work, you know that? I can't imagine anyone thinking you're a damsel, a sidekick or a prop. You know what people are going to think when we walk in a room together? They're going to be amazed a bozo like me could ever be with a woman like you."

She felt herself blush and turned her face back to the window hoping that would hide it. It was his charm coming out, nothing more. Trent was a charming guy. He'd probably inadvertently left a trail of broken hearts all over past undercover missions.

"I promise you, the fact that you're posing as my fiancée won't have any impact on the fact that I see you as an equal partner," he said. "I won't start acting like you're my property. I won't sideline you, take over your conversations or fight your fights for you, unless you ask me to. I won't even try to rescue you unless you're in actual danger. I promise."

That helped. She let out a long breath. "Thank you."

"Now, are you sure that's all it is?" he asked. "Is there anything else you're not telling me?"

What could she possibly say? That he was a good-looking guy and she was really attracted to him? She knew that he wasn't relationship material and that he didn't actually have feelings for her. She did a pretty good job of tamping down her feelings for him and not letting them show. But asking her to spend an entire day, hanging on his arm, pretending to be in love with him?

That might be more than her foolish heart could take.

Chapter Six

"You're the one who taught me every good cover is based on some truth," Chloe said. "Have you ever had a cover that hit a little too close to home?"

He watched as she turned back toward him, her body framed in the early morning light that spilled from the window behind her. There was an earnestness in her face that made him want to pour his heart out on the floor at her feet.

He wanted to tell her what made him so good at pretending to be a gang member was that he understood the anger and pain that welded a heart so firmly shut that eventually all it ended up knowing how to do was to lash out in anger.

He wanted to admit that while she'd been a responsible kid from a messed-up family, he'd been the kind of selfish and irresponsible bad boy who had punched holes in walls, cut classes and broken the hearts of good girls like her.

He wanted to confess that while he'd played several different types of criminals, the hardest thing he'd ever had to do was to pretend to be a more broken and less kind version of himself.

He wanted to tell her all about his family.

He wanted to tell her about his sister, Faith, and how she'd died at the age of twelve because he'd not been there for her when she'd needed him and a killer had grabbed her on her walk home from school.

It was like he couldn't open one door to his past without inevitably opening them all. But if he did, how would she ever look at him the same way again?

"Yeah," he said. "Some covers are definitely harder than others. A three-month stint as a hockey coach is pretty easy. But there've been some that have lasted so long and sunk so deep that I found myself questioning who I really was."

"Well, I can't imagine you've ever started a fight or committed a crime in real life." A mild smile crossed her lips. Then it faded just as quickly. "How do you do it? How do you pretend you're somebody you're not or pretend you don't feel things you do, without it driving you crazy?"

"You're overthinking this," he said. Or maybe he was. "It's just a day. Shut your feelings behind a big metal door and don't let them out until your cover is done." No matter how much he might hear them trying to rattle the doorknob.

He left her alone in her house to get changed and make the phone calls she needed to her superiors, and headed out to his truck. Along with his superiors and hers, he also needed to call the crime scene investigation team to come in and sweep her house. Not that he expected they'd get anything usable. When his calls were done, he stared at his cell phone a long moment, debating dialing one final number.

Lord, I need guidance. There's nobody in the world I trust quite like Jacob.

He dialed. The phone was answered before it had even rung once. "Jacob Henry, RCMP Criminal Investigations."

"Hey, bro." Trent leaned back against the driver's seat and stared up at the ceiling, listening to the sound of heavy snow buffeting the truck. The eldest of the Henry siblings, Jacob was sixteen months older than Trent and half an inch shorter. Jacob had a lot of heart for a cop and a passion for justice. If things had been a lot different when they were younger, they'd probably have been best friends now instead of feeling more like slightly strained, friendly acquaintances. But still, there was nobody Trent respected more. "I'm sorry to bug you about work, but I have a favor to ask."

"Anything." Now that sounded exactly like something Jacob would say.

"As you know, I've been undercover as a hockey coach in Bobcaygeon trying to track down the person who's been making and selling payara. OPP Detective Chloe Brant is helping me on the case now and she was attacked this morning. She's all right and we've already got a team coming to go over the house. There's also a cell phone she recovered from a Gulo that's being processed. I don't know exactly what I'm asking of you. But RCMP Criminal Investigations is a small world…"

"I can keep an eye out," Jacob said. "I can double-check everyone involved in processing physical evidence is on the up and up."

"Thanks." Trent blew out a long breath. Footsteps

crunched in the snow outside the truck. He looked up. Chloe was coming down the long drive toward him. She'd changed into a tailored wool jacket, blue jeans and smart leather boots. Through the open top buttons, he caught a glimpse of a crisp white dress shirt and navy blazer. Her hair was tied back in a long, loose braid with wisps falling down around her face. She looked absolutely perfect.

"Chloe Brant is the red-haired detective, right?" Jacob said. "This'll be your third joint operation."

"Fourth, actually," Trent said. He couldn't remember what he'd told Jacob about Chloe. But he could hear that same admiration in Jacob's voice that most people had when they mentioned her. He wasn't sure if that was because of some outside knowledge or something he'd said.

"Have you told her about your new undercover mission?" Jacob said. "The one Mom and Dad might not be too happy about?"

Yeah, nothing like ruining family Christmas like showing up and announcing that he was going to disappear again the first week of January. And this time he would be totally disappearing.

North Jewels Diamond Mine was located in a very remote area of Canada's arctic. Rumors had been rumbling for years that someone had secretly been siphoning diamonds from its operations to fuel organized crime. Proving it and taking them down could cripple multiple crime rings, including the Wolfspiders. It would mean weeks of specialized mining training and cutting off all external contacts for months, maybe even a year or more. A mining operation was a tight ship, ironically to prevent the kind of smuggling he'd be there to investigate. All his communication could be spied on. His belongings could be searched. He would need to go dark.

This time he wouldn't even have a picture of Chloe on his phone to gaze at.

Chloe opened the passenger's-side door and hopped in.

"I've got to go. Talk soon." He ended the call, slid his phone into his pocket and turned to Chloe. The thought of telling her about Jacob flitted across his mind. But Chloe was all detective. Admitting he had one brother would just lead to questions about his two younger brothers, his parents and the sister he'd once had. That was more than a can of worms. That was opening up an entire worm farm. "Good to go?"

"Absolutely." If Chloe had any lingering hesitation about the investigation, her eyes didn't betray it. She reached out her slender, gloved hand. He took it in his and shook it. His hand lingered on hers and he could feel the smooth curve of her pretend engagement ring under the leather. Then he dropped her hand, put the truck into Drive and pulled out onto the snowy rural highway. Chloe pulled out her cell and opened it to a note-taking application. "Okay, tell me the plan."

"My first class is at nine thirty this morning," he said. He could feel himself grinning but wasn't exactly sure why. "Basically it's a physical education and sports psychology class. I get a quick lunch and then go to my second lecture. Then we go grab a very early dinner with the entire team at Nanny's Diner.

"The owner, Eli Driver, also owns the coffee stand at the sports center and works part-time for the college as the hockey team's assistant coach. He's not the easiest man to deal with and doesn't have a lot of time for weaker players. Although we do have Eli to thank for the fact that we can isolate the person who left the payara bag in the locker room to being one of the third-line players. He was running practice a few months back, got frustrated, and decided to make the four of them stay behind after practice and skate laps. He just left them there. Janitors didn't even realize they were still in there until they turned off the lights and heard the guys hollering to turn them back on. They'd already locked up the locker room and had to reopen it."

"And sometime between reopening the locker room for the third-line players and locking it back up again after them, a baggie of drugs appeared?" Chloe asked.

"Pretty much," Trent said. "Like I told you, I've spent three months trying to get chummy with Third Line and so far have discovered diddly-squat. Third Line at Trillium is more like a designation for trouble players and, because there's only four of them, it's not even a full line.

"Aidan's the center. He's a good guy and a natural leader. The rest of the guys would follow him anywhere. He's at Trillium on a full scholarship and when his grades started slipping he couldn't keep up Eli's demands to stay in the first line. He lives with his mother and I get the impression that money's a big problem for them."

"A big enough problem that he'd sell payara to keep a roof over his mom's head?" Chloe asked. She was typing notes on her phone. He was amazed her thumbs could move that fast.

"Maybe," he admitted. "But he's a genuinely good guy, so he'd have to be pretty desperate."

"Any female friend or girlfriend who could be Trilly?"

"Not that I know of. Not that I claim to know everything about the players' social lives. Brandon is the only Third Line player with a sister."

"You mean Lucy." Chloe's smile tightened. "You think she's Trilly and the man she's protecting is her brother, Brandon, or Frank himself? Because she didn't sound like she was talking about a grandfather."

"No, she didn't," he admitted. Not that it wouldn't tie things in a neat and tidy package if Trilly had been calling about the uncomfortably anxious staff sergeant. "To be honest, Brandon is a good guy, too. He tries very hard. I can't imagine him selling drugs. How did Frank seem when you talked to him yesterday?"

"Uncomfortable and distracted." Chloe frowned. "I don't get it. He was always so stern and focused when I worked with him. Not warm, but professional." Her jaw set. "Then again, he's still mourning the loss of his wife. That has to be hard on anyone."

There was something impressive about her trust and loyalty, even if he thought it was misplaced.

"Now, Hodge is dating Poppy, and she was there yesterday," she added. "She could be Trilly. What can you tell me about him?"

"Hodge is your typical potentially strong guy who just needs to brush up his skills. He was suspended already for fighting—"

"He seemed shy," Chloe interjected.

"He is. He's a sweet kid, actually, with impulse-control problems. He gets frustrated too easily, especially when people taunt him. Contact sports are great for a person like that because it gives them a healthy outlet. If a gang had ever gotten their claws into him, he'd have made a great enforcer. Get him worked up enough and point him at someone, and he'll charge like a bull. But I can't imagine him masterminding a drug-dealing operation."

He looked straight ahead through the windshield. Royd of the Wolfspiders was an enforcer, too.

"I could see Poppy being Trilly," Chloe said. "Hodge would be the logical person for her to want to protect. I didn't get the impression she liked that blowhard from the Haliburton team, Johnny, enough to want to protect him. It was more like he was relentlessly trying to impress her. He tried to flirt with both of us."

"If Johnny's involved, it wouldn't explain why the payara only appeared after Third Line was in the locker room," Trent said. "He's a braggart who hits on a lot of women and thinks a lot of himself. I can definitely imagine him dealing drugs. But we'd still need some connection to Trillium College and Third Line."

He eased the truck to a stop at an intersection.

"Can't tell you much about Milo," he added, "except that he's studying electrical engineering and is really into fixing and building things. He's very quiet and keeps to himself."

"Do, you think Nicole could be Trilly?" she asked.

"Honestly, I think the idea of a fellow cop calling you to report that she knows of a secret drug cover-up is too good to be true," he admitted. Snow crunched beneath the tires. "But it's very possible. Maybe another cop is working with the drug dealers, or being bribed to look the other way, or is somehow compromised by the payara investigation. She could be afraid of the damage it will do to her career if she reports a superior officer. I know you're afraid that if Butler is found to be corrupt they're going to reopen and reexamine all the old cases you worked on together. But, trust me, you can't underestimate the amount of damage a single bad apple can do."

"In my experience, actual bad apples are so rare they're almost a myth," Chloe said. "Cops are human. People make mistakes. But have you ever actually met a rotten-to-the-core cop who used their position to break the law?"

His mouth twisted into a grimace. Knew one? One of his cover identities had meant pretending to be one. "You don't think Frank Butler would bungle an investigation to protect Brandon?"

Chloe stared out through the windshield. "The Frank Butler I served under was a stone-cold sergeant who'd send his own grandson to jail."

Trent lapsed into silence again. Whatever she'd said to trigger him this time, their conversation was over again for now. She glanced at him sideways.

When she'd first met Trent, it had been in the middle of summer. He'd been undercover with the Wolfspiders and had met her in a dingy roadside diner to pass off information he'd gathered from Uncle. His black hair had been buzzed short that day and soaked with sweat. The strong lines of his form had been perfectly framed by a plain white T-shirt that cut across his broad chest and muscular shoulders, like something carved out of marble.

Trent had looked like danger then. It had radiated from him in every move and every glance. He'd looked like the kind of man she'd have to be on her defenses against. The kind who'd pull a gun on her the moment her guard was down. The kind she'd inevitably find herself tossing to the ground and handcuffing before carting him off the jail. His current beard and toque softened him. It made him look like the kind of caring man who'd hold a steady job, make sure the bills got paid, remember to empty the dishwasher and play with the kids after school. It made Trent look like the kind of man she'd never thought she'd ever have in her life, let alone a future with.

A sign welcoming them to Bobcaygeon appeared ahead. Trent navigated the main streets, until he reached Trillium Community College. The building was smaller than she remembered. It was brown and flat, spread out in three rectangles, with a parking lot to the side and a forest to the back. How had she felt about starting courses here? Determined. Like Trillium was just one more challenge she'd needed to get through to be where she wanted to be.

Trent's hand brushed her shoulder. "Ready?"

"Absolutely." She met his eyes. So what if shivers were moving through her arms again? She could handle shivers. "We've got this."

The afternoon passed in an unending series of seemingly unremarkable encounters. She'd showed her fake engagement ring off to the staff in the office and hung on Trent's arm when they'd paused to grab coffee in the staff room. She'd sat in the very back of the room at his first lecture and listened as Trent talked about how the body reacted to adrenaline and danger. His facts were bang on and all stuff they'd learn at the academy. But his delivery was dry, stilted even. She'd never known Trent to be anything close to stilted.

She'd spotted Poppy in the second row, in a clump of Trillium players that included Hodge, Aidan and the shortest of the third-line players, who she knew by the process of elimination had to be Milo. But besides a sunny smile from Poppy and quick hello from the players, none of them had wanted to stick around to chat.

First class was followed by a quick trip through the cafeteria, where she spotted Lucy in the corner, curled up by herself with a textbook on perfume and cosmetics. Chloe waved. Lucy smiled shyly and waved back. Yes, Chloe remembered hiding in the corner to study all too well.

Milo was also in Trent's next lecture, as were a clump of first-and second-line players, although she noticed that Milo didn't sit anywhere near them. Once again, while technically accurate, Trent's delivery was so awkward it was like he was a robot who'd never spoken to people before. He wasn't connecting. Most of the class wasn't even listening. It was beyond baffling. How could a man of such endless talents and irresistible personality be so terrible at talking to students?

Class finished. Students fled the room and new students filed in, like two currents moving at once. Trent tossed his arm lightly around her shoulder. His face bent toward her. "See anything interesting?"

"Plenty." She smiled benignly as he planted a light kiss on her cheek. "Nothing suspicious."

"Well, let's get out of here." His voice rose to a normal level. "I've just got to grab my stuff and then let's head to Nanny's Diner. I don't know about you, but I'm starving."

They navigated the hallways and he steered her into an office barely larger than a walk-in closet, with a large glass door looking out into the hallway on one side and a huge glass window looking out into the trees on the other. There, on his desk, sat their picture. They were standing on a ski gondola, with snowy, tree-lined slopes spread out beneath them. His arms were around her waist. She was leaning back into the strength of his chest. The smiles on their lips and twinkles in their eyes were so convincing they looked to anyone like a real couple in love. It was all so fake. Yet looked so real. Right down to the piece of costume jewelry on her finger.

"How are you holding up?" Trent's voice was soft behind her. Then she felt the warmth of his hands on her shoulders as his strong fingers squeezed the knots and tension from her muscles.

"I'm good." She stepped forward, out of his hands, and turned around. The office was so small she was practically sitting against the desk with her knees inches from his legs. "Nothing major that stands out. But, to be honest, today was all about maintaining our cover before I meet up with Trilly tonight. I'm really pinning all my hopes on what happens at the hockey game." Maybe Trent would be more engaged with the players then and less like the stiff and awkward oddity she'd seen in front of the class.

"You're frowning," Trent said. "You had that same pained look on your face when I was teaching. Care explaining why?"

He was looking at her intently and she was torn between the desire to be honest and the desire to be polite. She knew which one Trent would prefer. "Your choice on how to play Coach Henri was really odd to me. It wasn't anything like any other cover I'd ever seen you do before."

"Well, of course. Because Coach Travis Henri is a college professor and hockey coach. He doesn't have a shaved head and a motorcycle, with an illegal-looking shotgun on the back."

"He's boring and stiff," she said. His eyes widened. "And that has nothing to do with the fact that he's a professor. I know you, Trent. I've seen how many incarnations of you so far? Four? Five? And you know what each of them had in common? They were likable. They were dynamic. But, Coach Henri—"

"Is boring." He finished the sentence for her.

"Well, maybe I wouldn't want to put it that bluntly—"

"You just did."

She ran both hands through her hair and felt her elbows graze his folded arms. "You said yourself that you had trouble connecting with people on this assignment and getting the players to trust you."

His brow furrowed. His mouth opened.

The window behind her exploded.

Chapter Seven

Glass showered the room around them. Trent pulled her into his arms and spun her around. They hit the floor. She landed on her elbows and knees. Trent crouched over her, one arm around her waist and the other on her shoulder, cradling her and sheltering her with his body. Freezing wind whipped at them through the broken window. She glanced back, past Trent's forearm. The window had completely shattered.

"You okay?" he asked softly. His fingers touched the back of her neck. It was comforting and protective.

"Yeah, I'm fine," she said. Except for the fact that her heart was racing. He'd grabbed her, reached for her, sheltered her and pulled her from danger. She flexed her legs to stand.

"Hang on. Don't move." Trent's deep voice filled her ear. He braced himself with one hand, slid his other hand into his pocket and pulled out a leather glove. He tugged it on with his teeth and then picked something up off the floor. He held it so she could see it. "See this?"

She looked down. A smooth, symmetrical white stone lay in his palm, wet from the snow. Smudged words were scrawled on the surface in black marker that was quickly running into an illegible smear.

Mind your own business or your fiancé dies!

Someone was threatening to kill Trent? She nodded. He slid the rock into his pocket. Then he stood, and she let him pull her to her feet.

Jagged edges of glass stood around the window frame. The tree-lined lot was empty. Whoever had pitched the rock through the window had bolted. On the other side of them, a handful of students now stood around the office doorway, although Chloe was amused to see that even more were moving past blithely. Most of the students who had noticed the broken glass were now taking pictures with their phones.

"Now, everyone step back!" Trent said. "Don't want anybody cutting themselves. Can somebody run and let the office know what happened? They're going to want to call the police and send down Maintenance." Students stepped back. A few were typing on their phones, but none were specifically dialing. Then she noticed the young man, with a thin frame and serious eyes, slip away at the back of the crowd. She glanced at Trent. He'd noticed him, too.

"Hey, Brandon!"

The young man froze and, for a moment, she thought he was about to bolt. Instead he took a step toward them. "Hey, Coach! What happened to the window?"

"Somebody threw a rock through it!" Trent said. "Just glad nobody was hurt. Can you do me a huge favor and call your grandfather?"

Brandon hesitated. His eyes darted from the floor

to the broken window and then back to the floor again. "You don't have to call him, though, right? You can just call the division and they'll send a regular cop."

Was it her imagination or was sweat actually forming on the young man's brow?

"Well, somebody should call the police, right?" Trent's arm slid around Chloe's shoulder. "Your grandfather worked with Chloe years ago, so I figured he might want to handle it personally."

Trent pulled her in for a hug. But she could tell in an instant that he was doing so to position himself so that they could whisper without being heard. Yes, this kind of Trent hug she knew well and had experienced before. It was all tactics and no warmth, unlike the confusing way his fingers had touched her skin after the home invasion. Trent rested his head on top of hers. She tucked her head into his neck.

"They used an erasable whiteboard marker on a wet rock," he said softly. "The rock is from one of the planters out front. The marker could be from any classroom. It's a total crime of opportunity." She could hear the frown in his voice. "Thankfully, it gives us an opportunity for you to talk to Butler about the payara situation, and judge where he's at with that for yourself. Certainly, I think something's off with him. But you might disagree. When he gets here, I'll talk to him and then I'll make myself scarce while you talk to him. We can compare notes afterward."

"Sounds good." A sigh of relief filled her body and she found herself moving deeper into Trent's chest before she caught herself and pulled back.

Trent detangled himself and walked over to talk to Brandon. By the sound of things, Brandon still hadn't called the police but was reluctantly agreeing to give Trent his grandfather's cell phone number.

Chloe turned back to the glass-strewed office. A silent prayer of thanks crossed her lips. She was more than grateful Trent had suggested she talk to Butler alone. She was almost surprised at the thoughtfulness of it. A larger task force would inevitably be formed to investigate the payara situation in the future, even if Butler didn't face an internal affairs investigation.

Trent's undercover mission into the third-line players was just the first step of a much broader and larger operation that would be launched. Her conversation with the staff sergeant after the Gulos' attack on the sports center had been rushed. Her top priority had been protecting Trent's cover, even though she barely understood it, so her own reasons for being there had fallen completely by the wayside. But now, thanks to a rock through the window and its hastily scrawled message, she had the opportunity to have a real conversation with her former training officer about the whole situation without threatening Trent's investigation.

"Clo?" Trent's hand brushed her shoulder. She turned. He was holding out his cell phone. His brow furrowed and she could tell by the set of his jaw that he was working at finding the right words to say. "I'm going to head to the front office and fill them in on what's going on. Brandon's grandfather says filing a report over the phone is fine for vandalism. But I wondered if you wanted to talk to him, too? You know, cop to cop."

Really? Trent handed her the phone. She took it. "Hello, Staff Sergeant Butler?"

"Detective Brant." The older officer's voice was

rushed and breathless, like he'd been interrupted while running on a treadmill. "I understand you want to talk to me about the vandalism at Trillium College?"

She stepped deeper into Trent's office. Glass crunched under her feet. Cold air stung her skin.

"It goes much deeper than that, Sir," she said. "Are you free at all this afternoon? I'd really appreciate being able to talk to you about it in person."

"It's my day off, Detective. My grandson should never have given his coach my personal number. A vandalism report can be filed directly with the division. I hope you have a nice day—"

"But, Sir, it was a threat. There was a warning written on the rock. The words were pretty smudged but I was able to make them out."

"What did it say?" he asked. Was it her imagination or had his tone grown sharper?

"'Mind your own business or your fiancé dies,'" she said.

"Mind your own business about what?"

She didn't know. But it wasn't a big stretch to presume it had something to do with the payara and maybe even her secretive informant, Trilly.

"I don't know for sure, but I suspect the fact that I cleared out the Gulos from the sports center yesterday has something to do with it. It was clear they were looking for payara." She waited for him to answer. Instead a long pause waited on the phone line. "Look, Sir. It's no secret that a baggie of payara was found in the sports center a few months ago. Rumors are swirling around other divisions that the investigation is stalled, and it's been leaked to the press. You and I have worked together well in the past, I know this area well and I'm already on the ground. I'd like to be considered for a transfer to work on this case or at least to be more involved in the investigation of what happened yesterday."

Another pause filled the line. Suddenly a memory came back to her mind of standing awkwardly in a small meeting room as Butler reprimanded her sternly and at length for some minor mistake she'd made. He hadn't ever been a warm man when they'd worked together. He'd been downright cold at times. But he'd been incredibly professional, his standards had been high, and at that time in her life she'd appreciated that.

"Thank you for your offer, Detective," Butler said, "but I assure you all of our active cases are well staffed within the division, and I'm not in the habit of commenting on ongoing investigations. Have a good afternoon."

The call ended. She turned back. Trent was gone, but Brandon still stood there, one arm crossed in front of his chest. "Coach said he'd meet you in the head office. I'll show you the way."

"Thank you," she said.

He walked with her to the office, in silence, his lanky form dipping with each step like he was self-consciously trying to shrink. She tried to do some quick mental math to figure out how old he must've been when she'd worked with his grandfather. Six maybe? Seven? Yet none of her memories of Butler had included pictures of his grandchildren on his desk, or a small family visiting the office. "I worked with your grandfather a long time ago. He was a good man to train under. He was very hard on rookies."

Brandon nodded. "He has pretty high standards, yeah."

The question was, had her standards been too low?

Had she been so eager for her life to have some order and structure that all it had taken to win her admiration was a cold demeanor and strict dedication to the rules?

She found Trent in the head office talking to a slender, blond, uniformed cop.

"Constable Docker, right?"

"Call me Nicole." She turned. "Nice to see you again."

"That was fast." Chloe reached out to shake her hand before realizing it was holding an evidence bag containing the white, smudged rock.

"Oh, I was just around the corner when the call came in." Guilt flickered in Nicole's eyes, so quickly it was almost unnoticeable. Guilt about what? What was around the corner from Trillium exactly besides the sports center?

Chloe smiled and nodded, then stood back to let Nicole take their statements.

It was her first real, hard look at her beyond a very quick introduction they'd had at the sports center yesterday, when Chloe had been looking for Butler. She'd have pegged Nicole to be in her early twenties. The rookie cop had curly blond hair scraped back into a ponytail at the nape of her neck and the kind of bright blue eyes Chloe had longed for as a preteen.

"If you're free, I'd love to grab a coffee and talk more," Chloe said. "Staff Sergeant Butler was my training officer when I was a rookie, too. I'm sure we have a lot in common."

Was it her imagination or did slight panic flicker in Nicole's eyes?

"I'm sure you would both enjoy that." Trent's arm slid over Chloe's shoulder. "But sadly, my fiancée and

I have to hurry over to Nanny's Diner. The whole team is waiting for us. Maybe you two gals can meet up at the game." He practically steered Chloe out of the office and toward the front door.

The winter sun sunk low in a pale gray sky. Their footsteps crunched across the snow-covered parking lot. His head bent toward hers. "I appreciate your impulse to chase leads, Detective. But for today you're my fiancée, and we are on a very tight timeline. Not showing up at Nanny's for the team meal would raise some pretty major eyebrows." They reached his truck. He slid his arm off her shoulder and opened her door for her. "If it's any help, I did find out she's single."

Chloe felt her eyebrows rise. "How did you find that out?"

Trent chuckled and walked around to his side of the truck. He whistled something musical under his breath. If he was trying to make her jealous by implying Nicole had asked him out, it wasn't going to work. But that would explain why she'd looked vaguely guilty. He hopped into the driver's side and looked at her. She had no idea what the expression on her face was, but whatever it was made him laugh.

"Don't worry. I'd never date a cop who tried to arrest me without first reading me my rights." He draped his hand over the back of her seat and backed up. "Even if she had, I don't have time for a girlfriend. I simply don't date or do relationships."

An odd heaviness settled into the pit of her stomach. She wasn't sure why. Trent had never showed any interest in dating her, with the one notable exception of the coffee date that wasn't. Surely the knowledge he didn't date anybody at all would make her feel better.

"I spoke to Staff Sergeant Butler," she said. "It was disappointing. I asked him if I could assist on the payara case, and he was curt. But I still don't like thinking he's a bad cop. His standards were insanely high. I can't imagine he'd be open to blackmail or greed, or allow corruption in his ranks."

"You can't make blanket statements about bad cops. Like you said, cops are human and make mistakes." Trent pulled onto the road and drove. His hand remained on the back of her seat. His fingertips brushed the back of her neck. "But I wouldn't blame you for being miffed that he wouldn't come down to the college. Your life was threatened, after all."

"Miffed?" She pushed his hand off her seat back, feeling the tension his hand had begun to brush away snap back with a vengeance. "Trent, I'm a cop. I've had my life threatened more times than I can count, in far more disturbing and graphic ways. Besides, it was your life that was threatened. Not mine. Even with the marker smudges, it was pretty clear they wrote 'fiancé' with one *e*, not two."

"Because criminals are such great spellers," he said. "They threw the rock in my office window—"

"When we were both in clear view of the window. I haven't left your side all day, so it's not like it would be easy to threaten me alone. I'm the cop. You're the mild-mannered hockey coach."

"You left out 'boring,'" he added.

"I'm sorry if using that word bothered you," she said. "But you were incredibly awkward and uncomfortable just being in that lecture hall."

He didn't answer. Instead he just stared straight

ahead, with both hands on the steering wheel, as they drove through the small-town streets.

It had been an act, right? She'd seen him face down armed criminals without so much as breaking a sweat. So it was hard to imagine being in front of a classroom would intimidate him.

He pulled into the parking lot of Nanny's Diner. They got out of the truck and walked toward the blue-and-white-striped awnings.

Two people stood near the entrance, arguing by the look of things, and it took Chloe's eyes a moment to realize what she was really seeing.

Lucy stood in the doorway, dressed in a waitress's apron and holding two jugs of pop as if someone had called her to the door while she was waiting tables. A tall man with gray hair and a baseball cap was talking to her, his hands shaking in the air and his voice a low hiss. It was clear whatever he was saying was upsetting her almost to the point of tears.

What was this? Chloe's footsteps quickened, feeling Trent match pace.

"As long as I'm paying for your schooling, young lady, you're staying in Bobcaygeon and going to Trillium, and that's final!" The elderly man's voice rose.

Chloe's heartbeat stuttered. It was Frank Butler. The staff sergeant didn't seem to notice their approach. "I don't care how many letters you get that university in Vancouver to send about deferring your acceptance. You are not going. Makeup making or perfume mixing, or whatever it is you call it, is a garbage waste of an education and I'm not throwing my good money away on it! Period."

"Good afternoon, Frank," Trent said loudly. Their

footsteps paused in the snow. Then his voice dropped softly. "Hi, Lucy."

Lucy looked up nervously and the tears in the young woman's eyes shook something inside Chloe's chest. Had her former training officer always been so volatile?

Frank turned and stumbled as his foot slipped in the snow.

"Afternoon," he said and nodded curtly without meeting their eyes. The unmistakable stench of liquor rose from his breath. He walked off.

Lucy paused for a moment, turned and bolted into the diner. The door swung shut behind her.

Chloe turned to Trent. "I had no idea Butler drank. Did you?"

"No, I didn't." Trent's head shook. "But, the only time I saw him out of uniform was at hockey games and I kept enough of a distance not to notice the smell of whatever was in his thermos."

He sighed. If Butler had a drinking problem, it would certainly go a long way in explaining how he'd botched a crucial investigation and why he was so jittery. Despite what Chloe might've hoped, an internal investigation would be for the best, especially if it got the staff sergeant the help he needed.

Trent turned to Chloe and reached for her hand, ready to walk with her into the diner. To his surprise, as his fingers brushed hers, he could feel her shaking beneath his touch. He pulled her close.

"Are you okay?" he asked quietly.

"I just can't believe I never saw it," Chloe said. "My father was the same. He was one way in public and another in private. I could never understand how he fooled people. But he was very charming and outgoing, and Butler was this cold, hard stickler for rules…" Her voice trailed off.

"Listen to me," he said, "everybody has ugly and unpleasant parts of themselves that they try not to show to the wider world. It's possible Butler might not have been like that when you worked with him. Sometimes grief hits people hard. Or early onset dementia can cause angry outbursts and emotional issues. You can't know. We shouldn't guess without knowing more. And you definitely can't blame yourself for not knowing."

Even though he could tell that, in a way, she was.

Lord, I don't know what she's lived through or what battles she's fighting on the inside. Please, heal her heart. Please, help me help her.

She met his eyes and smiled weakly. There was a slight quiver to her lips that made something thud inside his chest.

"Maybe," she said. "I'm just suddenly doubting everything I thought I knew about him. Sometimes when you've seen the very worst side of someone it changes everything and there's no going back from that."

Yeah, that's what he was afraid of.

They pushed through the door to the diner. His hand was still loosely holding hers and he told himself it was all for the sake of his cover and not because of how comfortably her palm fit into his.

He scanned the room. Most of the Trillium hockey players were crammed into three large, yellow-vinyl booths in their usual place at the far side of the wall.

Aidan looked up and waved. There was an unmistakable tension in the third-line center's face, and he wasn't the only member of the team who was scowling. What was that all about? Trent waved back. Then he leaned toward Chloe and whispered, "Game time."

They started across the floor through the tables. But they'd barely taken five steps when a burst of arrogant laughter to his right made his head turn. He frowned.

A couple of the Haliburton players were lounging at a tall table by the jukebox, cracking jokes under their breath and tossing glances in his players' direction.

The Haliburton coach was a foulmouthed man who'd never really done much to encourage sportsmanlike behavior from his players, as far as Trent could see. It wasn't the first time a couple of players from their rival team had wandered into Nanny's before a game looking to psych his players out and goad them into a fight, or even just to test how long they could hang out and talk nonsense before Eli got frustrated and kicked them out.

It was an immature posturing thing that had been going on for far longer than Trent had been on the scene, and he got the impression that with the number of regional hockey teams that bussed in to practice at the Bobcaygeon rink and college students from neighboring towns that drove over to work out at the elite sports center, Eli couldn't exactly afford to refuse to serve them all. Trent was just thankful his guys were usually too good to take the bait.

"That's Johnny." Chloe gestured subtly to the blond jock. "He's the guy who was in the exercise room yesterday with Poppy."

He nodded. "I figured. The other player's the Haliburton goalie. His name is George."

The ice cubes rattled in Lucy's jug as she poured pop into their glasses. George ran his eyes over her and snickered. It was an ugly sound. Then Johnny leaned over and whispered something in Lucy's ear. Her cheeks went crimson.

"Hey, Johnny!" The tone in Chloe's voice told Trent she'd noticed the interaction, too. "I see you made it out safe and sound yesterday."

"Detective!" He stood and glanced at her hand holding Trent's. "You didn't tell me you had a boyfriend."

There was a hint of reproach in his voice. Trent didn't much like the sound of it. But at least now Lucy had stepped away from them and moved on to another table.

Trent leaned his head toward Chloe, keeping his mouth close enough to her ear that they were unlikely to be overheard. "Do you want me to handle this?"

Chloe snorted and shook her head. "No. Thanks. Let me. After all, he might have seen something, yesterday." She pulled her hand out of his and stepped toward the Haliburton players.

"Coach Henri is my fiancé, actually," Chloe said. "I hope all that chaos at the sports center didn't throw you off your game. I'm looking forward to seeing our team beat yours fair and square."

A smattering of laughter came from the Trillium players.

Johnny's eyebrow quirked.

Trent grit his teeth as he felt something fierce and protective rise up inside him. He didn't like the way this student, fifteen years his junior, was looking at Chloe.

God, I know I should ignore him, just like I always tell my players to. I promised Chloe that I wouldn't fight her fights for her. And if I tell a college student off for looking at Chloe the wrong way, I'm going to end up looking like a possessive jerk in her eyes.

"You sure she's a cop?" George pivoted in his seat. "She doesn't look that tough to me."

"Oh, yeah." Johnny sniggered, like he didn't believe it, either. "Apparently she took down a knife-wielding gang member in an elf mask."

"Her?" The goalie looked Chloe up and down. "Nah, that didn't happen. What she do? Throw her purse at him?"

So, this was what it was like being a female officer. Sure, Trent had heard the stories from women he'd served alongside about dealing with a steady stream of disrespect from stupid punks, but still he'd never gotten over the shock of seeing it firsthand.

George slid off his seat, grabbed a dull butter knife off the table and waved it around theatrically, like a bad television ninja, complete with sound effects. "Watch out, girlie. I'm a mean gang elf and I'm coming to stab you!"

A grin turned on Chloe's lips. She stepped forward, knocked the knife from the young man's grasp with one hand and caught his wrist with the other. Then she spun him around, twisting his arm behind his back and forcing him down until he was kneeling on the floor.

The Haliburton goalie swore and looked up at Trent. "Tell her to let go!"

"You'll have to talk to her. I don't tell her what to do." Trent chuckled. He could hear a smattering of laughter and the murmur of gasps coming from the Trillium players. "Looked to me like you just threatened to stab a cop in front of a room full of witnesses."

"Coach Henri!" Eli rushed through the diner toward them. "What is going on? I was on the phone and suddenly one of the waitresses comes rushing into the office in saying there's a fight about to break out."

Chloe let go of the goalie. He scowled, stood and stuffed his hands into his pockets.

"Not a fight," Trent said. "One of the Haliburton players was acting foolish and waving a knife around. My fiancée stepped in before the situation could escalate."

Eli nodded to Chloe. "Thank you."

She smiled. "No problem."

Trent stepped back and watched as Eli escorted Johnny and George from the diner. The chorus of Trillium players laughing and clapping behind them seemed to be growing. Then, to his surprise, Chloe threw her arms around him and hugged him tightly. His hands slid about her waist.

"That was fun," she whispered. "Thank you."

"For what?" he asked. "For letting you take down some arrogant college kid? You asked me to let you handle it, so I did."

"I know." She looked up into his eyes. Something sparkled there, like happiness mingled with gratitude. "I also know just how badly you were itching to jump in and take over. It was written all over your face."

Well, he'd made the right decision by the sound of it. The applause had turned into a thunderous wave of students stomping on the floor and banging on the tables. Her hands slid up around his neck. He found himself pulling her closer into his chest. "I think they're chanting for me to kiss you."

"Do you think you should?" she asked.

They were still whispering, her face just inches from his, although he was certain nobody would be able to make out their words over the sound of the racket his players were making. He could feel his heart beating like a drum in his chest, matching the rhythm of the percussion around him.

"Maybe. If that's okay with you."

What are you doing? the voice of logic shouted in his head, struggling to be heard.

They were on an undercover mission. Yes, they were pretending to be a couple. But the desire to kiss her was stronger than that. He wanted to kiss her for real. Like she was really his. And he was really hers. He couldn't let himself get emotionally compromised like that. Not by her. Not now. Not ever.

She bit her lip, just a little. Then she nodded. "Yeah, I think that's okay."

Her fingers brushed the back of his neck and curled through his hair. He pulled her close. His lips met hers and he kissed her.

Chapter Eight

Kissing Chloe was like coming home to a place where he'd always hoped to belong. He felt her kiss him back, sweetly and gently. The clapping turned into a roar of applause. Hands banged on the table like the beat of dozens of drums. He could even hear some of his players whistling.

Then Chloe pulled away, ending the kiss. She hugged him, tucking her head into that old familiar and practiced spot on his neck that meant she wanted to talk without being overheard and suddenly the full weight of what he'd done hit him. For the first time, in his entire life, he'd kissed someone not because he'd felt obligated to, or because it was what his cover identity would do, but because he'd wanted to. He tilted his head toward her, thankful for the wall of noise because it would hide his words. "I hope that was okay."

Her breath tickled his ear. "It was the right thing for Coach Henri to do."

But was it the right thing for Detective Trent Henry to do?

She pulled out of his arms, brushed a quick kiss on

the scruff of his cheek and sat down in the booth. She flushed, smiling, and waved her hands at the players. "Oh, you guys are being ridiculous! It's like you've never seen a man kiss his fiancée before."

Laughter rippled through the room. Trent sat down. Milo reached across the table and shook her hand. Aidan flashed Chloe a thumbs-up. "I can't believe you took George down like that!"

She laughed. "It was nothing. People like him and Johnny are all bark and no bite."

Eli came over and thanked her. Lucy brought a platter of wings to the table. Then it was like something broke in the air and the players all started talking at once. Watching Chloe take down the rival goalie in the middle of the diner had somehow chipped a hole in the invisible barrier that had always stood between him and the four of them.

Milo told a ridiculous story about trying to talk his way out of a driving ticket when he was fifteen and had borrowed his older brother's car without permission even though he didn't have a license.

Aidan started teasing Hodge about dating Poppy.

Brandon stopped checking his phone.

Conversation flew around the booth as smoothly and easily as a well-passed puck and, for the first time since taking on his cover, he felt like he was really getting to know who these young men were.

When the wings were done and the players started filing out, Trent helped Chloe into her coat and they walked outside. His arm slid around her shoulder again, effortlessly and almost unconsciously, as they walked to his truck. He opened the door for her again, they got in and he peeled out of the parking lot, thankful for the few minutes they'd get alone before they reached the sports center.

"I feel like I should thank you," he said. "I don't know how you did it. Those young men opened up more to you tonight than they ever have to me."

"They felt like I had their back and that I was one of them." She leaned against the seat, looking far more exhausted than he'd expected her to feel. "I don't blame them for being suspicious of people, especially outsiders. If you're right, at least one of them committed a major crime having that much payara in his possession, and at least some of the others are covering for him. If Aidan's involved, it could cost him his scholarship. Hodge already has a record. And judging from how we saw Butler yell at Lucy, I can't blame Brandon for wanting to keep his head down. They have no reason to trust me, you or anyone. They need to know that we have their back and that we're on their side. Or, at least, that we're willing to listen and hear their side of the story."

She was right, of course. He'd even go so far as to say that many of the criminals he met had gone through childhood traumas as bad, or even worse, than the murder of his sister, and talking to them about how he'd gotten lured into petty crime by Royd and snared by the Wolfspiders had helped get them to trust him. But what could he say that would possibly connect with these bright and shiny college students?

I've always hated school, so it feels like I'm suffocating every time I walk into Trillium. I have three amazing brothers and two incredible parents, who I think have all given up on me. I used to have a sister, too, but she was strangled to death by some creep when I was thirteen, because I was hanging behind the school with idiot Wolfspiders when I was supposed to be walking her home...

Her hand lay in the empty space between them just resting on the edge of the console. He resisted the temptation to reach for it. The kiss at the diner had been too real, at least for him. But she'd kissed Coach Henri. She hadn't kissed the real him. Like she'd said, once she knew his entire ugly story, there'd be no going back.

He pulled into the sports center parking lot. "I'm going to suggest we split up," he said. "I'll go be with the players. You hang out in the stands. See if you can strike up a conversation with Nicole. I'll keep an eye on the clock once the third period starts. When you slip out, I'll give you exactly fifteen minutes to either text or reappear. Anything longer than that, I'm putting Eli in charge and coming out. Okay?"

"Got it," Chloe said. "Hopefully, Trilly will come through for us and in a few quick hours we'll have enough information to pass it up the chain of command, they'll form a task force and authorize a raid and then it will be out of our hands."

"Agreed." And then what? Then he'd assume another cover identity and plunge into specialized mining operation training for his next investigation, before flying off to the remote mine in the Arctic, and he'd be stuck figuring out how to say goodbye to Chloe again. His phone started to ring. He glanced down at the name on the screen. Jacob.

"Who's Jacob?" Chloe asked.

"The guy I told you about with RCMP Criminal Investigations. I should take it."

"Understood." Chloe brushed her lips over his cheek, in a gesture he was certain was for the benefit of the gaggle of players and students already gathering in the sports center parking lot, and hopped out of the truck. He tried not to watch the swing of her hair brushing her back as she walked away.

Then he answered the phone. "Hey, bro. What's the news?"

"All good," Jacob said. "Everyone on the team who's processing the cell phone and Detective Brant's house is aboveboard and someone I'd professionally vouch for. If there is a corrupt element impacting your case, it won't come from within our part of the police world."

Thank You, God. Trent sighed and leaned back against the seat. "Thanks, I appreciate it."

"No problem," his brother said. "Mom and Dad are wondering when you're arriving at the farm. The rest of us are here already and tomorrow's Christmas Eve."

Not that Trent needed the reminder. "I'll be there for dinner on Christmas Day."

"Then you're going to disappear." Jacob said it like it was a statement of fact.

So much for thinking they were going to save this argument until Christmas. Then again, the eldest Henry brother had always been the family peacemaker.

"I've spent my whole professional life fighting gang crime," Trent said. "I'm running around out here, cutting the heads off snakes, only to have six more grow back in their place before I can even turn around. If a diamond mine is funneling money into organized crime, and I can take it out, I'll be chopping down the Wolfspiders, the Gulos and countless other gangs at the roots."

"Those were some impressively mixed metaphors." Jacob chuckled. "But, seriously, why does it have to be you?" Sounded like he really was getting the prefight out before he had to explain it to the folks. Maybe it was Jacob's way of helping.

"Because I'm good at what I do, and I have no relationship entanglements." Not to mention he was really good at closing doors and walking away. "The tech crew is already erasing any trace of me online. I have no digital footprint. The mining company can search my picture online all they'll want and they'll never find me. I'm off the grid. I don't exist. I'll be cut off from the world up there, and I'll be watched constantly. They'll invent a fake relationship for me, a parent most likely, and send me carefully crafted messages from that person with cyphers hidden inside incase of emergencies."

"I know. I looked into that, too," Jacob said. Trent could almost hear him nodding. "Sounds like an impressive investigation. I just know what Mom and Dad are going to say and your voice sounded a bit off when we last talked. I want to make sure that you're sure."

"Of course I'm sure. We can talk a lot more at Christmas. But right now I've got to go."

"Got it," his brother said. "If you need anything, feel free to call."

"Thanks." The call ended. He put his game face on and walked into the sports center, feeling an odd and uneasy ache in his chest. He blamed Jacob. Sure, his older brother meant well, but it wasn't exactly helpful to have him planting doubt in his mind. In a few hours the case would be over, he'd be saying goodbye to Chloe again and she'd never know just how many nights he'd probably end up lying awake on his bunk at night, listening to the sound of dozens of burly men snoring, missing her face.

Trent found the team in the locker room, abuzz with

fresh energy and enthusiasm. As much as he enjoyed it, he couldn't help thinking Chloe was the reason why.

They stood in a circle, Trent stuck his hand in the middle of the huddle and they all piled their hands on top. Then the team hit the ice with more hustle than they ever had before. But only half of his mind was on the game. The other half kept glancing up to the stands, instinctively seeking out Chloe's face. She was sitting one row behind Nicole, who was in uniform and with a young male officer. Chloe had somehow also acquired a Trillium College team banner. She waved it at him. He waved back.

Then Chloe glanced at her phone. Her brow furrowed. She gestured to the exit, he nodded, and she slipped out of her seat and disappeared behind the stands. Where was she going? She wasn't supposed to meet the informant until the third period and the game had barely started. A shout broke out from the bench. He spun back just in time to see Hodge haul himself over the boards and pelt across the ice into the middle of a face-off, like a cue ball shooting across the table.

"Hodge, what are you doing?" Trent bellowed. "Get back here!"

But his words were swallowed up in a chant of "Fight! Fight! Fight!" erupting from the stands as Hodge ploughed into Johnny.

Hodge grabbed Johnny by the jersey and yanked him sideways as Johnny's fist ploughed into the side of his head. The ref's whistle blew. Eli and the coach from the opposing team were already pelting toward the scrum. Aidan, Brandon and Milo were tumbling over the boards, too, yelling at Hodge to stop.

Trent grabbed the boards and leaped over after them,

feeling automatic prayers for wisdom cross his heart as he strode across the ice. *Lord, what's happening? I've always known Hodge had issues. But to lose it like this in the middle of a game?*

Johnny was punching back as good as he got, pummeling Hodge with a blistering force that was all brute strength and no skill. A crowd was forming now as parents, refs and coaches tried to pull them apart. Players on both teams exchanged pushes and insults as the energy seemed to spread.

Trent grabbed Hodge by the collar with one hand and Johnny with the other and physically yanked them apart. Then he straightened his arms, giving just enough torque on the back of their jerseys to make sure they felt the pinch, and marched them to the penalty boxes. He'd broken up wilder fights with killers twice their size. They were just fortunate he didn't knock their helmeted heads together. He tossed the guys into opposing penalty boxes.

"Sit!" he ordered. Johnny glared at Hodge. Hodge stared at the ground. Trent could hear Eli, still out on the ice, now bellowing at the other team's coach and the ref. Third-line players skated up and leaned over the boards, waving something at Hodge and yelling. Poppy, Lucy and a handful of other students had run around the stands and yelled at them from the other side, leaving him stuck in the middle.

He didn't have the patience for this level of angst and hormones. His eyes rolled to the stands and Chloe's empty seat. Where was his fake fiancée when he needed her? He just had to pray her meeting with Trilly was going better than this. His eyes locked on Hodge.

Hodge's pupils were so large his eyes seemed to bulge. "What did you take? What are you on?"

"Nothing!" Hodge spluttered. "Johnny kissed Poppy! Somebody posted it to social media!"

Johnny swore. "You're a lunatic."

Trent was almost tempted to agree. He'd charged into the middle of a hockey face-off and started throwing punches like a caveman because a known player had kissed his girlfriend? But Trent also didn't believe for a moment that Hodge was sober. Aggression, suggestibility and an adrenaline-like rush, Hodge was practically an advertisement for payara.

"I didn't kiss Johnny!" Poppy's voice rose to a wail. She bent over the railing and tried in vain to grab hold of Hodge's shoulder. "You've gotta believe me! We just work out together!"

Aidan launched himself over the boards almost vertically and pushed a cell into Hodge's hands. Hodge thrust it in Poppy's face.

"Then explain this!" he demanded. A picture filled the screen that sure did look like Johnny and Poppy locking lips. "Why did somebody post this?"

Why did anybody take it? Trent shook his head.

"That's not me!" Poppy shouted. "Someone Photoshopped a picture of Johnny kissing somebody else to look like me and then posted it online!"

"Oh, yeah, that's really logical." Hodge tried to stand. Trent pushed him back down. "Why would somebody do that?"

"Because they're a troll, you're rival teams and they're trying to cause chaos," Trent said. It had worked, too. But was that all it was? A fight had broken out on the ice while Chloe just happened to be meeting her informant, because someone had just happened to post a picture of the girlfriend of the worst hothead on his team kissing one of the opposing team's star players?

"Hodge and Johnny, stay here and don't move," he said. "Now, does anybody want to admit to doping Hodge with payara? Or, Hodge, do you want to admit it yourself?"

Hodge glared and shook his head. Nobody else met Trent's eye. Right.

"Who posted the picture?" he asked.

"I don't know." Hodge grunted.

"Somebody anonymous," Aidan said.

Of course. Trent turned to face the other players.

"Brandon, go grab Hodge's water bottle and bring it to me," he said. Brandon took off across the ice. "The rest of you, get back to your own bench and sit down. Aidan and Milo, I expect you to set an example. Lucy, take Poppy back to her seat. She can sort things out with Hodge after the game."

Brandon sprinted back with the water bottle. At a glance, Trent could see faint sediment swirling at the bottom.

"Brandon, I'm putting you in charge of that bottle. Hold on to it until Chloe can take it from you. Don't let anybody else so much as touch it until it can be tested by police. Hodge, you're going to need to take a drug test. When Eli stops pushing and shoving the opposing coach, tell him I'll be back in a minute."

He could hear voices clamoring behind him. He didn't look back. Instead, Trent sprinted through the risers, through the change rooms and into the hallway. He checked his phone again as his feet pounded down the hall. Nothing from Chloe. *Lord, please may I be wor-*

ried about nothing. He pressed his feet faster, prayers pushing through him with every step. He burst through the emergency exit door and out into the alley. But saw nothing, except garbage cans and piles of snow. *Help me, God. Where is she?*

Then he heard the sounds of a struggle and ran around the corner just in time to see Royd, the very same thug that had introduced him to the Wolfspiders so many years ago, hold a knife against Chloe's throat as he dragged her backward toward a van.

If he tried to stop Royd, his former friend would recognize him and his cover would be blown. But if he didn't, Chloe would die.

The knife pressed against her skin, threatening to end her life if she made one wrong move. A huge arm tightened over her chest, squeezing the oxygen from her lungs. Her eyes looked up to the snow-filled sky as her neck was forced upward by the prick of the blade digging into her skin. Desperate prayers filled her heart.

It was the same man who'd broken into her house and attacked her. She'd barely seen his face over her shoulder as he'd leaped on her from behind and jammed a weapon into her neck. But everything she'd suspected in the glance had been confirmed with terrifying certainty when she'd smelled the rancid odor of his breath and heard the same rough voice threatening that if she didn't hand over the Gulo's cell phone immediately, he'd take her somewhere remote and hurt her until she told him everything he wanted to know.

"Leave her alone!" Trent's voice seemed to rise on the bitter wind.

"Back off! Or I'll slit her throat right in front of you!"

"She's my woman, Royd!" Trent shouted. What was Trent doing? How did he know her kidnapper? She didn't know if he was blowing his cover just to save her life or because he knew he'd be recognized if he tried to help her. "Did Uncle really give you permission to off a Wolfspider's lady?"

"Trent?" Royd swore. His voice shook with disbelief and rage. "Nah, it can't be. I gotta be seeing things."

Confusion bordering on panic threatened to steal her breath from her lungs. How did this criminal know Trent's name? None of this made any sense. But she could also feel the knife had slipped an inch away from her skin. Barely more than a breath lay between her and the weapon. But it was all the space she needed.

Chloe jammed her thumbs between her throat and the knife handle, prying the blade away from her body just long enough to pivot sideways and wrench the knife from his grasp. They struggled for the knife, even as she could hear Trent's footsteps pelting across the ground toward them. She wrenched the blade from Royd's grasp. His fist made contact with her jaw, filling her eyes with stars and knocking her body to the ground. She fell hard on the frozen cement. Royd loomed over her. She kicked up at him, forcing him back. Trent's footsteps grew closer.

Royd hesitated. Then he turned and ran.

"Chloe!" Trent dropped to the pavement beside her. "Are you hurt?"

"No, I'm okay. Thanks." She gasped. "Trilly texted and said she needed to meet me right away. I ran outside and into a trap. Who is that man? Why does he know your name?"

"He's a Wolfspider I crossed paths with in the past."

Worry pooled in the depths of his eyes, making something ache inside her chest.

Something was wrong. Very wrong. The man who'd broken into her home was somebody Trent knew. The informant she'd planned to meet had turned out to be a trap.

Trent was still kneeling beside her in the snow. His fingers brushed her hair from her face and warmth filled her body. This whole mess had become intensely and dangerously personal. Trent had kissed her. He'd held her. She'd been emotionally compromised. She'd just been reminded yet again how little she knew Trent. And it had put her life in danger and blown his cover.

She shoved his hand away. "What are you doing? Go! Go after him! Don't let him get away!"

Trent blinked and it was like a switch had flicked inside his mind. Then he leaped to his feet and sprinted after Royd. "Stay back unless I give the signal! Stay out of sight if you can. Don't let him see you!"

"Will do." She stumbled to her feet and forced herself after him. Trent would need her for the arrest. He could hardly do so himself without blowing his cover.

Her body ached. Her head swam. She watched as Royd yanked a van door open and leaped in. She heard the sound of the engine turn over. Trent yanked him from the front seat and tossed him to the ground. Royd swung back hard, and then it was a battle of blows and limbs. She slipped around to the other side of the van, staying low and out of sight, hiding from Royd's gaze as Trent forced him to the icy ground.

"What are you doing here?" Trent pinned him there with his forearm over his throat. "What do you know about payara?"

Royd swore and barked out a laugh, like he was staring down something that was anything but funny. "I could ask you the same thing. Are you really involved with that cop?"

As she watched, it was like Trent's body transformed in front of her. His shoulders drew back wider. His jawline tightened and a colder, meaner look than she'd ever seen before filled his eyes. Did Trent know she was there, close and listening in? Surely he had to know she would be. "Don't make me ask you again. If we didn't have history together, I wouldn't be asking so nicely."

Royd's eyes narrowed. "I'm not talking till you tell me why you're with that cop."

"You mean instead of your sister?" Trent snapped. "Savannah and I are done!"

Who was Savannah? She crouched lower, thankful Royd hadn't noticed her.

He spat out another swear word. His eyes rolled back in his head. "So, you moved on to a cop? Come on, Trent. I know you. You gotta do better than that."

Trent leaned forward. His voice grew deeper, more dangerous. "My relationship with her is my business, not yours!"

Shouts filled the air behind them. She looked back. It looked like players and spectators were spilling from the building. How long until somebody walked through the parking lot enough to see Coach Henri pinning a man to the ground on the other side of the van? Royd laughed so hard he was spluttering. "O-oh, yeah, like I'm gonna believe you have a thing with Detective Brant. You think I didn't do my homework before I paid her a visit? She's fierce and she's totally clean. You're no way near at her level. You don't have the smarts to either turn or play somebody like her."

Trent's eyes grew dark. With one hand he shoved Royd back into the ground. The other swung back and his fist flew hard and fast at Royd so quickly the criminal's face went white in fear. Chloe's hand rose to her lips. But Trent pulled the punch, stopping mere inches from the criminal's nose.

"First you hurt her and then you insult me?" Trent snarled. "I'm gonna take pity on you because Savannah and I've got history. But you're gonna forget seeing me here. The payara deal is my business. You think Uncle's got you looped in on every deal he's got going?"

"You're nothing to Uncle—"

"Oh, yeah, then how come I'm still walking around alive with my heart still beating inside my body?"

Shouts were coming behind her now. Then she saw the smart, blue, uniformed form of Nicole and the male officer she'd been sitting with running toward them, a plain-clothed Butler two steps behind.

Looked like listening in was over and she was going to have to come out of her hiding place. Chloe ran around the van, holding out her badge. "We've got company!"

Trent leaned in toward Royd. "This isn't over. Keep your mouth shut." Then he grabbed Royd by the collar and yanked him to his feet. He thrust him at Chloe. "Cuff him. If anyone asks, he attacked you and I came to your defense. That's the truth. Now, I gotta go. Don't follow me. Don't call me. Don't try to come find me."

Her eyes searched the man standing in front of her. But Trent was gone and the hard man who stood in his place was nothing more than a stranger.

"But what about the hockey game?" Chloe said. Trent turned on his heels and strode off.

What about his cover?

"I'm sorry." He shook his head. "But I don't trust Royd to keep his mouth shut, and now that Royd knows I'm here, I can't be here anymore."

Chapter Nine

That was just Trent's cover talking, Chloe told herself. It had to be. Trent had seen a criminal from an old case and so he reassumed an old identity. He had to have said he was disappearing just for Royd's benefit. He didn't actually mean he was abandoning his Coach Henri identity, the Trillium players and moving on without her, right?

Yet, no matter how firmly she told herself that, something twisted in her chest as she watched Trent disappear around the side of the building, slinking like a wounded animal that didn't want to be seen. *Lord, what just happened? What do I do? I need a whole bunch of wisdom and clarity right now.* It was like Trent had transformed into a stranger right before her eyes and then abandoned her to handle the mess he'd left behind.

Butler had picked up his pace and overtaken the uniforms. She spun Royd around and pressed him against the van, feeling her brain go into autopilot as she recited the words she'd been saying to criminals for years. "I'm arresting you for assault with a weapon, assault of an officer and attempted kidnapping. It is my duty to in-form you that you have the right to retain and instruct counsel without delay..."

Usually, this was the point of an arrest that whoever she was arresting pointed out the Canadian version of reading them their rights didn't match what they were used to hearing on American television. But Royd merely grunted. This almost certainly wasn't his first arrest on Canadian soil. Not to mention something had seemingly sapped his will to fight. Just who did Royd think Trent was? What side of him had he seen? She didn't know. She just had to trust that Trent had blown his cover to save her life and that he would fill her in as soon as he could. Chloe turned Royd around so that he faced her. "Do you understand?"

"Do you?" He scowled. "Word of advice, lady. Don't trust Trent. He uses women like you. He'll cut your heart out, chew it up and spit it in the gutter, just like he did to my sister, Savannah."

Another mention of Savannah and yet another reminder she didn't really know Trent at all. He'd told her he didn't have relationships.

"Detective Brant!" Butler arrived at her side with Nicole and the second uniformed officer now one step behind. "What do you think you're doing, arresting someone in my jurisdiction when you're off duty?"

"Sorry to interrupt your day off, Sir." She straightened. "This man is a member of the Wolfspiders. Goes by the name of Royd. I stepped outside and he jumped me, held a knife to my throat and demanded I tell him about payara. Thankfully, Coach Henri, was there to assist. You're right, I am off duty, so do go ahead and let Constable Docker take over the arrest. But when you question Royd, I want to sit in."

She stood back and let Nicole and the male officer who introduced himself as Constable Don Walleye, lead Royd toward a police cruiser.

"Where's Coach Henri now?" Butler frowned. "I told him we don't want civilians trying to do citizen's arrests on criminals."

"I honestly don't know where he is." Chloe crossed her arms and stared down her former training officer. The smell of alcohol surrounding him was even stronger now. "But don't start with me about people stepping out of bounds. You were my training officer. I know you're a sticker for the rules. But, like I told you, there's been gossip circling for weeks about the baggie-full of thousands of dollars' worth of payara pills found on these premises and the bungled investigation.

"Your division apparently failed to find out who's making the payara and now the Gulo Gulo Boys and the Wolfspiders have descended here, as well, trying to track that person down, too. You should be thankful it seems neither of them has succeeded. I'll cooperate with your investigation. But with all due respect, Sir, from what I'm hearing, your badge and reputation are on the line. Some random hockey coach tackling a thug who attacked his fiancée is the least of your worries."

Butler had gone white. His hands were shaking and she suspected he'd had more than one drink during the game. He started spluttering something about protocols and investigations taking time.

But she was done arguing. This whole situation was out of control. She'd come here hoping to help find the source of the drugs. Now the entire mess had spiraled so badly she didn't even know what she was supposed to do anymore. She took a deep breath and let it out slowly. Her job. She would do her job. She paused long enough to give her statement to Nicole's partner and then she turned and strode back to the sports center.

A small cluster of Trillium players, including Third Line, had gathered by the back doors. What were they thinking about all this? What could she possibly tell them? It was all fine and good of Trent to just snap from one cover identity to another on a dime, like the plastic doll with snap-on clothes she'd had as a child. What about the young people who'd spent three months building a relationship with Coach Henri only to have him disappear?

"Who was arrested, miss?" Aidan called.

"A Wolfspider gang member named Royd," she said, going for blunt honesty and deciding to give the "miss" a pass. "He tried to attack me. He didn't succeed. Now, who wants to tell me why you all stampeded out here when you're supposed to be in the middle of a hockey game?"

There was a long pause. Feet shuffled. Eyes darted right and left. Finally, Brandon blurted out, "Hodge charged out onto the ice during a face-off and sucker punched Johnny."

"Because somebody posted a picture of him kissing Poppy!" Hodge snapped.

"You shouldn't have been looking on social media during a game, anyway," Aidan said.

"I wasn't! But everybody else in the arena was and the next thing I know, like, six people were leaning over the back of the box shouting it at me."

"And I told you, that picture is a faaaaaaaake!" Poppy shouted the word like it had six syllables.

"Really?" Chloe looked around the crowd for Johnny.

She didn't see him or any of the other Haliburton players. She turned to Poppy. "Who's behind it then?"

"I don't know!" Her voice rose to a wail but Chloe wasn't sure if she believed her.

"Hodge took payara before the game," Aidan added.

"No, I didn't!" Hodge spun on him.

Aidan didn't even blink. "I didn't say you did it on purpose!"

"Coach said somebody might've drugged him," Brandon explained. He held up a water bottle. "Coach said I should give you this and that Hodge should get a drug test."

Voices rose in a babble as multiple students started talking at once. Chloe raised a hand. "I got it. So a fight broke out and then you all collectively decided to run outside here at once because…?"

Her words trailed off. Voices fell just as quickly as they'd risen. Her question hung in the frozen air.

"I dunno," Milo said eventually. "People started yelling there was a fight outside and running for the exits. So I followed."

Crowd mentality. Super.

"Let me guess. None of you know who started the stampede for the exits, either?" she asked. No answer. Right, so this was how it was going to be. Chloe pulled her badge out again and held it up, making sure everyone saw it. "As you guys all should know by now, I'm a detective with the Ontario Provincial Police. Most of my work is with the Special Victims Unit, which means it's not just my job to stop criminals. It's also my job to take care of people and protect them." She dropped her badge and crossed her arms. "So, I'm going to be straight with you. And I expect you to be straight with me.

"I know that a baggie of a new designer upper drug named payara was found in the locker room a few months ago. I know several of you were questioned about it. I also know the police didn't come up with enough evidence to arrest anyone, probably because you're all busy protecting each other. But that doesn't change the fact that someone in your community is cooking the stuff and somebody else is selling it. I wouldn't even be surprised if some of you have theories about who that could be." Her eyes fixed on Third Line. "I also wouldn't be surprised if it turns out more than one of you has tried it."

Nobody's eyes were meeting either hers now or even meeting each other's. Some scanned the snow falling from the dark sky above. Others scanned the edges of the parking lot. Hodge's face reddened as he stared directly at the ground.

"Now, maybe you think this isn't your problem and that it has nothing to do with you," she went on. "Maybe you only know rumors or don't want to get anybody else in trouble. Or you're worried about getting in trouble yourself. But yesterday three gang members took baseball bats to your sports center and threatened your lives. Today, somebody from a different gang tried to kill me. That same big, creepy jerk broke into my house early this morning and attacked me."

Eyes grew wider. About half of them were meeting hers now. Poppy made a sound like a whimper. Lucy hugged herself. Aidan looked ready to punch someone.

"Frankly, I don't care what story you've been telling yourself about why this isn't your problem. Your community is in danger and it probably isn't going to stop without your cooperation. So, here's what's going to happen. Right now, each and every one of you is going to take out your cell phone and add my phone number into your contacts. Text it to all your friends. Post it on the school message board. Give it to everyone you know.

"Then, go away and think long and hard about whether you really want criminals tearing up your community. When you decide the answer is no, text me everything you know. I'll find you a lawyer if you want one. I'll put you in touch with Victim Services or a social worker. You can block your number and text me anonymously, I don't care. Just give me what I need to protect you. Phones out. Now."

She waited as one by one the clump of students pulled out their phones. Then she recited her number slowly, watching them like a hawk. "Thank you. Now, unless any of you feel like confessing right now, I'm going to get out of this cold and get someone to process this water bottle and a drug test for Hodge. Any questions?"

Brandon raised his hand. "Where's Coach?"

"Honestly? I don't know." She waited while the youth dispersed slowly back into the building like shadows disappearing into the sun. Then she ushered Hodge over to Nicole's partner, Constable Walleye, handed him the water bottle and explained about the drug test. Thankfully, Hodge cooperated, although part of her suspected it was to get away from Poppy's attempts to pull him aside to talk.

There were no messages from Trent on her phone. She crossed the parking lot and walked around the front of the building. Trent's truck was gone.

She nearly screamed at the sky. So, Trent really had

left, then. He'd dropped Coach Henri, switched covers and disappeared from her life without explaining what was happening or telling her why. She didn't even know why she was surprised.

A car honked at her twice as it drove out of the lot. Johnny was hanging out of a silver sports car. "Hey, Detective, I'm sorry for what happened earlier at the diner. George was being a fool. I saw Coach Henri pull out of here like his feet were on fire. Everything okay in paradise? Can I give you a ride anywhere?"

She nearly laughed in his face. From where she stood that flirtatious and cocky young man had caused more than enough trouble. "I'm good, thanks. Tell me, did you really kiss Poppy?"

"A gentleman doesn't kiss and tell!" Johnny slid back into the driver's seat.

Like he was a gentleman.

He lit a cigarette and puffed it out the window as he peeled out of the lot.

Now there was someone she'd have suspected of dealing drugs in a heartbeat, if she could figure out how Third Line fit into it. Trent was certain one of the four third-line players had hidden the payara in the locker room, and she didn't believe for a moment any of them would lie to police to protect Johnny, especially not considering how Hodge had pounded on him and apparently none of the players had tried to stop him. Had Trent been wrong about the timeline? Was Poppy really Trilly?

The taxi she had called took twenty minutes to arrive. Then it was an eighty-dollar fare back to her house. She spent it looking out the window and staring at the darkness rushing past. She never should've let herself kiss Trent. She never even should have let herself hold his hand. She never should've let Trent slide himself back into her life and infiltrate her heart.

Hers was the only vehicle in her driveway when she got home and her small hatchback was buried under a foot of snow. Her footsteps crunched on the cold, snowy ground. She undid both sets of locks on her front door and eased it open.

A tall form with broad shoulders sat silhouetted in her living room.

She yanked her service weapon and pointed it at him. "Hands up! Don't move!"

"Clo, it's me." Trent switched on the lamp. Her gaze fell on the short, buzzed hair and smooth, clean-cut face. Gone was the softness of the beard and the gentle curl of his hair. Now shadows sharpened the lines of his jaw and traced along his cut shoulders and bulging biceps. A black T-shirt covered his chest. He leaned forward like an alpha animal. Torn jeans covered in motor oil stains gave way to the outline of a handgun near his ankle, just above a pair of steel-toed work boots. "Look, I'm sorry, but you have to trust me—"

"No, I don't." The gun held firm in her grasp. "I don't even know who you are anymore."

Chapter Ten

"Come on, Chloe. You can't possibly mean that," Trent said. Could she? He watched as Chloe holstered her weapon. Then she smacked on the switch to the main lights. Light flooded her living room.

"You broke into my house," she said.

"You left a spare key for the crime scene investigators." He stood. "I just picked it up from them, let myself in and locked the door behind me. They didn't find much but they'll have what they found analyzed in a few days—"

She cut him off. "Which hardly matters now that you clearly know who my attacker was."

Okay, she was angry. He'd expected as much. He bit his tongue and kept from pointing out that any evidence that Royd had broken into her home would still be helpful in getting a confession and conviction.

"Why didn't you tell me you knew him?"

"Because all I had was a suspicion." His jaw set. "There's more than one bald and bulked-up man out there with a spiderweb tattoo. Royd's full name is Roy Denver. He's low-level Wolfspider fodder that Uncle throws at problems sometimes to see if he'll come back alive."

Trent wasn't even sure what he was doing in her living room. He had to drive two hours to Huntsville, find Uncle and get him to believe his side of the story before Royd managed to get word to them of what had happened.

As Chloe had slapped the handcuffs on Royd, he'd run back to his rented apartment, shaved off every last trace of Coach Henri and transformed into the version of himself he most hated looking at in the mirror. He'd been motoring down the highway, twenty minutes passed her house with Bobcaygeon in the rearview mirror, when he'd suddenly found himself turning his truck right back around and heading to Chloe's. Couldn't say for sure why. He just knew there was something inside him that kept kicking his brain like an old boot, telling him he needed to at least try to give her an explanation for his sudden shift in gears.

"I don't know what Royd's doing here," he added, "but I need to find out. Yesterday we had one gang involved in this payara mess. Now we have two—"

"So, you just took off?" Flames blazed in the green depths of her eyes.

"I came back!" he said.

"You blew your cover!"

"Because I had to." His arms crossed in front of his broad chest. "Royd and I have known each other for a long time. The moment I tried to help you he would've recognized me. But part of my arrangement with Uncle is that my family and girlfriend—if I ever had one—is off-limits. Either way, I was made. My cover was going to be blown. I couldn't just keep pretending to be a mild-mannered hockey coach.

"Yes, Royd was arrested and that will complicate my situation with the Wolfspiders. Royd'll probably get bail, and he'll most definitely get a phone call. Who knows how long it will be before he tells someone he saw me in Bobcaygeon and they figure out I was posing as a hockey coach. Or, for all I know, he might've even had someone else on the inside. I didn't come to town to coach hockey. I came here to stop the spread of payara. Sure, when this mission started my job was to get close to the third-line players. But the second I knew the Wolfspiders were involved, and that one of them would recognize me, then the mission changed. Don't you get that? I texted Eli, told him I had a personal emergency and needed him to take over the team, and also emailed my resignation to Trillium. It's done. All of it—Coach Henri, Trillium hockey, Third Line and the coach's cute fiancée—is over."

"Because that's how this works," she said. "You just snap your fingers and everything changes. Too bad for anyone who might care about Coach Henri or miss him."

"I'm an undercover cop. You know this. It's my job. It's never personal."

"Royd says you broke his sister Savannah's heart," Chloe said.

He winced. Yeah, he wasn't exactly proud of that. "Savannah has a crush on the person I pretend to be for my Wolfspider cover. Not on who I actually am. I promise I never intended to lead her on."

"He knew your real name, Trent. Not a cover name."

"Because, as we've covered, the best cover stories have a kernel of truth," he said.

Fact was, he'd been fourteen and still an uncontrollable ball of rage and pain about the death of his sister, when the students he occasionally hung with behind the gymnasium had introduced him to Uncle. Uncle had taken a liking to him and started giving him odd jobs to do, like picking up packages, looking out for cops and destroying things. Until, at seventeen, Trent had been arrested and scared straight by an understanding cop and gotten his life back on the straight and narrow. He'd never imagined his work as an undercover cop would mean using the shell of his teen life to concoct a new cover, based on a version of himself that he'd never really forgiven himself for.

"The Trent they know is a fixer," he added. "I randomly show up, after being away for months or even years, and use Uncle for information. He's a source and a gossip. He tells me what other gangs are doing because he knows I'll take care of it."

Chloe's eyebrows shot up.

"By getting them arrested! Sheesh, don't look at me like that! Uncle is a vital informant to our police operations and has absolutely no idea. Thanks to the information I've weaseled out of him, the RCMP have taken out human smuggling, child abuse rings, weapons trafficking and all sorts of other horrendous crimes that give cops nightmares. Even you've used information my cover has gotten from Uncle. When we first met, I was giving you intel I'd gotten from him about a Gulo operation."

But what he really wanted was to take Uncle down. Yes, Uncle was too clever about keeping his own hands clean, and Trent understood why his superiors believed an arrest shouldn't happen until they were confident the charges would stick. Not to mention that once Uncle believed Trent was no longer usable, he might come after Trent's family. But when Uncle finally slipped up, Trent wanted to arrest him personally.

"That's what's in jeopardy right now," he went on. "I don't know what Royd and the Wolfspiders have to do with payara, but it's a lead I can't afford to ignore. Uncle doesn't exactly trust me, and he won't be happy that I let you arrest Royd. I don't know what Uncle is going to think when he finds out that you and I have been telling everyone around town that we're engaged. Maybe he'll laugh it off like Royd did. But maybe he won't."

Or maybe, the Wolfspiders had an informant inside Bobcaygeon who'd seen them lock lips at the diner. "Either way, my roughing up a Wolfspider to save a cop looks really bad. In fact, it could destroy my Wolfspider cover for good. Not to mention it basically announces that I'm an obstacle in Uncle's way of getting his hands on payara. But I can probably manage to convince Uncle to tell me everything he knows about both the dealer and drug lab if I can spin it right."

Which he couldn't do as long as he stood around arguing in her living room. At least Chloe seemed to be listening now.

"Either I get the intel I need from Uncle tonight to find the payara dealer," he said, "or he discovers I've been playing him for years and he puts targets on both my back and yours. Those are the stakes. So, I've got to make tracks to get to Uncle first and spin him some story about how I've been romancing a pretty but foolish lady cop who doesn't realize I'm using her to get my hands on the drugs. No offense."

"None taken." A smirk turned at the corner of her lips that he didn't think he liked the look of. Then she turned and walked into the bedroom. The door slammed and locked behind her. "Give me thirty seconds. I'm coming with you."

"No, you're not!" He called through the door, "This is still my case, and there's absolutely no way that you're walking into a Wolfspider den with me."

"I'm going." It sounded like she was tossing the contents of her drawers and wardrobe on the floor. "My home stopped being safe when Royd broke in. Uncle could've sent someone else by now. Besides, someone needs to have your back."

"My back is just fine!" He paced to one side of the room and back again.

Help me, Lord, what am I doing here? Why did I even turn the truck around and come back? Why can't I walk away from this fight?

"The case might've changed, but we're partners." She pulled the door open so suddenly he tumbled to the floor, landing hard on one knee at her feet. He looked up and blinked.

Thick, knee-high combat boots encased her legs, over a pair of leather motorcycle pants. She wore a black tunic dress over top, which fell all the way to her knees, with a studded leather bag that was half purse and half gun holster around her waist. A black leather motorcycle jacket completed the biker look but was almost swallowed up with the wild tumbling mass of thick red hair, now with unexpected shocks of pale blond extensions. Electric-blue eyes, framed with thick, artful dark lines met his.

"Stand up," she said. "And let's go. We can argue as we drive." Her lips were painted the same flaming red as her hair.

He stood slowly, opened his mouth and had to swallow twice before any words came out. "Who are you and what have you done with Chloe?"

"You think I've never walked into a room full of criminals who'd kill me as soon as they look at me?" She tossed her hair and it fell around her shoulders like a cape of flames. "Who do you think the Special Victims Unit sends in after those girls trapped in the kinds of nightmarish places you get intel from Uncle about? Detectives like me. I'm the one who walks through that door. I've been the one inside, providing surveillance, providing cover for the girls and giving the Emergency Response Unit the signal to burst in."

"The plan is to convince Uncle that I've been using you—"

"The plan is idiotic and going to get you killed." She cut him off. "Then, after they kill you, they'll send someone to kill me. You think Uncle is really going to believe that you're so smart and irresistible that you charmed a fierce and dedicated detective into spilling classified information without her knowledge. You really think you can sell that?"

Well, not to anyone who'd actually met her. But still.

"I don't have any other choice," he said.

"Yes, you do." Her hands snapped to her hips. "You keep trying to convince me that you're some expert on corrupt cops. We go in together, you introduce me as a bad apple and we tell them I only arrested Royd because there was a bunch of people coming my way and I needed to maintain my cover."

His eyes opened wider. "You expect me to walk into the middle of the Wolfspiders, right up to Uncle, with you on my arm, and tell him that the detective who Royd tried to rough up was just posing as my girlfriend because she's corrupt and wants a piece of my payara money?"

"Not quite." Her eyes fixed on his face through the blue contacts and he realized he'd know they were hers anywhere, no matter what color they were. "I'm going to walk in there and do what I don't believe you can. I'm going to convince Uncle that I sold out my badge, my honor and everything I believed in for you. We're going to tell them I'm your fiancée, and then I'm going to convince a roomful of killers that I've fallen head over heels for you, Trent. I'll make Uncle believe that he has nothing to fear from me and that he can still trust you. Because if I don't, you'll die."

Chapter Eleven

The Pit 11 Grill was a low, nondescript, squat structure that sat on a strip of highway outside Huntsville, Ontario. It was only about a twenty-minute drive from the warm family farmhouse where he'd grown up and would be going for Christmas dinner. But it felt like an entire world away. Yellow light seemed to drip in puddles from the sparse lampposts. The electric sign flickered blue through the thickly pelting snow. The parking lot was packed with battered Wolfspider vehicles.

Trent pulled to a stop at the far end of the lot. Then he felt his hand reach for Chloe's and squeeze it while he prayed. "God, help us in there. Keep us safe. Keep us smart. Keep us honest and honorable. Help us do what needs to be done, with as few people getting hurt in the process as possible."

"Amen," Chloe said.

He looked up through the windshield at the place that had harbored so many of his worst memories. He hated the Pit 11 Grill. He hated what he'd heard in there, what he'd seen in there and everything the dingy restaurant represented. A person like Chloe didn't belong in a place like that. Yes, as a cop she'd walked bravely into even uglier places for the sake of justice and mercy. But the dirt of what Pit 11 stood for was like a stain on his heart. She deserved better than to be led by a man like him into a place like that.

"Any last words?" she asked.

He winced. He wished she hadn't put it like that. He looked down at her slender gloved hand enclosed in his and felt the lump of the engagement ring beneath the leather. He wanted to tell her that the story of his life had some ugly chapters he hoped she'd never read and that his heart had some dark places he hoped she never saw. He wanted to tell her that as grateful as he was that he'd turned his life around, he wished there was a way to scour every corner of his past so that he'd never even needed that forgiveness God had offered him. "If you sense your life is in danger, I want you to get yourself out of there, okay? Don't hesitate. Don't look back. Got it?"

"Got it." She pulled her hand from his. "But for the record, if anyone pulls a gun on you and threatens to kill you, I'm shooting them first. Even if it's Uncle."

He chuckled. "Deal. You can shoot only if he tries to kill me. But only then."

As they walked toward the building, he could feel his shoulders roll back, his chest puff out and his gait slow to a cocky saunter. They reached the door and he felt Chloe's left arm drop possessively around his shoulders, as confident and smooth as if it belonged there. His arm slid around her waist. Her lips brushed his cheek and an odd warmth filled his core as he realized that for the very first time, when he stepped through those doors, he wouldn't feel utterly alone.

They stepped over the threshold into a dark space filled with wobbly round tables and even wobblier patrons. The air stunk of alcohol spilled long ago. Faces he recognized and strangers whose types he knew all too well cut him furtive glances. His eyes narrowed and locked on the white-bearded, barrel-chested man nursing something in an unmarked bottle at the counter.

Uncle glanced up.

Trent counted at least two enforcers flanking him—a tall one to his left and a shorter but heavily armed one to his right. Trent kept his eyes locked on his target and strode toward him with the swagger of a man who knew every crack in the counter and the kinds of deals that had been made over them.

He made it six steps from the place where Uncle sat before the taller enforcer leaped in front of him and lobbed a sucker punch at Trent's jaw, knocking him clear out from under Chloe's arm. Trent took the blow and staggered back. Then he reared forward, grabbed the enforcer by the throat and shoved him hard against the counter. Trent glanced at Uncle. "What kind of welcome is this for an old friend?"

Uncle snorted. "What kind of old friend disappears for months and drops off the grid?"

"The kind who's been busy and had things to do." Trent stepped back. The enforcer hesitated. Uncle nodded at him. The enforcer slunk to the end of the counter and glowered at him like a guard dog. Trent reached for Chloe's hand and pulled her over to stand beside him.

"Heard you'd tried going straight again," Uncle said. He cast his eyes over Chloe then back to Trent. "Let me guess. You ran out of money and so you're back asking for work."

"I'm here to find out why you sent Royd to rough up my woman!" Trent swept Chloe's hair back off her throat and showed the dark bruises Royd's fingers had left on her skin. He let her hair fall. "Babe, take off your gloves."

She did. Trent held up her left hand and showed Uncle the bruises on her wrist just long enough to make sure he also saw the engagement ring on her hand.

"I don't know what Royd's got against your woman." Uncle shrugged. "Maybe Savannah's mad you moved on, so she put him up to it."

"You mean Royd just decided to try to rough up and kidnap a cop all on his own?" Trent's voice rose.

The room froze. Uncle turned. His face went white. "You brought a cop into my business?"

"I brought my woman into your restaurant, because you and I have a history and she asked to meet you. She's been poking around Bobcaygeon trying to find out how to get her hands on payara. She took out a group of Gulos because they were after the same thing. Then you send Royd after her? You have any idea who this woman is? Or how solid her reputation is? She's connected. She's fierce. She could've been a major asset to you, for the right price. She could've helped you out and worked with you to get you whatever you needed. Instead you sent Royd to take her on." Trent shook his head.

"You must be Detective Brant." Uncle stretched a large callused hand toward Chloe.

She took his hand and shook it. "Call me Chloe."

"My apologies, Chloe. I had no idea you and Trent were an item, or that you'd be interested in doing business. You two set a date to get hitched?"

"Not yet." Chloe smiled. It was a look full of confidence and courage, and incredibly attractive. "Trent's pretty stubborn when he wants to be."

Uncle laughed. Trent couldn't believe it. Chloe was actually charming the head of the Wolfspiders. "Remind him that a married woman can't be forced to testify against her husband in court, but a girlfriend can."

She grinned wider, then shot Trent a glance that made him suddenly realize just how helpless he'd be if she ever really did turn her will against him. "Will do."

"Give me a moment with your boy?" Uncle gestured to the back of the room. "He and I have some business to discuss alone. Then you and I can sit down and see about making a deal."

The hair rose suddenly on the back of Trent's neck. No, this wasn't the plan. But Chloe had already slipped from his side and brushed her lips against his cheek, filling his senses with the scent of her skin. "No problem. It was a long drive and I could use some freshening up. Don't make any decisions without me."

She turned and headed toward the back. All eyes in the room watched her go.

"You've got it bad," Uncle said. "How do you know she's not planning on arresting you?"

Trent snickered. "She wouldn't. I can trust her."

"How would know?" Uncle turned back to his drink. "You're head over heels for that chick. Not to mention she's way out of your league. A woman like that doesn't take up with a guy like you without a really good reason."

Trent held his tongue. He knew Chloe was far better than a man like him deserved. He didn't need a criminal like Uncle reminding him of that. *One day, Lord,*

I will get a warrant to arrest Uncle and take down the Wolfspiders for good. One day, I will close this chapter of my life for good and never use this cover again.

"So what does your family think of her?" Uncle raised an eyebrow. "You going to pop by with her for a visit while you're in town?"

"Wasn't planning on it." Trent's jaw clenched. He didn't even want to imagine how that would go down. They'd probably love her. "But I'm not here to talk about her. I'm here to talk about payara."

"Oh, but I think the bigger issue is family, don't you?" There was a mocking tone in the old man's voice, but the hint of something evil glinted in his eye. "I saw your dad just recently."

Trent felt his face go pale. His father? His parents were in their sixties and the nicest, most honest, caring and down-to-earth people anyone would ever want to meet. Not to mention, their farm was less than half an hour's drive away. Uncle had never made a move against his family, and Trent knew he never would as long as he thought Trent was useful to his operation. But Trent had tried to warn his folks and brothers, more than once, that when the day finally came that he took Uncle down they should sell the farm and move out of Wolfspider territory. He just had to pray they would. His eyes narrowed. "What are you playing at?"

"Nothing," Uncle said. "I happened to be in the Huntsville cemetery and saw him laying flowers on your sister's grave."

Anger built like heat at the back of Trent's neck. Was this Uncle's way of tightening his stranglehold on the man Trent pretended to be when he was undercover? *Lord, I do this job to save lives and protect the inno-*

cent. Please, don't let one more person I love get hurt because of me. "Are you threatening my family? We had an arrangement, Uncle. The day I became a Wolf-spider, you promised my family would be off-limits."

Uncle had to know that if he ever went after his family, Trent would slap the cuffs on him.

"I'm just making friendly conversation." Uncle slapped his empty bottle down on the counter and another one appeared. "When I sent Royd to see what he could about getting me into payara production, I knew that the Gulos had staged a failed attempt to get their hands on it. I knew there was a cop involved. I didn't know it had anything to do with you, or that you were even there. If I had, I'd have given you the opportunity to handle it. But since you didn't, I've now got a race on my hand to see which one of you can deliver first."

He took a long sip from the new bottle then fixed his eyes on Trent. "Because, make no mistake, I am taking over the payara operation, one way or another. I am getting hold of that lab and convincing whoever's working the drug to come work for me. Our arrangement still stands. You stay out of my business, I'll stay out of yours. But if you try to double-cross me, or take that payara distribution for yourself, you just might have to get used to visiting a whole row of new headstones in the family plot, starting with that pretty cop you think you're going to marry."

Chloe leaned back against the cracked counter in the surprisingly large but dingy women's washroom and peered through a crack in the door. Something was wrong. Trent's shoulders were hunched like a protective lion. Whatever Uncle was saying had angered him. She watched as the enforcer who'd sucker punched Trent by way of a welcome left his post at the end of the counter and shifted closer to Trent and Uncle. Another enforcer had materialized behind them. She took a deep breath and reminded herself that Trent knew exactly what he was doing and if he needed her, he'd find a way to let her know. She didn't know which was worse—throwing off a seasoned detective in the middle of the undercover interrogation of a gang leader, or staying back, when every beat in her chest told her he needed her by his side? She knew the answer. She was going out there.

The door flew inward. A woman stood in the doorway, a snarl on her lips and her hands on her hips. She was brunette and curvy, with the kind of face classically considered quite beautiful and a stance that implied she thought Chloe had invaded her territory.

"Excuse me," Chloe said. To her surprise, the woman stepped out of the way to let her pass. But as Chloe's hand brushed the door frame, the brunette slammed it shut again so quickly and violently that the speed of Chloe's reflexive move to leap back was the only thing that kept her from having her fingers broken. The brunette closed the door behind them. Chloe felt her green eyes narrow behind their blue contacts. "Do we have a problem?"

The attractive brunette snorted. "You're not welcome here. Get out before I hurt you."

Chloe planted her feet. "Let me guess, you're Savannah? I hear you and my man have history."

Savannah's eyes widened, just long enough to let Chloe know she'd hit her mark. Chloe shook her head. Savannah was a distraction. Nothing more. Chloe pitied her, even knowing what Trent's cover had done to her feelings. Maybe they had that much in common.

"You're the cop who thinks she's going to marry Trent," Savannah said. Seemed news traveled fast. "Let me guess, you think you're in love with him?"

Yes was the word Chloe knew her cover required her to say. During the drive she'd even rehearsed in her head how to say that she had feelings for Trent. Yet, as she stood there, in the dingy washroom of a run-down restaurant that served as the front for a gang operation, she couldn't do it. Whatever it was she felt for Trent, it cut way too deep just to be blurted out meaninglessly on an undercover mission. "Well, we're getting hitched."

"No, you're not," Savannah said. "There's no way Trent Henry's ever marrying anyone. If you think he is, you don't really know him."

Chloe almost laughed. This woman's jealousy was ridiculous. "And you do?"

An unsettling confidence flashed in the depths of Savannah's eyes. "I've known Trent since the second grade."

The words hit Chloe's ears like a thunderclap. Her knees almost buckled. "You're lying."

"Oh, no. Trent was my high school crush!" Now it was Savannah's turn to laugh. "He didn't tell you, did he? We've been on and off since we were teens. We used to go around Huntsville hot-wiring cars and going on joyrides. Who do you think introduced him to Uncle and got him in with the Wolfspiders? My brother, Royd, did. Who do you think he called when being a cop got old and he wanted back in? Me."

Pieces of the picture that was Trent turned and clicked into place in her mind. No wonder he'd been able to return to the Wolfspider cover more than once. No wonder Royd knew his real name. Trent had gone undercover with a deadly gang, time and again, by playing a corrupt and twisted version of his younger self. Her eyes dragged her gaze back to the closed door that blocked Trent from her view. Why hadn't he told her? She might not know his whole story or the cover roles he played, but she knew the man he was on the inside.

"You're right," Chloe said. "I haven't known Trent as long as you have. I don't know his history or everything he's done. But I know his heart. That's good enough for me." It was high time she got back out there and by his side. "Now, are you going to step aside and let me out? Or am I going to have to move you?"

"You can't rescue him," Savannah said. "The best you can do is cut your losses and run. I know about Royd's arrest. I know Trent chased him down and held him for you."

"How?" A chill spread through Chloe's limbs.

"Royd has friends. One of them already called me. My brother is moving up in the world. Royd knows who's selling the payara. It's only a matter of time before he gets him to cut a deal for Uncle."

Savannah was still smirking. She clearly didn't understand the importance of what she'd just said or that she was telling Chloe something she didn't already know. But Chloe's blood ran cold. Uncle already knew who was selling the payara. That meant Uncle didn't need Trent for anything. Uncle was just lying to Trent for his amusement or to find out what the police knew. Trent had walked right into a trap and he didn't know it.

Chloe shoved Savannah aside, yanked the door open and strode back into the dining room. Her fingers snapped. "Trent! Honey! Toss me the keys. We're leaving! Now!"

Her voice rang like a bell through the crowded room. Trent frowned. Then he grabbed his keys from his pocket and pitched them to her. She caught them one-handed.

"Go do what you need to do," he said. "I'll join you in a bit."

"No, you're coming with me now!" Her hands were planted on her hips. Was it her imagination or were the men closing in tighter around them? "I've just been talking to Savannah and she's been filling me in on your past. You come now or you can forget about marrying me."

Trent glanced at Uncle and shrugged. Then he cut his eyes over her shoulder. Savannah had followed her. He groaned. "Look, whatever Savannah said to you, it doesn't matter. Just ignore her."

He meant it. She could read that much in his eyes. He thought she was making a mistake.

"Trent, trust me, if you don't come talk with me, you're an idiot." Glimmers of a warning pushed its way through her words, begging to be heard. She strode over to him, weaving her way through the gang members that stood around him like a pack of animals waiting to strike. She stopped, her toes inches away from his. They were so close that all she had to do was lean forward and their lips would be touching. "I'm not your sidekick. I'm not your woman. I'm your equal. And I'm telling you, I want to go talk."

"Is there a problem, Trent?" Uncle raised an eyebrow.

She took a step back and almost felt the wall of gang members hemming them in. *Help me, Lord. I can't stop the danger. And Trent's too confident in the strength of his cover to see it's about to self-destruct around him.*

She grit her teeth. Well, if they were going down, then she was going down swinging.

"I didn't come here to be treated like this!" Chloe yanked the ring off her finger and flung it at him. To her surprise, Trent leaped off the stool and scrambled for it. She swung back toward Savannah. "Why didn't you tell me you and Savannah had a history? I thought I knew you. But I don't and I never will. Because you're so determined to shut people out, you hurt everyone who cares about you and wreck everything you touch. And I'm done with it."

Chloe spun around so quickly that her flailing arm made contact with Savannah's jaw and knocked her back a foot. No one watching would've believed it was on purpose.

But that hardly mattered. The profanity that escaped Savannah's lips was primal. The blow she leveled across Chloe's cheek was even more so. Then Savannah leaped at her, yanking out Chloe's clipped-in hair extensions and trying to dig her nails into Chloe's face. Chloe reared back, tossing Savannah into the nearest enforcer. Before she could take another step, she felt Trent's arms around her waist, lifting her feet off the ground.

"What are you playing at?" Trent snapped. "You actually trying to start a fight?"

He pulled her backward toward the door. His voice rose. "Uncle, I'm sorry, just give me a minute."

He kicked the door open and they tumbled outside. Trent dropped her into the snow. Frustration filled his gaze. She looked back over his shoulder. Uncle was standing. A crowd of Wolfspiders was watching them. She threw her arms around Trent's neck and hugged him, feeling for that familiar space in his shoulder that meant safety. But his arms weren't about to yield.

"Chloe, my past with Savannah is none of your business—"

"Royd has already found out who the payara dealer is and has been negotiating with him. He has a contact on the inside in Bobcaygeon who called Savannah tonight. I don't know if Uncle knows that Royd's already found the dealer. If he does, it means Uncle knows he doesn't need you and we've walked into a trap. If he doesn't, you don't want to be sitting there making him promises when he finds out the truth."

Trent pulled back. His eyes met hers. He believed her and he was sorry. She could see both truths clearly in a single glance. That was all she needed. Then he leaned forward and kissed her on the forehead and whispered, "We gotta run."

She turned and ran for the truck, knowing without a moment's hesitation that Trent would be right behind her. She heard voices shouting and the Wolfspiders pouring through the door. Then she heard Trent grunt as an enforcer leaped on him from behind. She looked back. Trent was down on his knees, struggling as the large man tried to choke him. Trent reared back and shook him off. An agonizing pop filled the air. Trent howled in agony. He'd dislocated his shoulder. "Trent!"

"Don't stop!" He struggled to his feet. "I'm right behind you!"

She reached the truck first and yanked the passenger door open for Trent. Within seconds he was inside. She slammed the door and sprinted for the driver's side, wiping as much snow off the back window as she could with the palm of her hand. The keys slid into the ignition. The engine turned over. Her eyes slid to the rear-view mirror. Wolfspiders were jumping into vehicles. She glanced at Trent.

"Don't worry," she said, "we'll get you to a hospital and they'll pop your shoulder back in."

Engines roared behind them. She fired back, barely missing a van, then yanked the steering wheel and gunned the truck onto the narrow country road. The windshield wipers worked hard and fast against the falling snow.

"They're not going to let us go that easily," Trent said. "Uncle's going to get them to run us off the road."

"I didn't hear him say that." Her fingers tightened on the wheel.

"He doesn't need to," Trent said. "Nobody just gets up and walks out on a conversation with Uncle without paying a price for it. Car crashes are one of the ways Uncle deals with people and why I've never been able to pin a murder or an assault on him. He orders people to drive someone off the road and then gets them to ditch the vehicle, leaving him untouchable."

"He's not untouchable." She looked up. The bright glare of high beams filled the rearview mirror. "We're going to get out of this, and you're going to be the one to eventually take him down."

A vehicle bumped them hard from behind. Her body slammed against the seat belt. Trent shouted out in agony. His face was paler than she'd ever seen it before. How many jolts could his body take before he passed out from the pain? A white van was riding her back bumper. A large red truck was coming up on her left. Trees and a frozen lake lay to her right. The van bumped them again. The truck swerved. She prayed hard, struggling with the steering wheel and fighting to keep them on the road.

Trent dropped his cell phone onto his lap. "Call Jacob."

From Criminal Investigations? "I'll call 9-1-1."

"No!" Trent's shout echoed through the cab. "Call Jacob! Tell him everything. He knows who you are. He knows I'm undercover. He'll know what to do."

"But—"

"He's my brother!"

"You have a brother?"

"I have three. I grew up on a farm not twenty minutes from here. Tell my family that I'm sorry."

Sorry for what? The red truck sideswiped them so hard she felt the steering wheel yanked from her grasp. They spun. She grabbed for the wheel. But it was too late. The road disappeared from under them. She was thrown against the door as Trent's truck began to roll, tumbling down the hill.

Help us, Lord!

They were going to crash.

Chapter Twelve

Darkness swept over Trent in waves, with fractured thoughts slipping through the gaps of unconsciousness. The truck was rolling. Prayers slipped like screams through Chloe's lips. They were upside down. Right-side up. Sideways. Then they stopped. Pain smashed into his body like a sledgehammer. He passed out.

Gunshots yanked his mind back to consciousness. Chloe had crawled out of the vehicle and was firing her weapon in the direction of the road.

"Stay back! You come one step closer and I'm going to shoot!" A long, tense silence fell as he lay there in the vehicle, helpless as she faced down the criminals who had run them off the road.

Suddenly he felt Chloe's strong, determined hands pulling his body from the wreckage and out into the snow. Coldness pressed against his back and flakes were falling on his face.

"They're gone," she said. "A red truck without legible plates ran us off the road. An enforcer from the grill got out and doubled-checked that we'd really crashed. I fired at him. He took off."

So today wasn't the day he was going to die. Uncle had ordered his enforcers to run Trent off the road as a punishment or warning, but not told them to finish the job. It wasn't unusual for Uncle to "warn" someone several times before finally coming to kill them. It was one of the ways he kept people in line and terrified of him. He should probably be thankful this was the first beating Uncle had ever meted out on him. Seemed whatever business Uncle had with him, he wasn't through with him yet.

He heard Chloe on the phone with Jacob, telling him where they were and what was happening. *Thank You, God.* Jacob would know what to do. But how could Trent ever forgive himself for dragging Chloe into danger?

He felt the warmth of Chloe curling her body against his chest and pulling an emergency blanket over them both. He groaned.

"You're not allowed to die, Trent! You hear me?" Her stern voice cut through the darkness and pain filling his mind. "You're going to stay that same stubborn man I care about who's too pigheaded to die. You got that? You're staying alive! I need you and I don't want to live without you. You hear me?"

I hear you, Chloe. I'm here. I'm so sorry I didn't listen sooner.

Words filled his mind, but before he could get his mouth to work, unconsciousness swept over him again. Then he heard more voices. Deep, strong, familiar voices were shouting his name and filling his chest with hope. A pair of large hands felt for a pulse.

"Yeah, he's alive," a male voice said. It was Jacob, his older brother. "Hang on, bro. Max's going to give you something for the pain."

Max? His younger brother, the paramedic?

Hey, guys, I'm fine. This darkness just keeps taking over and I keep passing out.

"If you want pancakes, you're going to have to wake up eventually," Jacob said.

Trent opened his eyes. He was lying on a bed. There was a blanket draped over him. Bright morning sunshine streamed through a window to his right. His eyes focused slowly as shapes swam before him. A row of plastic dinosaurs growled and snarled down at him from a shelf at the end of the bed. He groaned and leaned back against the pillow. He was home. He was lying in his very own childhood bed at the Henry family farmhouse.

"Look, I'm just warning you, as your big brother," Jacob added, "it's Christmas Eve brunch and Mom's pulled out all the stops. So the fact that you were run off the road by an evil, criminal gang isn't going to keep us from eating all the good stuff and leaving you with nothing but cereal."

He glanced sideways. A tall man, with broad shoulders and chestnut hair, was sitting on a single bed on the opposite side of the bedroom that had been way too small for them even as kids.

"I'm saying we split his pancakes and just don't tell him." A second voice dragged his attention to the doorway. Max's strong bulk leaned against the frame, his short black hair a mass of curls.

"Nobody eats my pancakes," Trent muttered. He tried to roll over onto to his side and almost yelped in pain as his shoulder hit the mattress. There was a sling wrapped around his arm and shoulder. No doubt his paramedic brother's doing. "What's going on? What am I doing here?"

"Steady there, buddy," Max said. "You have a dislocated shoulder and a nasty concussion." He crossed the floor in two long strides, crouched beside his brother's bed and helped him sit. Then he glanced across the room at Jacob. "If I'd known the threat of stealing his pancakes was going to wake him up, I'd have done it twenty minutes ago."

"No, you wouldn't. You'd have gone ahead and eaten them before he could stop you." Jacob chuckled then leaned forward, resting his elbows on his knees. "We got there less than twenty minutes after the truck crashed. Max and I dragged you up the hill, took you home and got you patched up. Max and Nick popped your shoulder back in. You were conscious. But Max warned us you might not remember much. You've been asleep for about nine hours."

"Last thing I remember, I was in the truck," Trent said as his mind filed the pieces back into order. "We were being chased by some vehicles. I was in pain. I told Chloe—" He leaped to his feet so quickly his head swam and his knees buckled. "Where's Chloe?"

"Downstairs in the kitchen having breakfast with the family." Max caught him by his good arm before he crumpled to the ground.

"Is she okay?" Trent asked. "Is she hurt? Was she injured?"

"She's fine." Max firmly guided him back down to the bed. "A few bruises from the crash. But in way better shape than you. You need to take it easy. You're going to want to avoid any strenuous physical activity for the next few days. Nothing involving your shoulder for at least two weeks."

He nearly groaned in frustration. This was no time for him to be out of commission. Trent glanced at Jacob. "How is Chloe, really?"

Jacob glanced at Max. Neither of them spoke for a beat. Then Jacob said, "Max, why don't you go get some pancakes and tell the rest of the fam that Trent's awake? We'll join you in a moment."

Max nodded and headed down the stairs, with a parting reminder not to mess with the shoulder sling.

Jacob turned to Trent. "Chloe's fine. Really. She's strong and resilient. But as you can imagine, she's got a lot of questions. I take it you never told her about any of us."

No, he hadn't. Now Chloe was sitting in his parents' kitchen, on Christmas Eve, eating pancakes with his parents and his two younger brothers. "I take it she knows everything now?"

"No, we dragged her to a houseful of strangers, put her to bed on the foldout in the den and fed her breakfast without telling her that we were your family." Jacob laughed. Trent didn't. "Of course she knows who we are. She's now met all of us. She knows this is the farmhouse where you grew up. That's where things are at. But we respect your privacy, so the rest is up to you."

Trent winced. "So, you didn't tell her about Faith?"

The smile faded from Jacob's face. "We figured that was your story to tell."

There was a more than ten-year gap between the oldest and youngest of the Henry brothers. Max had just been a toddler when Faith had died. Nick hadn't even been born yet. But Jacob had been fourteen when their sister had been killed. He'd been the one standing out-side when Trent had sauntered home, waiting to explain why there were cop cars parked on the lawn, and the crying from the house was so loud he could hear it from the driveway. The death of their sister was a shared but mostly silent bond between them, even as they each pursued a career in law enforcement.

"Thank you." It was a conversation he knew he needed to have with Chloe. If he was honest with him-self, it was the one topic that every other conversation he'd ever avoided having with her had come down to. He'd once had a younger sister. She'd been murdered by a killer who'd never been caught. He'd blamed himself.

"Chloe saved your life, you know." Jacob's voice cut through Trent's thoughts. "If she hadn't steered the truck clear of the trees before the crash, or dragged you out of the truck, or kept you warm until we got there, or called me..."

Or caused a scene to get him out of the Pit when he was too stubborn to listen.

"I'd be dead twice over," Trent said. "I know. She's a spectacular cop and I owe her my life. Did she or you file a police report?"

"Against Uncle and the Wolfspiders, no. She informed the higher-ups, of course. But she said whether actual charges are pressed is your call. She said you guys never heard Uncle give the order to cause the accident and that when she challenged the criminal who'd run you off the road, he just turned and walked away. My guess, and hers, is that the vehicle's already been ditched by now and they staged it to look like an accident. It's your inves-tigation and taking down the Wolfspiders is your deal."

That was one way of putting it.

"It was a warning," he said. "If Uncle wanted to kill us, we'd be dead by now. He's probably still hoping he can use me." Trent stood. So did Jacob. Was it his imagination or had the room shrunk even more since they were kids? They were both practically hitting their heads on the slanted ceiling. "Chloe probably thinks I've acted like an idiot."

"Well, maybe you have," Jacob said. He smiled.

"Maybe." Trent chuckled and ran his hand over his jaw. The stubble he'd shaved off yesterday was already starting to grow back. "Chloe doesn't let me get away with anything."

Then the smile faded from his face. "I've been undercover with the Wolfspiders for years, and this is the first time Uncle has turned against me. I can't assume it'll be the last. Knowing him, he'll probably lay low for a bit and wait to see what my next move is. Hopefully the fact that I'm going to disappear and fall off the map again when I head to the diamond mine will be enough to make him think he's scared me into hiding. If he still truly believes I'm dirty, he'll think I'm more use to him alive. He won't make a big move against the family if he thinks he can still use me. But when I finally do take him down, it will put a target on the backs of everyone I love."

His brother nodded. "We'll discuss it with the family. I'll try to convince the folks to take a holiday somewhere warm for a few weeks while we wait to see how this is all going to play out. Then maybe I should move home for a bit to keep an eye on the folks while you're away."

"Maybe," Trent said. *Lord, am I overreacting? Was Uncle just meting out a beating on me to remind me who's in charge? Or does last night mean everything's changed in my game of cat and mouse with Uncle, and he'll come after me again?*

Jacob went downstairs, leaving Trent to get dressed in a borrowed pair of jeans and a plaid shirt. Of the four Henry boys, only the youngest, Nick, still lived at home, and even then only between stints of military service. But the four bachelor brothers always returned home for Christmas. He never imagined he'd be the first one to bring a woman home for the holidays, even if he hadn't done it on purpose.

His feet walked slowly down the wooden stairs and crossed through the living room. A fire crackled in the redbrick hearth, filling the space with warmth. A real and towering Christmas tree stretched up to the ceiling. The sound of laughter and the smell of bacon floated toward him. He paused in the doorway. Mom and Dad, Jacob, Max and Nick all sat around the old kitchen table passing plates of food, eating and talking. And there, in the middle of it all, sat Chloe, clad in one of his old gray sweatshirts and a pair of his jeans from high school days, when he was still all stringy limbs and before he'd put on any bulk.

He watched as she laughed and smiled, bantered with his family about her plans to spend Christmas dinner with her sister's family and accepted the bacon Max dumped on her plate before drizzling a dose of his mother's maple syrup over it. Chloe fit with his family, somehow. She belonged there, in that happy mass of Henry family breakfast, in a way he was never sure he had.

"Trent! Sit! Eat!" His father's voice boomed through the kitchen. Trent felt all faces turn. But no sooner had Chloe's eyes met his than she looked back down at her plate again. His father crossed the room toward him.

"Food's getting cold. I was just about to throw some extra bacon on."

"Dad, Mom, guys, I'm sorry to cause you all so much trouble. We need to talk about what last night could mean, for all of us."

His dad's large, callused hand landed on his shoulder.

"I know." His dad's voice dropped. "Jacob's already briefed us. He's called someone from Victim Services who can come brief us later, and we will talk more. In the meantime, stop blaming yourself for things out of your control. Sit. Eat. Talk to your family. It's Christmas Eve." He steered him toward the seat beside Chloe, even as Nick rose to vacate it and pull up a chair on the other side of the table. "You're home now."

Home. In Dad's way of thinking that meant the place where some things didn't have to be said and long explanations didn't have to be given, because being sorry was enough to be forgiven, and forgiveness was all that mattered. But what happened when someone did something bigger than a mere apology could cover? How did a person just accept forgiveness, drop their baggage at the door and take a seat at the table?

Sure, he'd physically stepped through the door and joined the family, dozens and dozens of times, acting like he was one of them. But somehow it had never been enough to fully remove that invisible barrier he'd felt spring up and block off his heart from theirs in the terrible moment he'd learned that Faith had died.

No matter how many times he'd told them he was sorry for not keeping her safe and they'd assured him he was forgiven.

No matter how many times his father told him he was home.

His father's hand was still resting kindly on his shoulder. Trent sat beside Chloe and said sheepish hellos around the table, thanking them all for what they'd done last night. He took the food his family passed him and the coffee Jacob poured into his cup. His good shoulder brushed against Chloe's.

"I'm sorry," he said. "This isn't how I wanted you to meet my family."

"They're really rather wonderful." She smiled. But her gaze seemed to sweep in everyone but him.

"Are you okay?" he asked. Was she hurt? Was she angry or disappointed in him? Were they still okay?

"I'm a little sore," she said. Her eyes were green again, without the colored contacts she'd worn the night before. "As I gather Jacob told you, I called the powers that be and filled them in on what happened last night and the state of our investigation. Apparently the Wi-Fi went down in the night, so I've only been able to use your family's landline. Your brother Nick is hoping to get the Wi-Fi back right after breakfast."

She smiled and yet her eyes stayed silent. As if that secret and unspoken connection they shared—the one that enabled them to read each other's thoughts in a glance—was gone. She held up her mug toward Jacob for a refill of fresh coffee.

"Fresh cream and maple syrup, right?" Max asked.

"Oh, absolutely." She reached out her hands as they were passed down the table to her.

Trent watched as she poured both into her coffee and stirred it slowly, turning it from her usual plain black to the color of caramel that, to her, meant comfort and home.

Conversation flowed again around the table like an

invisible current of warmth and happiness, sweeping Chloe up along with it and carrying her along. As breakfast finished, he stood and reached to help clear the dishes. But his mother waved him down. "Don't worry about it, Trent. We've got more than enough hands. Why don't you go show Chloe the barn?"

The barn. In other words, she was suggesting he take Chloe to the one place on the family farm where he used to go to deal with the loss of his sister, Faith.

It was a conversation he and Chloe needed to have, and should have probably had long before this moment. Now, with everything crashing around him, could he really afford the time to open his heart to Chloe?

"Don't worry," Jacob said softly, as if reading his mind. "Whatever we do next, it can wait twenty minutes. Nick's busy working on the phones. I'm going to sit Mom and Dad down to talk about that vacation we talked about. There's only one road into the farm and the barn's close. You'll be in sight lines of the farmhouse the entire time. I've got things covered."

Right. But still, the sooner he left the farm the safer his family would be.

He glanced at Chloe. She nodded. "Sounds good to me."

He found his coat hanging on his childhood hook by the back door and his boots in the cubby with his name on it. Chloe helped him zip it up over the sling. They pushed through the back door. Bright sunshine met his eyes, filtering through thick flakes that danced in incongruously from pale clouds to the north. Snow lay thick and white in pure unbroken sheets at their feet, spreading out to the horizon.

Trent and Chloe walked, in silence, their footsteps

crunching in the snow, past the frozen pond and toward the barn. His eyes searched her face as they walked. But her features were so emotionless it was like she was carved from ice.

"I'll be honest, Chloe," he said. "So much has happened in the past twenty-four hours that I literally don't have a clue what to say right now. Two days ago, I was a hockey coach, facing down the end of my investigation into which of four young men in Third Line had a connection into a dangerous new designer drug. It was supposed to be a quick and simple assignment.

"All I had to do was find out who was making and selling the stuff then I could move on to my next investigation. But then the Gulos attacked the sports center and threatened Third Line. You sprung to their rescue and mine.

"Then you were attacked, a potential informant reached out, we went undercover together, Royd attacked again and suddenly I discovered the so-called simple case I was working on was actually linked to the biggest, meanest, nastiest gang I knew and their leader, Uncle. It's like an onion that keeps having layer after layer and each one is worse the deeper it goes. Then the Wolfspiders drove us off the road and you saved my life, called my brother and brought me home."

Chloe stopped walking. He stopped, too, and she turned toward him. And for the first time since the moment they'd met, he saw an emotion in the depths of her eyes he'd never seen directed at him before. She was angry and something about that knocked him back further than a physical blow ever could. "Why are you angry?"

"I never said I was angry—"

"You didn't have to. Chloe, it's me. I can usually read your face. Just like you can usually read mine."

She shook her head, like she was trying and failing to shake the raw emotion from her gaze. "This is probably going to sound pretty petty. But spending time with your family makes me feel even worse about mine. Yes, I have Olivia and I love her more than anything. But you have no idea how much I'd have given for what you have."

Her hands swung out as if painting the farmhouse and scenery around her. "This is perfect. This is ideal. You have a home, Trent. You have two parents who still love each other. You have three brothers, all of whom have dedicated their lives to taking care of others. The six of you are actually able to sit around a table and enjoy a meal together without bragging, competing, guilt-tripping or resentful silences. It's like something out of a fairy tale. Yet you spent your teen years rebelling like a brat and hanging out with people like Savannah?"

"I never dated Savannah!" His voice rose. "I know that probably doesn't seem important right now, but I need you to understand that. In her mind, we had a relationship. But my heart doesn't work like that. It doesn't connect with people. It can't. I can't explain it."

She stared at him. Wind tossed her hair around her face. "Try."

She really wanted to hear it? Fine.

"You think my family is perfect and ideal? Well, it's not. It's broken. And I'm the one who broke it. I'm really good at pretending to fit in. I'm good at talking to people, making superficial connections, getting people to like me and then moving on. But I don't do real relationships and I sure don't do vulnerability or romance.

It's like the part of me that knows how to give and receive love is broken."

At least, it had been until he'd met her. Something about being with Chloe had kicked the dust off his heart, pulled on its chain and tried to get it running again. Chloe had made his heart feel like it was capable of love. Until he'd gone and ruined everything with her, too.

"You've done and said a lot of foolish things since I've met you, Trent, but that lie you've somehow convinced yourself of is the worst!" Raw fire filled her gaze, burning a hole through his rusted chest. "Your heart isn't broken. You shut it off. You're like a kid who put himself in time-out, when nobody asked him to, and now has forgotten that all he has to do to get out of the corner is turn himself around. Don't forget, I was there when you passed out in the snow. I was there when your brothers brought you home. I was there when your mother and father saw them carry you in. I saw the looks on all their faces. More than that, I know you, Trent. And I know you have the biggest, strongest heart of anyone I've ever met—"

"Just a few hours ago, at Pit 11," he said, "you were shouting that I was so determined to shut people out, that I hurt everyone who cares about me and that I wreck everything I touch—"

"That was my cover talking!"

"Every good cover is based on a hint of truth!" He had to tell her. His mother was right to tell him to take her to the barn. He had to show her. It was the only way she'd understand. He stretched out his hand. "Come with me, please. There's something I need to show you."

She took his hand. They broke into a jog as he led

her to the barn and they burst through the door, out of the snow. The warm, welcoming smell of hay filled his senses. They stood there in the darkness for a moment, panting, their eyes on each other as they waited for their vision to adjust to the lack of light. Then he slowly pulled his hand from hers, slid it onto her shoulder and turned her toward the side wall.

There, painted on the wood, was the outline of a girl, willowy and tall, carrying an old-fashioned torch in one hand and a schoolbag in another. A dark maze of lines spiraled down around her protectively like branches, joining more branches and flowers that grew up from the base.

Underneath read one word. *Faith.*

"Mom painted this," he said. "I used to have a sister. Her name was Faith. She was so unbelievably smart. She was always reading, and teachers loved her. We were in the same grade, even though she was over a year younger than me, because she was so quick at learning stuff, and I was so slow that school was like painful gibberish half the time.

"She'd make these supersmart jokes that I didn't understand. Then she'd laugh really, really loudly at them, even if nobody else was laughing. She had the loudest laugh of anyone I'd ever met and she never cared if she was the only one laughing.

"She died when she was twelve and I was thirteen. I was full of anger and full of pain. Uncle and the Wolfspiders took advantage of that. Because it was my… because I'd…"

He couldn't say the words. He couldn't tell the rest of the story. He'd never told it to anyone before and now the words wouldn't cross his lips. The old familiar sting of pain, anger and shame filled his core.

He turned away from Chloe and toward the wall that had born the brunt of his anger so many times as a teenager. His hand rose. His fingers balled into a fist. But he stayed his hand and wouldn't let the blow fly. He wasn't a young man anymore. He wasn't the person he'd been.

There was a dent in the wall in front of him, inches from where his fist would've landed. There was another dent, a few inches to the right and another a few inches to his left. He saw more dents, above him, below him, spreading out on all sides, and realized with a start that his father had never asked him to repair them or done it himself, but had left them there as a testament to the grief Trent had felt.

Emotion choked his throat, but not like the blind pain of the young man he'd been, more like the grief of a grown man who'd seen countless families torn apart by similar pain, violence and evil, and who knew he'd given every breath in his lungs to fight it.

His fingers unclenched. He braced his open palm against the wall.

"I've blamed myself for my sister's death," he said. "Because I wasn't there for her. She was murdered by a monster, because I let her down when she needed me the most."

Pain pierced Chloe's heart. Her hand slid over his back and up to his uninjured shoulder. He didn't flinch, but he also didn't turn. He stood there, his palm against the wall.

"I was supposed to meet up with her after school so we could walk home together," he said. "It was one of those rules that meant a lot to my parents, but from my perspective as an arrogant kid it seemed like nothing but a hassle. So I gave her the slip because I wanted to hang out with the cool kids behind the gym and bum a smoke without getting caught. I hid from Faith and made her walk home alone. Then I sauntered home an hour late, feeling cocky and like I'd pulled something off. Only, when I got here, Jacob was waiting outside for me, there were cop cars everywhere and my mom was... crying, howling, like I'd never heard anyone sob before.

"I didn't know that adults had been worried because some car had been seen cruising back roads, like a predator hunting for someone to hurt, or that two girls from another school had already been harassed by him but had gotten away. I never imagined that when Faith was walking home, alone, some predator would stop his car, grab her and try to...take...her..." Unshed tears choked the words from his throat.

"I'm so sorry," Chloe whispered.

She'd known so many girls and women like Faith. She'd dedicated her life to saving them, seeking justice for them and punishing those who'd hurt them. She'd hugged countless survivors and relatives as they'd grieved. She'd cried for them in the privacy of her own room and then come back, stronger, ready to fight another day. Now here she was, seeing the strongest and most amazing man she'd ever known being broken down by that same pain.

Lord, what a horrible weight and burden he's carried all these years. Help him to forgive himself. Help me to help him bear it. Help him to know he doesn't have to carry it alone.

She slipped into the space between his body and the wall and stood there, her back to the slats that had borne the brunt of his pain. Her arms slid around him.

He bent down, until his forehead brushed hers. Her eyes closed. Tears slid down her face and onto his. They stood there, their foreheads touching and their chests beating into each other.

"The monster didn't succeed in abducting her," Trent whispered, his voice hoarse. "She fought back hard. She fought for her life and refused to let him take her. Police said she died quickly. That he choked her out in seconds and left her there. They said she died fighting."

"Sounds like she was very strong and very smart," Chloe said.

"Yeah, she was pretty tough." He chuckled, sadly. "Typical Henry."

His palm slid off the wall and around her waist. He held her there for a moment and she leaned up against the gentle rise and fall of his chest.

"They never found the guy," Trent added. "They found his skin under her fingernails and his blood on her hands. Police think it was because of her that he disappeared after that and left the area. His car was never seen again. They did DNA tests and compared him to everyone who could possibly be connected with her life. Nothing was a match. Jacob hasn't given up on finding the guy, though. That's part of what led him into Criminal Investigations."

"You realize that Jacob probably blames himself, too, as do your parents." She opened her eyes. Her hand brushed his jaw. "Look at me. You can't live your life punishing yourself for this. It's not what your smart, strong sister who loved to laugh would've wanted. You were just a kid. You had no way of knowing anything like that would happen. A predator like that was probably watching the area for weeks or months. If it hadn't been her, it would've been someone else or he might have targeted her another day in another place. You're a cop. You know this. We do our best, but sometimes we can't stop all evil from ever happening."

"I know." Blue eyes looked deeply into hers. "But in a way, knowing that makes it worse."

"I don't understand," she said. How was blaming himself better than accepting some things were out of his hands?

"Because as long as I keep blaming myself and telling myself that it was my fault, I can fool myself into thinking I had the power to stop it." His thumb brushed the trail of tears from her cheeks. "What's the worst option? Believing I failed? Or accepting that no matter how hard I fight and how hard I try, there are some villains I'm never going to catch and sometimes there's no way to prevent those I care about from getting hurt? How do I let myself care about anyone knowing I'm incapable of protecting them?"

He closed his eyes again and she felt his breath on her lips. She closed her eyes, too, and Trent let out a long sigh that bordered on a groan. "How do I let myself love someone knowing I might lose them?"

"I don't know," Chloe whispered. "All I know is I can't control when I fall. I can only control where I land."

"Well, it feels like I'm falling," Trent said, "and all I know is that with you is where I want to land."

Trent's mouth brushed over hers, soft and deep. He kissed her in a way that felt like a request for forgiveness and a desire to be known. He kissed her like he'd meant it, and he always had, but had been too afraid to say so. She kissed him back, her hands in his hair and her body in his arms, like they were both falling and holding on to each other as they fell.

Her phone buzzed in her pocket. Then it buzzed a second time, a third and a fourth. She pulled away from the kiss. He stepped back and let her out of the embrace. She took out her phone. It kept buzzing. Message after message arriving. "Nick must've gotten the Wi-Fi working."

She had twenty-seven texts. From at least six different numbers.

Hey. I think I know who has payara. Hodge.

Hi, it's Aidan. Can we meet up and talk? I know who had the drugs. I didn't tell because he said they weren't his and I believe him. Also, have you seen Coach? They rescheduled the Haliburton game for tonight because of the fight and everything yesterday.

Hello, Detective. It's Brandon. If I talk to you, will you promise not to tell my grandfather?

'Sup. It's Johnny. Wanna talk? Want coffee?

Hi. It's Poppy. I think Johnny does steroids. I don't know about other drugs, though. Also, I'm really not dating him. He dates a lot of girls. He's kind of a player.

Hi. Can we talk? It's Lucy.

Hi, miss. I think I saw some pills in Brandon's bag one time and he tossed them in the garbage can. He said he thought someone had been messing in his bag. I didn't tell the police because I didn't know for sure and his grandfather is a jerk who'd stop paying his tuition and throw him in jail. Also I'm Milo.

"It's Third Line!" She laughed in a mixture of relief and amazement. Her thumb scrolled through the messages. Then she held up the phone and let him read. "I gave them this big speech last night after Royd was arrested about responsibility and stepping up. I told them it was up to them to stop the flow of payara and save their community. I told them all to text me whatever they knew about payara and they are!"

Trent stepped back and ran his hand over his jaw. "The third-line players are texting you about payara?"

"Yes." She watched as he read the messages. "See? They want to talk. They want to help. We have to question them again. If it's true that Brandon threw the drugs in the garbage can, that's a major breakthrough to finding out who's selling them. We have to go back to Bobcaygeon."

"No, we don't." Trent shook his head. "We have to follow the investigation and the investigation has moved so far beyond mere college students using pills at this point. It's not about Third Line anymore.

"It's about whoever Royd is working with and whatever he and the Wolfspiders are planning. We have other leads now. Like I told you, Coach Henri is gone. Eli has taken over the team and I sent in my resignation to Trillium."

"But the third-line players—" Chloe started.

"Were a means to an end," he interrupted softly. "You know that. I wasn't ever really their coach. I was there to get information out of them when we thought they were the best lead we had. Now we have better leads. This case isn't about four mediocre hockey players from a small-town community college anymore. Now we know the Gulos and the Wolfspiders are both somehow involved. The Wolfspiders ran us off the road last night. Not to mention, I'm injured. I'm not going back to Bobcaygeon."

"Well, I am." Chloe's chin rose. "You might be used to walking out of people's lives without saying goodbye and dropping your mask at the door. But I'm not, and that's not how I do my job. I made them a promise that if they were honest with me, I'd help them."

Cold wind rushed in through the door, sending it flying back on its hinges.

Trent was still shaking his head. He didn't get it. He probably never would. But she still had to try to explain.

"The story of my life is littered with people who just disappeared," she said. "People who promised to write letters I never heard from again. Friends who stopped talking to me because of some argument my father had with their father. Relationships that vanished overnight.

"We talked about broken parts of ourselves? Well, my father's shenanigans broke the part of me that knew how to trust. I asked these students to trust me. They are. I'm not letting them down. I'm going to listen to them. Maybe it won't help solve the payara case. But I can still put them in touch with lawyers, social workers, therapists, churches, support groups, Victim Services or whatever else they need. I'm going to show them that cops are worth trusting."

"I can't go back," he said again. His shoulders flinched and he winced, as if he'd tried to cross his arms before remembering his injured shoulder wouldn't let him. "For me, when a door is closed, it's closed. If you go back, I can't protect you."

"I never asked you to protect me." She slipped the phone in her pocket and grabbed his free hand in hers. "I don't need you to promise to keep me safe—even though I adore the fact that you want to try. What I need is someone who's there for me, day in and day out, who I can count on not to just disappear."

She watched as his eyes scanned the barn wall, as if drawing lines connecting all the holes he'd punched there.

"Let's walk," he said. "We need to talk. I told you this payara case was supposed to be just a short-term assignment tiding me over until a big gang investigation started. Well, it's pretty far away."

Her heart stopped. "How far?"

"Pretty far," he said. They stepped out of the shelter of the barn and back into the snow. "I'm going to be a long ways away and we won't be able to communicate while I'm gone."

Her eyes rose to the snow falling from above. Trent was disappearing from her life yet again. "How long will you be gone?"

"A really long time," he said. "I'm sorry. But I'll be going after a source we suspect is funding a lot of organized crime. It could be my opportunity to cripple the Wolfspiders, the Gulos and countless other gangs. It'll be a huge investigation."

"And you'll be the one on the inside," she said. "Why? There are dozens of excellent undercover officers. You could be leading them, guiding them, training them and overseeing their missions. You could be the running point from head office as part of a team, making the difference you want to make and still coming home at night, instead of walking away from everything you've got."

"What am I walking away from, Chloe? What specifically? Tell me. What's here that's worth staying for?" Something deep and aching echoed in his eyes and shook something inside her. There was a question there. One that he wasn't ready to speak and she didn't know how to answer. How could she tell him she loved him and ask him to stay, when he'd just end up leaving, anyway?

The sound of motors filled the air. Trent turned. A motorcade of beaten-up vehicles pulled into the driveway.

His face paled. "I'm so sorry, I was wrong! Run! Call the police. Tell my family to hide. Get them to safety." He pushed her shoulder. "Go!"

She turned and ran. Her footsteps pelted toward the farmhouse, even as questions swarmed her brain like the vehicles converging around the farmhouse. Then she saw the dented red truck that had run her off the road and the white van that had bumped them from behind. She saw the enforcers from the night before spilling from the vehicles and standing shoulder to shoulder like a shield.

Then she saw Uncle climbing out of a truck behind them.

"Trent!" Uncle called. "Glad to see you're still standing. Sorry for the unexpected house call, but I've got a brand-new problem, and you are going to be the solution. You have five minutes to tell your family and girlfriend goodbye, and then we're going for a drive." He turned to a large man holding a semiautomatic and gestured to Chloe. "Shoot her in the leg and then grab her. Trent's stubborn and will need to see what the penalty will be of him saying no."

Chapter Thirteen

Prayer filled Trent's heart as he watched the large, ugly gang enforcer set Chloe in his sights. What was Uncle doing here at his family's farm? How had he been so wrong? He'd believed all this time Uncle would keep to his word and leave his family alone.

"Stop!" Trent called. If he got in the vehicle with Uncle, he'd never make it out alive. But what other choice did he have? He couldn't let Chloe get hurt. He'd give up his own life, if that's what it took to save hers. "I'll go with you."

Uncle smirked, like a hunter that knew he'd finally found his prey's weakness. "Good. Tell your girlfriend to stop, drop to her knees and raise her hands."

"Chloe, stop!" Trent begged. "Trust me. It'll be okay."

But Chloe didn't stop. She ran, strong and straight, with her head down and elbows up, toward the enforcer like a linebacker. The enforcer fired. Chloe leaped. Bullets hit the snow beneath her. Her body struck the enforcer, knocking him back into the snow. He swore and leaped to his feet. But it was too late. Chloe had already scrambled up the front steps and through the front door as someone on the inside flung it open for her. The enforcer spun and shot at the space on the porch where she'd been just seconds before. The farmhouse's front window shattered.

"Uncle! You came for me! Here I am!" Trent shouted. His free hand rose. Could he take an armed Wolfspider enforcer down with a dislocated shoulder? Maybe. But there was no way he could take an entire army of them. Even if Chloe or Jacob was already on the phone with Dispatch it would take police at least fifteen minutes to get vehicles out to the farm. His best hope was to stall. "Are you really so scared of me that you had to bring everybody and his brother to talk to me? Come on! It's Christmas Eve. People have better things to do than stand around in the snow."

Ugly murmurs rippled through the crowd. The Wolfspiders knew as well as Trent did that if the man who never got his hands dirty was making a house call, it could only mean one thing: execution.

Lord, I knew from the first day I decided to walk back into the Wolfspiders' den as an undercover cop that my life could end like this. If I die today, let me die protecting those I love.

Uncle smirked. "What happened to your shoulder? Don't tell me you got into some kind of trouble after you left the grill last night."

"Fender bender with a reckless driver." Trent's smile grew tight. He prayed that the police were on the way and that his family had gotten to safety. Sure, Jacob was a decorated cop, Max had seen more than his fair share of trauma as a paramedic and Nick had served a term in the military. But they were grossly outmatched and this was his fight. "I thought you said you were

going to let me and Royd sort things out between ourselves."

"I'm having a bit of a problem with Royd." Uncle's
mouth curled into a scowl.

"Oh, really?" Trent blinked. "What kind of problem?"

"Our boy Royd called me this morning from jail and
told me he'd found the payara dealer and the location of
the lab." Uncle looked like even the memory of the conversation had left a bad taste in his mouth. "He claims
he's made a deal with them to take over the operation.
Thought it gave him leverage. Thought he could use it
to negotiate with me for a new role in my organization."

Really? Wow. Well, Royd never had been the sharp-
est knife in the drawer and preferred brute force over
thought and precision. But if Uncle thought that he
could use Trent to teach Royd a lesson—let alone hurt
whichever Third Line player was involved—he had another thought coming. He prayed it wasn't Brandon. Or
Aidan. Or Milo. Or Hodge. It was funny. For months
he'd been looking at the third-line players as suspects.
Now he found himself hoping he'd been dead wrong.
The thought of any of them being in trouble, like he'd
once been, was unthinkable.

"Sounds like Royd betrayed you. I don't see what
any of this has to do with me."

"Oh, you're going to fix this for me." Uncle's sneer
grew into a vicious grin. "Obviously, I need to teach
Royd a lesson. I reached out to the Gulos. Figured if
they wanted payara so badly, it gave me a sweet opportunity to broker a deal. So we're going to team up, go
after the supply chain together, find the lab, convince
the manufacturer to work for us instead and then split
the distribution."

Right, of course he was going to sell Royd out to a rival gang, leave it to them to track him down and kill him, once again keeping Uncle's own hands clean.

But what Uncle was describing was no less than a major shift in Canada's gang warfare power structure.

He couldn't imagine what leverage Uncle could have possibly used to make the Gulos agree to it, and the truce would be unlikely to last once Uncle had his hand on the payara supply. But until they did, it would be carnage. Finding and destroying the lab would be just the start, as they flushed out the next lab and the next, and took out anyone in their way. Who knew how many civilians and police would die and how much property would be destroyed in the process? What had happened at the sports center in Bobcaygeon was only the beginning.

Help me, Lord. Help me stop this.

Trent walked forward, knowing his voice was the only weapon he had left. "Again, what are you doing here? What does any of this have to do with me? I'm not about to help you kill Royd or broker a deal with the Gulos."

A chuckle spread through the crowd. It sent shivers up his spine and he didn't know why.

"Oh, yes, you are!" Uncle said. "You couldn't imagine how interested the Gulos were when I told them that the Wolfspiders had their very own undercover cop. One who'd also arrested countless Gulos and ruined several of their major operations. Not to mention someone who knew everything there was to know about drugs, weapons and human trafficking in Canada, including the location of secret dens, trade routes, where the various people have hidden their money and the identity of other undercover cops. A treat as sweet as a dirty cop like you was just too good for one gang to keep all to themselves. Just imagine what they'd do to a cop like that and the information they'd pull from him once I turned him over."

So, Uncle hadn't just negotiated a truce with the Gulos to punish Royd and take over the payara operation. He'd offered up Trent as bait. No wonder they hadn't come back sooner to finish the job after the crash. He was confident Uncle wasn't foolish enough to give up Trent's actual identity without a deal being made, so he was going to deliver Trent to the Gulos himself. Trent grit his teeth as his eyes rose to the sky in prayer.

Lord, I can't let them take me. I can't let the Gulos force me to tell them all I've learned during my career. Too many lives hang in the balance. But if I don't, what happens to my family and Chloe?

"My promise not to harm your family as long as you obey me still stands," Uncle said, as if reading his mind. "I won't touch them, even after you're dead. Everybody knows I'm a man of my word. But, you try anything, and we'll swarm your parents' house and burn it to the ground. Now, hands on your head. You're coming with us."

The door creaked behind him.

"He's not going anywhere." Chloe's voice filled the air.

Chloe, please, go back inside. Can't you see how outnumbered we are? You can't give up your life for me.

He turned. Chloe stood on the front porch of his family home, her service weapon held strong and firm in one hand and her badge in the other. But she wasn't alone. Jacob stood beside her in full uniform, holding his service weapon. Nick stood beside him in his fatigues, armed with the gun he'd gotten for his nineteenth birthday, and Max stood beside him, his paramedic's bag at his feet and Dad's new hunting rifle at his shoulder. Then Trent saw his father holding his older hunting revolver and this mom with the family's shotgun in one hand and the phone to her ear. His whole family—everyone he loved—stood on the front porch of the farmhouse, weapons at the ready, willing to defend his life.

"Go back inside!" Trent yelled. "Now! Go inside and lock the door! This is going to get ugly and none of you are going to die for me!"

"We're Henrys, son." Tears filled his father's eyes. "Henrys never go down without a fight."

"Don't you get it? I need to protect you!" *Like I didn't protect Faith.*

"No, you don't!" Jacob cut him off firmly. "Don't you get it, Trent? We already lost one of us. We're not losing another."

He did. Suddenly and overwhelmingly, as he looked from face to face and saw that same fierce, protective love he felt for each one of them filling their eyes for him in return. He could see the forgiveness he'd never let himself see. He could feel the wall he'd built around his heart crumbling in rubble at his feet.

"Enough!" Uncle snapped. He pushed past the Wolfspiders protecting him. "You're outnumbered. Trent, I own you. I will always own you and I will kill you when I'm ready. And if any of them try to get in my way, I will kill them, starting with your detective fiancée."

The single gunshot rang loud and clear, striking Uncle in the shoulder, and Trent watched as the man who'd threatened his life ever since he was a teenager crumpled to his knees in the snow.

The Wolfspiders hesitated. The large enforcer raised his weapon and aimed it toward the house. Trent leaped on him from behind, knocking him to the ground one-handed. The sound of police and emergency vehicles filled the air. A pair of handcuffs appeared at the corner of Trent's vision. He looked up, expecting Chloe. It was Jacob. Trent let his brother take over the arrest and cuff the enforcer. Then he pulled himself to his feet.

A mass of shouts and motors filled the air. Wolfspiders rushed to their vehicles even as police poured down the driveway, cornering them. Then he saw Max down on his knees beside Uncle, tending to his wound. Chloe was at Uncle's other side, arresting him.

"Chloe shot the bullet that took down Uncle," Jacob said. "It's a nonfatal through-and-through. She said something about how you'd told her not to shoot him until he actually explicitly threatened to kill either one of you. Her nerves are amazing."

"She's incredible." Trent stood there for a moment and watched as Chloe read Uncle his rights. Then he stepped back and waited while Jacob handed the enforcer off to another officer. The sheer volume of vehicles swarming the farmhouse lawn was unbelievable. There were dozens of officers in full riot gear, taking down criminal after criminal. It was like something out of a dream. He watched as Chloe went over and introduced herself to the officer in charge. Jacob came back to Trent. "How on earth did you make this happen?"

"Don't look at me," Jacob said. "Chloe made all the calls. I was busy giving the rest of the family a crash course on the Criminal Code of Canada sections on reasonable force in terms of self-defense and protections of others. Dad wasn't about to let some Wolfspiders storm the old farmhouse or kidnap you."

"You didn't think try to convince our family not to get into a standoff with criminals?" Trent asked.

"What can I say? We're all Henrys." Jacob chuckled. "But in all seriousness, Chloe mobilized this operation. People came out of the woodwork in an instant to make this happen, like nothing I've ever seen before. Your fiancée's reputation is stellar."

He could tell his big brother was trying to make a joke. But it wasn't funny.

"You know that Chloe and I aren't actually in a romantic relationship," Trent said.

"Whose fault is that?" Jacob said. "You do realize you're just standing here, while she's over there making what should be the biggest arrest of your career?"

"I know." He guessed that under any other circumstances watching another cop take down the man he'd waited years to arrest would sting somewhat. But somehow this was better. "It's okay. It's good for her to have Uncle's arrest on her record. You know she's in the running for the next detective sergeant post that opens up? She'll get it, too. Only like twelve percent of all senior officers are women. She'll be one of them."

Jacob's eyes searched his brother's face. "And what do you want?"

"I want to marry her," Trent admitted. "Not that I'd ever ask. And not that I expect she'd ever say yes. I've never even really admitted to her that I have feelings for her. It's all push and pull with us. One step forward, two steps back.

"We had a moment in the barn where I told her about

Faith and it was like something changed between us.
But when I told her that I was heading off on another
undercover mission, the roller coaster crashed right back
down again. She needs someone steady. I'm not steady.
I assume a different cover identity every few weeks."
Or at least, that's what he'd always told himself.

Jacob didn't answer. Instead the two cops just stood
there for a long moment and watched the police operation unfold around them. Then Trent ran his hand over
his head. "I need to think and I need to pray. Can you
cover for me if I take a walk? I won't leave the farm. I
just think that Chloe and I need to have a long talk, and
I want to get my head on straight first."

"Sure thing." Jacob clasped Trent's good shoulder
in a quick half hug.

Trent turned and walked up the hill to the tree line
of the Henry farm. He brushed the snow off a log and
sat gazing down on the scene below.

*Lord, I don't even know what to pray for right now.
To ask You for a happily-ever-after with Chloe feels
selfish. But, if You help me find a way, I'll love and protect her with all the strength You've given me.*

The wind whistled in the trees. The number of lights
circling below slowly diminished as vehicle after vehicle pulled out of the driveway. Finally he saw a solitary
figure, tall and strong in dark green fatigues, climbing
up the hill toward him. He stood. "Nick, hey!"

"Chloe took off," Nick said. "One of the other officers lent her their personal car to drive to Bobcaygeon."

"What?" Trent leaped to his feet. Chloe was gone?
Just like that? "Did you guys tell her where I was?"

"Of course we did." His little brother shrugged and
ran one hand through his chestnut hair. Nick wasn't

much older than the third-line players. "But she's as stubborn as you and didn't want to be convinced. Not that we didn't try. I don't pretend to get it. I'm the wrong person to ask about what women mean when they say things. Mom or maybe Jacob could explain it better than me. I got the impression Chloe thought you'd done a disappearing act on her and she said she was in a hurry to get to a hockey game."

The youngest of the Henry boys could understand anything mechanical or practical. But relationships weren't his strong suit.

Trent groaned. "I'm guessing you all had a quick family meeting and you drew the short straw to come be the one to tell me that Chloe'd left me?"

"Nah, bro." A grin filled Nick's face. He reached into his pocket and pulled out a pair of car keys. "I pulled the long straw! I'm the one who gets to drive when you go chasing after her."

Chloe locked the doors of the borrowed car and walked through the parking lot toward the Bobcaygeon Sports Center. It had been a long, silent drive through the snow. She'd kicked herself the whole way.

Driving away from Trent had been painful, agonizing even, and his family's attempts to delay her hadn't helped. What would the point have been? Trent had taken off, and she wasn't about to go chasing after him, just so they could have yet another argument hashing out what she already knew. Trent was leaving, no matter what she said or did.

And she loved him, no matter how hard she'd tried to stop her foolish heart from falling. She loved him for all his strengths, all his faults and everything about him that drove her crazy.

Something inside her had started falling for him that very first moment she'd seen those fierce, brave and compassionate blue eyes shining through the rough exterior of his Wolfspider cover. It had only continued to grow through every new and complicated version of Trent she met, like each cover he'd worn had revealed a new truth about the heart of the man who lay inside. But she also knew that her own heart was going to keep breaking over him, unless she was the one who finally gave up and walked away. She'd hung on for far too long to a dream that wasn't ever going to come true.

She stepped into the front entrance and joined the throng of people pressing toward the hockey rink. Her phone rang. She glanced down. It was a blocked number. Hope leaped in her chest. She stepped into an empty hallway and raised the phone to her ear. "Hello? Trent?"

"Hi? Detective Brant?" The voice was young, female and frightened. "Is that you?"

"It is." Chloe's voice dropped. She walked deeper into the empty hall. "Who's this?"

"Lucy... Brandon's sister..."

"Hi, Lucy, of course I remember you..." Chloe walked farther down the hall. The sounds of the crowd faded. "What's up?"

"I made the payara."

"You did what?" Chloe's footsteps froze. Lucy had been making the payara? The young woman behind the coffee counter that she'd saved from the Gulos? Staff Sergeant Butler's timid, nineteen-year-old granddaughter? "I needed money to move to Vancouver to go take cosmetics chemistry, and someone told me there was big money in inventing new pills. He told me he'd pay me really well if I did. So, I made payara."

"Who was that someone?" Chloe could feel her heart beating like a warning drum against her rib cage. Lucy didn't answer. "You're Trilly, aren't you? What happened last night?"

"The guy I told you about found my phone and made me text you. I didn't know that other guy was going to attack you. I promise I didn't! Now he's says he's made some business deal, and we've got to pack up right away and go somewhere. And I don't want to go."

"Who? Who's making you do this, Lucy?" Her brother, Brandon? Her grandfather, Staff Sergeant Butler?

"I can't tell you!"

"Yes, you can!" Frustration and compassion merged in Chloe's heart. The complex relationship between abusers and victims was one of the hardest and most agonizing parts of her job. She'd lost count of how many young women who'd begged to be rescued then went back to their dealer or abuser before the trial. She prayed to God for patience and wisdom. "Where are you now?"

"In the sports center." There was a pause and then a sniffle. "I'm in the basement in the storage room where we keep things for the coffee stand. I was making payara there."

Chloe looked down at the tiles. The payara lab was in the sports center. It had been underneath them the whole time. Her footsteps quickened. "Stay right there. I'm coming to you. Just hang on, okay!" She found a utility door and pushed through into the stairwell. Her feet pounded down the stairs into the basement. The door swung shut behind her. "I'll be there in a moment—"

"Detective!" A voice boomed behind her as she watched the rectangular light cast by the open door grow wider. She turned. Johnny was standing at the top of the stairs, holding the door open. "I was hoping I'd see you! Where are you going? Thought we could grab a coffee or something."

"Johnny, hi!" Was he kidding her with this? A young, male lothario was exactly the kind of distraction she didn't need right now.

She turned back to the phone. "Don't go anywhere, please. I'll be there in a minute." But the line had already gone dead.

"What are you doing hanging out down here?" Johnny lumbered down the stairs toward her. Light dimmed as the door swung shut again. "I was keeping an eye out. Then I saw you and waved. But I guess you didn't see me." He stopped one step above her. "So is it true you and Coach split up? I heard he just quit and took off."

"It's complicated," she said, and nothing she planned to discuss now. "Please, just head back upstairs to the game."

He stepped closer, his head tilted to the side. "But what are you doing down here? You sure you don't need somebody to keep you safe?"

"I'm meeting someone. It's police business. You understand."

"Yeah, I understand." He pressed a gun into her side. "And I'm sorry. Because I really don't want to hurt you."

Chapter Fourteen

Nick pulled his truck to a stop in the sports center parking lot and turned to Trent. "Do you want me to come in with you? Because I should really go get gas and maybe a bite to eat."

"Nah, thanks, I'm good." Trent leaped out the passenger door. "Just don't forget to come back. I might not find Chloe and even if I do, she might not feel like driving me all the way home. I still have no clue what I'm going to say to her."

His little brother chuckled and leaned over the front seat. "I'll tell you a secret, but you gotta promise not to tell the folks. I had a girlfriend on base. Not too proud of how it all went down. Never told Mom and Dad, because I knew they wouldn't approve. It ended badly, and she was so mad I thought for a moment she was going to stab me with a pair of scissors."

Trent's eyebrow rose. "The moral of the story is don't let Chloe near scissors?"

"No, it was just something she said to me. She told me she'd didn't care what my words were, she'd just always hoped I would fight harder for her." He grinned, but his gaze ran to the sky above. "Maybe I should've. But, anyway, my point is that you should go fight for Chloe. Maybe it's not about knowing what to say. It's about just showing up."

"Thanks. I'll give you a call in a few, hopefully with good news." Trent slammed the door with his good hand and walked through the parking lot. *Lord, I wasn't joking. I don't know what to say to her. I don't know what to do. I just know that I love her. I don't know if that's enough.*

His phone began to ring. His heart leaped. It was her. He answered. "Hi! Chloe, I'm here—"

But instantly his voice faded as he heard the steady tap of her fingers drumming SOS in Morse code against the microphone.

"Johnny, put the gun down!" Chloe's voice was muffled. "I'm just putting my phone in my pocket, like you told me to."

Johnny? The Haliburton team center?

His footsteps quickened across the parking lot. Nick's truck was already disappearing down the road. Chloe was in danger and had called him for help. But where was she? He closed his eyes and listened. An ache filled his heart. She had no idea he was even there. She'd called him to give him information about the case. Maybe she'd even called him to say goodbye. Then he heard the sound of footsteps echoing down an empty hallway.

"Johnny, what is this?" Chloe asked. "Why do you have a gun? How did you even convince Lucy to create a payara lab in the basement of the sports center?"

"You've got this all twisted," Johnny said. "I'm not a bad guy. I threw a rock through the window at you when

I found out Lucy had called you, because I thought that might convince you to leave it alone. Now everything's a great big mess and I've got some major problems. I'll get you out of here. We just need to get Lucy first."

"Put the gun down and we'll talk. You don't want to hurt me. You're not a killer. You told me in the gym that you're a tech genius and an entrepreneur."

"I am!" Johnny's voice grew defiant. "I just did business with the wrong people and got in some trouble. But I'm going to fix it. And it'll be fine."

"What kind of wrong people? You mean a gang? You mean the Gulos or the Wolfspiders? I can help you. But not until you put the gun down."

Trent paused outside, beneath the lights of the Christmas tree. People were still streaming through the front door. He wanted to be in the building. But once he joined the crowd he'd lose his ability to hear her. *Keep him talking. I'm here. I'm listening. Tell me what I need to know. Tell me how to rescue you.*

"So, this is your grand plan?" Chloe asked. "Forcing Lucy to make drugs for you? Becoming a common drug dealer?"

"I'm not a common drug dealer!" Johnny's voice rose. "I came up with the idea of inventing a new designer drug. I talked Lucy into it. I found sellers. I got Nicole's passwords to get access to the police computer systems and police scanner, so I always knew what they knew—"

"Constable Docker was helping you? Why?"

Johnny snickered. "She thought we were dating."

"Lucy thinks you're dating, too, doesn't she?"

"Maybe," Johnny said. "And don't believe Poppy.

That picture is totally her. But it was a one-off just to get Hodge to fly off the handle, to create a diversion."

He laughed again and Trent's blood boiled. He looked up to the snow falling from the dark purple sky. Was that how he'd come across? Using people and not realizing who he'd hurt? *Forgive me, Lord.* If so, it had never been on purpose. But it would never happen again. He'd get down on his knees and ask Chloe to make an honest man of him. Just as soon as he found her.

"You found out Lucy had contacted me," Chloe said. Was it his imagination or had their footsteps slowed? "So you tossed me to Royd to take care of. I'm guessing you also overheard that Gulo bellowing that I had his phone, and tipped Royd off about that, too."

Trent nodded as he listened. It was all making sense now. He just wished he'd realized this sooner, before Chloe's life was on the line.

"Royd's crazy." Johnny's voice darkened. "I thought I could play him, but he's a psycho. He told me he's going to make the Gulo attack on the sports center look like child's play. He said he wired bombs to the fire alarm system, so if anyone pulls a fire alarm it sets off the timer to go into countdown mode, giving him just enough time to run out of the building. If you call the police, he'll know. He has my police scanner. He gave us twenty minutes to get all our lab stuff out of the building and leave with him, or he'll set the bomb and *ka-boom*."

Trent's footsteps hurried toward the sports center. A scenario unfolded in his mind. So, Chloe was being held captive by Johnny and presumably they were going to wherever Lucy was. That meant only one hostile who was in over his head. That also gave him twenty minutes to evacuate the building, disarm Johnny, rescue Chloe and Lucy, and call the police. Not easy, but doable. The sound of footsteps slowed. Wherever in the building they were, they'd arrived.

"What is this?" Royd's voice boomed down the phone line. "What is she doing here?"

Royd was already out of jail? Had someone inside the police messed up his arrest or not charged him correctly? Or did Royd have a connection on the inside? Anything was possible. Any faith Trent had in Butler's division had been steadily disappearing ever since this whole mess had started. True, it had been over twenty-four hours since Royd's arrest, so likely he was just out on bail. Trent knew the police might not hold him for long if they'd booked him for assault and not attempted kidnapping. Still, he had hoped that Butler's division would have tried to find a way to hold him longer.

Trent's footsteps quickened.

"I thought we could use her or something," Johnny said.

"You thought wrong," Royd snapped.

Then he heard the sound of a struggle, the phone fell and a gunshot echoed on the line. Chloe cried out. The phone went dead. Trent's heart leaped into his throat. *Oh, Lord, what do I do?* He could save an arena full of people. He could try to save Chloe and Lucy. He couldn't do both. He needed backup. He needed help. He grabbed his phone and dialed.

"Hey, Coach," Brandon answered. "Look, I really don't know what you want but none of the guys want to talk to you right now."

"Listen to me, I need Third Line. Right now. All of you. Meet me in the alley behind the sports center."

"We're already getting changed and I really don't know if I can convince the guys. Everyone's still pretty angry at you."

"I know," Trent said. "I don't blame you and I can explain. But Chloe and Lucy are in danger. Please."

"I'll see what I can do."

Trent ran for the alley. It was empty. He paced while he prayed.

The door creaked.

"Hey, Coach." Aidan's voice came from behind him. "You got some nerve disappearing like that. What happened to your beard?"

He turned, hope filling his heart as Aidan, Brandon, Milo and Hodge filed out into the alley, in various stages of street clothes and hockey gear. Four pairs of skeptical eyes focused on his face. Arms crossed. Mouths frowned. He took a deep breath and pulled out his badge.

"My name is Detective Trent Henry. I'm a detective with the RCMP. I've been undercover as your coach for the past three months, because police thought one of the four of you was selling payara."

Various stages of anger and denial filled their faces. He was surprised none of them swore at him.

"You what?" Hodge found his voice first. "What is this?"

"I get that you're angry," Trent said. "Believe me when I say I understand. You're all great people and I was wrong to think any of you was behind payara. But Johnny talked Lucy into making it. He has her and Chloe trapped somewhere in the building with a criminal named Royd, who wired a bomb to the fire alarm and is threatening to blow the whole place up."

"I don't believe you!" Aidan snorted. "You're trying to tell me that Brandon's little sister is involved in a drug scheme?"

But one look at Brandon's pale face and Trent could tell that he believed it.

"You're the one who left the payara in the locker room, weren't you, Brandon?" Trent said. "You found it in your bag and didn't know how it had gotten there, so you just hid it a garbage can where it was found by the janitor and turned over to police. The rest of Third Line covered for you. Right?"

Brandon looked down but didn't argue.

Trent took that as a yes. "Well, if your sister didn't put it there, who did? My guess is that she used your bag to get drugs to Johnny during a game, or one of you two grabbed the wrong bag somehow, but either way you had no idea what they were doing there, so your friends agreed to cover for you."

"This is nonsense and I'm not going to stand around listening to it!" Aidan turned to leave. "None of us had anything to do with making or selling payara. So what if Brandon found pills in his bag one time and we all covered for him? We all knew they couldn't be his. You've been lying to our faces for months. Why should we believe anything you say now?"

"My little sister was murdered when I was thirteen and I blamed myself," Trent said. "Trust me, even if this isn't your fault, you don't want this on your conscience.

"You're right. I haven't been straight with you. But Chloe has. She came back here to help you. Now she and Lucy are in trouble. Everyone in this building is in danger. I'm taking a huge risk in blowing my cover to you guys, because if you tell people who I am, or post anything about this online, my days of working under-cover taking down gang operations are over. But I need your help. I can't do this alone."

Silence fell. The guys were looking from one to the other. This was hopeless. They had no reason to trust him.

"Tell me one thing you've said to us since the day we met that wasn't a lie," Hodge said.

"I really do want to marry Chloe. She's not really my fiancée or anything. That part was a cover. But my feelings for her are totally real, and I'd like her to be my wife."

There was another pause that lasted a lot longer than he liked. He could almost feel the moments ticking by.

Then Brandon nodded. "Okay, I'm in. What do you need?"

"I need you to help me find Chloe and Lucy, and someone to evacuate the building without pulling the fire alarm so it doesn't set off the bomb."

"I'll disable the fire alarm," Milo said. "Then if anybody pulls it, nothing will explode."

"I can help you to find Lucy," Brandon said. "I know roughly where in the building she hangs out. But I didn't know what she was doing."

Trent let out a long sigh. "Okay, that leaves Aidan and Hodge to evacuate the building. Everyone good?"

They nodded. Then Aidan stuck his hand out in the middle of the circle and Third Line piled their hands in. Trent placed his hand on top and whispered a prayer. Then they ran.

Pain shot through Chloe's right leg, from where Royd's bullet had grazed it. Her arms ached from the zip tie fastening her hands together behind her back. She was down on the damp, concrete floor of a storage room, watching helplessly as Johnny and Lucy packed equipment into crates and Royd supervised, gun in hand.

Please, Lord, whatever happens to me, may my phone call to Trent have given him enough information to make sure justice is done.

"Lucy, Johnny, you don't have to go with him," she said. "You have a choice."

"Shut up, you!" Royd turned and focused his gun on Chloe.

Johnny's face had gone pale. Royd had taken his gun. "It'll be fine," he said. "Royd knows people. He'll set us up somewhere where Lucy can have a lab and he'll help my business expand. We'll be fine."

"You'll be owned by a gang member!" Chloe's voice rose. "What do you think life in a gang is like, Johnny? Because it's not all fancy parties and flashy cars. It's violence, ugliness and constantly looking over your shoulder wondering who you've got to be afraid of hurting or killing you."

"I said, stop talking!" Royd cuffed her across the face. Pain exploded through her jaw. He glanced at the clock. "Hurry up. I'm not waiting all night."

Lucy's hands shook so hard the glass beakers rattled.

"Listen to me, Lucy, Johnny's just using you." Chloe grit her teeth and talked through the pain. "Just like he used Poppy and Nicole. He doesn't love you. He's never going to protect you from people like Royd."

Lucy didn't look at her. She was on her last box now. The fire alarm switch loomed bright and red on the wall, like a giant self-destruct button.

"That's it," Royd growled. The gun jabbed hard into Chloe's forehead. "I thought maybe I could use you for some kind of leverage. But you're just too much trouble."

Her eyes closed. Silent prayers fell from her lips.

"Royd, put the gun down. This isn't going to end well for you." The voice was deep and strong, and it filled her heart with hope. She opened her eyes.

Trent was standing in the doorway, with Brandon behind him. Trent's eyes met hers. His voice dropped. "Hey, Chloe."

"Trent, you're here."

"Well, seemed only fair to return the favor," he said. But his eyes were serious as they looked at the gun digging into her flesh. Then he turned to the criminal behind it. "Royd, you and I go way back. So, I'll make you a deal. If you let Chloe, Lucy, Brandon and Johnny leave, I'll let you take me as a hostage in their place."

"On your knees, both of you." Royd's eyes cut toward the doorway. "You're in no position to bargain and nobody's going anywhere. You so much as move and I'm going to put a bullet right through her head. Got that?"

"Got it." Trent knelt. His eyes closed and she watched as a silent prayer moved across Trent's lips. Then his eyes met hers. Worry filled his gaze. She had a bullet wound in one leg, her hands tied behind her back and a gun aimed at her forehead, while Trent still had his shoulder in a sling and was down on his knees. But somehow, through all that, she felt safer than she had in a long time.

"Johnny," Royd snapped. "Handcuff them."

The athlete grabbed a zip tie then hesitated, looking at the shoulder sling. He handcuffed Trent to the metal shelf by the door. Then he glanced from Trent to Brandon and back again, and reached for a new zip tie. "I'm sorry about this. But I kind of have to."

"Guess dabbling in crime isn't turning out to be as much fun as you hoped," Trent said. He glanced sideways at Johnny, like Royd wasn't even there. This was one of his favorite tactics—verbal warfare, using his words as a weapon to get under a criminal's skin. "I've been there. Believe it or not, Royd here got me messed up and involved in crime when you all were still babies. Don't worry. I'm going to cause a distraction in a minute. When that happens, Brandon I want you to grab Lucy by the hand and run. Johnny, I sure hope you wise up and run, too. Trust me, you don't want to work for Royd."

Johnny paused inches away from Brandon. The zip tie shook in his hands.

"Are you trying to anger me, talking like that, Trent?" Royd snapped. "I don't know what game you think you're playing. But if you try anything, I'm going to shoot Chloe." He glanced at Johnny and Lucy. "Now, see how big a mess you two caused by involving a detective in this?"

"Now!" Trent shouted.

Royd glanced toward him to stop whatever he thought he was about to pull. Chloe dove forward, head-butting Royd in the chest. The gun fired into the ceiling. Lucy ran toward her brother. Brandon grabbed her by the arm. Their footsteps echoed down the hall. Johnny paused. His eyes darted around the small, collapsing empire he'd created. Then he turned and bolted after them.

Royd scrambled to his feet. The barrel of the gun

swung from Chloe to Trent and back again. "Nice trick. You think this is funny? Neither of you are making it out of here alive. I'll set the timer and go after them, leaving the two of you to blow up in this building."

He yanked the fire alarm. Nothing happened. He swore.

Trent glanced at Chloe. "Milo really is an excellent electrician."

"I've had enough of you, Trent." Royd swung around and pointed the gun at him. "All my life you've acted like you're somehow better than me. When you quit the Wolfspiders and joined the police, I thought you were gone from my life for good. But you came back, and you kept coming back, again and again, convincing everyone you were special. Well, now I'm the one with the power. I'm the one that's going to run payara distribution in Canada. You've got one arm in sling and the other tied to a shelf. Your girlfriend has been shot in the leg and has her hands tied behind her back. I've got the only gun in the room. And I'm going to destroy the only thing you've ever cared about right in front of your eyes."

A fierce and determined grin curved Trent's lips.

That dangerous spark she loved so much flickered in his eyes as Chloe pulled herself up onto her knees. Her eyes met Trent's. He held her gaze.

Royd turned and aimed the barrel of the gun between Chloe's eyes.

Trent roared in pain as he yanked the shelf from its bolts so hard the handcuff snapped free.

Royd fired.

Chloe dropped to the floor and rolled.

Trent threw himself on Royd and wrestled the gun

from his hand with one hand. Then he rolled Royd onto his stomach and pinned him to the ground with his knees and one good hand.

"What happened to those zip ties Johnny was holding?" Trent grunted.

Royd was still struggling and swearing.

Chloe tuned him out like white noise. "By the door," she said. "But what do you expect me to do with them, Cop Boy? My hands are still tied behind my back."

"Okay, fine," Trent said. "Turn your back to me. I'll pin him with my legs and cut your hands free."

"Got it!" She spun her back to him and waited as he yanked a knife from his pocket. The blade slipped between her wrists. He cut her hands free. She lunged for the zip ties and, with Trent's help, forced Royd's wrists together and cuffed them. "What's his full name again?"

"Roy Denver. Teachers would call out 'Roy D' in class, so he insisted we call him Royd, even before he started using steroids."

"Got it." Chloe pulled out her badge and stuck it in front of his face. "Let's try this again. Roy Denver. I am arresting you…"

Her eyes met Trent's. The affection and respect echoed there filled her heart with joy. But still there was a question hovering in their blue depths that gave her pause.

Now what? Now that the case was over and the source of the payara had been found, what happened now?

Chapter Fifteen

Snow fell in thick white flakes, swirling down from the dark sky above. People huddled in clumps behind the safety tape as police swept the sports center for both the remains of the drug lab and the hidden explosives. Flashing lights from emergency vehicles spun white and red, casting the scene in an odd, ethereal glow.

The staff of Nanny's Diner was serving hot chocolate and cookies. A group of the sports fans and players had gathered around the Christmas tree, phones raised above them like pinpoints of light as they sang Christmas carols. Christmas was only a couple of hours away and in the midst of the chaos the community had gathered together.

Trent paced in front of the yellow police tape like a tiger prowling his cage, his eyes scanning the emergency vehicles and staff for one face—Chloe.

After calling 9-1-1, he'd dragged Royd's squirming and defiant form out of the sports center while Chloe hopped alongside him, using a broom handle as a crutch. Thankfully the gun wound had been not much more than a surface scrape and the police had arrived quickly.

"Go," Chloe had told him. "None of these cops know you as anything more than a hockey coach. You might as well try to preserve as much of your cover as you can."

He'd tried to argue that now that Third Line knew the truth of his cover, it was probably spreading like wildfire through the student body, until it ended up online, killing any opportunity of future undercover work. But Chloe had been insistent. So he'd waited until the paramedics reached her then he'd slipped back into the crowd and found his brother Nick and filled him in. That had been almost an hour ago. Nick had wandered off into the crowd, either because he realized his older brother needed space or because Trent's restlessness was driving him nuts.

It was Chloe's case now. She got the glory. He prayed it would lead her to the promotion she'd earned and deserved more than any cop he'd ever known. And when she was done and came looking for him, she would find him there, waiting for her.

Lord, what will I say to her? Where do I start?

"Um, Coach?" Aidan's voice came from behind him. He turned. All four members of Third Line stood in the darkness.

"Guys! You were incredible!" His head shook, as he looked from face to face. "I'm in awe. Seriously. You disabled the alarm. You evacuated the arena." He glanced at Brandon. "You saved your sister's life. I'm so sorry I didn't have faith in you all before. I've never met a more impressive group of young men."

Feet shuffled. Eyes glanced at the ground, at the sky and at everywhere but him.

"It was nothing," Hodge said.

Right, he knew that tune. He'd played it many times himself. "How's Lucy?"

"Good." Brandon nodded. "She's shaken and scared. I'm not excusing what she did, but when she got in over her head with Johnny she was too scared of my grandfather to get help. Chloe introduced her to someone from Victim Services and also a detective friend of hers, and promised she'd be taken care of."

Trent let out a sigh of relief and nodded. "That's good."

"Johnny tried to run," Aidan said. A slight smirk turned his lips. "But Hodge and I saw him running. We caught up with him and made sure he stayed put. But just until the cops could arrest him, of course."

Trent chuckled. His eyes instinctively turned back to the flashing emergency lights. Chloe wouldn't leave without saying goodbye again, would she?

"Coach?" Brandon's voice dragged his attention back to the group. "One more thing. We all talked and decided, collectively as a group, that none of us are going to ever talk about anything you told us about yourself in the alley. Not a word.

"We told the police the truth—that you were our hockey coach and that you'd told us Chloe and Lucy were in trouble. But they didn't ask us if we knew anything else about you and we didn't volunteer that we did. We just wanted you to know that. You can trust us. We have your back. You are Coach Henri to us, and always will be. End of story. We promise."

Trent swallowed hard and let out a long breath. They were protecting his cover. He'd put his life in their hands and given them the opportunity to both blow his cover and ruin his career. Instead they'd promised to protect his cover and guard his secret. "Thank you. I really appreciate that."

"No problem," Aidan said. "We owe you that much."

Trent stuck his hand in the middle of the circle and they piled their hands on top, like a team huddle or sealing a pact. "If you ever need me, for anything, you call me, okay? I'll keep this phone number forever."

There were more nods and a couple of claps on his good shoulder. Then they glanced at something behind him and, as if with one mind, disappeared into the crowd. He looked back. Chloe was making her way toward him on crutches. Her eyes met his.

She smiled. He leaped the police tape and ran toward her. But before he could reach her, she raised one crutch and waved him off. "Don't you dare try to pick me up or I'll throttle you."

His hands rose. "But you're wounded."

"I'm fine. I'm just limping a bit."

"Got it." A grin turned the corner of his lips. "Well, there's a bench over there by the tree. Can I at least convince you to limp over there with me?"

She pretended to frown but the smile in her eyes gave her away. "Sure."

They walked slowly through the snow together, side by side, toward the sparkling swell of lights around the Christmas tree. He lifted the police tape to let her pass underneath, feeling something swell in his chest as her head brushed against his arm.

"I was just talking to Brandon," he said. "He said that Lucy is willing to cooperate fully and you found her help?"

"She's still a bit uncertain, and I understand," Chloe said. "Trust can be hard. Johnny's been arrested. I don't know what hope there is for him, but people do change and he's young.

"Butler is definitely going to be facing an internal investigation now. Nicole Docker probably will, too. It's her fault Royd got bail after just one night in jail. She knew he was a friend of Johnny's, so just booked him on a basic assault charge. But with everything we have against Royd now, he'll be looking at being behind bars for a very long time." She waited while he brushed the snow off the bench. They sat. "How's Third Line?"

"They seem determined to protect my cover," he said. "They're pretty amazing people."

"They are," she said softly. "So, I guess this means there's nothing to stop you from taking that big and long case somewhere far, far away."

"It was in the Arctic, actually," he said.

Her green eyes looked deep into his. "That's pretty far."

"It is." He took her gloved hand in his and held it. His fingers stroked hers. "And I've decided I'm not going."

Her eyes grew wider. Something flickered in their depths. It was beautiful and something he'd rarely seen there. Hope. He knew in an instant he'd move heaven and earth to see it there every day. He took off his gloves. "You made a good point about letting someone else go undercover for once and my becoming part of the planning, training and coordinating team. I've got a lot of experience and there are a lot of young cops who could benefit. My shoulder's wonky. Plus, it would be nice to have a job that enabled me to still come home at night."

"I understand the feeling," she said. "If I get this promotion to detective sergeant, then I'll be a lot more stable, too."

"Oh, you'll get it," he said. "I have faith in you, and I'm willing to fight for you any way I can."

Slowly he pulled her gloves off and cradled her hands

in his, sheltering them from the cold. Then he pulled the ring of emeralds and diamonds from his pocket. "I think you should go back to wearing this again. It looks good on you and I kind of like telling people you're my fiancée. I was thinking we could go back to my parents' house tonight. Then tomorrow, head to your sister's house for Christmas dinner."

She looked down at his fingers cradling hers. "I thought you didn't date and don't have time for a girlfriend."

"Who said anything about dating?" He slipped the ring over the tip of her third finger and let it hover there. "I'm asking you to become my wife."

Light danced in her eyes. "Trent Henry, are you actually trying to propose to me with a ring you found in a mud puddle at a truck stop?"

"Would it help to tell you that I followed proper procedure?" he asked. "I turned it in to local police, waited to see if anyone claimed it and when they didn't, I tried to trace its rightful owner. Then when I knew for sure it was mine, I gave it to you."

"All that for a mud puddle ring?" Her eyebrows rose.

"Darling, I had it appraised. This ring is worth what I make in six months."

"You mean it's real? All this time I've been wearing real diamonds and emeralds?"

She pulled back, as if the ring was on fire. He caught her hand.

"It is. And you threw it at me in the middle of a dingy grill in front of a bunch of criminals." He gently slid the ring over the tip of her finger again. "It is as real, special, exquisite and precious as the woman I am trying my best to propose to right now."

She pulled her hand away again and crossed her arms. "Really? That is your best?"

He groaned. Then he got down on one knee in the snow at her feet and took her left hand again. He held it firmly.

"Chloe Brant, you drive me crazy. You challenge me, aggravate me, inspire me and invigorate me, more than anyone I've ever met. I'm crazy about you. I'm in love with you. I promise I will do my best to protect you, respect you and always be the steady, dependable rock you can rely on. Right now, I'm kneeling before you in the dark, in the very cold and very wet snow, on Christmas Eve, asking you very nicely to marry me. So, please, my love, my partner, my favorite person on this planet...please put me out of my misery and tell me you'll marry me."

A smile brushed her lips and filled her eyes.

"I love you, Trent, even when you drive me crazy. And I will love you for the rest of my life."

"And you'll marry me, right?"

"Of course I'll marry you!"

"Good!" He slid the ring onto her finger. Then he lifted her up off the bench, swept her into his arms and kissed her. Somewhere in the distance, he was sure he could hear Third Line cheering and whooping, and spurring the crowd on to clap. But all he knew for sure, was that Chloe's hands were in his hair, her lips were kissing him back, his heart was filled with more joy than he'd ever imagined feeling and he was going to love the irresistible, irrepressible woman he held in his arms for the rest of his life.

* * * * *

Get 4 FREE REWARDS!

We'll send you 2 FREE Books plus 2 FREE Mystery Gifts.

FREE
Value Over
$20

Both the **Love Inspired**® and **Love Inspired**® Suspense series feature compelling novels filled with inspirational romance, faith, forgiveness, and hope.

YES! Please send me 2 FREE novels from the Love Inspired or Love Inspired Suspense series and my 2 FREE gifts (gifts are worth about $10 retail). After receiving them, if I don't wish to receive any more books, I can return the shipping statement marked "cancel." If I don't cancel, I will receive 6 brand-new Love Inspired Larger-Print books or Love Inspired Suspense Larger-Print books every month and be billed just $6.24 each in the U.S. or $6.49 each in Canada. That is a savings of at least 17% off the cover price. It's quite a bargain! Shipping and handling is just 50¢ per book in the U.S. and $1.25 per book in Canada.* I understand that accepting the 2 free books and gifts places me under no obligation to buy anything. I can always return a shipment and cancel at any time by calling the number below. The free books and gifts are mine to keep no matter what I decide.

Choose one: ☐ **Love Inspired**
Larger-Print
(122/322 IDN GRDF)

☐ **Love Inspired Suspense**
Larger-Print
(107/307 IDN GRDF)

Name (please print)

Address   Apt. #

City   State/Province   Zip/Postal Code

Email: Please check this box ☐ if you would like to receive newsletters and promotional emails from Harlequin Enterprises ULC and its affiliates. You can unsubscribe anytime.

Mail to the **Harlequin Reader Service:**
IN U.S.A.: P.O. Box 1341, Buffalo, NY 14240-8531
IN CANADA: P.O. Box 603, Fort Erie, Ontario L2A 5X3

Want to try 2 free books from another series? Call 1-800-873-8635 or visit www.ReaderService.com.